BRIGHT CITY
DARK LOVE

A Luke Kelly Crime Story

Graham Storrs

This Edition, Copyright © 2021, Graham Storrs

ISBN: 987-0-6484329-8-2

Published by Canta Libre
Cover art and design by Craig Johnson (windowgazing.com)
Interior design by Write Into Print (writeintoprint.com)

Dedication

Another one for my wife, Christine, who, it turns out,
I have now loved for more than half my life.

Chapter One

The office phone rang. As with everything else after the worst of the pandemic, the demand for private investigation services seemed to be bouncing back with a vengeance. The calls had hardly stopped coming in for months and I'd taken on two full-time investigators and a receptionist, Desdemona Wataubi – Desi to the world – to manage the load. I wouldn't have paid that particular call much attention but I could tell by the way Desi reacted that it was something special. She stood up at her desk and stared at me wide-eyed and open-mouthed as she listened.

"I'll put you through now, sir," she said and gestured frantically for me to pick up.

"Luke Kelly," I said.

"Hi, Dr. Kelly, my name is Aikenhead, Vincent Aikenhead. I'm the General Manager at Eastern Island Resorts Limited. I wonder, would your company be interested in taking on a murder investigation?"

I fought down the urge to shout "Yes!" and said, as calmly as I could, "Perhaps you could give me a few details?"

"Well, I'd rather not go into it on the phone. Can we meet? I'm in Brisbane today, at the Hyatt Hotel. I've got back-to-back meetings all day but if you could come by after work, maybe I could buy you dinner or something."

"That's very kind of you but maybe just a few details, before we meet?"

"Oh. Okay. Do you remember the Harold Cross murder from last year?"

I did. As a matter of fact, I had become a keen student of unsolved murders in the past couple of years. I said, "He was stabbed through the heart on Murdock Island in April, last year, just before the lockdown. The police made a couple of arrests but neither of them went to court."

"That's the one. I'm not surprised you know it. Everybody knows it. Well, the Board feels it is time this whole thing was cleared up. It's been hanging over our Murdock Island resort like a bad smell ever since it happened. The police don't seem to be able to sort it out. We feel a fresh set of eyes is needed and, well, you have an excellent reputation for solving cases the police can't."

I grinned, always happy to hear how good our reputation was. "I'll meet you in the hotel bar at about six then, Mr. Aikenhead, if that's OK?" We said goodbye and I set the phone down carefully, staring at it, almost afraid to believe what had just happened.

"Oh my god, oh my god, oh my god!" Desi squealed. She came rushing over for a hug. She was a big girl and enthusiastic. I was what my mum generously described as "slender". So I braced myself for cracked ribs. "A murder!" she sang. "You must be so happy!"

I was but, somehow, just ordinary happy seemed to pale into insignificance around Desi's extravagant emotions. She was a great receptionist-cum-office manager, don't get me wrong – she was conscientious and organised and bright – but her extroversion bordered on pathological and I sometimes found myself yearning for the days when the Featherfoot Agency had no work and I could just sit alone in a silent office enjoying the peace and quiet.

"I'll call everyone and let them know," she said, heading back to her desk.

"No, wait. Just let them carry on with their assignments. They'll find out when they check in."

"Everyone" didn't amount to much. Harper was an ex-cop in her forties who was out trailing an unfaithful husband. Noah was a former would-be tradie who had given up his life as an electrician's apprentice to spend his days spying on insurance fraudsters. Apart from Desi, that was it.

Oh, and Ronnie.

"I'll call Ronnie," I told Desi. She frowned at me, clearly disappointed.

I reached for the phone and hesitated. It wasn't that Ronnie wouldn't be pleased we had the chance of a murder investigation. He'd be all over it like a rash. It was just that I wasn't sure I wanted him involved. It was more than a year since he and I had brought down the killers in what the papers had called The Tontine Murders. In the final confrontation with one of the murderers, he'd taken a shotgun blast to the chest at close range and I'd rolled my car crashing into a light aircraft. My broken bones had mended in a couple of months and I was back in action long before that. Ronnie, however had taken a long time to get back on his feet – even longer to get back to some semblance of his former self. He'd lost weight, he'd become withdrawn, his usual bad-tempered grumpiness had become a snarling, vitriolic savagery that I struggled to get past. I think he'd assumed he'd bounce right back after his injuries. When he didn't, it hit him hard.

"Tell you what," I told Desi, grabbing my jacket. "I'll go and tell him in person."

* * * *

Ronnie's front garden, usually so neat, was showing signs of neglect. Just seeing how long the grass was made me realise how long it had been since I'd last called. I rang the bell and waited. And waited. I rang again and knocked. Knowing Ronnie's habits, I walked around the house to the back and found him on a sun lounger on the patio. He was reading something on his phone and looked his usual self in board shorts and a Tee, bare feet and a pair of thongs on the floor beside him. An empty coffee cup and an empty side-plate were on a small table nearby.

"Most people would just bugger off if no-one answered the door," he said, not looking up.

"I'm good," I said, pointedly answering the question he hadn't asked. "How are you?"

He put down his phone and looked at me. "Is this a social call, or are you here to persuade me to help you find someone's lost kitten?"

I pulled up one of the other loungers that littered the patio and sat on the edge of it, facing him. It was a bright winter's day. Typical Brisbane. Still warm enough to walk around in shorts but cold enough for people to huddle on their sofas at night with a blanket.

"You're looking good. The exercises are really paying off, hey?"

He studied me for a while then said, "Go get yourself a drink. You know where everything is. Then you can come back and tell me whatever it is that's got you so excited you're wetting your panties." He picked up his phone again and went back to whatever he'd been reading.

I got up and went into the house. After more than two years of working with Ronnie, I'd finally learned that the best way to avoid endless, distracting rows with him was to ignore his barbs and stay on topic. Of course, it wasn't a foolproof technique. I'm only human and Ronnie was an expert at pushing people's buttons.

I came back with a cup of his awful powdered coffee and a packet of biscuits. I wasn't hungry. The biscuits were partly to take away the taste of the coffee and partly as a way to keep Ronnie quiet. That was another thing I'd learned; if you kept the beast fed, it was less likely to bite you.

"Go on, then, tell me," he said. "You've been to the animal shelter and brought home another stray to help with your heavy caseload of persecuting poor, unemployed invalids on behalf of our dear, compassionate government."

"Harper and Noah are good, hard-working detectives. I wish you wouldn't denigrate them like that. Besides, the arrangement was that you were going to train them. What happened to that? And as for Centrelink... well, they may not be dripping with the milk of human kindness, but they're a good, steady customer." I realised, too late, that I had taken Ronnie's bait and was already going off at a tangent.

Ronnie nodded sagely, "So, not that, then. I suppose you got laid again and rushed over to tell me. That's so sweet."

"I didn't get—" Damn it, why couldn't I just ignore him?

"It's been a long time," he said. "How long is it since Meg dumped you?"

"Megan didn't dump me. I mean, she did but... it's complicated." Which was the understatement of the year. "Look, we've got a new job. A murder case. I need you to go to a meeting with me tonight to see what it's all about."

He opened his mouth to make some kind of wisecrack but then closed it again. His brows dropped in to a sceptical frown. "Why would anyone give a murder investigation to a chickenshit PI company like the Featherbrain Agency?"

"Foot. It's Feather*foot*. And we got the job because of our stellar reputation, apparently."

He looked away, scowling. "So put Harpy and Nowhere on the case. They're good, hard-working detectives. They'll soon crack it."

I was losing my patience. "Will you stop pissing about? You know you want it. We both do. And you know I need you. So stop screwing around and say you'll come to the meeting."

He kept up the scowl but said nothing. Eventually, I lost my rag and stood up, ready to go.

"So, who got murdered?" he asked, not looking at me.

I sat down again. "Harry Cross," I said.

He gave me a sharp look. "From last year? The Murder Island case?" All the tabloids – which is basically the entire Australian media – had called it "Murder Island". It's no wonder our prospective client thought the publicity had been less than stellar.

"That's the one."

"Who's the client?"

"The company that owns the Murder Island resort. Only they would like everyone to stop calling it that and go back to booking holidays."

"What's the background?" he asked, reaching for his phone and, just like that, he was on the case.

* * * *

The bar at the Hyatt was like any bar in any hotel anywhere. Ronnie and I arrived fifteen minutes early and took a table where we could see the entrances. That was typical Ronnie. Old habits from his special forces days. A kind of generic paranoia that made everyone a suspect. Finding our new client in a pre-meeting meeting with someone shady was what he was hoping for. On this occasion, however, all it got us was fifteen minutes of listening to muzak in the sterile luxury of an almost empty room. Conversation would have been nice but the total output from Ronnie was the occasional ironic remark ("Nice here, isn't it?") or muttered exclamation ("Jeez these places give me the shits!").

At last, Vincent Aikenhead turned up. He was easy to spot because he stopped in the entrance and peered around the place, studying each of the half-dozen or so customers. I stood up and waved him over. He was a tall, slim man in his early fifties, wearing a well-fitting suit. His greying hair was cut short and neat and added to the overall impression of fastidious and expensive grooming. I felt self-conscious about my cargo pants and hoodie and wondered what our prospective client might make of my even more dishevelled companion.

Aikenhead had a woman with him, a tall, elegant creature, twenty years his junior who I assumed was a girlfriend or a trophy wife but whom he introduced as Victoria ("Call me Vicki,") Finn, his Head of Legal Affairs. Ronnie dragged himself to his feet and we all refrained from shaking hands as we introduced ourselves.

"So you're the Genius Detective," Vicki said with a charming smile. Ronnie snorted.

"That newspaper has a lot to answer for," I said. And it did. For some reason the idea of a philosopher detective bringing down a serial killer had caught the public imagination and the local tabloids had milked it for all it was worth. The "Genius Detective" label had seemed cool at the time but, more than a year on from the event, I just felt embarrassed now when people dredged it up. To make matters worse, Desi had had a load of T-shirts printed with, "I work with the Genius Detective," and a picture of Socrates. She had been handing them out to staff and clients alike until I found out and stopped her. She still wore hers to work now and then.

We ordered drinks, sat down and exchanged pleasantries. Yes, the start of the winter had been unusually warm. No, it didn't bode well for next year's bushfire season. Yes, I was Brisbane born and bred. No, I'd never been to Murdock Island resort but I'd heard it's lovely. And so on. Perhaps picking up on how bored Ronnie was looking, Aikenhead started to run through the details of the Harry Cross murder.

About a year ago, Cross, the CEO of a company called XtraVirtual, had taken rooms for a staff retreat at the resort. He'd also brought along some family members, including his wife, his two young children, his mother and even his grandmother. There were about twenty employees and they were holding meetings in one of the resort's conference rooms to discuss strategy for the coming year. It was during a rest period on the second day that Harold Cross was stabbed through the heart with a carving knife from one of the resort's three restaurants. There were no witnesses, no clues, no particular motive – except that Harry Cross was a nasty piece of work whom everyone hated, including his family – and the police and reporters had given up after a few weeks and gone away, leaving the hotel to deal with its new and unpleasant reputation.

We moved into the dining room – Aikenhead had made a reservation – as Vicki was explaining that the press had made the Murdock Island resort famous as the place where people are murdered in mysterious circumstances.

"There was all kind of wild press speculation at the time," she said. "And they dug up or simply made up some very unpleasant facts about the staff there. One of the sous chefs had a criminal record for assault that the resort management had not known about. One of the maintenance staff had outstanding warrants for domestic violence in South Australia. They also said – but it wasn't true – that there had been other unsolved murders and disappearances on the island over the past fifty years."

"Bookings went down to zero..." Aikenhead said, "...apart from a few weirdos who wanted to hold murder weekends there and that kind of thing. One couple, just a couple of months ago, tried to stage a satanic ritual in the woods near the resort. A security guard caught them dancing naked with a dismembered chicken." I tried not to laugh. Aikenhead did not seem amused in the least.

"Bookings are up to about thirty percent again," Vicki said. "But the resort isn't viable at that rate."

"We need to do something," Aikenhead said, sounding angry. "The whole thing is ridiculous. It's not our fault some bloody idiot got himself stabbed there. From the sound of it, he was going to be stabbed somewhere, sooner or later, and I don't see why we have to bear the cost."

Ronnie, who had been almost silent throughout, put on a big smile and addressed Aikenhead.

"Mate, that is such a load of bollocks." He waited while Aikenhead and Vicki sat back in open-mouthed astonishment, and I nearly choked on my Moreton Bay bug, then he went on. "There is no way that raking up all the muck yet again is going to do anything for your resort's reputation. Even if we find the killer, do you think the media are going to throw up their hands and say, 'Yeah, sorry everyone, we shouldn't have said all that crap, Murdock Island resort is really a nice place and you should all go there for family vacations.'? Nah, they're just going to double down on their bullshit and make things worse." He looked from Aikenhead to Vicki and back again. I took a look too, to see how bad things were. Oddly, our potential clients looked more shifty than furious.

"So what's this really about? And why did you bring a lawyer to meet us and not someone from Marketing or Operations?"

Vicki stole a glance at Aikenhead and I realised Ronnie was right on target.

Aikenhead shifted uncomfortably and turned to Vicki. "The NDAs please."

The lawyer reached into her copious handbag and produced an A4 envelope. From this she drew two documents.

"These are non-disclosure agreements," Aikenhead said. "If you will kindly sign them, I will explain everything and you will get the job. If you won't, this conversation is over and so is our business."

"What?" I said, mainly because it was the word echoing in my head at the time.

Ronnie smiled. "You guarantee that we get the work, at our usual rates plus expenses, and that we get at least one month to complete the investigation?"

"What?" I said, this time to Ronnie.

Aikenhead barely hesitated. "Agreed."

Still grinning, Ronnie stood up. "If you'll excuse us, I need to talk to the Genius Detective for a minute." He tapped me on the arm and flicked his head towards the entrance. "Come on."

In a daze, I got up and followed him out into the hotel lobby.

"What?" I demanded.

"We've got the job," he said. "If we want it. Do we want it?"

"Well, yes, but…"

"So we sign the NDA."

"No! They're up to something."

"So what?"

"So what? I'll tell you what…" But then I saw what he meant. Eastern Island Resorts could re-open the investigation for any reason they liked. Why should their motives matter to me. I'd become a PI to solve murders. That was the sole reason. And, in the two years I'd been in business, I'd had exactly one murder case. One. And here was number two. Someone was offering me the chance to find Harry Cross's killer, to bring a murderer to justice, and I was cavilling because their motives might not be pure?

"Right," I said. "I see what you mean."

"It's always a joy to work with such a great mind. Shall we go back?"

"But…" I realised that, while I didn't actually have any coherent objection, I definitely had a feeling of unease. "They lied to us. They tried to con us."

Ronnie nodded. "Yeah, the CEO of a big business and his head shyster turn out to be devious shitheads. Who could ever have seen that coming?"

I gave him a taut smile and headed back to the restaurant.

Aikenhead and Vicki had their heads together, deep in conversation, but stopped as soon as they noticed us. The plates had been cleared away and a copy of the NDA for each of us was on the table where the seafood had once been, along with an Eastern Island Resorts biro.

"Everything all right?" Aikenhead asked.

"No worries," said Ronnie. He picked up the pen, flicked to the second and final page of the document and signed without reading it.

I began scanning down it, getting bogged down in untangling the very first paragraph which was only trying to explain who the parties to the agreement were and what they would be called "herein".

Ronnie said, "Just sign the stupid thing. Vicki, tell him what's in it."

Coolly, she explained it was purely to prevent anyone from the Featherfoot Agency from speaking to the press – or anyone else – about the results of our investigation, or to pass on anything revealed to us by agents of Eastern Island Resorts.

"What about the cops?" I asked.

"What about them?"

"If we find the killer – or evidence of any crime – we need to talk to the cops about it."

Patiently, she explained that an NDA could not remove any of our statutory duties.

"J.F.D.I.," Ronnie said, impatiently.

Reluctantly, I picked up the pen, made a show of reading through the rest, and signed.

"Good," Aikenhead said as Vicki collected the documents. "Vicki?"

The elegant lawyer settled herself and nodded to her boss.

"Murdock Island resort is a lost cause. We need to sell it for what we can get and cut our losses. It goes on the market later this year. Meanwhile we want to sue two of the parties involved in reporting the Cross murder." She named a couple of very large media companies. "We believe we have a very strong case that their wanton speculations and historical inaccuracies destroyed a viable and thriving business. We have already begun proceedings. However, our case would be much stronger if we could show that the real murderer was not among the people they suggested and never could have been. That's where you come in."

"Bit of a punt, isn't it?" Ronnie said.

"Yes, it is." Aikenhead seemed more relaxed now that the NDA was signed. "But, in the scheme of things, your fees – even for a month – are small potatoes and Vicki estimates we could double our damages if we knew who the real murderer was. Also, it's a legitimate business expense we can write off against tax."

"And what if we find out the killer was one of the people the papers named?" I asked. "Wouldn't that destroy your case?"

"I really don't think that's going too happen. In fact, after so much time has passed, I don't think you are going to find the killer."

"But you just said…"

"It's more evidence that we've suffered reputational damage and that we've tried everything we can to fix the problem," said Vicki.

"If it makes us look a bit desperate," added Aikenhead, "then that's all to the good."

"What?" I said, completely bemused.

"Why us?" asked Ronnie.

Vicki and Aikenhead exchanged glances. Vicki gave a small shrug and Aikenhead said, "You were the first company to even consider taking it on. All the others dismissed it out of hand."

"It seems private investigators don't like to work on murders," Vicki added. "Or very cold cases."

"Or without knowing what's really going on, without having to sign an NDA?" Ronnie suggested.

"That too," said Vicki.

"Our criteria are not a hundred per cent commercial," I said, feeling I needed to defend us for some reason. A small frown crossed Aikenhead's brow. Perhaps he found the notion difficult to process.

"We. Love. Murder," said Ronnie, grinning broadly. It added a hint of alarm to Aikenhead's expression.

But Vicki just smiled. "Then I hope you have lots of fun. When can you start?"

"First thing in the morning," said Ronnie. I opened my mouth to protest that we couldn't just drop everything for this but, of course, we could and we would.

"Wonderful," said Vicki. "The project is being run from my department, so I'm the one you send your reports and invoices to." She handed Ronnie her business card. He pushed it along the table so I could see it but it contained no new information, just confirmation that she was located at Eastern Island Resorts' head office in Sydney. "The manager at Murdock Island will be your primary contact there. Day-to-day reporting will be to Shirley Stephens who runs our Queensland office. She's in Little Edward Street. They both know everything so you don't need to tiptoe around with them. I'll send you an email with full contact details."

Now that we were doing business, she was totally

businesslike. With a glance, she passed the floor back to Aikenhead.

"Any questions?" he asked.

"We'll need you to sign a contract," I said.

"Shirley can do that," he said. There was something in his tone that said we were well within Shirley's discretionary spending limits.

"We'll need to travel to the island at some point," I said. "Perhaps more than once." I suppose I was stalling, bringing up a trivial detail. For some reason I was feeling railroaded. There was something about the way these two had recruited us that I didn't like.

"Again," said Aikenhead, "see Shirley. She'll organise that kind of thing. If there's nothing else…" He took our silence for agreement and stood up. We all stood and remembered a time when people shook hands.

When they'd gone, Ronnie and I wandered back into the bar.

"Don't you just love corporate types?" Ronnie said after a brief discussion with the barman about what kind of beers they had. He picked up his bottle of Belgian lager and studied it suspiciously. "Their whole lives are spent working out how to meet their performance targets and get their bonuses. It's all about who you can screw and what you can get away with."

"Do you suppose those two are sleeping together?"

He shuddered. "Can you imagine that? It'd be like a couple of lizards clambering around on each other."

"Vicki didn't seem that bad," I said, weakly.

"Jeez, mate, get a couple more drinks in you and give Megan a call, you're clearly not getting enough."

I felt my jaw clenching. "I can't give Megan a call. She's

gone back to her husband, remember?"

Ronnie shook his head in despair but said nothing. I knew his feelings on the matter. Megan and I had dated for about six months. It had seemed to me that we were on a trajectory that would soon see us moving in together and maybe making it permanent. Then the coronavirus pandemic had hit. While my business had started to pick up and thrive, hers had been wiped out. She produced marketing material for research labs, which had seemed like a great little niche to corner the market on until the pandemic hit the universities. In a time of mass redundancies where most universities were fighting for their very existence, spending on third-party consultants became an unaffordable luxury. She signed on the dole and became morose and withdrawn. I didn't realise at the time but her husband, from whom she was separated, awaiting a divorce, had also lost his job. While I was becoming more and more occupied with my work, the two of them had been growing closer in their common misery. When he started begging her to give their marriage another go, she agreed that they should. She explained it all to me on a Skype call, which, even in those times, seemed harsh.

Ronnie, when he heard, took time out from his own wallowing self-pity to be furious with me. He explained, at length, my various inadequacies as a man and told me if I didn't "get round there right now, coronavirus be damned, and demand she stop seeing that dropkick she's married to," he'd never speak to me again. "Be a fucking man!" he yelled at one point. It was her decision, her life, her marriage, I explained. In reply, he called me a "whacker" and a total waste of oxygen.

It was one of the reasons Ronnie and I had not spoken all that much over the past year. I took his point, that Megan and I were great together and I'd be very unlikely ever to find a woman so compatible with me again, but what could I do? I really believed the choice was not mine and, if I thought marriage meant anything – which I did – I should stay out of it and let her make a go of hers if she could.

"What the hell are we getting ourselves into?" I asked Ronnie, trying to change the subject.

He gave me a long look to let me know he knew what I was doing, then said, "Why should we care?"

"I dunno. I thought both his versions of the reason for hiring us were dodgy. I mean, do you buy that it's all about suing media companies for a drop in customers? I'm no legal eagle but if I were defending the case, I'd point out that we'd just had the worst pandemic in a hundred years and maybe that was something to do with the drop in tourist numbers. No court would be able to untangle that from some supposed effect of bad press."

"Yeah." Ronnie grinned. "It was nice to watch the performance, though. Word perfect, both of them. What a double-act."

"So? Shouldn't we give the whole thing a wide berth?"

Ronnie took a swig of his beer, grimaced at the bottle and said, "I have never met anyone so easily discouraged as you. How you manage to get out of bed every morning is a mystery, what with the air being so cold and the floor being so far down. Look, Aikenhead's little intrigue is his own business. Our business is catching killers and, whatever is really going on here, we've been handed an incredible opportunity to do our thing, all expenses paid. Aikenhead can blow smoke up my arse all day every day for all I care, somebody murdered Harry Cross, somebody stuck a kitchen knife in his chest and, for a year now, they believed they got away with it. But they didn't – not for much longer, anyway – because we're going to hunt them down and lock them up."

I could see the old light in his eyes and, I have to say, it was good to see. For all that Ronnie was a miserable, abrasive old mongrel, I sort of missed him. The past few months, without him and Megan, had been a pretty lonely time. I hadn't really admitted that to myself until just that moment and maybe I hadn't actually seen it all that clearly until this sudden flash of excitement illuminated the dullness of my recent life.

"All right," I said, grinning back at him. "Let's catch the bastard."

Chapter Two

The house was new – to me, anyway. I'd bought it with my share of the annual profits of Chelsea's old company just a couple of months ago. I didn't want it. I didn't want the money. I'd had the usual argument with Kazima Abbas, the company CEO.

"It's way too much," I said.

"You own sixty-two percent of the company," she said patiently. "The profits go to the owners. That's how it works."

"But I don't do anything. I don't contribute in any way. You do everything – and the others who actually work here – I just sit down once a month and listen to you telling me all the great things you're doing. It's not right."

She sighed and looked at me with her big, dark eyes. "Luke, it's just capitalism. Your contribution is the investment that got this all going. Now you reap the rewards."

But I hadn't even done that. My late partner, Chelsea, did that. Chelsea had started the company, worked her socks off getting it going, put in all the "sweat equity" that turned a few good ideas, hammered out on second-hand computers, into a thriving IT business that now employed almost forty people and was still growing. In the past two years, Kazima had managed that growth while I sat back and collected obscenely fat cheques, just because Chelsea had left her majority shareholding to me when she died.

"But what would I even do with all that money?" I asked. I had never expected to be rich but it looked as if I would be by the mere accident of falling in love with a woman who had built a money-making juggernaut.

"If it really upsets you, give it to charity," Kazima had said, losing patience for an instant. Apparently regretting her lapse, she said, "Or, look, why don't I hook you up with my financial adviser. He's a good bloke."

The adviser, an ex-pat Brit called Philip, told me to buy a house, invest in a pension fund, and try to get a bit more enjoyment out of my growing wealth. So I did. Except for the enjoyment part. The only luxury item I might have wanted was an electric car and someone had already bought me one of those would you believe? Unto those that have, more shall be given, right?

In pursuit of a serial killer, at the end of my last and only murder investigation, I had driven my car into his light aircraft at high speed to stop him taking off and getting away with a thirty million dollar painting he'd stolen. It worked a treat but I also wrote off my car and put myself in hospital. However, there was a super-rich guy in Sydney who had been on the killer's hit-list and who was a part-owner of the painting. He was so grateful for what I'd done, he offered to replace my car with a much better one. He had a fancy muscle-car in mind but I said I wanted an electric one, so he said he'd get me a Tesla Roadster. I told him I couldn't drive around in anything that flash and talked him down to an electric BMW SUV.

So now I had a house in walking distance of the office and a fancy car sitting in the garage being charged by the solar panels I'd had installed on the roof. I liked to think Chelsea would be happy about that but the truth is, it made me really uncomfortable. I didn't earn any of it and I didn't deserve it. My own company – the PI business – barely broke even. That's all I should have had, really, and even that had been heavily subsidised by the proceeds from Chelsea's company for more than a year until business had picked up. Standing in the kitchen of my new house, making myself a cappuccino, I felt like a fraud. A fat cat, capitalist rent-taker. Marx and Engels would have despised me.

On the other hand, I did like my new place. I had tons of space and even a small garden that was lush and green the way only sub-tropical Brisbane gardens can be. There were trees along the boundary that the estate agent who sold it to me said included a paw-paw, a macadamia, and a tibouchina. I'd forgotten quite which was which but I looked forward to them coming into flower one day and then, as appropriate, producing fruit, nuts and whatever a tibouchina produced. I also had birds; lorikeets, eastern rosellas and little scaly-breasted lorikeets. They came to a feeder the previous owner had installed and which I dutifully kept supplied with fruit and sugared water. They were noisy and squabblesome but astonishingly beautiful and I watched them in awe whenever they were around. I even talked to them. As I said, the past few months had been very lonely.

I finished my coffee and set off on foot to the office. It was literally five minutes away, so I usually left the car at home. Desi was already there – she normally opened up the place – and gave me a lot of silent, swivelling eye gestures, which meant nothing until I followed her gaze and saw Ronnie at a table in the common area.

"Wow, you're a bit keen," I said, joining him.

"You're not?"

"Well, yes. Anyway... I'll just get a coffee and we'll get down to it, then. I just need to let everybody know what's going on." While my cappuccino machine worked it's magic, I got on my phone and sent out a group message explaining we had a big new job and that Ronnie and I would be focusing on that for the next few days, if not weeks. I got an immediate reply from Noah wanting to be part of it. I told him we'd see how things went but that I was relying on him and Harper to keep everything else going while we worked on this. He sent back another reply but I didn't look at it.

Ronnie said, "We need to get over to see the regional manager... whatshername."

"Shirley Stephens," I said. I'd spent yesterday evening setting up the case files and I'd already done some background on the people we knew about.

"Right. And we need to get up to Murder Island and check out the crime scene."

"It's Murdock Island. We should probably agree to use it's real name, to avoid any slips in front of the client."

"Fair enough, Genius Detective. Have you looked at the victim and the suspects yet?"

"Not really. I read some news reports from the time but there weren't many actual facts in there. Just the usual guff." One of the big revelations of my time as a private investigator had been how unreliable, sensational and ridiculous the popular press was. What little truth there was in most news pieces was basically just a peg on which to hang a load of opinion, speculation and distortion. Oddly enough, my new awareness had not changed my habit of reading the papers every morning.

Ronnie nodded. "Yeah I saw your notes in the file."

"That's funny, I haven't seen any from you, yet."

Ignoring me, he said, "Right-o, here's what we know. Harry Cross was a self-made man – meaning he was given a truckload of money by his family and turned it into many more truckloads. He started with a company making iPhone accessories, began buying up other companies and diversifying in the high-tech area, then hit paydirt with XtraVirtual."

"Yeah, I saw that. Any idea what they do?"

"Augmented reality," he said.

"Yeah. Still not actually getting what they do."

"What, and you're asking me? How the hell should I know? It's the next big thing in IT. Go ask Karen, or Kazima. Anyway, he got rid of all the dross and turned XtraVirtual into a national, then an international success, floated it on the stock exchange for gazillions of dollars but kept complete control of everything."

"Smart guy?"

"Nah, just ruthless. He had a rep for never paying his suppliers, suing all his competitors out of business, treating his staff like slaves and being best mates with dodgy politicians. Frankly, it's a miracle he lived as long as he did. There were rumours he beat his wife. He was always being pictured with beautiful bimbos. And, you remember that big scandal where that federal politician was caught on camera at a dinner with one of our most notorious mob bosses?" I did. It had been front-page news for all of two days. "Well, Harry Cross was also at that very same dinner."

"Did you sleep at all last night?"

"What?"

"You seem to have done a lot of work and I last saw you about twelve hours ago."

"Your concern is touching. Can we get on with the job?"

"Sure." I wasn't really concerned. Ronnie didn't sleep much anyway and, when he got into a case, he could go days without more than a couple of hours a night.

"So, we have a victim that everybody hated. Meaning everyone he knew was a potential suspect – including his wife, his brother and members of Brisbane's organised crime syndicates."

"But only the people on the island could have killed him."

"Correct but that gives us six members of his immediate family, twenty-one XtraVirtual employees, and god knows how many resort staff. There were also dozens of other holidaymakers staying there at the time, as well as day visitors. Any one of them could have done it and, of the scores without any obvious motive, any one of those could have been paid to do it."

"Jeez. It's no wonder the cops got nowhere. Where do we even start?"

Ronnie didn't even hesitate. "With the family. Then the employees. Then everyone else."

"O-kay. Because the usual motives are love and money and the family probably has both?"

"Yup. Cross died intestate, meaning the wife got everything. The brother, Richard Cross, is contesting that in court. He claims he was instrumental in growing the business and deserves a cut. There's also a mistress, Carla Ventura, who reckons she deserves a slice of the pie, too."

"Carla Ventura the actress?"

Ronnie grinned. "Yeah. Bags I get to interview her."

I rolled my eyes. "What about the others – the kids, the mother?"

"The kids were five and three at the time. Doesn't completely rule them out but… The mother is a possibility. The granny…" He pulled a face. "She's eighty-odd."

"OK, what about servants, personal assistants, the nanny, all that stuff?"

"Yep, definitely a bunch of those on the island. There was Harry's personal assistant, the kid's nanny, Granny had a nurse, and probably others I don't know about. We'll need a definitive list."

Vicki Finn had already emailed us a lot of information about who was there on the island at the time of the murder but we needed to check it and add to it ourselves. Getting hold of the police files would be a huge help since they would definitely have done all the checking and chasing already. Which reminded me…

"Who was in charge of the investigation?"

Ronnie grinned and I felt my stomach sink before he said it. "That would be your old friend Detective Inspector Trevor Reid." The man who had tried very hard to arrest me for murdering my girlfriend Chelsea. It was bad news because it was unlikely we'd get any friendly co-operation from that quarter. On the other hand, his right-hand man was Detective Sergeant Alexandra Bertolissio, as intelligent and reasonable a police officer as you are ever likely to meet. If Bertolissio had been on the case, it was quite possible we could get lots of detail directly from her.

Ronnie interrupted my chain of thought. "Mate, if you're thinking your old sweetheart Al Bertolissio will be there to feed you the inside dope, you can think again. She was on secondment to Organised Crime at the time of the investigation. Trevor Reid had to do it all on his own. Which is probably why the killer is still out there."

"Bugger. Reid hates me."

Ronnie laughed out loud. "After all that Genius Detective crap in the papers, he probably sticks pins in Luke Kelly dolls these days."

"Yeah, well, I seem to remember he didn't exactly warm to you, either."

He seemed to find that hilarious too. "Can you imagine his face when he finds out we're working on this case? Jeez, I'd love to be around when he gets the news."

I couldn't help smiling. It was nice to think how furious he'd be. "Still, not funny, mate. We're going to need information from the cops." And then I burst out laughing, despite myself. "How long do you reckon before he arrests one of us for the murder?"

It actually took Ronnie several minutes before he remembered to be miserable again.

* * * *

The Cross family lived in and around Brisbane. They had a sprawling farmhouse out near Gatton somewhere, where four generations of them presided over well-manicured acreage, a penthouse in the CBD, and a beach house near Tweed Heads for weekend breaks. They may have had other properties, too. Those three were all I could discover by trawling through the Web.

The business, XtraVirtual, was also based in Brisbane, with a head office in the CBD and an office for the plebs on an industrial park in Archerfield. There were other offices in other states, a couple in the US and one in the UK. The big

BRIGHT CITY DARK LOVE

bash at Murdock Island resort had been for head office managers, and the managers of the interstate Australian offices.

Before we went to see anybody in the family or the business, we went to have a chat with Kazima Abbas, the woman who managed Chelsea's company. I should start calling it mine, I suppose, but it just felt like Chelsea's. Kazima wasn't a tech-head like Karen Cha, who was the systems administrator for the company and who also did sundry IT jobs for my PI business – and the occasional spot of illegal hacking on the side when Ronnie and I needed it – but Kazima knew the Brisbane IT world inside out.

The place was in chaos when Ronnie and I arrived. Kazima hurried us through to her office and closed the door on it all. I remembered, too late, that the whole company was reorganising its premises. It had expanded rapidly over the past couple of years, filling all the space on one floor of the building they were in, then another, and now they were contracting back onto one floor since the pandemic had given staff the habit of working from home.

"I'm sorry to bother you while all this is going on," I said, waving an arm at the rewiring and desk moving going on beyond the glass wall. I noticed a large board with the removal schedule mapped out in detail and an A4 sheet taped to the glass that had the floor plan and seating allocation for the new office. It dawned on me, vaguely, what a complex job moving office could be when you had almost forty staff, half of them now working off-site, and you couldn't stop development or production for a minute without losing money.

"No problem," said Kazima, as if it really wasn't. "How are you? Keeping busy, I hope."

"We've got a murder case," I said, knowing she would understand the importance of that to me. Kazima had been Chelsea's closest friend. She had been supportive and helpful while we tracked down Chelsea's killer and had continued to be supportive ever since.

"Ah," she said. "Please don't tell me you need Karen." She looked through the glass. "We cannot do this without her."

"No, no. We just need to ask you a few questions."

"Me? How can I help?"

Ronnie spoke for the first time since arriving. "You can tell us what you know about XtraVirtual."

"The AR company?"

"That's the one."

"Oh my god, is it Harry Cross? Is that the case?"

"Yes, it is."

"Wow. Talk about high profile. Whew!" She blew out her cheeks. "Let me see now. XtraVirtual. About twelve hundred employees, ASX listed – I don't know what today's price is. At least a billion a year in revenue. Offices—"

Ronnie interrupted her. "I mean the stuff we can't get off the Internet."

She frowned. "Like?"

"Like how are they really doing? Who really has the power? Who did Harry Cross cheat and trample on his way to the top? That kind of thing."

"Ah. That kind of thing. All right. Well, there are really two XtraVirtuals. One was the company before Cross was murdered. The other is the one you see now. Before the murder, it was all about acquisitions and asset stripping. Cross liked to spread a wide net across many promising new technologies, pick out the best bits from his catch and throw the rest back into the water. It can be an extremely successful business strategy, but only if you're a ruthless ratbag who doesn't care about the cost to your workers. The market loved it, though, and kept on supporting him. Since Cross died, XtraVirtual is pretty much an ordinary sort of company. In fact, its share price took a dive during the pandemic and hasn't recovered at all. They'll be shedding staff and cutting costs, soon. The AR business is new and exciting but, without all the buzz that used to surround Harry Cross, XtraVirtual is increasingly seen by the market as speculative and a bit too risky. They won't keep pumping up the share price the way they used to. I think the company has had a bit of a grace period in this past year. People have been waiting to see what it will do next but, honestly, it doesn't seem to be doing much at all, just sitting there, losing value."

"So who's running it, these days?"

"Well, the wife got all the shares but that's part of the problem. There's a couple of court cases going on and no-one really knows how that will leave the ownership. I think most investors want the brother to win. What's his name again?"

"Richard."

"Right. But that's only because he might be a better bet than the wife – or the mistress. At least Richard might keep control of the company and try to do something with it. The other two would most likely just sell up and walk away."

"Do you know Richard Cross?"

"Not really. I think I met him once at a bidder's conference." To Luke, she said. "We are very small fry compared to the likes of XtraVirtual. If you were hoping for an introduction, I can't help."

"Tell us about augmented reality," Ronnie said. "I looked it up online but it didn't make much sense. Is it just some kind of sci-fi nerd's wet dream, or is there anything to it?"

She thought for a moment. "You're ex-military, right?" I don't know how she knew but Ronnie nodded. "So you've probably seen heads-up displays."

"HUDs? Sure, tactical and other data projected onto an aircraft's windscreen so the pilot doesn't need to look down at their instruments."

"And sometimes they project it onto the pilot's face mask," she said. "It's a simple idea. You augment the reality the pilot is looking at with overlays of useful information. Except it's very hard to make it work. You need to know where the user is looking and what they're looking at. Putting up an altimeter is pretty trivial, but if you want to put an X on a target – or an advert on a city wall – you need to do some fancy, real-time 3D modelling to get it to look right. But the good news is, you don't need a billion-dollar aircraft to make the technology work these days, you can fit it all into a pair of goggles or spectacles."

"But who'd need that?" Ronnie wanted to know.

"Everyone," Kazima said, smiling. "Haven't you ever used Google Maps? Well, imagine getting directions through your glasses, rather than through a phone, overlaid on the actual street you're looking at. Or imagine meeting someone at a conference – at a party even – and you can get their name, age, occupation, whatever, to appear as a block of text floating next to them. Or what if you're trying to assemble some flat-pack furniture and you can see the part name and assembly instructions overlaid on each piece you look at? Or what if you could see your spreadsheets, word processor, accounting software in virtual windows that floated in the air in front of you instead of having to use a computer or a phone?"

"OK. I get it. It's the kind of tech that will change everything. So, if you've got a handle on how to do it, you'd be worth a fortune, right?"

"Correct. And that's what XtraVirtual brought to Harry Cross. They came with eye tracking, object recognition, lots of the bits and pieces you need to make this a viable technology. Cross already had a games engine that could do the spatial modelling and super-fast processing. He bought a software company that could put it all together and, hey presto!" She looked at our faces, both scrunched up with the effort of making sense of what she was telling us and said, "I could get Sanjay in. He's our chief architect, very bright. He could give you a quick tutorial if that's what you need."

"No thanks," I said, quickly. I'd met Sanjay Patel before. He was one of those super tech wonks, so in love with his own brilliance he couldn't explain a toaster to a starving man. "I think we've got what we need."

A young man poked his head in the door and apologised for doing it.

"Yes, Yoham?" Kazima said, cutting him off.

"Oh, sorry. We need a decision on the servers. Susie's getting uptight about the shut-down sequence." He rolled his eyes.

"I'll be right there." The young man vanished. She gave us an apologetic smile and we all stood up. "It's all going to be worth it in the end," she said. "That's what I keep telling myself."

Outside, in the car, I asked Ronnie whether he thought that had helped.

"Yeah, maybe…"

Which I took to mean no. "So, who's next? The wife?"

"The widow."

"Right. Widow."

He grinned, coming out of a reverie. "She's young and beautiful and rich. Perhaps I'll get lucky."

I laughed. "Why don't you make the call? Tell her we'll be about fifteen minutes. Unless you'd like to stop at a barber's, get yourself prettied up? Shame they don't do drive-through plastic surgery. I can see how a bit of nipping and tucking might take twenty years off that crumpled old mug of yours."

"Hey, this face might have the odd line or two but that's just wisdom and experience, mate. At least I don't look like I appear in brochures for adoption agencies." He put on a soppy, TV ad voice. "Could you provide a home for little Lukie and the many poor lost boys like him?" He sat back grinning, apparently well pleased with his little riposte. I grinned too, just happy to see Ronnie back on form.

Chapter Three

XtraVirtual Tower was as upmarket as Brisbane got. It was the centrepiece of a riverside development that housed posh restaurants and fancy boutiques but it soared, literally and figuratively, above them all. Every unit in the building – sorry, I should call them luxury apartments – was beyond the reach of any but the richest; the casino owners, the mining magnates, the crime lords and the foreign autocrats. And at the very top of this steaming heap of money and privilege, was the penthouse residence of the Cross family. They hadn't built the tower and they didn't own it but they had bought the naming rights. Sadly for them, a local standup guy had taken to calling it "The Extrav", which undercut the advertising message somewhat.

The lift, which a ground floor flunky had to enable with a special code after thoroughly checking our credentials, took us all the way up and opened onto a world of breathtaking splendour. I take it all back; "luxury apartment" did not do this Wonderland justice. I gazed, open-mouthed at the wide-open spaces, the giant artworks, the islands of sofas and tables, the... Let me stop myself there. If you've ever been inside one of those up-market home furnishing stores that are so cleverly lit and so full of exquisite design choices in every nook and cranny of their broad acreage, you can probably imagine the XtraVirtual Tower penthouse. Just take out seventy percent of the stuff, add floor-to-ceiling windows on three walls, replace the discrete shop assistants with a discrete housekeeper, and you get the picture.

The housekeeper greeted us in hushed tones and led us through the magical realm to one of the enchanted islands of furniture. There, an ethereal young beauty, dressed entirely in white, floated to her delicate feet and greeted us. We introduced ourselves.

"I'm Cassandra. I don't have long, I'm afraid," she said. Her voice was a languorous drawl. "My trainer is coming…" She consulted a golden artwork on her wrist. "…in about ten minutes. Is that enough time?"

"No worries," Ronnie said. He held out a hand. She regarded it sadly.

"My physician advises that I don't make physical contact with anyone while the pandemic is still active."

"But… the vaccine," I blurted. The roll-out of vaccinations was not yet more than half completed but I'd assumed the Cross family would have been disdainful of the queue, getting their jabs at a private clinic in Switzerland, or wherever.

She smiled and walked over to a sofa. "I won't let them put that poison in my body," she said. "Please, have a seat."

She seated herself. Actually, she sort of curled up on a sofa like a kitten. Somehow, her every action made me feel clumsy and brutishly masculine – not a feeling I was used to.

"We'd like to ask you a few questions about your husband's death," Ronnie said.

Cassandra looked away, striking a tragic pose. "Why do you want to drag up all that horribleness?"

"Because the killer is still free," Ronnie said, firmly. "And he –" He glanced my way. "– or she needs to be brought to justice. I'm sure you agree."

She turned to look at Ronnie and, for the first time, I saw some actual interest in her big, almond eyes. "Of course. But why now? And why you? The police failed. They told me they couldn't do any more unless some new evidence turned up. Do you have new evidence?"

"No, we don't. But we have a fresh pair of eyes and, on previous cases, we've been able to find things the cops have missed. So tell us what happened the day your husband died."

She studied him for a moment, then said, "We were at that awful resort place. Harry said it would be nice. I hated it. It was scruffy and the amenities were so basic. We were staying in some kind of horrible wooden hut they called a chalet. Jenny and her mother were in the hut next door."

"Jenny?" I asked. Ronnie winced. "Oh, right. Jennifer Cross, your husband's mother."

"Please go on," said Ronnie in a tone that said I was going to hear from him about that afterwards.

The lovely Cassandra gave a delicate shudder. "It was all very primitive. Even so, I stayed in the horrible shack thing and had them bring me food and drinks there. I was not going to eat in one of those disgusting café things they had. Harry said I should go for walks in the hills or sunbake on the beach but there were dingoes just roaming loose out there. I might have been eaten alive. And the children! What kind of mother would expose her children to such risk?"

"So you were in your chalet when it happened?"

"Yes, I was. They sent a secretary to tell me. Can you believe that?"

"Were you alone?"

"Yes. Oh, I had the children with me." She waved a hand as if it was inconsequential. I suppose, as far as an alibi went, it probably was.

"Did you go to see what happened?"

"Good grief, no! Why would I do that? I stayed where I was until Richard came to console me."

"When was that?"

"I don't know. It felt like forever. I mean, I'd just lost my husband and they just left me there in that wooden shack, all alone."

"Do you not get on with Jenny and Richard?"

"I used to. Richard was always so sweet. And Jenny... well, she tended to side with Harry, but, otherwise, she was nice enough to me."

"Did you and Harry argue a lot?"

"What? Whatever gave you that idea?"

"You said Jenny tended to side with him."

A little frown creased her perfect forehead. "We had the usual disagreements, like all married couples."

"But Richard is contesting your inheritance now."

"Yes. Isn't it horrible how greed will bring out the worst in people? I've seen such an unpleasant side of him since... you know."

She took another look at her watch. "I'm sorry but—"

"And, speaking of your inheritance... Did you know about Carla Ventura and your husband before she staked a claim to Harry's money?"

Cassandra stood up. Her face was set in an angry pout. "My therapist and I are working through all that. I don't see that it's any of your business. Now, if you'll excuse me." I stood up too and, reluctantly, it seemed, so did Ronnie. "Sandra will see you out."

As if by a secret summons, the housekeeper materialised beside us. We said our goodbyes pleasantly enough and followed the skivvy. When we reached the lift, Ronnie stopped and turned to the woman.

"Were you with Mrs. Cross when her husband was murdered?"

"Yes, sir."

"So you can verify that she was in chalet when the body was found?"

"Of course."

He nodded to himself. "What's she like to work for?"

"Mrs. Cross is an excellent employer," she said. But, as the lift doors opened and we stepped inside, she added. "But I will tell you this: my name is actually Susan."

* * * *

"O-kay," I said as we headed back to the car. "That was strange."

"Yeah? Well make the most of it. We'll be lucky if get an audience with the great lady again."

"Is it just me, or did she seem… well…?"

"Nuts? Bonkers? Off her trolley?"

I grinned. "I suppose you're rethinking that plan to marry the rich widow, hey?"

"Oh, I dunno, she was definitely hot."

"Anti-vaxxers give me the creeps."

"As long as I get my shots why should I care what a bunch of nutters do to themselves."

I opened my mouth to argue about the ethics of putting other people's health at risk for the sake of some conspiracy theory but changed my mind. "So we believe her alibi?"

Ronnie thought about it. "I find it hard to imagine that woman pushing a kitchen knife into a man's chest."

"Even if he was abusing her?" It was just hearsay but, from what I already knew about Harry Cross, it seemed quite possible. "Even if he had a mistress she'd just found out about?"

"Yeah, nah. It's always possible she could have snapped but, as the papers tell it, the knife was brought from somewhere else and was wiped for prints after it was used. That doesn't sound like our little princess. She's more the kind who would have found a big strong man to do the job for her."

"You didn't like her much, did you?"

"Jeez, what's to like?"

We got in the car and Ronnie told me to take a left out of the car park.

"Where are we heading?"

"Head for the Warrego Highway. We need to get to the Cross homestead before the princess tells Jenny Cross we're nasty little trolls and she shouldn't talk to us."

"Morlocks," I said. "That's how she sees us. She's one of the Eloi and we're Morlocks." Disturbingly, it had felt a little like that to me too when I was in her presence.

"Is this some more of your intellectual crap?"

"Yeah, if reading a book counts as intellectual crap."

"Just drive the car."

∗ ∗ ∗ ∗

It took more than an hour to reach the township of Plainland, a little east of Gatton, and then another thirty minutes to locate the Cross farm. It was a huge place, about a thousand acres, with forests and a broad creek and dams bigger than the reservoirs of some small towns. The farmhouse was a massive, two-storey Federation beauty that looked more like a country hotel than someone's home. It was spoiled by a couple of wings someone with no taste except for comfort had added in the century since it had been built. There were other buildings, too, some more modest houses, some gigantic sheds and stables. Most were at a good distance. The main house, gleaming in the sunshine, was surrounded by beautifully-kept lawns and faced a large set of fenced paddocks in which horses grazed. Even a tractor we passed on the way in looked clean and new.

We pulled up at the house and got out. Neither of us had spoken since the palatial 'farm' had come into view. Above us, on a broad balcony, I heard voices and looked up. A tanned and handsome woman in a long, loose dress appeared at the rail and smiled down at us. She looked about fifty but if, as I guessed, this was Harry's mother, she must be more like sixty-five.

"Are you Luke Kelly?" she called down to Ronnie.

"Yes," I called back. "Jennifer Cross?"

"I'll be right down. Let yourselves in."

The front door was, in fact, wide open behind the screens. The interior was dim and cool after the brightness of the day outside. We walked into a large, open area with a huge stone fireplace and polished wooden floors. The ceilings were high with authentic pressed steel mouldings and big, slow fans. Everything looked grand and expensive, yet there was a cosiness about the place that was completely absent from the XtraVirtual Tower apartment. I heard footsteps on wooden stairs and Jennifer Cross appeared from around a corner. She moved with long, easy strides. *Good genes*, I thought. It struck me that she must have been a beauty in her youth. I wondered whether Harry's father had acquired her as a trophy wife. If he had, I suspected he'd got more than he bargained for because there was a vitality and intelligence about her that did not suggest meek subjugation.

"Please sit," she said, waving towards a big, brown leather sofa that looked so deep and soft it might swallow a man whole. She went to sit in a matching armchair. Ronnie sprawled comfortably on the sofa while I perched cautiously on its edge. "Can I get you something? A drink? A snack? It's quite a long trek out here."

I started to say we were fine but Ronnie told her we'd like something cold and long. "And if you've got a couple of biscuits or something…"

She didn't seem to make any sign but a young woman appeared who was clearly a servant. Did the rich control their minions with their thoughts now? She asked the girl to fetch us things and settled back.

"You said on the phone you want to ask me some questions about Harry's death."

"That's right," I said.

"And you're private investigators?"

"I am, Ronnie here is a consultant to my company." I always made a point, if asked, of being explicit on that point. I knew there were cops who would just love to take Ronnie down, and me with him, for misrepresenting himself as a licensed investigator. She looked at Ronnie as if his consultant status had made him particularly intriguing. I pulled out my licence and offered it to her but she waved it away.

"Who hired you to look into my son's death?"

"Eastern Island Resorts," I couldn't see any reason not to

tell her. From her expression, she didn't seem to know the company. "They own the Murdock Island resort," I explained. Still no particular reaction, just a nod. "They're concerned that wild and speculative media reports at the time of the murder have damaged their reputation and they'd like the matter cleared up."

She raised an eyebrow. "The matter?"

Shit! "I – er – I'm sorry. An unfortunate choice of words. Obviously this was a deep personal tragedy for you and your whole family."

She held up a long-fingered hand. "Please. Don't. I quite understand. To you this is a job. A case. Just one among many, I suppose. You didn't know Harry. You don't know any of the family."

I opened my mouth to make some kind of protest but Ronnie said, "Don't mind Luke. He's an academic. You know the type: social idiot, no friends, no girlfriend, but good at solving puzzles."

She stared at Ronnie and I saw a smile slowly grow. "But you're something else, aren't you?" Ronnie smiled back. "So, you tell me then, why should my family subject ourselves to having all this raked up yet again, just so Eastern Island Resorts can make a bit more money?"

"You shouldn't," Ronnie said. "Frankly, I don't give a stuff about Eastern Island Resorts, either. You ever met their CEO?" I goggled at Ronnie, stunned by whatever the hell he was doing. Jennifer shook her head. "Yeah, well, don't bother. Complete wanker. If they weren't paying us, I'd give the bloke a wide berth. But…" He raised a hand, index finger up for emphasis. "Someone out there killed your son. Someone took a knife and stuck it through his heart. Someone stood there and watched him die. Then they wiped the knife walked away and went back to living their life. It was probably someone you know, almost certainly someone he knew. Someone planned to kill him. Someone executed that plan in cold blood. Someone who is still out there, still free."

I watched Jennifer's face slowly morph from mild amusement to grim anger. Her lips thinned, her nostrils flared, her eyes hardened.

"The cops were useless," Ronnie went on. "But we're not. We're hunters. To the cops, it's just a job. Nine to five. Clock on, clock off. Check the in tray, go through the motions, go to budget meetings, go home to the wife and sprogs. But this is what we live for. This is why we get out of bed in the morning. Hunting down killers and throwing that scum in jail where they belong is how we get our rocks off. And we are good at it. That's why you should care that we're on the case. That's why you should let us open those old wounds and probe them no matter what the pain. Because someone murdered your son and we are going to catch that evil bastard. And that's what you want. Isn't it?"

She regarded him long and hard. I felt for sure she had been moved by his speech and would declare herself solidly on board. But, as she continued to study him, she visibly relaxed.

At last, she spoke. "What an interesting person you are. I think you actually believe what you just said. The only problem is, you didn't know my son." She stood up and walked a few paces away from us. "Harry was a cruel and violent man," she said, not looking at us. "For everyone in the family – for everyone at the company – his death has changed things. For the better. In every case, for the better. Even I feel it." I couldn't be certain, her face was turned away from us, but I had the impression she was crying. "Whoever killed Harry did us all a favour."

Ronnie and I exchanged glances and I could see that he was as surprised as I was.

"But you're still going to help us, aren't you," Ronnie said. "Because whatever Harry was like, he was still your son."

Without turning, she nodded. Then she wiped her cheeks with her fingers and turned. "Yes. He was still my son." She walked briskly back to the chair and sat down. "So, ask me your questions."

I was about to suggest that maybe she'd like a few minutes to compose herself, or something, but Ronnie jumped straight in.

"Where were you when your son was being stabbed?"

"I was walking on the beach. Alone. I only found out when I got back, about an hour later, and saw all the fuss that was going on. The hotel manager broke the news. She was in a terrible state. They were keeping everyone out of the meeting room where it happened and were waiting for the police to arrive. I went to check on Mum. She and I were sharing a cabin. There was a woman from the company sitting with her – some assistant manager type. I shooed her out. Mum was shaken and seemed a bit confused about what was going on. She's eighty-six. Not senile or anything but the shock of it seemed to have sent her a bit... She hasn't been right since. Not really.

"Anyway, the police finally showed up and we were all interviewed by some great oaf."

"Detective Inspector Trevor Reid," Ronnie said.

"Yes, that's him. How did you know?"

"Your description was spot on."

"And that was it, really."

"Did you talk to Cassandra?"

"After it happened, you mean? Not really. They let us go later and we all shared a boat back to the mainland. Richard had gone to see she was all right and he'd stayed with her. The children didn't really know what was going on, bless 'em."

"You don't like Cassandra," Ronnie said.

"Whatever makes you say that?"

"She doesn't seem like your type."

She bristled a little. "And what's my type?"

"Oh, you know, grown ups." Jennifer suppressed a smile and Ronnie went on. "How did Harry and Cassandra get on?"

Jennifer shrugged. "Like most married couples."

"Were they in love?"

Jennifer laughed. "Are you married, Ronnie?"

"I was. It didn't take."

"If you'd been very rich, do you think she'd have stuck around?"

Ronnie nodded. "Good point. So, you think Cassandra is a gold-digger?"

"I'm just saying women find they can put up with a lot more from their men if they're wealthy."

I wondered if she was speaking from personal experience.

"Did he hit her?" Ronnie asked.

Jennifer's face fell. "You should ask her."

"What about the kids?"

"You sound like the tabloid reporters. It's all they could talk about. Australian newspapers are such garbage these days."

"Yes, but is it true?" Jennifer's face became set and angry. "I'm trying to establish a motive, Jennifer. I don't mean to be rude about your son but a lot of people disliked him. I need to find some reason why someone disliked him enough to kill him. It sounds to me as if your daughter-in-law might have that reason – if the gossip is true."

Jennifer shook her head, clearly not wanting anything to do with this line of questioning. "You'll have to take that up with Cassie."

Ronnie gave her a long look then asked, "What about Richard?"

"What about him?"

"I dunno. Younger brother, wanting to get out from under Harry's thumb, felt he could run the business better, long-term grudge about Harry being your favourite, all that kind of thing. What's Richard's story?"

Her eyes flashed anger again but then her mouth turned up at the edge – not exactly a sneer but getting on for it. "You're way off the mark there. Richard is one of the nicest, sweetest men you'll ever meet. His friends adore him. The staff at the company think he's wonderful. It's true that Harry didn't really take him seriously but that was Harry. Richard still loved his brother. Their little blues didn't mean anything. If you had a brother, you'd know what I mean."

"As it happens, I have got a brother," he said. I almost jumped out of my seat in surprise. In over two years he'd never mentioned him. "He's a complete dickhead, runs a car dealership in Leeds. We haven't spoken in twenty years. We used to have our little blues all right. Last one was when our mum died. I ended up decking him at the funeral and putting him in hospital. I bet if you'd asked Mum she'd have told you it was all good natured banter between us. And that's because we always lied to her to keep her happy."

Jennifer studied him, carefully. Eventually, she said, "Your mum knew the truth. You and your brother were kidding yourselves if you thought she couldn't see right through you."

Ronnie smiled. "You may be right. She was a wily old bird. So, a mother knows her children and Richard is a sweet little lamb. OK. What about granny?"

"My mother? Now you're being ridiculous. My mother is a little old lady with arthritis in every joint and no reason at all to go about stabbing her grandchildren."

Ronnie didn't press it. "Just covering all the possibilities. Somebody did it and it's most likely someone in the family. Just statistically, you know."

"In that case, you've missed one of us out."

"Yes, I have, haven't I? But you were walking on the beach, weren't you? Did anyone see you out there?"

"I believe the police found a couple of witnesses."

"And you didn't have any motive, did you?"

"None whatsoever. Harry could be a difficult boy but, even when I was furious with him, the worst I ever contemplated was giving him a good spanking. Forty-year-old boys still need a good spanking now and then, you know – probably more than when they were bubs."

"And what kind of thing made you furious with him?"

She smiled. "He could be... inconsiderate of people's feelings, sometimes. Well, all the time, really. Sometimes it was just infuriating."

Ronnie stood up. "Thank you, Jennifer. That was great. I won't keep you any longer."

Surprised, I stood up too. So did Jennifer.

"Do you really think you'll catch him?" she asked, herding us towards the door.

"Him?" I asked.

"Or her."

"Yes," said Ronnie. "We will."

"How can you be so sure?" She seemed genuinely interested.

"Because this is an easy case."

Jennifer and I both goggled at Ronnie.

He smiled. "The murder took place on an island. Our entire pool of suspects is, say, three hundred people. We can get the names of every single one of them. Eighty percent of those people – maybe ninety – will have a solid alibi. So we have a pool of just thirty suspects. We will delve into the lives of each and every one of those people until we are certain they are innocent, or until we find the one who is guilty. If it is none of these, we will begin picking at the alibis of the others until we find the one that unravels."

"Goodness," she said. I could see she was appalled but whether it was at the amount of work implied – as I was – or at the absolute determination in Ronnie's tone, I couldn't say.

We pushed open the fly screen and walked out on to the verandah.

"Just a couple of questions before we go," Ronnie said. "One, where do we find your son, Richard, these days?"

She seemed a little taken aback. "At the office, I suppose. Or at home."

I handed her a business card. "Could you email me his contact numbers, please? It would save us some time."

Ronnie said, "By 'the office' you mean the Brisbane office of XtraVirtual? Even though Cassandra got the shares and Richard is suing her, he still works there?"

"Of course. Why wouldn't he? He took over as Managing Director when Harry died. Cassie doesn't want to run the business. Not that she could. She's more than happy for Richard to have day-to-day control. She's Chairman of the

47

Board, now. She even turns up to Board meetings, I'm told, for whatever that's worth. If it wasn't for her majority holding, I'm sure they'd be rid of her like a shot."

"Why didn't your son make a will?" I asked. It was a question dear to my heart. The fact that Chelsea had made a will and given me everything had changed my life completely. The story I'd had from Kazima after Chelsea died was that the company managers making wills had been a requirement of a venture capital deal they'd done to raise money for an expansion. I wondered why no one lending XtraVirtual money or investing in the company had ever insisted on tying down the succession.

"Because Harry Cross was never going to die," his mother said, her voice heavy with the irony of it. "Plenty of people asked for him to sort it out – not least Richard – but he shut them all down. He was going to outlive everyone and, when he died, he would take the whole damned lot with him. He was quite clear on that point. Contemplating his own death was something Harry found impossible to do without growing extremely emotional."

"So, my last question," Ronnie said. "Who do you think killed your son?"

Jennifer's eyes lost focus as she thought about it. "I don't know," she said. "I really don't. Someone I know, perhaps. Maybe someone I love. It just doesn't make any sense. I'm sometimes glad I don't know. Perhaps knowing would be even worse."

Chapter Four

By the time we got back to Brisbane, it was too late to see Richard Cross. So we went straight to the office. I called Richard on his direct number – already there in my email thanks to his mother's secretary. He was too busy to talk but seemed keen to meet, so we set up an appointment for the morning. Then I bent to the dual task of writing up the case notes and fending off Desi's endless questions. After a while, Ronnie went off in search of food and beer and returned with lots of both. Desi went home, frustrated, and Ronnie wrote names and drew arrows on our new digital whiteboard.

At about six thirty, Noah came in begging to be allowed to do something on the murder case. I was diplomatically telling him he had other projects on the go that couldn't be dropped just because something more interesting had come up, when Ronnie told him to "fuck off and stop whining like a little bitch." Noah, shocked into silence, turned on his heel and walked out of the office.

"Mate, for fuck's sake, you can't talk to the staff like that. What if he resigns?"

"He's not going to resign. Why would he leave the cushiest job in Queensland? You're too soft on these drongos."

"Yeah, it's called being a good boss."

"It's called being a bloody doormat. You need to grow a pair, mate. They'll never respect you if you let them get away with all that shit."

"What? Shit like showing enthusiasm? Shit like wanting to do exactly what you want to do?"

"Trouble in paradise?"

We both turned to see who had spoken. Harper strode into the office. She was a nondescript, scruffy woman in her forties, still trim but her face was already craggy and careworn. If you passed her in the street, you wouldn't notice her except that Harper had that swagger and self-confidence that only twenty years of working as a cop could bring. She'd butted heads with the meanest, toughest crims in Brisbane and lived to brag about it. She'd made Detective quickly enough but had since been passed over for promotion so many times she'd left the police service early, feeling nothing but bitter disdain for the whole organisation.

"Hi," I said, hoping she hadn't heard too much of that. "How are you doing?"

"Can't complain. Well, I could, but who'd listen. So, you got a murder at last. Solved it yet?"

"Not quite. Ronnie reckons we need to check the alibis of three hundred people before we'll get anywhere."

She went to her desk and rummaged in the drawers. "Yeah, well, give me a call if you need any help. The only part about being a cop I miss is getting heavy with suspects to break their stupid lying alibis."

"Speaking of which," I said. "Do you suppose any of your old mates would slip us the files on this one. It's a closed case. Well, dormant, anyway. What harm could it do?"

She laughed. "'Slip us the files'? You know the files for a

case like that would run to twenty boxes of crap? Maybe more. You think someone's going to sneak that out under their jumper?"

"Just a thought. What about someone who worked on the case that we could talk to?"

"You know whose case it was, don't you?"

"Yeah, Reid's."

"Right. And you know what he thinks about you guys. Anyone who so much as looked in your direction would risk becoming Reid's personal punchbag. I'm not going to ask any of my old mates to hang their goolies where Reid can kick them. Also…" She looked from me to Ronnie and back again, drawing out the tension. "I heard a rumour that Gomez is retiring next year." Gomez was what the cops in homicide affectionately called their boss Chief Inspector Adams. "And Reid is preparing to pounce on the old bastard's empty chair. You know what would look really bad for him right now?"

I sighed. "A bunch of amateur sleuths swooping in and solving the highest-profile murder Brisbane has seen in a decade."

"Especially since you did the same trick on DI Marr last year and that's why she's definitely not in the running for Gomez's job."

"She was pretty decent about it," I said, reminiscing.

"Yeah, well, the brass wasn't so understanding. Look, I've got to shoot through." She stuffed some documents into her bag and headed for the door. "Needless to say, if there's any chance of a role in the Cross case, even a bit part, you know how to reach me. Lots of valuable police experience, blah, blah, blah."

She left without waiting for a reply. I looked around for

Ronnie and found him hanging up his phone.

"Right," he said. "Grab your wallet, you're taking a beautiful woman to dinner."

"Great," I said. Then a horrible thought struck me. "You didn't call—"

"Megan? Nah, mate. That's your job. Tonight, you are dining with Detective Sergeant Alexandra Bertolissio." He grinned. "And me, of course."

"You remember she wasn't part of the original investigation, don't you. She was... I dunno... seconded or something."

"To Organised Crime. Of course I remember. Better than you, as it happens. But Al's been Reid's bag man forever. There's no way she doesn't know every detail of the Cross case. She's read the file front to back and she's talked to everyone involved. She's the kind of copper who likes to make her boss look good. If she could have solved it on the basis of the evidence they gathered, she would have. The fact that she didn't tells me the cops missed something important. And, tonight, I want her to tell us where to look for the missing piece. So, come on, get a shuffle on."

"Right-o. You told her this isn't just a social call, hey?"

"It must have slipped my mind."

"Look, I don't want to—"

"Just stop worrying and get your arse in gear. Bertolissio is the smartest woman I ever met. She knows damned well why we want to buy her dinner all of a sudden. She's probably been waiting for our call all day."

* * * *

Alexandra Bertolissio may or may not have been the most

intelligent woman I knew but she was certainly the widest-read and best-informed. I'd first met her after Chelsea was murdered, when she was one of the detectives working the case. Since then, she had almost become a friend. Over the past couple of years, I'd sought her out for advice and I'd had several stimulating and wide-ranging conversations. She was the only person I knew – outside my former university department colleagues – with whom I could discuss epistemology without having to explain every concept. Which, when you think about it, is quite amazing. She was about ten years older than me, late thirties, and Ronnie was not wrong in describing her as a beautiful woman – something you had to look closely to notice because she was petite, dark, always dressed practically and quietly, and never wore makeup. When her sister, Mel, was around – tall, blonde, stunningly attractive and gorgeously displayed in designer outfits – Alexandra almost faded into the background. And yet, male hormones aside, I'd give you a hundred Mels for one Alexandra. The fact that a woman like that was stalled in her career at Detective Sergeant said some very bad things about the Queensland Police Service.

We found her sitting demurely at a table in her favourite CBD restaurant. I'd been there before and had nearly been given the bum's rush by the management for being too scruffy. But, the story went, Alexandra had saved the owner from some terrible fate or other and, since then, he and the whole staff at the restaurant always treated her as visiting royalty. I saw the head waiter frown and begin a manoeuvre to intercept us as soon as he noticed Ronnie but, when Alexandra stood up and greeted us as friends, he changed direction and sent a waitress over to take our drinks order.

"Well, I wonder what this is all about," she said, smiling.

"You know you don't need an excuse to invite me to dinner?"

Ronnie grinned back at her. "Yeah, but it's good to have one, hey? Especially when it's a fatal stabbing."

I don't suppose Ronnie and Alexandra could ever be friends. They were just so very different. But they each shared a mutual admiration of the other's skills as a detective. They also shared a passion, bordering on mania, for catching killers. I'd seen Ronnie's obsession up close and I'd heard several stories of how Alexandra had put her life and career on the line to bring down the bad guys. Of course, I can hardly talk. The only two murders I'd ever investigated ended up with me almost getting myself killed. Sometimes, I found that deeply disturbing. Other times, I felt a wild pride that it made me part of a club that had people like Ronnie Walker and Alexandra Bertolissio in it.

"Tell you what," Alexandra said. "Let's not talk about the Cross murder while we eat. Afterwards, I'll tell you whatever you want to know."

"Yeah, no worries," said Ronnie. "What's good here?"

For a while, we discussed the menu, then we moved on to social topics. Alexandra's boyfriend – a Russian violin player called Pyotr Somethingorother – was visiting soon for the first time in eighteen months.

"The closure of international borders has been especially difficult for Pyotr," she said. "He's used to travelling with his orchestra and being invited as a soloist all over the world. He loved it. And it brought him to Australia at least twice a year, sometimes more, when he could arrange it. But now he's talking about taking a job over here. Any Australian orchestra would be very glad to have him." She probably wasn't exaggerating. I'd looked up his Wikipedia entry one time and the bloke was some kind of international superstar.

"Luke's love-life is in the dunny too," said Ronnie. "Did he ever tell you abut the lovely Megan?" Alexandra nodded. I was grateful for her discretion. The truth is, when Megan dumped me and went back to her husband, I'd turned up on Alexandra's doorstep, a blubbering mess, needing someone to tell me what to do. She'd been perfect: cool and sensible, and had taken my pain seriously without being either indulgent – as my parents would have been – or mocking – which would have been Ronnie's approach.

"Yeah, well, she fell for her emotionally abusive jerk husband's sob-story about needing her to give his life meaning – or some such dingo's droppings – and went back to him…" He made disdainful air quotes. "…to give their marriage a second chance." He looked at me angrily. "Tell the little drongo he needs to get round there, give the jerk a good walloping and get Megan back."

Alexandra laughed. "I'd never advise anybody to break the law."

"Why do you care so much anyway?" I asked him. "What the hell business is it of yours?" It was embarrassing to have this row in front of Alexandra but I was growing more irritated with Ronnie every time he brought this up.

Ronnie shook his head, looking for all the world as if he was angry with himself, not me. "You're right. I should stop bringing it up." He bent to his food and I glared at his head, noticing his hair was getting thinner.

"How's your chest these days, Ronnie?" Alexandra asked and the conversation moved on.

After the meal, we went to sit in an area with deeply-cushioned cane armchairs and had coffee and liqueurs.

"Right-o," said Ronnie, putting down his Bundaberg

Royal. "Tell us who killed Harry Cross."

Alexandra, who was sipping a Kahlua, put it down and said. "I really have no idea. The case focused on Grigor Mostek, the wife and the brother, but there wasn't enough evidence against any of them even to make an arrest – well, one that would stick – let alone get a conviction. Trevor is convinced it was Mostek or the brother. Richard and Harry had had many very public arguments over the years and many witnesses said that Harry treated Richard abominably. But Harry Cross treated everybody abominably, including his wife, his mother and his friends."

"His mother tried to tell us his spousal abuse was all just tabloid rumour-mongering," I said.

Alexandra pursed her lips. "I can't really say much about it but the investigation found plenty of evidence that there was more to it than that. In fact, before we get any deeper into this, I have a condition to place on you for any information I give out."

Ronnie held up a hand. "Yeah, yeah. We won't reveal our source. Anything you say is in strictest confidence. All that crap."

A small smile of amusement grew on Alexandra's lips. "I would hope that your discretion need never be bargained for." Ronnie shut up and looked a little abashed. "No, what I want is this. Contact Trevor Reid, tell him you're working on the case, tell him you'll keep him informed of any findings, and, if you do find the killer and if it is at all possible, make it work out so that Trevor gets at least some of the credit – no matter how he behaves, no matter how he treats you. That is my condition. Promise that and I will break all the rules and support you any way I can."

Ronnie sat back in his chair, looking stunned. I felt pretty shocked myself. On the one hand, Alexandra was offering us the crown jewels – access to inside knowledge of the case. On the other, she wanted us to play nice with Trevor Reid and to make him come out smelling of roses even if we solved the crime after he had failed miserably.

"So," Ronnie said. "The rumours are true. Reid is up for the Chief Inspector's job."

"I cannot confirm or deny any such rumours."

Ronnie rolled his eyes. "So why do you want him to get it? Would they make you a DI?"

She laughed. "I suppose anything is possible."

"Do you think he deserves it?" I asked, appalled that someone like Reid could fail upwards.

She gave me a long look. "It's complicated. I know you had an unfortunate experience with him but he's basically a decent man – unlike many I know – and he does listen to advice. Eventually. Anyway, that's the deal. What do you think?"

I sat back and thought hard. As reluctant as I was to help DI Reid in any way, what Alexandra was offering was definitely the good oil. And yet…

I realised I'd been brooding for quite a while. I looked up and found Ronnie staring at me with his eyebrows raised. It was obvious he'd reached his conclusion quickly and was impatiently waiting for me to catch up.

"OK. It's a deal," I said.

＊ ＊ ＊ ＊

"So what do we know?"

Ronnie stood by the whiteboard, stylus in hand. It had been his idea that we go back to the office to get everything sorted out before we forgot anything. Personally, I was dead tired and would much rather have gone home to bed. The answer to his question was, "A lot." Alexandra had given us a long and comprehensive summary of the investigation. The most impressive thing about her dissertation was not how clear and coherent it had been but how incredibly detailed. She had remembered names and times, personal histories of obscure and minor characters, who could alibi whom, who had seen what and when, and where everyone had been at all the key moments. I'd taken a notebook and pencil in case she'd dropped any useful information but I hadn't expected to spend the whole post-dinner period scribbling furiously, filling page after page. And all this from a woman who had not even been part of the investigation but had merely read the files later and chatted to her colleagues.

I said as much to Ronnie and he said, "She really wants to get that promotion for her boss."

Which made everything make sense. She hadn't just casually skimmed those files, she had sat down with them, probably for many hours, poring over them, trying to solve the case so that she could make Reid look good.

And yet she'd failed.

And, if Alexandra Bertolissio had failed to find the killer, it had to mean that the key to the case was not in those files. Everything she had told us, everything she could ever tell us, was not going to help – except to steer us away from all the many dead ends Reid and his team had gone down. In an instant, all the excitement I'd felt at being given that torrent of information, evaporated. Alexandra had saved us a massive amount of time, no doubt, but she had not helped us find the killer.

"OK," I said. "Let's start with the family."

Ronnie wrote the names in a column on the board, starting with "Granny" at the top (we still didn't know her name) and moving down through Jennifer, Richard and Cassandra. At the bottom were "The Kids" (we didn't know their names either). We wrote down a few facts about each and, importantly, their alibis. Granny had none because Jennifer had gone out for a walk. Jennifer had the alibis of two day-visitors to the island who had seen her on the beach. Richard was in his room, alone, so no alibi there. Cassandra was also in her room but her housekeeper vouched for her and Alexandra had confirmed that she had made a statement to that effect. So ruling out Granny and The Kids, of the family, that left only the victim's brother with no alibi.

Ronnie started a new column for motive. Again, excluding Granny and The Kids, Cassandra had by far the best motive – her husband had been beating her and she inherited everything. Richard had the possibility of taking over the firm, and the possibility of deep sibling conflict, but that all seemed a bit speculative. Only Jennifer, Harry's mum, didn't seem to have any motive at all. According to Alexandra, a detailed study of everyone's movements showed that all of them (including Granny and The Kids) had had the opportunity to acquire the knife that had killed Harry.

Ronnie saved the contents of the board and wiped it. "OK, that's the family. Now for the company execs."

My only exposure to any of the people who had been with Harry Cross on that ill-fated company retreat was through Alexandra's mention of them at the restaurant. I ran through the names from the barely-legible scrawls in my notebook – only listing the ones Alexandra had said had no alibi. There were three of them. Ronnie wrote them up. Top of the list was Doug Fletcher, the Sales Manager and the only one who described himself as a friend of Harry Cross. They had a stormy relationship and there were rumours that Harry had slept with Doug's wife. Doug's wife denied it but, even if it wasn't true, it would still be motive if Doug believed it. Next was Sandra Tsai, the Chief Financial Officer. It was rumoured that Harry had slept with her, too, and had dumped her but, from what Alexandra said, it was the kind of company where that kind of rumour was rife. Basically, everyone hated Harry and wouldn't put anything past him. Sandra had been taking a nap at the time of the murder, she claimed. Others said that was really unlikely because she was a human dynamo and famous for only sleeping about four hours a night. Finally, there was Claudia Knecht, Harry's personal assistant. Oddly enough, there were no rumours about her and Harry. At the time of the murder, Claudia had been in another meeting room, next door to the one in which Harry had been stabbed, preparing materials for a different presentation that Harry was to give to the board a few weeks after the retreat. She had been alone throughout the stabbing and had heard nothing. In fact, she said she only learned of the killing when the body was discovered and a commotion broke out. She had worked for Harry Cross for five years and was said to be fiercely loyal. So, plenty of opportunity but no motive.

There were a couple of others the cops had looked at. A bloke who worked in the kitchens, Mike d'Angelo, had a criminal record for violent assault – which he'd lied about to get the job. It would have been simple for him to get hold of the knife and he had no alibi for the time of the murder. Reid had tried hard to find some connection between him and the victim but came up empty-handed. There was no money trail to suggest the man had been paid to kill Harry. They'd found snuff movies on the man's laptop and a few grams of methamphetamine in his room and Reid had had to settle for that.

The only other person of interest Bertolissio had thought worth mentioning was Grigor Mostek. This was a man who had brought his wife and two friends to the island on a day trip. They were driving around on sandy tracks miles from the resort in Grigor's new Lexus SUV according to the three witnesses in the car with him. However, the cops had discounted the alibis on the grounds that Grigor Mostek was an enforcer for the Novaks, a prominent Brisbane crime family and, by a strange coincidence, was well-known for favouring large knives when pursuing his trade. He had also been at dinners and other get-togethers with Harry Cross on more than one occasion over the past few years. Most recently, they had been part of a group that had shared the XtraVirtual corporate box at the Gabba to watch the Lions play. The investigation into Mostek had soon hit an impenetrable wall of lawyers and the cops had beaten their heads against it to no avail. It didn't help that several independent witnesses remembered Mostek's car being exactly where he said it was, even though none could swear they'd seen Mostek at the wheel. A forensic examination of the car had revealed no traces of the victim's blood or DNA. Mostek's lawyers had brought a harassment suit against Reid and the QPS which they later dropped after Reid delivered a personal apology to Mostek and his wife.

"I almost feel sorry for the big tosser," I said, imagining how hard it must have been for a man like Reid to deliver that apology.

Ronnie grinned an evil grin. "I think we should mention that when we see him. In fact, I think we should mention it often."

"You know, we haven't actually talked about what we're doing here, you know, helping Reid get the Chief Inspector job. Do we really think that's the right thing to do?"

Ronnie shrugged. "Better the devil you know. Reid might be a prick but at least he's an honest cop. I can think of lots of worse candidates. Anyway, we're not doing this to help Reid, we're doing it to put a murderer away. Reid's ascension will be on Al's conscience, not mine. She's the one who insisted on us helping him. And, what's more, we've got to solve the thing first or nobody comes out of this looking good."

I studied the board, each name representing a dead end the cops had already gone down.

"What do you think?" I asked. "Do you have, like, a gut feeling or something?" I have to say, I was feeling a bit overwhelmed. There were too many suspects, most of them rich or dangerous. I had a sudden flashback to being a boy of ten or eleven, playing with my mates at the local swimming pool, standing at the edge of the deep end as they all leapt in, knowing my swimming skills were barely up to the job of keeping me afloat but that I had to go in because the social cost of backing down was even scarier than all that deep water.

Ronnie got up and stretched. "I think we need to sleep on it. It'll look better tomorrow."

I didn't move. "Why couldn't the cops solve it?"

He looked unhappy. "I dunno, mate. Incompetence? Lack of motivation?"

"No, seriously."

He gave a heavy sigh. "Too much noise."

"What?"

"You know, like in signal-to-noise ratio. The noise was too

high and they couldn't find the signal."

"What the hell do you mean?"

"Look, there's only four main reasons for murdering someone: sex, money, fear and revenge. Well Harry Cross was getting lots of sex, he had tons of money, he was a powerful and cruel man, and he'd upset everybody who ever met him. Too much noise. You remember the Tontine Murders?"

"I wish you wouldn't call it that." It was our only other murder case since I'd become a PI and it had nearly killed both of us, so, yes, I remembered it.

"Well, there, the first victim was a bloody saint, loved by everybody, we floundered around looking for a motive. Just no signal at all. Here, we've got the opposite. Everybody had a motive, most people had the means, and lots of people had the opportunity. We'll wear ourselves out sifting through that lot. What we're looking for is why one of those people went ahead and killed the bastard instead of just hoping someone else would do it."

I struggled to see what he was getting at. "So, you mean, like, a trigger of some sort?"

"That's it. Something happened. Something changed. Somebody snapped. That's what we should be looking for."

"But..." What was it Ronnie had said? Sex, money, fear and revenge? "Surely there are other motives for murder? Like love. You know, like a mercy killing, or to protect someone."

He waved it away. "Yeah, yeah, of course, but I was just listing the main ones. Can we go now, or do you want to discuss theory all night?"

With a sigh, I shut up the office and we left.

Chapter Five

Richard Cross was a tall, rangy man. The minute I saw his soft brown eyes, I thought, *Now here's a man who might kill for love of someone else.* I tried to imagine him with his beautiful, shallow sister-in-law but knew by instinct he was not her type. Despite his position at the head of a multi-billion-dollar company, he was not the kind of man who could have fought his way to the top of the pile and held that pinnacle against all comers. He was the kind of man who got the job because his brother was the kind to fight his way to the top and didn't trust anybody else to have his back. As we said our hellos in the spacious luxury of his corner office with its spectacular river views, I wondered how long he could stay in charge of XtraVirtual without his brother around to deter challengers.

"I'm so glad that someone is working on this again," he said. "The cops say the case isn't really closed, they would never close it, but they've stopped actively investigating it. Honestly, I can't see what they think the difference is."

"Of course, we can't promise anything," I said, shifting into my company owner persona. "But we'll give it our best shot."

He led us over to a seating area with a huge glass coffee table and leather chairs. There were documents on the table in two piles. He'd prepared briefing materials for us. On the phone, setting up the meeting, I'd asked for a list of the employees on the island on the day of his brother's death. He'd obviously felt he could do better than that. On top of each pile was a non-disclosure agreement and a pen. He must have seen me looking at it.

"Your information packs include the full personnel files for each of the people involved in the Murdock Island company retreat. There is also quite a lot of company information. I intend to be as open with you as I can. I want my brother's killer found. However, I do need you to sign an NDA before I can share this with you."

"No problem," said Ronnie, already signing. Suppressing a sigh, I picked up the one-page document and read it. It seemed innocuous enough, barring us from disclosing anything that we were told by company employees, or that we learned through documents we were given.

"You understand we might learn things that we'd be obliged by law to disclose to the police," I said.

"I understand. Partly, this covers us for privacy legislation purposes..." He gave me a weak smile. "...and it keeps you away from the press."

I signed it. "I might need other members of my staff to be brought in on the investigation."

"That's no problem. You have a copy of the NDA in the pack, just make more copies if you need them."

"Right," said Ronnie, with the air of a man who wanted to get down to business if everybody had stopped messing about doing dumb admin. The moment he opened his mouth to ask a question, however, a woman came in with a heavily laden trolley. She parked it near a sideboard and began unloading goodies onto it. Richard asked us if we'd like a drink. We worked through the options – two kinds of tea, coffee, decaffeinated coffee, sugar, sweetener, cream, milk, milk substitutes, and so on – and the woman began preparing our requests, eventually bringing it over along with a plate of cakes and one of biscuits. While this was going on, Richard asked polite and neutral questions about our work.

As soon as the woman left, Ronnie asked, "Where were you when your brother died?"

Richard looked at him with a slightly hurt expression. "I was in my chalet, reading. On the balcony, actually. We were all taking a break from the proceedings and I chose to spend the time relaxing."

"How did you hear of your brother's death."

Again, he gave Ronnie a pained look. "Claudia came to my chalet – Claudia Knecht, Harry's PA." He pronounced the name in the German style – Clowdia. "She was in tears and I had to calm her down before she could tell me. As soon as I heard, we rushed back to the hotel building and to the room where it had happened. The manager there seemed to have everything under control. She'd sealed the room and had called the police. I went in briefly, to look—" He turned away and his jaw clenched. "I don't know why. I think it was just impossible to believe until I saw—" He studied the cup of Darjeeling tea in front of him for a moment. "I'm sorry. The memory of him lying on the floor with a knife in his chest and all that blood… It's still very vivid. I asked Claudia if anyone had told Cassandra yet and she said no, so I left the manager in charge and went off to Cassie's chalet to break the news."

"How long after the murder was this?"

"I don't know for sure. The manager told me they'd found the body about ten minutes before I heard about it. So maybe twenty, twenty-five minutes before I saw Cassie."

"And how did she take it?"

Richard frowned at Ronnie. "How do you think? She was distraught. I had to stay with her from that point on, until we were back on the mainland, in fact, hours later."

"What about the kids?" I asked.

"They went off with the nanny somewhere. Cassie was in no state to deal with them. It was far better to get them away from it all."

"What was the nanny's name?" It was the second time somebody had mentioned a nanny.

"I – I have no idea. You'll have to ask Cassie. Look, can I just say something?" We both waited for him. "I get it. You're questioning me like a suspect. And that's OK. But, look, I just want you to know that I want this investigation to succeed. I want to know who killed Harry. I want this awful business settled. The thing has been hanging over my family for a year now, with the bloody tabloids taking pot-shots at us whenever they feel like it. So, give me the third degree if you like. I suppose I would, in your position, but I just want you to know I'm going to help you as much as I possibly can."

"What about the rest of your family?" Ronnie asked, apparently unmoved by Richard's little speech. "Do they want this all cleared up, too?"

"Of course they do?"

"Yeah, mate, I'm not so sure about Cassandra. She seemed more eager to get rid of us than to talk to us. And your mother, she seemed a bit ambivalent, like she wasn't sure getting to the truth would be best. You know, just in case it was more bad news."

I had no idea why Ronnie was going in so hard with a

bloke who'd just said he wanted to help us all he could. I got the impression from his surprised expression that Richard Cross was wondering the same thing. He opened his mouth to make some comment but Ronnie jumped in with the next question.

"How did you get on with your brother? People say you argued a lot."

"What people?" The recent mention of Cassandra and his mother must have provided an unfortunate context for the question. He seemed quite rattled. Ronnie just looked at him, waiting for an answer.

"Look," Richard said. "Harry was a difficult person to get along with. If he was getting his way, he would be charming and amiable. Generous, even. Fun to be with. But, if he wasn't getting his way, he changed completely. People generally let him have his way. Yes, we had a few blues. Lots, probably. But, at the end of the day, Harry was my brother and I loved him."

Ronnie nodded. "Did he feel the same way about you?"

"Of course!"

"And yet he left all his property – including his share of the business – to his wife."

Richard's face did a funny little twitch and I wondered if it was a sign of his anger at his brother, or at Ronnie.

"It wasn't like that," he said. "Harry was sort of superstitious about death. He couldn't bear to think of himself dying. It was a real phobia. Everyone told him he should make a will. I told him, Mum told him, his lawyers told him, various institutional investors told him, the Board told him, jointly and severally. It was all a waste of breath. 'I'll make one when the time comes,' he'd say, or, 'Why does everybody want to see me dead?' He was quite irrational about it."

"Shame," said Ronnie.

"You could say that. It's left the business in disarray, the family in convulsions. All because he was such a sel—" He stopped himself. The words "selfish bastard" seemed to hang, unspoken, in the air.

Ronnie let it hang for a while before he asked, "And what about Cassandra? What's your relationship with her?"

Richard looked at Ronnie under his brows and chose his words carefully. "Well, having to sue her for control of the company doesn't help."

"So, what was it like before Harry's death? Were you two close?"

I saw Richard's jaw tighten. "She's my sister-in-law."

"You're not married, are you?"

"No, I'm not."

"That must make you one of Brisbane's most eligible bachelors – rich as Croesus, even without control of the company, still fairly young, no hideous deformities. I'd have thought you'd have been snapped up by some enterprising supermodel with a daddy complex. Perhaps some young beauty has already captured your heart."

"Are you asking if I was having an affair with Cassie?" I flinched at the anger in his voice but Ronnie was completely unfazed.

"Were you?"

"No, I was not."

"And now?"

"What?"

"According to what you told us, your first thought was to run off to comfort the grieving widow. You spent the rest of the day with her."

"Have we finished?" He stood up. I stood up too but Ronnie stayed where he was.

"Not yet? Who do you think killed your brother?"

"I haven't the faintest idea."

"Really? You haven't formed any theories in a whole year?"

"The police thought it was me. It sounds like you do too. Unfortunately, I don't have the luxury of being able to pick the easiest suspect because I happen to know I'm innocent."

"What about Cassandra? Could she have done it? I hear Harry beat her."

"Cassie's too... otherworldly. You've met her. The idea of her planning a murder, getting hold of a knife and then taking it to kill him in cold blood is... well, if you knew her, it wouldn't seem sensible. Besides, she's got an alibi."

I noticed he didn't contradict Ronnie about the wife beating.

"Alibis can be bought if you're a very rich person."

"I wouldn't know."

"Your mother then? Could she have done it?"

I thought a shifty look flitted across his face. He hesitated for a tiny fraction of a second.

"Don't be ridiculous. Look, I have other appointments."

"A few minutes ago, you were happy to do anything for us. Now you can't answer a few questions?"

"That was before you..."

"What? Started suspecting everybody? Even you? Started looking for motives? How else do you think we'll solve this?"

"You should—" He stopped, flustered. "It's just that—" Angry with himself now, he said, "It's your attitude. Frankly, I find your whole approach offensive."

Ronnie smiled and stood up. "It is. I'm in a business

where being offensive is unavoidable. Right now, you're my prime suspect. Cassandra's second. Your business colleagues are also on the list. Somewhere farther down are holidaymaking gangsters and disreputable sous-chefs. And your mother, of course. Right at the bottom are Cassandra's little ankle-biters. I probably won't even need to interview them until I've eliminated everyone else. If it offends you to be suspected, that's tough. My job isn't to worry about your wounded feelings, it's to pry loose the rock that Harry's killer is hiding under."

Richard looked abashed. "I – Of course. It's just— This whole thing has been so bloody awful and it never seems to go away. It just hangs over us all like a black cloud and it never ends."

"Oh, it'll end," Ronnie said. "It'll end when I catch whoever did this."

* * * *

We had lunch in the food hall near the station. Ronnie refused to discuss the case until he had a roast dinner inside him and had begun on the remains of mine.

"We need to eat better," I said, glumly regarding Ronnie's gravy-smeared plate.

"What's wrong with this?"

"We should cut down, at least. Well, you should. You're putting on weight."

He looked down at his belly where, for the first time since I'd met him, a slight paunch was visible. "Yeah," he said. "I'm not doing as much exercise as I used to. I get winded too easy."

Ronnie had been hit in the chest by a shotgun blast the

Christmas before last. By a miracle, helped along by a bullet-proof vest and extensive reconstructive surgery, he'd survived, but he'd come out of it all with about three-quarters of his former lung capacity. That and the long, painful recovery, had left him miserable and grumpy for months. More miserable and more grumpy than usual, I should say. If I'd known working on a murder case would cheer him up so much, I'd have gone out and shot someone myself.

"So, you need to eat less, right?"

"Nah, I need to find more ways to burn it off."

I gave up. "So, how come you went in so hard on Richard Cross?"

"That? That was nothing. He just needed to know who was boss."

"What? What the hell are you talking about?"

"Oh, you saw the way he was, with his information packs—" He accompanied the phrase with air quotes. "—and his NDAs and his 'I want this investigation to succeed' crap."

"You didn't believe him?"

"Believing him wasn't the issue. He wanted to own the investigation. He wanted to dominate it and steer it. It's probably something they taught him at business school but he's not cut out for it. I'm pretty sure his brother didn't let him get away with it and I'm damned sure I won't."

"But he was being helpful."

"Right. And now he'll go on being helpful but on our terms."

I frowned, deep in thought. "Do you practice that kind of macho bullshit psychology on me, too?"

He laughed. "Mate, I don't need to. You're one of the most omega males I've ever known."

"You mean I don't engage in pointless pissing contests all

the time?"

"Yeah, that's it. Whatever you need to tell yourself."

I shook my head and clenched my jaw. That old feeling of frustration and constant irritation was back. Somehow, I'd forgotten quite what it was like to work closely with Ronnie Walker. *Well, you're the idiot who wanted him to work on the case,* I told myself. *You could have used Harper or Noah.* But, of course, I needed Ronnie and there was no getting away from it. I didn't have the experience – or the self-confidence, for that matter – to tackle a high-profile murder without him.

"I'm off to look for a cake or something," he said, getting up. "What do you want?"

"I'm good."

He wandered off towards the food stalls and I sat back, pondering my inadequacies. I'd been idly staring at a woman a couple of tables away, sitting alone with her back to me, when it hit me it was Megan. My first instinct was to look away and pretend I hadn't noticed her. The I realised that, if she turned around and saw me, it would be obvious I had deliberately ignored her. I was only two tables away and facing right at her. How I'd missed her for so long was a mystery. But I really didn't want to say hello. She'd hurt me a lot when she'd gone back to her estranged husband 'to give it another go.' And it still hurt. It hurt just to see her. And I really didn't feel like talking to her. And yet, I didn't want to seem so petty as to be deliberately avoiding her. If I hadn't been with Ronnie, I'd have just sneaked away. Maybe I could still do that and phone him from outside. But the chances were he'd notice her on his way back to the table, then he'd talk to her and probably make jokes about my disappearance and make everything ten times worse.

I got up and went over.

"Hi, Meg."

She looked up at me and, for a moment, I saw something like horror flash in her eyes. Obviously, she didn't want this meeting any more than I did.

"I was just having lunch with Ronnie and I saw you. How are you doing? Back at work?"

She swivelled in her seat to face me, all smiles now. "I'm good. How's the detective business?"

"Pretty good, actually. We got another murder case. Harry Cross. Do you remember that from about a year ago?"

"Yeah, right. Murder Island? That one? So they never solved that?"

"Nah. No clues, no evidence, no witnesses, tons of suspects. Ronnie's loving it." She smiled, a little sadly, I thought. "How's married life?" The instant I said it, I regretted it. It was just a sore I couldn't help picking at. Megan's smile fell away. She struggled to find something to say, probably trying not to hurt my feelings. So I held up a hand and cut her off. "Stupid question. Forget I asked. Oh, look, there's Ronnie. I'd better go join him or he'll come over here and say rude things about me. Nice running into you. Catch you later."

Ronnie was, in fact, still at the food counter. I rushed over to intercept him before he noticed Megan. I left her looking slightly confused and distressed. I'd always known there was a chance I'd bump into her one day but, of course, I'd been completely unprepared. A hand had gripped my heart and begun squeezing the moment I saw her and it still hadn't let go. The look of her, the sound of her, were so familiar and normal. It felt completely wrong to be walking away from her. Some idiotic part of me that clearly hadn't been paying attention when we split up, was telling me to get back there and be with her, dragging at me like a toddler who couldn't understand why we were walking past the toy shop.

Ronnie, of course, wouldn't be dragged away without a full explanation and, when I refused, stood there looking around the food hall until he spotted Megan. Then he surprised me. With a sad shake of his head, he let me lead him out in to the square and away from my torment. He didn't even crack a joke about it, or call me a fool. We walked in silence in the warm autumn sunshine and wound our way through the busy streets.

We ended up outside the offices of Eastern Island Resorts before I even realised that's where we were heading. Ronnie stopped and looked at me.

"Get your head in the game, mate."

"I'm fine," I said. "When did you set this up?"

"I didn't. We're just dropping in on spec. The client said the manager here would give us whatever help we needed. So we'll see, won't we?"

"What was her name again?"

I pulled out my phone to look it up in the case file but Ronnie pushed ahead into the building saying, "Shirley Stephens," over his shoulder.

We got past reception and Stephens' personal assistant without much difficulty. It seemed Aikenhead really had smoothed our path, as promised.

Stephens had a small, cluttered office. It was the kind of place where real work was being done – unlike most executive offices I'd ever been in. Shirley Stephens herself was an energetic forty-something who reminded me of the smart and witty mother of one of my school-friends. She'd been a middle manager too, I recalled.

"How can I help?" she asked, once we were all seated.

"We need to get out to Murdock Island and take a look at the crime scene," Ronnie said, perhaps taking his no-nonsense, straight-to-business cue from Stephens. "Aikenhead said you could arrange things. Can we go tomorrow?"

I fought down an exclamation of surprise.

Stephens thought for a moment. "The first flight I can get you on is at 7:30 in the morning. Do you want to stay overnight or are you coming back the same day?"

"Same day," Ronnie said without hesitation.

"Five o'clock flight back?"

"That sounds great. Thank you."

"Our manager there is June Onbekend." She made a note as she spoke. "Lovely woman. She'll look after you. Anything else?"

"Just a couple of questions," said Ronnie. Stephens' face set into a ready, attentive expression. "Did you know Harry Cross?"

"What? No."

"Did you know any members of his family?"

"No. I don't exactly move in those circles."

"What about the staff at XtraVirtual? Know any of them?"

"No…" She seemed ready to ask Ronnie what the questions were about.

"How did they make the booking for their business retreat?"

"In the usual way. They have an agency that does their travel bookings. The agency contacted us through our corporate bookings program. It was just a routine booking."

I realised the cops must have asked already because she knew the answer.

"Whose idea was it to hold the retreat at Murdock Island?"

"I – I don't know. You'd have to ask someone at XtraVirtual."

"Who's your contact at XtraVirtual?"

"As I said, we don't deal with them directly. They do all travel-related business through an agency."

"So, who's your contact at the agency?"

In reply, she picked up the desk phone and punched a number. "Tony? Who's our contact at Faraway Travel?" She listened for a moment. "Well, who does bookings for XtraVirtual?" She listened again, repressing a sigh of frustration. "Well, when we used to do business with them, who handled it at Faraway Travel?" She waited a while, perhaps while Tony looked it up. "Thank you, Tony."

She made another note and this time tore off the page, handing it to Ronnie. "We haven't done any business with XtraVirtual at all since the murder, so I'm not sure if this Penny Wu person still works there but she used to be our primary contact for corporate bookings. Anything else?"

It was an interesting technique. Do what you're asked and say, "Anything else?" It seemed helpful at first glance but after only two iterations, it began to sound more like, "Is there anything else because I'm really busy and it would be good if you buggered off and let me get on with things."

"Nope," said Ronnie. "That covers it."

"Do you have a card?"

I handed her one. She glanced at it. "I'll send the flight details to this email addy within the hour." She stood up and the meeting was over.

"Jeez, talk about the bum's rush," I said to Ronnie on the way out.

"Good time management skills," he said. "We need someone like that in the office."

"Oh, here we go again. There's nothing wrong with Desi. She does a fine job."

"Adequate."

"Yeah, well, if she was Shirley Stephens, she'd be managing a regional office for a national hotel chain instead of working on reception for an obscure little detective agency."

"You don't have the right attitude to succeed," he said.

"What the hell does that mean?"

"It means if you start out intending to be The Rolling Stones, you might stand a chance of being the greatest rock and roll band in the world. But if you start out intending to be a third-rate Abba cover band, that's all you'll ever be."

"Is this some kind of special forces team-building bullshit? Be the best you can be? All that crap?"

"All I'm saying is, surround yourself with the very best people and then aim as high as you can."

"Yeah, yeah. Whatever. What do we do next?"

He glanced at his watch. I glanced at it too. It was early afternoon on the second day of the investigation and we'd done most of what we could with our victim's family. I expected Ronnie to say we should start interviewing Harry's business colleagues who'd been with him on the island but, instead, he said, "Let's go put our heads in the lion's mouth."

"What do you mean?"

"I mean, let's go see Grigor Mostek. You don't have to come if you don't want to. From what I hear, the guy's a complete psycho."

I felt the now-familiar flutter of anxiety. Every time we took on a murder case, there seemed to be organised crime connections somewhere. And our interactions usually ended up with me becoming a target. When we went after Chelsea's murderer, a bikie gang burned down my unit. When we were hunting the so-called Tontine Killer, a paid assassin took two shots at me and very nearly hit me. The thought of exposing myself to that kind of danger once again was not one I relished. The flutter in my guts quickly became a clenching fist. I swallowed against a suddenly dry mouth.

"Yeah, nah," I said, trying to sound relaxed. "I reckon I should be there." Ronnie glanced quickly my way but didn't say anything. "Any idea how we find him?"

"Sure. His home address was in the phone book."

Of course it was. One of the things I'd discovered working in the PI business but still couldn't get used to, was that even the worst criminals in the country seemed to live perfectly normal lives most of the time. Many of them were pillars of their communities, family men, with nice homes, smart cars, and kids at the best private schools. However grubby their working lives might be, their private lives were as clean and respectable as money could make them.

Ronnie gave me directions to a place in the leafy suburb of Camp Hill and we headed there as soon as we reached the car. We drove in silence for a while until Ronnie said, "Let me guess how it went with Megan."

"Please don't."

"You said hello and chatted about the weather. You were getting along fine until one of you – you, probably – mentioned her husband. Then there were awkward silences until you retreated in confusion and dragged me away from my iced doughnut with sprinkles."

It was so accurate, I wondered if he'd somehow been spying on us. It was such a miserable memory, I didn't have the strength to deny it. "Yeah, something like that, I reckon."

He shook his head, clearly despairing of me. "It's probably because there's no books about human relationships," he said. "That's why you don't know anything about it. Oh no, wait, there's fucking millions of the things. Practically every book ever written is about human relationships. I reckon it must just be that you're a fucking moron."

"Hey, Mr. Congeniality, the day I take relationship advice from a miserable old bastard like you, is the day it snows in Coober Pedy. What the hell do expect me to do? She's married. She's with her husband. She's trying to make a go of it. Just shut the fuck up."

He nodded to himself. "Right-o. I won't say another word. Maybe you'll meet a nice girl on Murder Island."

"Murdock."

"Cassandra seemed nice. And then there's Desi and Harper. Both just right for you."

I clamped my mouth shut. I suppose his heavily-laboured point was that the only women I met these days were crime suspects and employees. As true as it might be, I could not understand his obsession with me and Megan. I'd tried explaining it to him a hundred times. I only had one option and that was to move on. Move on to where was another matter.

For some weeks now, I'd been lurking on a dating site. There were lots of women on there who seemed nice – not special, maybe – but nice. The idea of dating a few was sort of tempting but not really. Just imagining the conversations, the awkwardness, the feeling of being judged, the knowing she knew I was judging, made it all impossible. I couldn't do that. I wasn't there yet.

Maybe I never would be.

Lightning had already struck me twice. Chelsea had been a miraculous stroke of luck; beautiful, intelligent, dynamic, loving, and way, way out of my class. And when she died, when I should have spent the rest of my life pining for an irreplaceable love, up popped Megan, another amazing woman, and filled me with hope that she could be the soulmate I thought I would never find. I'd been tentatively making plans, finally allowing myself to think about a lifetime committed to her, when she had dropped her bombshell and blown my dreams apart.

Twice I'd found women like that. Twice! It's incredible because, let's face it, I'm not much of a catch. I'm scrawny, introverted, and geeky to the point where my idea of a great night out is to go to a talk on existentialism and then discuss it for hours over a few cups of good coffee. It's true, I had some money – mostly thanks to Chelsea – but I knew full well that kind of thing can come tumbling down in a heap at any moment. A couple of bad decisions, another recession, some disruption in the market, and it could all just evaporate. Besides, if I had to rely on money to pull the chicks, I could say goodbye to ever finding one like Chelsea or Megan ever again.

Not that I hadn't tried. Well, to be brutally honest, I hadn't, really. I'd been on one date since Megan left me. No, not really a date, as such. I'd been feeling lonely, so I called an old university chum from the Philosophy Department. He was working in Environmental Planning now, for a mining company. He'd married and had a cute little home in Auchenflower. He'd invited me to dinner.

"Bring your SO," he said on the phone.

"My what?"

"Significant Other, mate."

"Ah, right. Look, I'm kind of in between SOs at the moment."

"No worries, mate. Just bring yourself then. And a bottle of vino."

I should have known the whole thing was going to be excruciating but I went anyway. From being a vaguely interesting PhD student specialising in environmental ethics, my old mate had transformed himself into a jovial yuppie with a detailed knowledge of the housing market. He'd also taken it upon himself to set me up with a woman. Her name was Tamara and she'd also been in the Philosophy Department, although, for the life of me, I could not recall her. She was small and fierce and seemed to take her role as my prospective partner for the evening very seriously. We managed to talk about things neither of us were very interested in for several hours.

As I was walking her to her car, she said, "This is our chance to cement our budding romance with a first, tender kiss."

Alarmed, I said, "Sorry? What?"

"Don't worry. It's not going to happen. You're not my type."

I admit, I was relieved. "You've, er, got a type, then?"

"Yes. Can I tell you why you're drifting about aimlessly with no girlfriend and no prospect of getting one?"

"I'd rather you didn't."

"It's because you're so wet."

"Wet?"

"Passive. Soft. Insecure. Indecisive. Needy yet indifferent."

"Hang on. You've only known me two minutes."

"Wishy-washy. Disengaged. Remote. Oh, here's my car."

We stopped beside an old Mitsubishi Magna that was clearly three sizes too big for her.

"Well," I said. "It was nice to meet you."

"You too," she said, presumably lying as much as I had been.

I went and sat in my own car and thought about what she'd said. In particular, I thought about how I'd been with Chelsea. *Passive, soft, disengaged, remote.* Had I been like that with Megan, too. Was that really why she'd left me? Or was it just why I hadn't fought to hang onto her? For all that I'd just had more company in any evening since she'd gone, the loneliness was more intense and painful than it had ever been.

Chapter Six

Grigor Mostek lived in a hideous MacMansion with statues of angels and fauns in the yard, and a Palladian arch over the front door supported by Corinthian pillars. Ronnie pushed the button besides a small screen above a little sign that said, "Please Ring." We waited for what seemed ages and Ronnie rang again.

This time the screen flickered into life. A woman's face peered through it at us, grossly distorted by a wide-angle lens. I assumed she could see us too because she seemed to spend a moment studying us.

"Yeah? What?" she said. I gathered we had failed the inspection.

"Mrs. Mostek?" Ronnie said in his charming voice. "My name is Ronnie Walker and this is my partner, Luke Kelly. Would it be possible for us to speak with your husband?"

"What about?"

"It's about your visit to Murdock Island last year."

She thought about that. "Are you cops?"

"We're private investigators. We just want to get your husband's perspective on what happened that day."

"You're private dicks? And you want to talk to Grigor about that stupid island thing?"

"That's right. We won't take up much of his time, I promise."

"We was just there having some fun. It's got nothing to do with us. We went through all this with the filth."

"I understand. We're not accusing anybody of anything. We just want to get your husband's thoughts on what happened that day."

There was a long silence while she squinted at the screen. Then she said, "Hang on," and disappeared. Two minutes later, a man's face appeared at the screen. Then the door opened. Grigor Mostek was a big man in his late thirties. He favoured the same kind of facial stubble and shaved head that Ronnie liked, had the same kind of deep chest and thick neck, too. Maybe there were style magazines for hired killers from which they copied their looks. He had on a bath robe, so I assumed he'd just come in from the poolside. The curly black chest hair visible in the deep V of the robe's front seemed calculated to emphasise the man's animal nature. I certainly took it as a warning.

"What do you wankers want?" Mostek said by way of introduction.

"Can we come in for a chat?" Ronnie asked, nicely.

"No you fucking can't." There was the faintest trace of an Eastern European accent in his voice, along with plenty of contempt.

"Then is it all right if I ask you a couple of questions about the Harry Cross murder?"

Mostek frowned. "You're PIs, hey? Who sent you?"

"We're working for the hotel chain that owns the island. Look, mate, you're not a suspect. We're not trying to put you in the frame for it, we've go no hidden agenda. We're just talking to everybody who was on the island that day to try to get an idea of what happened."

"Yeah? Well you look like filth. Sound like it too. Let's see some ID."

I pulled out my wallet and took out a business card. I also pulled out my PI licence and handed them both over. He studied them, studied me, handed them back, then turned back to Ronnie. "What about you?"

"He's not a private investigator," I said. "He works as my consultant."

With a sigh, Ronnie also opened his wallet and produced a Featherfoot Agency card. His said "Ronnie Walker, Consultant."

"I thought PIs were supposed to be tough guys," Mostek said, provocatively.

Ronnie smiled. "Yeah, I thought that about mob enforcers."

Mostek stared at him in silence for a moment – about the time it took for me to swallow hard – then he burst out laughing.

"All right, tough guy, ask me your questions."

I pulled out my note book where I'd scribbled down a few key names and times – the people with Mostek in the car, the time of the ferry they'd arrived on, the time the cops interviewed him, the time he was allowed to return to the mainland, that kind of stuff – but Ronnie didn't even notice.

"Right-o," he said. "Did you kill Harry Cross?"

Mostek's brows fell and my heartbeat kicked up a notch. "No, I fucking didn't."

Ronnie didn't look convinced. "Well, you would say that, wouldn't you? Maybe Harry Cross pissed off the wrong people. Maybe someone you work for decided Harry knew too much, or was asking too many favours. There's lots of ways a jerk like Harry Cross could make himself a target. What did Mr. Novak think of him? I gather they were big mates, always going out to clubs together and enjoying a few drinks."

Mostek's jaw was working as he listened to this. The mention of Mr. Novak seemed particularly to incense him. His eyes widened and he stepped out onto the porch. Involuntarily, I took a step backwards, but Ronnie did not move.

Nostrils flaring, Mostek spoke through clenched teeth. "Mr. Novak's social life is none of your fucking business, shithead."

"You're right," Ronnie said. "I should go and talk to him myself. I'll be sure to let him know how co-operative you were. He'll appreciate that."

Mostek stepped right up to Ronnie. They were practically nose to nose. "Maybe it would be best if you weren't around any more to annoy people with your fucking questions."

"Ronnie?" I said. "What're you doing, mate?"

They both ignored me.

"Tell me again," Ronnie said. "Were you on that island to kill Harry Cross?"

"It's time you and your girlfriend fucked off," Mostek growled.

"Or else?"

My breath caught. Even Mostek seemed taken aback. A frown crossed his heavy brows.

"Are you fucking mental, or what?"

"Are you going to answer my question?"

"I've told you. That bastard's death was fuck all to do with me." Pointedly, he added, "Or anybody I know."

Ronnie looked into his eyes for several seconds, then

stepped back. Breezily, he said, "You know what? I believe you. Thank you for your time, Mr. Mostek. Luke, do you have any more questions?" He must have taken my open-mouthed stare for a no. "Then we'll be off. Nice meeting you."

I backed away, heading for the car. Ronnie, recklessly, I thought, turned his back on the gobsmacked gangster and strolled past me.

I made it all the way to the car and had my hand on the door handle before Mostek bellowed, "Oi, cunt!"

Ronnie, on the other side of the car, looked back at Mostek. "Yeah?"

"You and me should get a drink sometime. Hang out. Get to know each other."

"Yeah," said Ronnie. "Sounds good. You bring your wife and I'll bring my girlfriend."

They both laughed.

I got into the car, scowling.

"What the hell was that?"

"Are we going, or what?"

I put the car in drive and set off. "So? What the hell did you think you were doing?"

"What do you mean?"

"Well, the dick-measuring contest, for a start. The man is a professional killer."

"So am I."

Which threw me a little. "Yeah, well, not recently – as far as I know. Then what about the Jaffa mind games?"

"The what?"

"Jaffa. You know, from *Stargate*."

"What?"

"It was a film and a TV show… It doesn't matter. I mean

all that staring into a man's eyes to read his true soul. That crap."

"Is that what I was doing?"

"And then, suddenly, you're best buds, swapping Telegram addresses and making each other little bead bracelets."

Ronnie was silent for a while. I glanced his way and found him grinning at me.

"Look," he said. "Mostek's a dead end. So is his boss. It wasn't a mob hit. Not by that mob, anyway."

"What? You're just going to take his word for it?"

"Yeah, pretty much. That, and the police investigation. There's no actual evidence that he did it, or the cops would have found it. I'm pretty sure they searched very hard. I just wanted to look Mostek in the eye and make him tell me he didn't do it." He shrugged. "And I believed him."

I felt a sulk coming on. "Yeah, well, not being part of this brotherhood of short-necked psychopaths, all I saw was a career criminal, probably lying his head off. 'Cause that's what criminals do, you know?"

Ronnie didn't deign to reply and we drove in silence for a while. I was heading towards the office, for want of anywhere better to go.

"Why don't we—?" Ronnie began and the phone rang. The screen in the car said it was DI Reid. We exchanged glances and I hit the pickup button.

"Detective Inspector," I said. "What can I do for you?"

"Are you with him, Walker?" Reid said, eschewing the social niceties. Maybe he'd picked up on the car noises.

"Yes, Trevor," Ronnie said. "What about your own better half? Is she there with you?"

There was a pause and some noise as Reid fiddled with his phone, no doubt putting it on speaker.

"Hi, Ronnie. DS Bertolissio, here."

"Well, this is nice," Ronnie said. "The old gang back together. Exciting, hey?"

"Shut up, Walker," Reid said. "What's all this about you two poking around in the Harry Cross case?"

"We're just doing our jobs, Detective Inspector," I said.

"I want the pair of you to know this is an open case and I don't want a couple of bloody amateurs screwing things up."

"Mate," Ronnie said. "You don't need us to screw things up. How long has the case been open?" He didn't wait for an answer. "And how many killers have you put behind bars?"

From the grin on his face, I could see Ronnie was relishing the chance to wind up DI Reid. Reid himself didn't sound too happy about it.

"I swear I'll do you both for obstruction if you give me any trouble."

I was about to explain to him that my license to practice as a private investigator gave me the right to pursue the investigation but Ronnie jumped in.

"Yeah, how's the promotion campaign going, Trev? I hear they're finally putting Gomez out to pasture and you're in with a shot. Scary when you think about it. I suppose the last thing you want right now is a couple of real detectives coming in and solving the biggest case of your career just before the selection panel signs off on making you chief. Wouldn't look good, right? Better if the case stayed unsolved, I reckon."

Bertolissio cut in. "Do you have any leads, Ronnie?"

"Hey, give us a chance! We're still eliminating some of the more obvious suspects. Like Grigor Mostek." I'm pretty sure he only added that to rub salt in Reid's wounds.

"We're heading up to Murdock Island tomorrow," I said,

throwing Bertolissio a bone. After all, our agreement with her was that we'd co-operate and try to make her boss look good. "We'll take a look at the crime scene, talk to the manager, get a feel for what happened that day."

"Tell you what," Bertolissio said. "We'd be interested in your findings."

I heard a scraping sound, as if someone was manhandling the phone. Then I heard muffled voices – Reid asking a question in an angry tone and Bertolissio explaining something. The scraping sound happened again – which, this time, I interpreted as Reid removing his hand from the mic – and Bertolissio said, "You'll be making reports for your client, I suppose. Perhaps you wouldn't mind sharing them with us?"

Ronnie grinned and shook his head as the pantomime played out. "What would be in it for us?" he asked.

"Oh, I don't know, maybe we could reciprocate," she said. "A bit of *quid pro quo*."

"We couldn't have done it without the extensive groundwork and support of DI Reid and his team," I said. "Just rehearsing what I'll say to the press if we solve this thing."

Ronnie rolled his eyes. I suppose I was laying it on a bit thick.

"I think that would be fair," Bertolissio said. "We scratch your backs, you scratch ours."

"I'm sure we can come to some kind of arrangement," I said.

"What about you, Trev?" Ronnie asked.

The big man's gruff voice came back on the line. "I reckon that'd be a great idea – if I thought for one second you clowns could find your own dicks with a searchlight and sniffer dogs. All I want from you two is for you to keep out of my way and – if by some miracle you do stumble on something useful – you pass it on right away. Got that?"

"Always nice to talk to you, Trev," Ronnie said and hit the end call button on the dash.

* * * *

"Weird," I said as we entered the office. "I can't get used to working on a murder case with no-one beating me up in the car park."

Ronnie just grinned and ambled off towards the electronic whiteboards while I stopped to talk to Desi and collect my phone messages. There was nothing important, so I went over to see what Ronnie was doing. He'd put up the list of suspects and put big Xs through Cassandra and Jennifer Cross and was just doing the same for Grigor Mostek.

"How can you eliminate all three of them on the basis of a single interview?" I wanted to know.

"Easy," he said. "Cassandra's a vapid airhead who probably thinks earthworms have souls, Jennifer wouldn't kill her own son, no matter how obnoxious he was, and Mostek passed my Jedi mind test."

"Jaffa."

"Gesundheit. Richard I don't really know about yet. He's being too helpful for my liking."

"Or he wants us to find his brother's murderer."

"And he's holding something back."

"Like an affair with his sister-in-law?"

We studied Richard Cross's photo for a moment.

"Anyway, we can't exclude anybody yet." I certainly had no reason to think any of them were innocent, alibis and relationships notwithstanding.

"OK," Ronnie said, ignoring me. "We'll be spending the whole day tomorrow on Murder Island. Don't forget to bring your Speedos. So we need to make a whole bunch of appointments with the XtraVirtual staff for the day after. Get Richard's secretary to set it up. We'll need a room in their offices, a constant supply of coffee and doughnuts, and an appointment every ten minutes from 8 A.M. until we've seen everyone. Get her to send a memo from Richard saying it is mandatory."

"Ten minutes? That doesn't seem much."

"Trust me, it will be more than enough for ninety per cent of them. And get her to lay on lunch for us. Something nice but we don't want to take more than half an hour. Some of the staff will have moved on to other jobs by now, you'll need to get contact details for all of them and set up meetings for the following day."

"And what are you doing while I do all this?"

"I'm going home. You should write up the notes from today, too. And drop the client a line saying we're making good progress. Bertolissio will probably call soon to tell you she's talked Reid round, so see if you can't get the police interview files out of her when she does. It would be nice to have them to check against our own interviews."

I was feeling a bit put-upon. "Would you like me to come round later and cook your supper?"

"No thanks." He either missed my heavy sarcasm or ignored it. "I've got Mary coming over. She'll probably bring something."

"You mean Maggie," I said, remembering the woman I'd met several times during his convalescence last year.

"No, mate. Mary. See you in the morning at the airfield."

* * * *

I actually did all the things he said I should. Hell, it was my business, my investigation, and somebody had to do it. Desi had just gone home when the phone rang so it automatically routed to my desk.

"Hello, Luke."

"Detective. I thought you might call." Well, Ronnie had thought she might.

"I hope you weren't put off by our call with Trevor earlier."

"You mean the one where he gave the impression he'd rather have sex with an echidna than work with Ronnie and me?"

"Well, on calmer reflection, he's decided that, in return for full disclosure from you, he might agree to a limited sharing of police intel from the case."

"Big of him."

"I'd say it was a major concession. So, what do you have to report?"

"We're scratching each other's backs, right?"

"Absolutely."

"In that case, what are the chances of us seeing the interview transcripts for the staff and guests you talked to on Murdock Island?"

"That's a lot of interviews."

"And it would save us a ton of time – and avoid us duplicating lots of effort."

I heard her make a blowing sound as if she was thinking it might be a lot of work.

"Here's what I'll do," I said, offering a sweetener. "I'll

send you and Trevor logins to our internal shared case file system. Everything we do will be on there – interviews, case strategy, profiles, client reports, everything. You'll both have full access."

"That's very generous."

"Yeah, well, I haven't talked it over with Ronnie, so it's probably really stupid. But what the hell? We're asking for a lot from you. It's only fair you should get as much back as we can give you. Deal?"

"You realise that what you're offering is only worth anything if you solve the case?"

I wondered at her hesitation but it struck me she was probably preparing her arguments for Reid.

"Detective—"

"Call me Al."

"Yeah, it doesn't really suit you. I'm not sure what would. Alexandra, maybe, or Xandra. That's kind of exotic. And feminine."

"Luke, are you flirting with me?"

"Good God, no! I mean, I was just…" Was I flirting? Surely not. Definitely not. Not with a woman who intimidated me so much. Seconds ticked slowly past. Feeling the silence, I started talking again. "Anyway, what I mean is, you realise that nothing you give us is likely to help us solve the case? You've had most of your evidence for a year already and it hasn't led to a prosecution."

"Very true." I thought I could hear the smile on her face. "So, you'll give us access to your potentially worthless case files, and I'll send you a bunch of completely worthless interview scripts."

"Which will, nevertheless, save us some precious time."

"It's a deal. I'll email you the transcripts."

"Thank you. Look, I don't want to sound like I'm flirting again. Which I'm not. Not that you're not— It's just… I'm looking forward to working with you again."

"Thank you," she said, graciously not laughing. "And I, you."

Bertolissio was my hero; a first-class detective, a cultured, educated woman who could converse intelligently on any subject, and a decent, caring human being, with the added bonus of being the only person I knew whose spoken English was more grammatically correct than my own written English.

I hung around at the office for another half hour after the call, during which time an email came with over two hundred interview transcripts, covering everybody the cops had spoken to about the case. I doubted that Trevor Reid would have approved of his Detective Sergeant's generosity, but she obviously felt she had sufficient cover and I wasn't going to tell him about it.

I moved everything into our file system, messaged Ronnie to take a look, and went home feeling like I'd had a successful day. The plan was to eat a frozen lasagne, drink a beer, watch some Netflix and crash early. But the plan drifted away like smoke as I stared at the note pinned to my front door. This was not good. There was no scenario I could imagine in which anyone pinned a nice note to my door two days into a murder investigation.

I looked around. It was dark but the street lights were bright enough. No-one was lurking in the street. No-one was running away. I looked back at the note. A single sheet of white paper, folded once and pinned at the fold with a single, plain drawing pin. There was no name on the paper, which had a slightly crumpled look, as if it had been sprinkled with water and left to dry. It hadn't rained. I reached out to the pin to remove it and stopped myself just in time. This might be evidence.

I opened the door and went inside, feeling the menacing presence of the note as I moved past it. I grabbed a pair of plastic gloves and a ziplock plastic bag and went back out. I put on the gloves and took hold of the note. The drawing pin was pushed in hard and took some effort to remove. I dropped it into the bag. Steeling myself, I unfolded the sheet of paper. Both times I had previously investigated a murder, the killer had threatened my life. Neither of them had sent me a note, of course, but maybe this was how the danger would start this time.

I was surprised to find printed words cut out and pasted onto the page, like a ransom letter in an old TV detective show. It explained why the paper was so uneven. The glue had spoiled the pristine smoothness of the page. I swallowed hard and read the words.

"if you want to know Who killed Harry cross look for the Man with the death's Head tattoo"

What?

I read it again, thinking there must be some hidden message. Maybe the weird capitalisation meant something. I read it over and over but, in the end, I had to conclude it was just what it seemed to be: a clue left for me to help me find Harry's killer. The capitalisation was just an artefact of having to find the right words in a bunch of magazines. And they had all come from magazines, judging by the glossy surface of the little cut-outs and the high quality of the print.

Was it a joke? Was someone pulling my leg? Ronnie, maybe? I wouldn't put it past him, except it had obviously taken some effort to make this note and I couldn't see

Ronnie going to so much trouble.

I put the note in the bag with the pin and sealed it. Then I went back out. I knocked on all my neighbour's doors, every house that might have been close enough for someone to notice a furtive stranger pinning something to my front door. As a way of meeting your neighbours for the first time, it wasn't the best. Most of them looked at me as if they were wondering what kind of trouble had come to live among them, although one friendly soul in the house opposite invited me to come over for drinks at the weekend. None of them had seen anything suspicious, however. So I went home and called Ronnie.

Chapter Seven

"It's bollocks," Ronnie said.

He hadn't been much interested in the note and my persistent attempts to get him to say why not had been a source of frustration for us both on the long, tedious flight up to the seaside town of Coomar. The plane was cramped and small. I wasn't much of a traveller – I'd only been on three planes in my life – and this was the first time I'd flown in a propeller-driven aircraft. I don't think we went above nine thousand feet the whole way and the views would have been great if the trip hadn't been almost entirely over water. Ronnie and I were the only two passengers but we still had to wear face masks. It was an airline rule. And don't get any false ideas about private jets or anything. Travelling on a city bus would have been a step up in comfort and space. From the almost-deserted airstrip at Archerfield, to the similarly daggy isolation of Coomar Airfield, the whole trip was an exercise in endurance.

"Maybe the cops will get a print or something," I said.

"No, they won't. The cops will get exactly what I got."

"And what's that?"

He sighed. "That the note was put together by a woman who lives in Brisbane and its only purpose is to misdirect us."

"How do you know it was a woman?"

"Because the words were cut out of a glossy magazine. Yes, before you say it, men read magazines too, but the giveaway is the capital letter on the word 'Harry', which I'm guessing is from a piece of crap article about the British royal family. You don't get those in Guns and Ammo, or Bondage and Boobies."

"That's a bit thin," I said, but he was probably right. Just to wind him up, I added, "And it's a bit sexist." He muttered something I couldn't hear over the engine noise. "So what if it was a woman? Maybe the killer's a woman."

"Jeez, not that again. Our killer is someone that stood in front of Harry Cross and, cool as a cucumber, pushed a knife straight into his heart. The woman who put that note together had craft glue and drawing pins and nice notepaper. She might know the killer, she might want us to look the wrong way to keep him safe, but she wasn't the cold-blooded murderer who took the trouble to get hold of a ruddy great knife and knew exactly where to stab a man to kill him instantly. It was a wide-bladed knife, remember, and the killer had turned it horizontal so it would fit between the ribs and not get snagged. That is not some soccer mom with craft supplies in her kitchen cabinet."

"So why did you tell me to take the note to the cops?"

Ronnie grinned, "Because it will give DI Reid something to get worked up about. Make him feel he's getting somewhere."

He was probably right. I'd taken the note in to Indooroopilly police station that night and handed it to my old mate Sergeant Tim Pearce. He'd been far too pleased to have an excuse to take it personally to Bertolissio. He and I had actually been out for a drink a couple of times since we'd had the chance to talk during the Sonny McKinley murder investigation. He was a nice enough bloke but we really didn't have much in common except an admiration for DS Bertolissio and her gorgeous sister, Mel. And that wasn't enough for a third outing, in my view.

I checked the time on my phone. It was after ten A.M. already. I reckoned that Bertolissio would have the note by now and shown it to Reid. Maybe Ronnie was right and Reid would be running around like a headless chook, feeling he'd got some valuable new evidence.

We were met at the aerodrome by a driver who took us to the harbour. The company that ran boats out to the island was owned by Eastern Island Resorts. They knew we were coming and they put us on a boat with a few dozen tourists to be taken out to Murdock Island. I was quite astonished by the VIP treatment but Ronnie seemed to take it all in his stride. We took seats on the aft deck, watching the massive wake and the receding land. The boat was loud and trembled beneath our seats. Cool air rushed past us, mitigating the already warm sunshine. We hadn't travelled as far as the Tropic of Capricorn, not quite, but we were close enough that the sun was already almost directly overhead and the day, like every day up there, promised to be hot.

"I suppose you're used to travelling around on boats," I said to Ronnie just to make conversation. He had been in the SBS, the UK's equivalent of the US Navy Seals – although if I ever mentioned the equivalence, he became mightily offended.

"Yeah, nah," he said. "Mostly the Navy flew us where we needed to go."

"Right."

I looked away. It was like getting blood from a stone,

trying to get Ronnie to talk about his past. I fished around for my earbuds, thinking I'd listen to some music.

"The dogs of fucking war, that's what we were."

Surprised, I turned back to him. He was still staring at the ocean.

"I used to have a dog," he told the hazy horizon. I resisted the urge to ask what the hell he was talking about. "An Airedale terrier. I got it after my wife left me. Best bloody decision I made in my whole life." I vaguely knew what an Airedale was – a biggish, brown dog with a beard that gave its head that square, terrier profile. I'd seen pictures of Airedales – probably the dog Ronnie used to have – hanging on his office wall. It seemed like the wrong dog for Ronnie. He should have had an Alsatian or a Doberman.

"We used to go out into the bush for walks and he'd go crazy, chasing after some poor bloody roo or feral cat. Jeez, that dog loved chasing things. Never caught a damned thing but it was everything to him. You could see the energy that ran through him, the sheer, indescribable joy he felt. He was born to hunt, literally bred for it."

He fell silent again but I kept watching him, sensing he hadn't said what he wanted to say.

"It wasn't like that with me. It never was. Me and my mates hunted in a pack. They dropped us in some crappy desert or poverty-stricken shithole town and set us loose to pursue our targets. And we did it with a grim professionalism, like fucking terminators. Sometimes we were up against real soldiers with training and proper weapons and tech – but never anything like us and what we had. Mostly the opposition was hardly better than civilians with AK47s. We went through them like targets on a training range. We did our hunting with cold, controlled ferocity. We did a job.

There was no joy in it. In the end, there wasn't even any satisfaction."

The air blowing past us felt cold. The subsonic growling of the engines was suddenly oppressive.

"But you did good, right? You helped people, made the world a bit better. All that."

He shook his head disdainfully, as if I'd said something really stupid. "Yeah," he said, almost too softly for me to hear. "There were rescues. We put down some feral scumbags. We did that too."

He stood up and walked away into the boat. His revelations were over. I sat alone and pondered them for a while. Whatever he'd done in his past life, I didn't suppose I'd ever find out. I was amazed he'd opened up as much as he had. It occurred to me how, if this case hadn't come up and I hadn't dragged him into it, Ronnie would still be sitting at home, alone, brooding in the tormented darkness of his bitter memories. *I should spend more time with him*, I told myself. *Make more effort to get him involved in the business.* But I knew how that would go. Ronnie could give master classes in pushing people away. Or maybe it was just me.

I started to get up and another realisation struck me so hard I fell back in my seat. Not only had Ronnie said more about his life in the past few minutes than I'd heard him say at any other time since I'd met him, he'd spoken eloquently. Well, not eloquently, exactly, but not in his usual expletive-laden, dinky-di, Aussie style. I realised what a chameleon Ronnie was. That day I'd first met him, sitting at the end of a bar in Brisbane, staring into a glass of rum, I'd barely noticed him. There was a grizzled old-timer like him in every bar in Australia. His accent, his constant use of Aussie slang, even his appearance pegged him for some bloke who'd worked in regional Australia, or out in the bush, maybe, and had somehow washed up in the city to spend his twilight years propping up a bar and looking for company.

It was all an act!

Wasn't it? Could it really be?

I tried to imagine Ronnie as a young man, working a mission in some North African city. Could I see him in cheesecloth shirts and linen slacks, sipping a glass of tea in a roadside café, passing the time of day in French with the long-faced waiter? Did Ronnie speak French? Or Arabic? Or anything other than English? It had never come up. I'd never thought to ask because the whole idea seemed so improbable. But now, maybe it didn't. Did it?

I decided to go find him and ask. But, as soon as I stood up and turned to face forward, I saw the island and forgot my resolve.

Murdock Island was a long, low smear of green-forested hills, separated from the grey ocean by a line of white sand. It stretched for several kilometres to each side of a solitary white jetty that was clearly our target. The jetty had a handful of small yachts moored nearby but the beaches looked empty and no buildings could be seen anywhere. The tannoy system on the boat was burbling out what might have been instructions for disembarking but I couldn't make out any of it. Looking around, I noticed other, much smaller islands dotted around in the ocean, all far away and beautifully exotic. Murdock Island itself was a picture-book tropical island, with streams running out of the hills into mangroves and pandanus trees lining the beaches.

Ronnie appeared at my elbow.

"Pity we're just here for the day, hey?"

The engine tone changed as we began to turn in a big arc

towards the jetty.

"Look at that lot," Ronnie said, pointing towards the jetty.

"What, the yachts?"

"Yeah, each one of them fuckers is a floating caravan. You could drop in here, from anywhere up the coast, stab an entrepreneur before lunch and be moored fifty kilometres away by tea-time. You wouldn't even need to touch land again until your tucker ran out."

"Do you think that's how it was done?"

"Nah, just saying."

"Why not?" It sounded like the perfect plan to me.

He actually thought about it for a moment, which surprised me. "Look, if it was a random killing, I might say yes. Some psycho, looking for a bit of fun, travels up and down the coast, hoping to get lucky, picks up a knife, finds Harry Cross all alone, does the deed and scarpers. It's possible; it's just not very plausible. It's too random. Also, in all my years chasing killers, I have never once come across a motiveless murder. Murder solves a problem. It doesn't merely scratch an itch." He shrugged. "I dunno. Maybe there really are loonies like that but it's incredibly rare. So, if we need a motive, we're better off looking at the people who were there with Harry – his family and co-workers."

"It doesn't have to be random. What if the killer had a good reason to stab him, wasn't part of the family or the company, and just happened to have a boat?"

"Again, it's just possible but I don't like it. They'd have had to know where Harry would be in advance, to make sure they were here with their boat at the right time. They'd have had to come ashore and get the knife, then get to the meeting room where Harry died, risking being seen and recognised, and then get away and off the island."

"Not impossible. We know someone did most of that anyway."

We were edging close to the jetty now. The other passengers were queuing up to disembark.

"All right," Ronnie said. "I don't think it's a goer but you can look into the enemy-with-a-boat angle if you like. I reckon the cops will already have taken a squiz at that, so you might want to ask Bertolissio."

* * * *

The boat's engines roared in reverse and we bumped the jetty with a casual delicacy that spoke of the helmsman's years of practice. The jetty was as broad as a two-lane road and paved entirely with grey weathered boards. The other passengers began the long walk to shore, dragging suitcases across the rattling planks, or boarded an open carriage pulled by an electric cart that the hotel had laid on. It made me think of children's train rides in parks. Ronnie and I had our own private cart, driven by a young woman in baggy green shorts and shirt and the word "Ranger" sewn on to her sleeve. She welcomed us to the island with such cheerfulness it made Ronnie wince. The manager, Ms. Onbekend, was waiting for us, she explained, in a strong Irish accent.

"First time on the island?" she asked.

"We're here to investigate the Harry Cross murder," Ronnie said, watching her eyes in the mirror.

"Yeah, before my time," she said, sounding regretful. "I've only been here six weeks myself."

"I bet the staff still talk about it," Ronnie said.

"Oh yeah! Old Wendy says there's a ghost lives down in the chalets."

"Any good theories about who done it?"

"They say it was the chef," she said, happily.

"Sous-chef," I said.

"No, the chef. But that doesn't make sense, now, does it? If it was the chef, why didn't he just poison the fella? He wouldn't need a knife at all, would he now?"

The short drive ended at the massive glass arch at the front of the main body of the hotel. We abandoned the cart and entered the gigantic foyer, our driver striding off across the wooden floor to a door beside the reception desk. The new arrivals from the ferry were gathered around the reception, being instructed by another woman in green shorts on how to register and find their rooms. Ronnie and I hung back, taking in the immense enclosed space. To our right were meeting rooms and beyond them a bar and the entrance to a restaurant we couldn't see into. There were other rooms to the left and a suspended mezzanine that seemed to have seats and shelving.

"Big, isn't it?" I said. Whatever I'd expected, it wasn't this vast glass and wood palace.

Ronnie didn't reply. He was watching the woman who had emerged from the door beside the reception desk, making her way towards us with our driver in tow. She was short and wiry, mid-forties, with sharp, piercing eyes in a face that suggested a Pacific Islander ancestry. In contrast to the "rangers", she wore a severe black pencil skirt and a striped blouse. Her black hair was short and, I couldn't help thinking, functional. She smiled when she got close enough to need to and studied each of us in turn before speaking to Ronnie.

"I'm June Onbekend," she said. She didn't offer to shake hands. Since the pandemic, the habit seemed to be dying out.

Ronnie introduced us. "Business looks good," he said,

nodding towards the newcomers.

"Never better," she said. "God bless the staycation, that's what I say. The border closures and the pandemic never really affected us." She paused, signalling the end of the chit-chat and the start of business.

"Now, Head Office has asked me to give you gentlemen every possible assistance, so I am completely at your disposal as long as you're here." She looked at our driver. "You've met Caitlin." Caitlin smiled at us. "She can take you anywhere you like – around the hotel precinct or anywhere on the island." She handed Ronnie a card. "That's my mobile number. Now, how would you like to do this?"

He explained we'd like to see the murder scene and for her to talk us through what happened. As he spoke, I felt the usual irritation that she had immediately pegged him as the one in charge and he, in his usual way, had failed to point out that I was the boss and he was my employee. Of course, it was just childishness on my part. I still had a great deal to learn from Ronnie and I was more than happy for him to take the lead in most situations. Even so, it would be nice if he at least mentioned my notional status now and then.

"We're actually standing almost right where it happened," June Onbekend said. She moved towards one of the meeting rooms – the "Robard Resolve Room" it said on the door.

"Odd name," I said as she rested her hand on the door handle.

"It means 'unknown' in Dutch," she said. "My family came here from Indonesia via the Netherlands. It was the Dutch authorities' way of coping with the lack of a surname. Lots of us in the Netherlands ended up with the name Onbekend."

Embarrassed, I said, "I, em, meant the room." I saw

Ronnie roll his eyes.

The manager just smiled. "Oh that. All our rooms are named after local landmarks. The Robard Resolve is the wreck of a cargo ship that went down at the north end of the island in 1932." She pushed open the door and went inside, still talking. "Foundered on a sand bar with a full load of timber. There were extensive logging operations here in those days. She's a rusted hulk now of course but very popular with divers."

We stood inside the door and looked around. The room was not impressive. About eight or nine metres square, it had a table in the middle with seating for about a dozen people. The table was a group of smaller tables pushed together and the chairs were middle-of-the-range tubular steel with upholstered seats and backs. Around the walls were large photographs of the wreck of the Robard Resolve and, on a long, veneered sideboard, a glass case containing a model of the ship.

"We replaced the carpet," Onbekend said into the silence, "but everything else is exactly as it was. I wouldn't get your hopes up about finding any clues. The room must have been cleaned a couple of hundred times since then."

"Where was the body?" Ronnie asked.

The manager went to stand at the far end of the room. "On the floor, here. He had a laptop and a projector on the table there and a screen set up against this wall. They said he was preparing a talk." Ronnie moved to join her. I followed him. Caitlin hovered in the doorway as if she were unsure she was invited to come in.

"You can't see the reception," Ronnie said, perhaps to me. I looked at the door. The angle to the outside was quite narrow and revealed only the glass outer wall of the building, some distance away. It would be unlikely that anyone out there would have been able to see much inside.

"That's right," said Onbekend. "Vince Collins was on the desk that day and he swore that he saw nothing. Of course, even when we're not busy with arrivals and departures, there's a steady stream of people coming to the desk to ask questions about the island, the restaurants, to book outings… You know. I can well believe Vince was so distracted he didn't see anyone going into or out of this room."

As she spoke, I got out my phone and checked the files for Vincent Collins' statement. It was as she said, Vincent had told the cops he had been dealing with guests all morning and hadn't seen a thing.

"It actually became a bit unpleasant," Onbekend went on. "Do you know the detective who was in charge of the case?"

"Oh, we know Trevor Reid, all right," said Ronnie.

The manager grimaced slightly, remembering. "He seemed to get it into his head that Vince had taken a bribe from some kind of gangster who was on the island for a bit of four-wheel driving. You know, to look the other way? Anyway, Vince was very upset. He was a nice boy and a very conscientious worker. I'm sure he would never have done anything like that but the detective wouldn't let it go. Vince resigned about a month into the investigation and, to be honest, I couldn't really blame him, although I wish he'd stuck it out. Good desk staff are like gold out here."

I was frantically searching through the files Bertolissio had sent us. Finally, I found it. "They checked Collins's bank accounts, searched his room, searched his parent's house in Brisbane, but they found no evidence of a pay-off. Poor bastard."

Ronnie nodded to himself, no doubt thinking, like I was,

that DI Reid had really, really wanted to put Grigor Mostek in the frame for this.

"So where were you when the murder happened?" Ronnie asked.

"I was in the office. That's behind the reception. We usually keep the door closed but you wouldn't see anything from in there, anyway. I was with Betty. She's our bookkeeper.-slash-accountant. She lives on the mainland and comes out a couple of times a week."

"Betty Cheng?" I asked, picking up the name from our file index.

"That's right. I left the office and came in here to check the room at about eleven thirty. XtraVirtual had the room booked for the full three days but I had their schedule of talks and meetings and I always make a point of looking in on things to make sure everything's tidy before a customer event. They were going to have their farewell presentation by the CEO after lunch, so I wanted to be sure everything was laid out properly. That's when I saw his body." Her face didn't change, she didn't show any emotion but she fell silent and the silence drew out until it became louder than her words.

I checked the police statements. The bookkeeper had followed her out of the office and had joined Vincent behind the reception desk. They had both watched her go into the Robard Resolve Room and then reappear in the doorway a few seconds later, backing up against the door post and standing there with her hand against her mouth. After a few more seconds, she had come out of the room, shut the door after her and called Vincent over. She had told him to call the police and an ambulance and had then locked the door. There was a nurse on the hotel staff and she asked Vincent to fetch her. She then waited outside the room until the nurse arrived, ten minutes later, and went back inside with her. By that time, Claudia Knecht, Harry Cross's PA had joined her at the door but the manager wouldn't let her go in. Eventually, the PA went off to find Richard Cross.

"I could see he was dead," she said, her gaze fixed on a spot on the floor. "I mean it was obvious. The knife was in his chest. There was blood… Even so, I felt for a pulse. Just in case, you know? I got the nurse to check him but she said he'd been dead a while before I found him. Then I got everybody out of there and locked it up again until the police came."

"It sounds like you did everything right," Ronnie said. She nodded, acknowledging his words of comfort, if not the truth of it.

"Claudia Knecht went to get Richard Cross, the dead man's brother," I said.

"Yes. Claudia was the one who had made all the arrangements for the company retreat, the one I dealt with, although I met Harry Cross when they arrived."

"How did Richard seem when he arrived?"

"Just how you'd expect: shocked, disbelieving, frantic to get to his brother. Claudia brought him back here – he'd been in his chalet – and he insisted on seeing the body, even though I told him we mustn't disturb the crime scene."

"You let him in?"

"I – I didn't have the heart to stop him. But he didn't touch the body or anything, he just stood over it for a long time, looking down."

"What do you think was going on in his head?" Ronnie asked.

She looked into his eyes, surprised by the question. "Why, horror, I suppose. Grief."

"You suppose?"

"Well, I—Isn't that what you'd feel, seeing your brother dead like that?"

"Did he say anything? Did he cry, or yell, or fall to his knees?"

"Well, no. He just stood there, like a statue, staring at the body. Then he said he needed to tell Mrs. Cross and left. I didn't see him again."

"And the police arrived about an hour later?"

"Yes, the local uniformed cops. The detectives from Brisbane didn't get here until maybe an hour after that. It was pandemonium by then. The guests couldn't leave the island, everyone wanted to cancel their bookings and go home but the ferry wasn't running. We had helicopters coming and going, more police kept arriving, then the press…" She shook her head as if to dislodge the unpleasant memory.

"What about his wife, Mrs. Cross," Ronnie asked. "Did she want to see the body?"

"I don't know. They told me she stayed in her chalet. The mother turned up, though. I saw her watching when they moved the body. They took it away in a helicopter, oh, hours later. She was crying, all right. She could barely stand, poor thing. Well, you can imagine."

I tried to imagine Jennifer Cross crying over the son that no-one but her could love.

"Who was she hanging on to?" Ronnie asked.

"What?"

"Well, it wouldn't be the other son, Richard, would it. He stayed with his brother's wife, not his mother. So who was she hanging on to when she could barely stand?"

"I – I don't know. Another woman, I think."

"A friend? A servant? One of the women from the company?"

June Onbekend retreated into herself as she searched her memories for the scene. Her head even moved from side to side a little, as if she were scanning the crowd. "It was an old woman," she said, remembering.

"The victim's grandmother?"

"I don't know. Maybe. She was very old. Small. But she looked..." She drifted away again.

"Yes?"

"I remember thinking it now. She looked as if she was made of stone. Hard. As if the world had thrown everything it could at her but she could endure anything. Even that."

Even a murdered grandson, I thought. *Even a family plunged into chaos and grief by the knife that had been plunged into Harry's chest.*

Ronnie asked a few more questions but it was clear that, once the cops had arrived, the manager had had little more to do with the family or the crime. She had focused on the guests, helping the ones who wanted to leave, trying to keep the hotel running as smoothly as possible for the ones who were staying.

"What about before the murder?" I asked, since Ronnie seemed to be losing interest. "Did you pick up on anything odd going on? Arguments? Disagreements? Indiscretions?"

She shook her head. "No, not really. I honestly don't have a lot to do with the guests unless they come to me with problems. Most of my work is focused on the staff. You should talk to them about the guests. They're the front line, really."

"Are there many staff from the time of the murder still working here that we can talk to."

"Sadly, no. It's the kind of business where we expect a

very high turnover anyway but, after the murder and all the media nonsense, even quite a few of our regulars didn't come back for this year's season. I don't suppose there are more than twenty here today that were here a year ago."

"Can we get a list and arrange to interview them today? Just very short interviews. Ten minutes each."

"I'll see what I can do. Caitlin, why don't you take Ronnie and Luke down to the Watering Hole for a complimentary lunch? I'll get those interviews set up for when you come back."

Chapter Eight

"I'm telling you, the chef's your man," Caitlin said, lounging back in her seat with a stubby in her hand. Being our chaperone seemed to agree with her and she had relaxed into the job during our large, carbohydrate-intensive lunch. The Watering Hole turned out to be a sprawling restaurant and bar that spilled into the bush that surrounded it. We ate burgers and chips and drank cold beers with our feet in the sand and a row of evil-looking kookaburras watching keenly from a nearby tree.

"So, where are you from?" I asked, not because I wanted to know, particularly, but it would at least stop her offering idiotic opinions on the case.

"Skibbereen in County Cork," she said.

"Sounds kind of exotic."

"That'd be because you've never been there," she said. "I swear to God I saw a fella at the Carbery Show having an orgasm over the size of some other fella's prize leeks. And that's when I told myself I had to get out of Skibb before I ended up as brain-dead as the rest of them. So I got myself a working visa and came out here as soon as the borders opened. I reckoned I'd go round the capital cities, do bar work, that sort of thing, and just have a good time."

Ronnie got up and went to the bar. I envied him his ability to just ignore people he didn't want to talk to.

"Yet you ended up here. Even Skibber – Skibb –"

"Skibbereen."

"– must have been more exciting than this place."

She made a face. "Yeah, well, I hooked up with a couple of fellas in Brissy and they said they had this great gig lined up on an honest-to-God tropical island and why didn't I join them? It'll be a laugh, they said. Bastards cleared off and left me here after two days!" She took a brooding suck of her stubby. "Still, it's not so bad. You meet a lot of people. I'll probably stick out the season."

Ronnie arrived with three more bottles and placed them on the table.

"Right, mate," he said, to me. "Get that inside you. I want you to go back to the hotel and do the staff interviews. You won't get them all done, but do as many as you can. Get June to give you a room with a desk and a couple of chairs and make it look a bit formal, hey? You're looking for differences between what they tell you and the statements they gave to the cops. See if you can work up timelines for all the Cross family and the XtraVirtual staff. Then we'll check them again when we get to XtraVirtual tomorrow. The cops missed something – someone where they shouldn't have been, an alibi that doesn't check out, something like that – so keep your ears open. We don't want to make the same mistake."

He looked pointedly at my half-eaten burger and I pushed the plate towards him.

"And what will you be doing while I do all the hard work?"

He grinned. "The lovely Caitlin is taking me for a ride on the beach."

"To check out Mostek's alibi?"

"They don't call you the Genius Detective for nothing. Then we're going to visit the chalets where the family stayed. Are you a good runner, Cailtlin?"

"Only if there's a dingo chasing me."

"Sensible but I want to check a few timings while we're out and my days of racing around in thirty-degree heat are well and truly behind me. So you're it, kiddo." To me, he added. "I'll meet you on the jetty at three-thirty for the ferry. Don't be late, or you'll be staying here tonight. Caitlin, let's go." He stood up, taking the remains of my burger with him. Caitlin hurried to down the rest of her beer and follow after him.

I sat for a while, keeping the hungry kookaburras at bay with a baleful glare, then got up and headed back to the main hotel building.

* * * *

Nobody had seen anything. Nobody was even there. It was a big hotel and an even bigger island. Taking a break after the first half-dozen interviews, I unfolded a map of the hotel I'd picked up at the reception desk, to help me make sense of what I'd been told. Walkways curved and wound away from the main hotel in three directions and each branched and looped its way through the guest rooms. These were arranged in rows of wooden structures on stilts that were two storeys deep and twenty or thirty rooms long. It was a complicated and difficult arrangement to get my head around and I imagined half the guests spent their holidays roaming around in that wooden labyrinth, lost and bewildered. Beyond the rooms there was a circular access road and, beyond that, set into the forest, were large chalets. It was in these that the Cross family members had stayed. The XtraVirtual execs had also been put up in chalets – up to six of them to a house, presumably to encourage "bonding" or "team building".

The people I'd interviewed had been almost all cleaners, with one barman from the Logger's Lounge – the hotel's most up-market bar and restaurant. The cleaners had been at work in the labyrinth, the barman had been off duty in his own room.

The interview room I'd been allocated was so large that the little table and chairs I was using were lost in it. Everyone who came in looked around at the big, empty space and shrank into themselves a little. I tapped in a couple of notes from the interview I'd just finished that said, "Not there. Saw nothing," and went to the door and opened it. Two men were on chairs outside. June Onbekend was doing a great job of keeping them coming.

"Who's next?"

"That'd be me, I reckon." One of the men got up and I stood back to let him in.

I went into my welcoming speech as we took our places opposite one another at the table. "And you are?" I asked.

"What I am is a busy man. You ever work in a hotel?"

I looked up from my notes and really looked at him for the first time. He was in his late twenties, a strong, vigorous type, with wispy blonde hair that was already thinning and a tan that suggested long hours outdoors. He wore green shorts and shirt like Caitlin and others I'd seen but his were faded and dusty and his arm patch said "Staff". He regarded me with steady, blue eyes and a sour expression.

"I'll try to be as quick as I can," I said. "What's your name?"

I looked down at the list Onbekend had provided, ready to tick him off, but he still wasn't playing.

"It's all well and good her volunteering me for this, she doesn't have a bunch of pipes leaking water all over a junction box in the fucking Logger's and fifteen other emergencies to get to when I get that sorted. I'm flat out like a lizard drinking and I don't need this bullshit. Do you know how many hours I've already wasted giving statements to the coppers?"

"I'm sorry about the—"

"Yeah, well, sorry isn't going to get my bitch supervisor off my back, or the power back on in the Logger's in time for them to cook dinner."

I have to say, a couple of years ago, I'd have just crumpled into a heap under this kind of belligerence but, since then, I'd interviewed quite a lot of unhappy and unwilling witnesses and I was finally developing a thicker, more crumple-resistant skin. Besides, this bloke was getting up my nose.

"OK," I said, sitting back. "I get it. You're busy and this is all a waste of your precious time. Well, frankly, whoever you are, you're wasting my time too. So why don't you just go back to your plumbing emergency and give us both a break." A small frown crossed his face and he made a tentative move to get up. "But, before you go, you should probably consider your position." He stopped moving. "I'm here at the direct request of Vincent Aikenhead, the CEO of the company that owns this hotel. I'm also working in cooperation with Detective Inspector Trevor Reid of the Queensland Police homicide division. The report I write will be sent to Mr. Aikenhead directly, along with copies to everyone in the management chain between you and him, as well as to the cops. Do you really want that report to say you came in here with a bad attitude and refused to answer any questions? Perhaps you'd like to discuss that with your union rep, or a lawyer, before you decide what you want to do."

He scowled at me and settled back into his chair.

"I was just... explaining," he said. "My name's Maury Ludgate. I'm a kind of handyman. Bit of everything."

"Thank you." I found Maurice William Ludgate in the files and pulled up his statement. "Where were you at the time of Harry Cross's murder?"

"I was out near the chalets. There was a couple of trees down in a storm. I was helping the groundsmen clear it up." A spark of rebellion flared in him. "I told all this to the cops."

"Well, the sooner you tell it all again, the sooner you'll be out of here. If you want to just leave, feel free."

His jaw worked. He looked like he wanted to reach across the table and rip my throat out. He took a moment before he started speaking again.

"We weren't anywhere near any of the chalets the cops was interested in – one to six – we were working behind the gas tank store past number ten. I was fetching and carrying stuff, taking rubbish to the dump, bringing tools and shit."

I unfolded my map of the resort and laid it on the table in front of him. "So, there's chalet 10," I said, pointing. "You were working back here somewhere. Where are the dump and the store where the tools are kept?"

"That's the dump. That's the shed."

"So, you had to drive past the other chalets each time you went." He shrugged a silent so what? "Were you driving a ute, or one of those little electric cart things?"

"A ute. The carts are just for the punters. Makes them feel more eco-friendly or some shit."

"And did you do any runs to the dump or the shed

between, say, half ten and eleven thirty that day?"

"I don't know, mate. It was a year ago."

I scanned through his police statement. "You told the cops you were working out there from about 9 A.M. until the cops came to bring you in for questioning at about noon. Is that right?"

"Yeah. So?"

"So how many times did you drive past chalets one to six in that time?"

"I don't know. I wasn't counting."

"Take a guess."

"I don't know. Half a dozen?"

"So the chances are good that some of those trips were during the period I mentioned?" He shrugged again. I tried not to lose my rag. "Think about it. You told the cops you were out there for three hours. During that time you drove past the chalets six times. That was your estimate, right? So, by simple mathematics, you probably drove past the chalets twice during the hour I'm interested in. Yeah?"

"If you say so." He made it sound as if I were the expert on these higher mathematical concepts and a simple man like him couldn't possibly be expected to follow my arcane reasoning.

"I do. And that means you passed the chalets four times between ten-thirty and eleven-thirty. Twice on the outward trip and twice on the return trip. Four times." He was still surly and hostile but I could have sworn there was a change in his demeanour – a certain shiftiness that hadn't been there before, he seemed uncomfortable in his chair and his eyes would no longer meet mine. On impulse, I said, "So tell me who it was you saw that day and why you didn't mention it to the cops."

"I didn't see no-one."

He was lying. I knew he was. "You can tell me now, or I can make a call and get the cops back here. I might be persuaded that whatever it is just slipped your memory until now. The cops are more likely to see it as withholding evidence and obstructing their inquiry."

He thought about it for a long time – plenty of time to convince me I'd been right. I gave him a nudge.

"You can see how this reluctance is going to look in my report."

He gave me a sour look but he started talking. "It was some old biddy. I was on my last run, so it was after eleven. I'd just taken a load to the dump and was on my way back. I suppose I might have been going a bit fast. There's a ten kilometre speed limit round the resort. It's fucking stupid. So I nearly hit this ditzy old bitch. Scared the life out of me. But I couldn't say anything 'cause of the speeding, right? I've had warnings. I thought they might sack me."

My heart was beating fast. I tried not to let my excitement show. "So, some time after eleven, you nearly hit an old woman on the road near the chalets?"

"Yeah, that's right."

"Which way was she going?"

"How should I know? I didn't see her till I was nearly on top of her."

"Which way was she facing?"

"Mate, it was a long time ago."

"But you've thought about it a lot since then. Was she facing towards the chalets or away from them?"

"Well… towards, I suppose."

"So that would mean she was heading towards the chalets from the direction of the hotel?"

"If you say so."

Annoying little shit! "I don't say anything. I'm asking you. Could she have been heading towards the chalets from the direction of the hotel?"

Again, the shrug. "Yeah, I reckon."

I grabbed a notepad and started writing. "All right," I said. "We're going to get this down on paper and you're going to sign it." A problem occurred to me as soon as I started writing that he'd seen an old woman. "How old did you say she was?"

"I don't know. Old."

This was a bloke a bit younger than me. Everybody over fifty looked old. "Was she old like June Onbekend?"

"Nah, mate. Older."

"So how old, exactly?"

"Like, you know, a real crumbly. Grey hair and everything."

"Over fifty?"

"Jeez, how should I know? If she'd been eighteen, I'd have had a good look. Gone back to check she was all right, if you know what I mean. Some of these tourist chicks…" He shook his head to dispel whatever fond images he'd conjured up. "But she was just some old biddy. OK?"

"If I came back with some pictures, do you think you could pick her out?" I already knew the answer.

"No fucking way. Are we done?"

"When we've got this in writing."

"Yeah, nah. I'm not signing nothing."

I didn't argue. I had it all recorded on my phone. So, I thanked him for his help and let him go.

* * * *

124

I hadn't got anything interesting from the rest of the interviews and had just decided to call it a day when Caitlin popped her head in the door.

"Your man Ronnie sent me to give you a lift down to the jetty."

I grabbed up my things and went out to find June Onbekend to say goodbye. She spotted me from the desk and came out to intercept me.

"That was great," I said. "You've been incredibly helpful."

"I hope so. We'd all like to get this cleared up."

"I'll be sure to let Mr. Aikenhead know we were very well looked after."

I followed Caitlin out to the waiting cart.

"So, who do you think did it?" she asked.

"Definitely the chef," I said and she looked at me sharply as if she suspected me of joking.

I noticed a couple in their fifties studying a map nearby and pointed them out as we climbed aboard. "How would you describe that woman?"

"What, me?"

"Yeah, you. Tell me about the woman."

"Well, she's old, a bit posh." She shrugged.

I tried to remember the words Maury Ludgate had used. "Would you say she was an old biddy? A crumbly?"

"Well, it's not very kind, but, yeah, I suppose so."

I let her set off and pondered the problem of relative ages as we went.

"Do you reckon that woman was as old as Ronnie?"

She laughed. "Are you thinking about fixing him up?"

I had to laugh too. "You're saying they're about the same age?"

"Yeah, more or less. What's going on?"

"How many old people do you get staying here? Like, what proportion?"

We pulled up at the end of the jetty. The ferry was already docked there. I didn't get out, waiting for her answer.

"A lot," she said. "Some days it feels like you can't throw a rock without hitting five old dears wandering about lost."

I smiled, weakly. I could probably get accurate data from Shirley Stephens – Eastern Island Resorts looked like the kind of outfit that would generate detailed customer segmentation reports – but Caitlin's response was enough to confirm my own impression that Murdock Island was very popular with the over-fifties crowd.

Before she let me go, she had a burning question of her own.

"Is it true what Ronnie says, that you're a doctor of philosophy?"

"Guilty as charged."

She seemed delighted. "That's amazing. You don't seem all that clever."

"Well, thank you!"

"No, I mean, it's a compliment, really. Like, you're not stuck up or anything. You're not rubbing it in people's faces and that."

"You're very kind," I said and made my escape before she thought of some other choice compliments to damn me with.

Chapter Nine

When I was a kid, we used to take caravan holidays at the beach. My dad always wanted to go camping but mum wouldn't have a bar of it. We couldn't afford hotels, so renting a caravan for the week was our compromise. My mum was always convinced that the sea air had some kind of magical effect on kids and made them sleep like the dead. I tried – even at the age of eight – to refute her, pointing out that we walked farther, swam, ran about like maniacs, and generally did so much more, there was no need to invoke the mystical powers of "sea air". But I could never convince her.

As my head hit the pillow on my return from Murdock Island and sleep came swooping in to claim me, I could almost hear Mum saying, "There, what did I tell you?"

I called Mum when I got up and put her on speaker while I ate breakfast in the garden. My new house came complete with a big old silk tree that spread its crooked limbs wide and shaded half the garden. I put a little table under it and a folding chair and it quickly became my favourite place to start the day. Magpies were bugling away somewhere nearby and a couple of noisy miners were shouting over some ancient dispute. It made it a little difficult to have a conversation.

"What do you mean?" Mum asked.

"Just that. Someone I interviewed said they'd seen an old woman and I don't know how old that might be. So, when do you think a woman starts to be called old?"

"I don't know... I'd have said fifty, when I was your age, only, these days, fifty seems far too young to be called old. Seventy, maybe."

"What are you now, fifty-five?"

"Cheeky beggar! I'm fifty-two, as a dutiful son would know."

"So, your perception of old is always, what, two decades past wherever you are now?"

She laughed. "That sounds about right. How old was your interviewee?"

"Bit younger than me. But he said she had grey hair, so mid-forties seems unlikely."

"Oh, now that's a big clue. None of my fifty-something friends have let their hair go grey, yet. That's something an over-sixty is much more likely to do."

"Doesn't hair just go grey when it wants to?"

"No, darling, it goes grey when the woman says it can."

I thanked her for her help and downed the last, tepid mouthful of coffee. By the time I got to the office, I was pretty sure of my conclusions.

"It has to be Jennifer Cross," I told Ronnie, who was already there and waiting for me.

"Oh yeah?"

"Yeah. Maury Ludgate saw an old woman with grey hair. My sources tell me that means a woman over sixty. Jennifer Cross is the only woman we've met so far who fits the bill. None of the XtraVirtual women are that old."

"But there were dozens of other older women on the island that day who'd also match the description." He gave me a sad look. "Mate, you're getting yourself excited over nothing. This guy remembering an old woman near the chalets, doesn't put Jenny Cross in the frame. She has a solid alibi, don't forget. And she's the victim's mother for God's sake. Where's her motive?" He moved to the whiteboard, agitated, but came back and sat down.

"All right, I agree, it gives us another line of investigation. We need to identify the mysterious old lady, if only so we can ask her about what she saw that day. But I wouldn't get your hopes up. If she was one of the hotel guests – which is a lot more likely than it was Jenny Cross – we need to get the numbers for every woman over fifty who was there that day and call each one to ask what she was doing and what she saw. And…" He paused for effect. "…we need to do the same for all the day trippers and all the former staff. In fact…" He flashed his wicked grin. "…we might consider giving the job to DI Reid and his crew. The cops love working the phones day in, day out, for little or no reward."

"But this is our first solid lead. We can't just throw it over the wall to Reid and let him solve it."

"Luke, trust me, this is not a great lead. It's a curiosity at best. At worst, it's a dead end that will consume masses of time we can't afford to waste."

"Yeah, well, it's more than you managed to get, driving up and down the beach with Caitlin."

"True. That was fun but not productive. All the timings checked out. Every movement of every suspect was absolutely consistent with the measurements we took yesterday. The only thing my trip with Caitlin achieved was to convince her that she never ever wants to become a private investigator. In her words, 'There's too much bloody running around for my liking.'" He smiled as if it were a fond memory. "However, we did make two very big and very significant discoveries while we were at the hotel."

He watched me in silence, eyebrows raised, until I was forced to ask, "What?"

"Well, the first is that June Onbekend could have done it."

"What?"

"Mate, it takes about one second to stick a knife in a man's chest." He mimed the movement. "She had plenty of time if she just walked straight up to him, stabbed him, wiped the handle and then staggered back to the door as if she'd just found the body."

"But that's…" Ridiculous? Was it? What did we know about the hotel manager?

"Then there's the other big thing."

I pulled my mind loose from June Onbekend.

"What's that?"

"I'll give you a clue."

"No, just tell me."

"Staycation," he said.

"What the hell has that got—?" And then I remembered June Onbekend saying, "God bless the staycation." It's not a word you hear often. Well, maybe if you worked in the tourism industry, you'd hear it every day. It means taking your vacation at home or locally instead of going far away or overseas. But why would Ronnie have thought it was such a big deal? Onbekend thought it was good because, she said, the border closures and the pandemic never really affected her business.

And, finally, it hit me.

"Shit! Aikenhead and the company lawyer were lying to us. And now we have proof!"

Ronnie was grinning again. "It's like watching paint dry,

sometimes. I can hardly believe you got through your PhD in just three years. Perhaps you should take the rest of the morning off, having worked your poor little brain so hard."

He had a point, I must admit. I should have noticed it straight away. Aikenhead had told us Murdock Island was losing money because of bad publicity after the murder. Our investigation was to help them make a case for compensation against a couple of media outlets. But he only told us that after Ronnie had called him out on his first lie, which was that our investigation was about rehabilitating the resort's reputation. It was quite staggering. He and Vicki Finn had come to our meeting with a lie already prepared and, I'm guessing from Aikenhead's performance, rehearsed. But they also had a fallback lie ready, in case we spotted the first one. Did they have more lies ready, too, in case the first two didn't work? What kind of people were we working for?

"I can see from your stunned mullet expression, that it's all sunk in at last," said Ronnie. "Quite a pair, those two, hey?"

"Jeez," was all I could manage in reply. "What does it mean? What should we do about it?"

"It means we have another new line of enquiry. Those two went to great lengths to sucker us into this investigation. So I want to know why. What are they hiding? Why is the Harry Cross murder really so interesting to them? So I'm going to focus on that while you do all the interviews at XtraVirtual."

I glanced at my phone. I needed to get moving if I was going to make it on time. I stood up again and cast a wistful glance at the coffee machine.

"So, you got out of the interviews yesterday because you had to be driven up and down the beach and you're blowing them off today to do what exactly?"

He leaned back in his chair and put his feet up on the table. "I think I might take a drive out into the country and say hello to Jenny Cross."

"Our chief suspect."

"Your chief suspect. I'm keeping an open mind."

"Yeah, well, make sure she doesn't stick a knife in your chest."

* * * *

As I expected, the organisation at XtraVirtual was superb. I had a nice little room, a printed schedule, a sideboard groaning with snacks and drinks, and personnel folders for every interviewee – even though the ones we'd been given at our last visit were still in my backpack. I was greeted and managed by Richard's PA, Claudia, an attractive thirty-something with a pleasant but businesslike manner.

"You're Claudia Knecht, right?" I asked. "You used to be Harry Cross's PA."

"Yes, Richard sort of inherited me." She suggested I take my seat and sat opposite me across the table. "I've put myself down as your first interview, so I suppose we could get started." She had a slight German accent but her English was flawless. I glanced at the schedule and there she was in the first slot.

"Okay…" I said, slowly, not quite ready and feeling a little railroaded. I tried to remember what I knew about her. "You organised the Murdock Island retreat, I believe."

"Yes."

I waited for more but that was all I was getting.

"And you organised the presentation Harry was about to give. You booked the room, arranged for the equipment…"

"And I put the preparation time in his schedule. I organised every last detail of his movements. I am absolutely responsible for him being there on that island that day and for him being in that room at that time."

She didn't seem at all perturbed by the fact that, by the means, motive and opportunity measure, she'd just put herself well up the suspect list. To be honest, I didn't know what to do with the information. So, I took a diversion.

"How long had you worked for Harry?"

"About five years."

"Were you close?"

"As close as we needed to be. He tried it on one time. I told him no. Things were fine after that."

"What about Richard?"

For a moment, her poise slipped. "We, er, we work well together. He's an easier boss than his brother was."

"Was it your idea or his that you become his PA?"

"Well, his, of course."

"Has he ever tried it on?"

"No. Never."

She was getting her balance back, so I went sideways again.

"So, Harry was a difficult boss."

She frown at me then relaxed. "Yes, I implied that, didn't I?"

"Was he?"

"I try not to speak badly about my former bosses. Or about the dead."

"That's great but it doesn't help me. In what way was Harry difficult to work for?"

She looked a little resentful that I was forcing her to break her rule but, finally, she said, "He had a temper. He could be… selfish."

"What does that mean? He used to shout at you? Throw things?"

"Yes."

"Did he ever hit you?"

"No! Never!"

"But he used to hit his wife, didn't he?"

"I never saw him do that."

It was frustrating that she was being so cagey. "You never saw it but you knew about it."

"Yes."

"How?"

"His wife told me."

I was surprised. "You're saying Cassandra confided in you?"

"Not exactly. She came here one afternoon. She was drunk and she had bruises on her face. She accused me of being his latest affair and wanted to tell me all about what a terrible man I had involved myself with." She paused, perhaps remembering the scene. "She apologised later."

I sat back to let it soak in. That little nugget wasn't in Claudia's statement to the cops. In fact, it was the closest to hard evidence I'd seen so far that Harry Cross really did beat his wife. I took another look at Claudia Knecht. She was quite beautiful and gave off a stylish and competent vibe. Yet there was something repressed in her manner, a buttoned-up quality that made me look for and find a little silver crucifix on a chain around her neck.

"You were OK working for a bloke who beat his wife and made a pass at you?"

She raised an eyebrow. "What, you're investigating my morality now?"

"From what you've said about him, in just the past five minutes, the man was a pig: a childish, selfish man, who threw tantrums and bullied people. I bet you saw plenty of other bad behaviour, working so closely with him."

"What do you want me to say? That I despised Harry Cross? Of course I did. Everybody did – except for his rich cronies, but I don't think men like that have friendships. Do you? Their whole lives are transactional. They scratch each others' backs. And they only like each other to the extent that they collude and enable and encourage one another."

She too sat back, her lips pressed together as if symbolic of the fact that she thought she'd said too much.

"What about Richard?" I asked. "Is he like that, too?"

I think I'd pushed her a bit too far. If I hadn't, she might have opened up and told me about her new boss. As it was, she was defensive and hostile.

"Richard isn't at all like that. He is a decent man. That's all I'm saying."

It was a shame and probably all my fault. Maybe Ronnie could have gotten more out of her but Ronnie wasn't there. He was taking his drive in the country.

"Are we finished?" Her tone suggested we were.

"Of course. Thank you for your candour. Will you give me two minutes and then send in…" I looked at the schedule. "…Ms Tsai?"

Alone, I thought about whether Claudia Knecht could have murdered Harry Cross. I was certain she could. There was a cold efficiency about her that meant if she thought the only way to proceed was by eliminating her boss, then that's what she would have done. It would have been flawlessly planned and she would never have been caught. But nobody murders someone just because they're a pig. Do they? Ronnie might know. And that seemed to be the only motive Claudia might have. Unless it wasn't. Maybe when Harry made his pass, Claudia had responded. As an abused or jilted lover, I reckoned she would be a dangerous woman. I made a note to look more closely at Claudia Knecht as my next interviewee entered the room.

* * * *

The rest of the morning became a blur of faces and stories. I was glad I had made recordings because I knew I wouldn't remember a tenth of who had said what about whom. I sat at a table in Richard Cross's office and flicked through my scant notes while a caterer from an outside company brought in a three-course lunch and laid it out. Richard hadn't arrived yet and I was glad to have that time to get my thoughts together. Claudia poked her head in the door at one point to say he'd be arriving in five minutes and I should start. So I did.

The two women and eight men I'd spoken to that morning were all managers in some capacity in XtraVirtual. They ranged from the small, withdrawn and defensive Chief Financial Officer, to the geeky Chief Technology Officer who mostly wanted to talk about what it was like to be a "private eye", to the big, avuncular Sales Director, who immediately made me think, "Buzz Lightyear". It was a struggle not to shout, "To infinity and beyond!" as he left the room. They all told basically the same story; no-one had seen anything, Harry Cross was a monster and the company was doomed without him. They all confirmed their alibis and a couple confirmed other people's.

I asked all ten of them "in complete confidence" who they thought had done it. Two said Cassandra, the wife, two said

Richard, the brother, two said Grigor Mostek, and four wouldn't say.

It was, pretty much, a waste of a morning.

All except for my conversation with Claudia Knecht. I couldn't get it out of my head that she had said, "I am absolutely responsible for him being there on that island that day and for him being in that room at that time." Claudia might well have been the only person who knew, to the minute, where Harry Cross would have been that day. Had she killed him? She had been working in the room next door when it happened. Not far to go. Had she conspired with someone else to kill him? She would have known everybody he knew, most likely. Perhaps she had been approached by an enemy – possibly a well-known local underworld identity. I needed to check her bank accounts. Or, had her traumatic encounter with Cassandra Cross, drunk and furious, ended in more than just an apology? Perhaps a friendship had grown out of it, or, at least, a pact to tackle their mutual problem.

"Sorry I'm late." Richard came in looking harassed and unhappy. "Couple of major shareholders wanted to make themselves feel better by kicking me around the room for a couple of hours." He took off his jacket and sat down opposite me. For a moment, he stared at the elaborate and excessive meal as if it were an imponderable question. Finally, he sat back without touching it.

"Claudia looking after you all right?"

"She's been brilliant. Thank you for setting it all up."

He nodded. "Getting her as my PA is the only good thing to come out of all this. Look, if you've had enough, let's go and sit over there and I'll call for coffee."

We decamped to a bunch of comfy chairs and Richard went out briefly to issue his commands.

"So, how'd it go?" he asked on returning.

"Everybody was very cooperative," I said.

"But useless, right?"

"No, no. They corroborated stories and confirmed timings. It's all important groundwork that has to be done."

He nodded again. It was obviously the thing he did while he thought about things. "And what about the case more generally? Any light at the end of the tunnel?"

"It's still very early days. There's plenty more groundwork to go before we can start to see what's what."

"It sounds… tedious."

"It is. Very. But, the thing is, there's so much at stake, everything is always tinged with a kind of terrible importance. Someone we talk to will know something. Someone might give away a vital clue at any moment – with a single word, a gesture even – and if we miss it, or fail to ask the right question… Well, it keeps you on your toes, hey?"

He nodded, processing what I'd said.

"Your colleague went out to the farm today."

"Yes, he did. How did you know?"

"Mum called. She wants me to stop the investigation."

"Ronnie can be a bit abrasive," I said, wondering what the hell he'd done to upset Jenny Cross so much. "But what he lacks in social skills, he makes up for in ability and experience as a detective." I should probably get that on a T-shirt instead of the "I'm with Stupid" slogan I usually thought I should be wearing.

"What did you tell your mum you'd do?"

"I asked her to be patient and reminded her that, however rude and ham-fisted you two and the cops are, we all want the same thing in the end."

I took the insult on the chin, like a pro. "I hope she'll see the sense in that."

"I don't know, she was ropeable but I'll go round and see her tonight, see what we can salvage."

I nodded, sagely, thinking I'd be having a few words with Ronnie that night as well.

My coffee was cooling and I'd have to get back to the tedious interviews soon, so I said, "At the risk of being even more rude and ham-fisted, do you mind if I ask you just a couple more questions before I go?" He looked as if he were about to make some excuse, so I jumped right in.

"We're working on getting the timeline straight and checking where everyone was around the time of the murder. So let me check this. After the morning's meetings broke up, Harry gave you a sort of free period to relax before his presentation. Harry went off to prepare his talk. You went back to your chalet and read a book. You were there, alone, until Claudia arrived to give you the news. Is that right?"

"Yes."

"What book was it?"

"What?"

"What book were you reading?"

"I – I don't remember. I read all kinds of things. It was a novel. Probably sci-fi. I read a lot of sci-fi. When I escape, I like to get as far away as possible."

"But you can't remember?"

"It was more than a year ago. I've read dozens of books since then. Is it important? It's probably still on my Kindle. Do you want me to look?"

"No, no worries. I was just curious. And you sat at the back of the chalet, on the verandah, to read it, yes?"

"Yes, that's right."

"Didn't all the sawing bother you?"

"The sawing? Wait! That's right. There were chainsaws going the whole time. It was bloody irritating. I thought I'd complain to the management but, well, I forgot about all that, later."

"Let me ask you another. You went with Claudia back to the hotel and she took you to see Harry. What were your thoughts when you saw him lying there?"

He frowned hard, as if he were trying to works something out. Then his face cleared and he smiled at me. "The book question was just to get me off guard, right? So I might let something slip."

"No," I lied. "I was just curious that you'd been out there reading despite all the noise."

He snorted. "Yeah, well, after two days cooped up on an island with Harry, they could have been sawing my leg off and I'd still have been glad to get away for an hour." He smiled again. "And there you are, an indiscretion, your little trick worked."

I gave him a taut smile in return. "People who saw you with the body said you didn't react much. You just stood there and stared for a while, then you left. What were you thinking?"

"I – I wasn't thinking at all really. Just things like, 'Oh my God!' and 'Harry's dead.' Stupid things, really. I suppose I was in shock."

"You didn't cry, or try to touch the body, or… anything, really."

The frown was back. "That would have been evidence of my innocence, would it?"

"No," I agreed. "I'm just trying to understand."

"I felt numb. The therapist I'm seeing suggested I clamped down on all my feelings because I was afraid to acknowledge to myself that I was glad that Harry was gone. Your friend Ronnie has nothing on my shrink when it comes to taking a wrecking ball to normal civilised interactions."

I wondered, idly, if that was the same shrink Cassandra Cross mentioned seeing. "Just one more question. After you saw Harry's body, you told Ms Onbekend, the hotel manager, that you were going to break the news to Cassandra."

"Yes? So?"

"So you went to her chalet?"

"Yes."

"Straight there. No detours?"

"What, to wash the blood off my hands?"

"I just want to get all the timings straight."

"Yes, I went straight there."

"Why?"

"Why?"

"Yes, why did you go to tell Cassandra and not, say, your mother?"

"I – I don't know. I suppose I felt Cassie would be the one who needed the most support. You don't know her. She's kind of fragile."

"And your mother's not?"

"No, far from it."

"And you stayed with Cassandra for the rest of that day, travelled back with her that evening to the mainland."

"She was a wreck. Someone had to stay with her."

"Did you visit your mother at all after you went to comfort Cassandra?"

"I – No. It was a strange time. I was in shock. Cassie was a mess. The cops were brutes. It was a nightmare. I barely knew what I was doing half the time. Harry was dead. I don't suppose you can begin to imagine just how huge that was."

Actually… I thought.

"So you didn't check up on your mother at all? Not even a phone call?"

His distress suddenly switched to anger. "What the hell is this? Now you're the Dutiful Son Police?" He stood up. It was time to go. I stood up too.

"I didn't mean to offend you."

"And yet, somehow, you always manage to."

"Thank you for your time," I said, weakly. "And for… lunch."

Chapter Ten

"I tell you, there is no love lost between Richard Cross and his mother. How else do you explain it?"

We were on Ronnie's patio, lying back on sun loungers, sucking on a couple of stubbies and watching the stars drift by overhead. It was something we hadn't done for months and I realised I'd been missing it.

"My guess," Ronnie said. "He believed his mum had stabbed his brother and he was hiding out with Cassie so Mummy Dearest couldn't confess to him."

"Jeez! But why would he suspect her? Do you think she'd said something? Had she been planning it?"

"Who knows? It's possible it was something as innocent as he saw her making her way back to the chalet – you know, when your handyman fella almost ran her over – and put two and two together, like you did."

"So you agree, it must have been Jennifer Cross on the road that day?"

He sighed, heavily. "Yeah, nah. Still not convinced but, I have to say, when I recounted the incident to Jenny, she got into quite a huff about it."

"Was that why she called Richard to try to get the investigation stopped?"

"Nah, that was something else. Are you hogging the macadamias again?"

I tossed him the bag. "So what was it?"

"Nothing."

"What did you do? Come on."

"She went out to make some tea or something and I sort of sneaked upstairs."

"You what?"

"I just wanted to take a look around."

"What, to see if she had any posters of Harry that she'd been throwing darts at?"

"Yeah, that kind of thing. Only I found the granny."

I could imagine the scene. "She screamed. And the rest is history."

"Not quite. She was laid up in bed with medical equipment round her."

"What, like a drip? A heart monitor?"

"Yeah, shit like that."

"So, she's really crook, then? Do you reckon her trip to Murdock Island was her last outing?" If so, it was a pretty dismal way to spend your last vacation.

"The thing is," Ronnie said. "She was kind of chirpy, despite everything. A little bit loopy, maybe. I wouldn't say she'd lost her marbles – not by a long way – but there's definitely a hole in the bag. Anyway, she wouldn't let her nurse shoo me out. She made me go and sit with her so we could chat."

"You didn't interview her about the case!"

He emptied a fistful of nuts into his mouth and spoke around them. "Nah, she wouldn't let me. Shut me down each time I went near it. Frustrating. I got the impression she knows something but will absolutely not say a word about it."

"What makes you think that?"

"I dunno. Something about her eyes. She got this look in her eyes when I tried to ask her about her grandson, or even when I just mentioned the island. I could swear it was fear."

"Fear? What's she got to be scared about?"

"Don't ask me. For all I know it's just that what happened is just too awful for the old dear to deal with. I asked Jenny before I left and she said Harry's death and all the crap that followed is what laid her mother low. She blames Granny's failing heart and a couple of small strokes on the way the family was treated by the media. Said arseholes like me barging into her sick-room didn't help. But she admits the old lady was pretty frail even before the murder."

I thought about it, saddened that an old woman's final years should be marred by such unpleasantness.

"So, what did you talk about?"

"Oh, all sorts, really. Lonely, I reckon. Poor bugger's in permanent lockdown and craving social contact. She really dotes on her family – especially the two great-grandkids. She's not wild about Cassandra but Richard is her pride and joy."

"And Jennifer?"

"They seem close. It's hard to tell without seeing them together. Anyway, I didn't get to chat to her much before Jenny came upstairs looking for me, found me chatting to Granny and gave me the boot. Seems I 'violated her trust' or something." He added the quotes with his fingers.

"Like she didn't want you talking to her. In case she told you something, perhaps? Like, something Jennifer had confessed? Or something Granny had seen?"

"Yeah, yeah. Don't get all excited. We've still got no evidence at all it was Jenny."

I didn't argue. After today's interviews, I could make just

as good a case for Richard Cross or Claudia Knecht being the killer. And, as Ronnie said the day before, the resort manager, June Onbekend, had the perfect opportunity. I rubbed my brows. It had been a long day – a long two days – and I was ready for bed.

"I'm going to shoot through, mate," I told Ronnie, setting down my beer. "What do you want to do tomorrow?"

"Tomorrow I've set aside for thinking. You've got a gazillion phone calls to make, so I'll let you get on with that."

"It must be exhausting watching me do all the work."

"You wrote up all your notes from today, right?"

"Yes, I did, in all the spare time I had between doing the interviews and coming round here."

"And indexed and filed the recordings?"

"Yes! Do you want to come home with me to check that I brush my teeth before bed?" I didn't need to ask Ronnie if he'd written up his visit to Jenifer Cross. For all his many faults, he was a meticulous record-keeper. I didn't even need to ask why he wanted to know about my notes: he would spend half the night reading through them and listening to the recordings. Somehow, he managed to survive on about four hours sleep a night. I liked ten, needed eight and, tonight, I'd be lucky to get six.

* * * *

There was another note pinned to my door when I got home.

As before, I went inside, got some disposable gloves and a ziplock bag and went out to take it down. *That's it*, I told myself. *I'm getting a security system. Cameras at the doors, alarms on the windows, the works.* I looked up and down the empty street but the only movement was a cat slinking along under a hedge.

Inside, I carefully examined my new missive. It was clearly the work of the same person: same paper, folded and pinned in the same way, same unevenness to the paper, same kind of words cut from glossy magazines. Only the message was different.

"you Have been warned death's head is coming For you"

Tired as I was, I knew I wouldn't get much sleep that night. So I photographed the letter and the pin and bagged it up. I put the photos into the company notes system with a few words explaining what they were. Then I drove off to Indooroopilly police station to hand them over to Sergeant Pearce. On the way, I got a phone call from Ronnie.

"I just saw the note you posted." he said. "Looks like the same person."

"What do you reckon?"

"A load of bollocks, mate. Don't let it distract you."

"Yeah? Well that's easy for you to say; you're not the one getting creepy notes pinned to their door."

"It's rubbish. Someone's trying to put the wind up you. Give it to the cops. Let them worry about it."

"I'm on my way now. You said the last one was probably from a woman."

"Yeah, one who watches too much TV."

"Do you think it's Jenny Cross?"

"Everything's Jenny Cross with you. Give me a solid motive for a mother to kill her own son and I'll start listening."

I pulled up at the station and grabbed the bag off the seat. "Gotta go. I'll see you in the morning."

Tim Pearce seemed genuinely pleased to see me.

"Did you just come for the coffee, or are you some kind of cop groupie?" he asked, cheerfully.

I looked around at the empty reception area and the dingy paintwork, looking grim under harsh fluorescent light. "What the hell did you do to piss them off so much that they put you back in uniform and gave you permanent night shift in this dump?"

He went round to the door and let me in. "It's not so bad. I get to read a lot and, every now and then, a genius detective drops in for a chat."

"Funny." I held up the letter. "I brought you a little something."

"Cool!" he said, his eyes lighting up. "I know a certain DI who's going to wet himself over this."

"Speaking of my good friend Trevor, how's his promotion campaign coming along?"

"How did you know about that?"

"Mate, I'm an integral part of Team Trevor. The case I'm working on is crucial to the promotion master strategy."

He nodded sagely and took the baggie from me, reading it in silence.

"Death's head?" he asked.

"Yeah, if you remember the first note, it said to look out for a guy with a death's head tattoo."

"Right. But the first one wasn't a threat, was it? This one definitely is. Kicks things up a notch." He started assembling papers and pens. "I'll need a statement."

"Yeah, no worries."

"Do you want a coffee?"

"Is the Pope Catholic?"

He found me a chair and went to fetch the drink. I sat in the glaring light and felt suddenly tired. Not just tired but bone weary.

"Looks like you need this," Tim said, holding out a plastic cup.

I took it and thanked him. "I wouldn't be making a fuss about this…" I waved my cup in the direction of the note. "Only my experience of investigating murders is that I get threatened and beaten up and even shot at quite a lot. Ronnie thinks it's a joke and I have to say, there's something almost childish about it, but I don't want to just ignore it and then wake up one night staring past a sawn-off shotgun at some bloke with a death's head tattoo on his forehead."

He seemed to understand. "Well, we'll get this processed and into the system. Tomorrow it will be in the hands of DI Reid and his team, and they can decide what's best to do about it. I have to agree, it seems a bit shonky. Not that I've ever seen an actual death threat but this one doesn't really feel right, does it?"

We chatted and filled in the paperwork and I left half-an-hour later hoping I could stay awake long enough to drive home.

* * * *

My phone woke me at nine the next morning. I was still in my clothes from the night before, lying on the sofa, with the TV playing a *Star Trek: Voyager* re-run. I vaguely recalled switching it on, thinking I'd watch a little before bed. Someone smart once described television as "bedtime stories for tired adults." I'd never before seen just how true that was.

The call was from Desi at the office, to let me know Ronnie was demanding to know where I was, and that Harper was in the office too and would like to get a few minutes and, oh yes, there was a strange woman there too who'd like to see me but Ronnie had grabbed her and was bending her ear.

"Did you get her name? Is it a potential client?"

"Ronnie got to her before I could ask her anything. I think they must be old friends or something. Should I go and ask her? I think he's showing her stuff from the Cross investigation."

"No, no. I'm sure he knows what he's doing. Give me half an hour."

"You only live ten minutes away."

"Yeah, well, you'll just have to hold all these people at bay until I get there."

By the time I'd showered and dressed and had a coffee and croissant in grumpy defiance – it was my damned business, I was the boss, they could all damned well wait – it was nearly ten o'clock before I finally reached the office. Desi glared at me but I ignored her. Harper leapt up to intercept me but I stopped her with a gesture. Ronnie was chatting to Megan and my heart was jumping about in my chest at the sight of her. She turned and saw me and her face lit up.

"Hi," she said. "Ronnie was keeping me amused. You didn't have to rush."

"Up all night fretting about Death's Head?" Ronnie asked.

I fielded his sarcasm with a "Yeah, nah," keeping my eyes on Megan. "What's up?" I asked her.

"It's nice to see you, too," she said.

"Right. Yes. Look, tell you what, why don't we go somewhere so we can talk?"

She picked up her handbag – she favoured large, leather sacks big enough to carry a week's supply of food, or whatever she kept in there – and we left without further discussion. Harper again tried to intercept me but I fobbed her off with a promise to be back soon. We took the lift down to the food court in the mall below and found a quiet spot to sit with a couple of coffees.

"So, what's up?" I asked again.

She grimaced in a how-do-I-put-this kind of way. "I've broken up with Donny," she said.

"Donny? Your husband? The bloke you left me for to go back to, to give it another chance? That Donny?"

"Yes."

I looked at her hard for a long time, neither of us speaking.

Eventually, she said, "I kept meaning to tell you but… And then, when I saw you the other day…"

"So, it had already happened by then?"

"Yes. It happened two weeks after I went back to him. It was a stupid mistake and we both knew it right away. The thing is, I—"

"Two weeks? So you broke up more than five months ago? And you didn't tell me? You just dumped me and left me to—"

I couldn't speak. I could hardly breathe. I definitely could not sit there and look at her stupid, pleading face. I got up, battered by a storm of emotions I couldn't even name but every one of which hurt in some deep and special way. We locked eyes. I don't know what she saw in my face – anger, betrayal, despair – but she opened her mouth to speak again. I shook my head. I didn't want to hear it. I just wanted to go. Without a backward glance, I barged through the busy food court, bumping into chairs and people as I went. I didn't think about Megan, or those long, apparently pointless months of pain she'd put me through, or even where I was going, until the lift doors opened and I found myself in the corridor outside my office.

I stopped. I couldn't go in there. There was nowhere private and at least three people who would see my shattered state and want to grill me about it, out of curiosity, or concern, or whatever passed for either in Ronnie's cryptic soul. But I had work to do. Lots of it. However much I wanted to just go home and pull the covers over my head, I had things I needed to get on with.

I walked over to the door of an empty office and studied my reflection. I didn't look too bad. I hadn't rent my garments or rubbed ashes in my hair like a character in a Greek tragedy. I looked a bit hollow-eyed, maybe, but maybe I always looked like that. I'd never been much to look at. My first partner, Chelsea, used to say I was cute, "like a big, skinny baby." Megan once said I looked like an androgynous rock star from the Eighties. I think they were both trying to make the best of a bad deal.

Whatever.

I straightened my back and set my shoulders. I hadn't been crying. I wasn't dishevelled. I'd just go in there and get on with it like nothing had happened. And, in truth, nothing much had happened. I'd always thought Megan was an idiot to go back to Donny. I never expected it to last. I'd always expected she'd give me a call one day to say it was over. It was just that two weeks thing. Two fucking weeks! All that heartbreak for two stupid, futile weeks.

I took a deep breath. This was not helping. *Just get on with it*, I told myself and set off towards my office.

"Oh God, are you all right?" Desi asked, as I walked in.

Harper, who had jumped up to intercept me, said, "It's all right. We can do this later."

152

"I'm fine," I said, glaring at each in turn. "Harper, what can I do for you?"

We sat together at the table near the door. I didn't want to take her to my private office because that would mean going past Ronnie.

"Bonking Barry spotted me," Harper said, without preamble. Barry was the unfaithful husband she'd been trailing for several days now. She'd seen plenty of evidence of his cheating but had been unable to get any decent pictures of it.

"When was this?"

She looked at her watch. "About two hours ago. He saw me taking pictures of him and his fancy piece and put two and two together straight off. I got sloppy. I'm really sorry. It was like everything was conspiring against me getting a good shot. I was pretending to be a tourist, just trying to hide in plain sight, hey. It was stupid. Once he spotted me taking his picture, he remembered seeing me before. Jeez, I could kick myself."

"Was it a good picture?"

"What?"

"The one he saw you taking."

"I – I don't know."

She pulled a compact DSLR camera from her handbag and peered at the screen. After a moment of flicking back and forth through the images, she turned the camera and showed me. Bonking Barry was a balding but athletic looking bloke in his forties. In the picture, he had his arm around a pretty young woman, half his age, whom we knew to be his secretary. They were looking sweetly into each other's eyes.

"That'll do nicely," I said, smiling. "Get over to the client right now, show her the picture and explain that he spotted you." I had no reason to believe Bonking Barry might become violent with his wife because she was having him followed but I had no reason not to believe it, either. "Take Ronnie, in case he's already there when you arrive."

She glanced across at Ronnie and I could see she was dubious. To anyone who hadn't seen him in action, he looked like a bloke who might once have been tough but who was now well over the hill.

"I can look after myself," she said, which was true. Harper was an ex-cop and had dealt with plenty of raging husbands at "domestics" in her time but maybe she underestimated the advantages of carrying a gun, a taser and pepper spray while wearing her old uniform.

"Yeah, I know. Just take Ronnie to make me feel better, hey?"

We got up and she went to tell Ronnie the news. I moved quietly to my office, hoping Ronnie would be sufficiently distracted. I needed a new job to put Harper on but that was no real problem. There was enough work on the Harry Cross case to keep her busy for now. In fact, I'd be very pleased to hand off a lot of the day's phone calls to ex-XtraVirtual and Murdock Island resort employees. However, as I tried quietly to close my door, Ronnie pushed it open and walked in.

"Don't do that," he said.

"Do what?"

"Hide in here all day, sooking like a big sooky sook."

"I wasn't – What the hell do you know about it, anyway?"

"I know Megan turned up with an olive branch and ten minutes later you're skulking about like a beaten puppy, hiding in your cupboard to lick your wounded pride. Is there any more to it than that?"

"It's compli – It's none of your fucking business! Are you

going with Harper or not?"

His eyes narrowed and his brows came down. He pointed a threatening finger at me and took a step closer. I moved as casually but as quickly as I could to the other side of the desk.

"This is not over," he said and stomped out.

As soon as he left, Desi came in with a cup of coffee and a plate of biscuits.

"Thought you might need these," she said.

I knew she was there mostly because she was burning with curiosity to find out what was going on, but I thanked her and took the offering with gratitude.

To stave off days of probing and hinting, I said, "Ronnie wants me to get back with Megan. I'm not sure that's possible after everything that's happened."

She nodded. "So that was the famous Megan. I thought it must be." She gave me a weak smile. "She seemed nice."

"Well, she's not." Even to me that sounded harsh. "Well, she is. But she's also an idiot who's put me through the wringer for months."

"I had a boyfriend who—"

I held up a hand. From bitter experience, I knew that, once started, Desi could talk non-stop for a full hour. "Can you get me the pending clients list, please? And, when Harper gets back, you can invoice her client and close the Bonking Barry file. Now, I've got a load of phone calls to make, so I don't want to be disturbed for the rest of the day unless it's something urgent. OK?"

She didn't look happy that I'd cut her off but I thought I'd been very generous with the information I'd shared about my private life, so she'd just have to deal, without telling a string of boring and largely irrelevant stories about every friend and relative she had who ever suffered romantic problems.

I got up my list of calls, got the files for each of them ready, and set up my desk phone to record it all. Then the phone rang. The caller ID was "Switchboard".

"Desi? Is this really an emergency?"

She sounded a bit huffy. "It's Detective Inspector Reid. He's on his way over and would like a chat."

Chapter Eleven

Although DS Bertolissio was her usual, friendly self, DI Reid was not a happy little Vegemite. On the other hand, that was pretty much his usual self, too. Had I ever seen the man smile? I don't mean a malicious grin. I mean an actual smile of happiness.

"These letters," he said, cutting across Bertolissio as she responded to my polite enquiry after her health. "They're bullshit."

"That's what Ronnie said," I told him, knowing it would wind him up.

"Yeah, well, for once, he's right. I thought there might be something in it with the first one but this last one..." He made a face that clearly showed his disgust.

"You think it's a prank?"

"I'd ask if you had any enemies who might be trying to make you look stupid or put the wind up you but we'd be here all day."

"So you're just going to dismiss it, even though, on the last two murder cases I investigated, my life was threatened and I was physically assaulted?"

He rolled his eyes. "Of course we won't dismiss it. It's just, as I said, it's bullshit."

"You're still able to access our notes?" I asked.

"So?"

"So you might have seen that three of our top four suspects are women?"

He looked puzzled. "So?"

"So, the letters were sent by a woman."

"We don't know that?"

"Ronnie's pretty certain."

"Yeah, well…" He looked like he was about to say something rather rude about my colleague but Bertolissio jumped in to stave it off.

"What the Detective Inspector means is that, while the choice of magazine is suggestive, a detailed forensic analysis of the first letter has revealed no evidence indicating either sex."

This was news. "So, what were the magazines?"

"*Vogue* and *Harper's Bazaar*," she said. "With one word not yet accounted for."

"The kind of thing Jennifer Cross might read," I said.

"Or any of the women in the case," Reid said. "Do you really think Jennifer Cross is trying to scare you off? She's the victim's mother, for God's sake. And she's old enough to be your grandma."

I looked at Bertolissio to see her reaction. She had a well-practiced straight face which she used a lot of the time when Reid was talking.

"OK," I said. There didn't seem much point in arguing. "I suppose you still think it's Grigor Mostek."

"Him or some other underworld scumbag. And just ask yourself, what kind of magazines do you think Mostek's wife reads? These crime families love that crap." He seemed very pleased with himself.

"So, you think Grigor Mostek's wife is sending me threatening letters?"

"Well, no. I'm just saying…"

"Does Mostek have a death's head tattoo?"

Reid looked taken aback. The question appeared to be one he hadn't considered.

"No," said Bertolissio, smoothly. "Unless he acquired it recently. His prison records show no such marking."

"Any hired killers in your database that have such a tattoo?"

"Yes, dozens. It would help if we knew what the death's head was like, exactly. We have plenty of basic skulls, some with crossbones, snakes through the eye sockets, impaled on daggers, wearing Nazi helmets, grinning, crying, appearing through flames… All kinds of stuff. We even have one on a bed of roses. Psychotic killers love body art and are very big on symbolism."

I gave her a smile. I liked her a lot. I turned to Reid. "So, to sum up. The letters are a dead end, no new leads, and you think they're probably some kind of hoax."

"That's right. A complete waste of our time. You don't happen to have any ex-girlfriends who read *Vogue*, do you?" I gave him a fuck you smile. It didn't faze him in the least. "You went to XtraVirtual yesterday. Dig up anything we missed?"

"It's all in the notes."

"Yeah, like I'm going to read everything you write. Just give me the gist."

I thought about telling him to root himself but decided I should probably try to keep as near as possible to the right side of him. His cooperation had been very useful so far – even if that was mostly down to Bertolissio.

159

"Claudia Knecht is an interesting character," I said. "Opportunity, means and possible motive. Also, a potential tie-in with Cassandra Cross. Any indication that those two might have been mates? Or collaborators?"

"You're clutching at straws, mate."

"Really? So you already knew about Cassandra accusing Claudia of having an affair with Harry? And that she confessed to her that he beat her?"

I glanced at Bertolissio. She was deadpanning again. She had read my interview notes.

"What does that mean?" Reid wanted to know. "Cassandra has an alibi. Her housekeeper confirms it. And the secretary's hardly likely to kill her boss because his wife's a bit upset. What else have you got?"

Enough compassion not to think being the victim of domestic violence, or feeling so insecure about your spouse you think they might be cheating on you, counts as being 'a bit upset', I thought. But I kept it to myself.

"Richard Cross also said some stuff. Did you look into the relationship between him and his mother?"

"Of course. Mother and son." Reid clearly didn't see where I was going with the question.

Again, Bertolissio chimed in. "It was pretty obvious to the investigating team that Harry was Jennifer Cross's favourite son – even though she didn't think much of Cassandra – but there didn't seem to be any more to it."

"What about the fact that Richard completely ignored his mother after the murder?" I asked Reid.

"So what? We thought it might be he was rooting the wife." He shrugged his regret. "But that didn't go anywhere. Just a crap son. World's full of them." He drew a breath making it sound disgruntled and unsatisfied. "Anything else? I read the interview where the kid said he nearly ran over some old girl near the time of the murder. There's always some fuckwit trying to hide something, however unimportant. So, other than that."

I shook my head, feeling tired. "Not unless you count June Onbekend."

"The hotel manager? What about her?"

"You didn't look at her for the killing?"

"Why would we? She barely knew the victim. She had no reason to kill him and the idea she'd have planned things far enough in advance, having only just met the man, to go into that room with a concealed knife, is ridiculous."

He glared at me as if defying me to contradict him. I could only imagine how much fun it was to work for a man like that. I switched my attention to Bertolissio.

"Have you guys dug up anything new in the past couple of days?"

"No," she said and, from her tone, I took her to mean they were not actively looking.

"Right-o, then," said Reid, getting to his feet and towering over us. "You've got nothing. We've got nothing. I reckon that's it for now, then."

Bertolissio stood, too. Finally, I joined them.

"Thanks for your time," Reid said and led his sergeant out of the door.

"Always welcome," I said to the empty doorway.

* * * *

By the time Ronnie got back with Harper, I was well into my calls. I saw them talking to Desi at reception, then Harper went to her desk and Ronnie made a bee-line for my office.

"What did the Lone Ranger and Tonto want?" he asked without preamble.

DI Reid, with his rangy build and square-jawed face, was so much like an old Western movie hero, we'd developed lots of cowboy-related nicknames for him. Ronnie liked to call him the Marlboro Man, which I'd had to google, being part of a mostly post-cigarette generation. The first time DS Bertolissio heard us refer to him as Rooster Cogburn, she'd had to bite her lip to stop herself laughing. That she suddenly frowned was probably because she'd guessed that made her Mattie Ross.

"Just a catch-up. Reid thinks the letters are bullshit."

"Yeah, well, he can't be wrong all the time."

"How did it go with the client?"

"Yeah, Bonking Barry hadn't turned up yet, so no-one got a walloping. Missus Barry wasn't so happy to hear we'd blown our cover but, when she saw the photos, she agreed it was all going to come out sooner or later. I told her to go stay with rellies until Barry calmed down but I think she was spoiling for a blue. She said she'd be emailing the pictures to her dad and her two brothers with an invitation come over to enjoy the fireworks."

"Hell hath no fury," I said.

"Too bloody true, mate. Any luck with the phone interviews?"

"Nah. Nobody saw anything. Nobody was there. Everybody confirmed their story. You know what? I think the cops did a pretty thorough job of extracting as much information as they could."

"Yeah, I told you Reid's not a bad cop. He just lack's imagination. Shame Al wasn't with him for this one."

I pulled a face. "Let's not call her Al, hey? If there's a

single female cop in the service it doesn't feel right to give a male nickname to, it's Alexandra Bertolissio. Only a bloke as thick as Trevor Reid would even think of it."

Ronnie gave me that puzzled look he seemed to reserve solely for trying to figure out what was going on in my impenetrable mind.

"Her sister calls her Lexi," I said. So did Sergeant Tim Pearce, although I wasn't sure he used it to her face.

He laughed. "I don't think a cutesy pet name suits her, either. Far too formidable. We'll just call her Bertolissio, hey?"

"Sounds about right. I didn't realise your feminist sensibilities were so attuned to my own." Why miss a chance to poke him with a stick?

But he didn't rise to the bait. Instead, he checked his watch. "Beer o'clock," he said. "If you want me, I'll be in the R.E. having a cold one."

The R.E. was the pub across the road from us. There was no invitation to join him and no chance that I could. It was only late morning and I still had tons more calls to make. So I got back down to it and he wandered off. At about twelve-thirty, Harper popped her head in to say she'd written up the case, sent off the invoice and was going down to get a sandwich.

"I'll bring you something back, if you like."

I pushed away my laptop. "Why don't we go and join Ronnie for a pub lunch? My treat."

On the way down, I described a couple of cases she might like as her next assignment.

"What about working on the Cross case?" she asked.

"You can do a couple of days but we need to take a new client off the stack." Unlike most private investigators I knew

163

of, we actually had customers waiting in line for our services. They were mostly corporate clients and the work was mostly really boring but it was a nice feeling to have a backlog of work. And this was a chance to make a customer happy because we'd finished a job early and could get to them sooner than we estimated.

She didn't look pleased but she nodded her agreement. One of the weird things about being the boss was that the people who worked for me tended to do what I asked them to do. Not Ronnie, of course, but everyone else. And it wasn't just that. They acquiesced not just because I paid their wages but because they actually seemed to believe that I knew what I was doing, that my assessment of priorities and roles and duties to clients was somehow superior to their own, just because it said "Managing Director" on my lapel badge. Not that I wore a lapel badge, but you know what I mean. On the other hand, maybe it was because they weren't as invested in the job as I was and were happy to let me make whatever stupid mistakes I liked. It was my funeral, after all.

The pub was busy and Ronnie was alone at the bar, swirling a glass of rum as he stared into its depths. He didn't seem surprised to see us. In fact, he might have been expecting us for all the reaction our arrival got.

"Pie and chips," he said to me by way of greeting.

I bit down a snappish response and asked Harper what she'd like. They went to find a table while I ordered drinks and food. By the time I rejoined them, they were talking about pandemics and vaccines and all the usual subjects of modern life. The conversation drifted around bushfires and climate change, economic crises and rising homelessness. The food came and went. So did another round of drinks. We got onto clients and surveillance techniques. Ronnie and Harper swapped a couple of cop stories. Then Harper said she'd get back and get started on some of those calls I wanted her to make. I wished her luck and, when she'd gone, turned to Ronnie.

"All right, what's up with you?"

"Don't know what you mean."

"You didn't have a go at me about Megan before lunch, and now you've been all normal and chatty while Harper was here. Something's not right."

"I'd have thought you'd be grateful. You're always whining like a little girl about how horrible I am to you."

"Now, that's more like it. And then there's the untouched glass of rum. Every time I catch you gazing into one of those, it means you're on the verge of some existential crisis. So what is it this time? You've been diagnosed with cancer? Your girlfriend lied about being post-menopausal and now she's pregnant? Your house has got a white ant infestation and it's a metaphor for the mental decay you've struggled with all your life? Come on, out with it."

He looked steadily back at me, his expression caught somewhere between wanting to laugh and wanting to smash my face in with a brick.

"You're a funny bastard," he said. "Not really my taste but I can see you going down well in some crappy comedy club full of bored metrosexuals. I bet the polite tittering would never stop."

"I'm right though, hey? So, what's the go?"

He sighed, heavily. "We're not getting anywhere with this case."

"What?" That was definitely not what I expected to hear.

"It's going nowhere. We're stuck. We're up a gum tree. Our wheels are spinning. We're paddling against the tide, stuck in neutral, bogged in the mud. Pick an idiom."

"We're not stuck. We've barely got started. I'm turning up all kinds of stuff."

He shook his head. "I can feel it in my gut, mate. I've read your interviews. I've read every word the cops wrote. I've been here before. I know how this is going. And I'm telling you: we need a lot more than we've got so far to reach any other conclusion than Reid's team did."

"Yeah, maybe, but… We've only been on it three days."

"Four."

"So what? That means we've got nearly a whole month before we have to start talking Aikenhead into giving us an extension."

"It won't make any difference. We need to kick this into a higher gear or we'll never find the killer. We need to shake the damned tree, Luke."

Willing as I usually was to defer to his long experience, all I felt was exasperation. We were just getting into our stride, doing the groundwork, getting all our ducks in a row… Jeez, Ronnie's spew of idioms was getting to me. I tried to be reasonable.

"Why don't we get all the interviews out of the way, then step back and take a look at where we are?"

"Because there's nothing there. Like I said: the cops did a good job. We're not going to pick holes in it. If they'd missed things, we'd have seen signs of it by now."

"But they did miss something: the odd job man and the old biddie he nearly ran over."

He looked away, squirming with irritation. "There was an old lady somewhere near a key location, sometime before or after an important moment, on an island swarming with old ladies."

"And Richard Cross didn't notice all the sawing going on near his chalet. And he ran straight to Cassandra and not his mother."

"Mate, you're clutching at straws."

I threw myself back in my chair, almost snorting with frustration. "All right," I said, thinking furiously. "All right. So, the cops did a good job. They wrung the cloth of truth dry, leaving barely a drop for us to find. Fine. Let's start there. Let's start with, we have all the facts and so do the cops. So the problem isn't one of finding new stuff but of using all the stuff we already have to solve the puzzle. Somewhere in those hundreds of interviews and case notes and statements and photographs, there is a pattern that the cops missed, a big, fat arrow that points to the killer, and all we have to do is to stop going over the same ground and focus on somehow seeing the bigger picture. We have the advantage of coming at this fresh."

He nodded thoughtfully and took a long pull at his stubby. "There is a problem with that," he said. "Bertolissio wasn't on the original case, either. And she's had the chance to go over all the police files and to talk it through with the investigating officers. I'm not saying she's as good as me, but she's probably the best detective the QPS has. If she hasn't seen whatever it is Reid's guys missed, I'd lay odds it isn't there."

I threw up my hands. "You just told me it was! You just said they'd done a good job and collected all the info they could. You just talked me out of doing any more field work on the grounds it was pointless! Now you're saying there's nothing in all those megabytes of data to be found even if we tried. Jeez, mate, I'm trying to work with you here but you just seem to be saying we should give up and go home."

"Yeah, well, maybe we should."

"What?" I was incredulous. "Are you kidding me? There's a murderer out there and you want us to just let them go free? You? Ronnie Walker? Ready to spit the dummy? It's like... like asking a cat not to chase a bird. It's like asking a toddler to leave the last biscuit in the packet. It's like—"

"All right! Maybe I was being a bit negative. Just having a whinge, hey? But you're not hearing me. This – the way we're doing the investigation – isn't working." He held up a hand to stop me interrupting. "I know you think we haven't given it a fair suck of the sav yet, but I'm asking you to trust my gut. We've pulled at a few threads and, far from it coming unravelled, the police investigation remains as tight as a drum. That's a bad sign – for us, anyway."

I studied him in silence for a moment.

"All right, then, what do you want us to do?"

He sort of slumped without actually moving much. A kind of spiritual slump, if you know what I mean.

"I don't know. That's why I need to spend some time thinking about it."

"And what should I do while your mighty brain is meditating on the ineffable depths of a glass of rum?"

He shook his head. "Carry on, I suppose. Finish the interviews. Go through the motions. There's always some small chance I got it wrong and the next person you speak to will blow the case wide open."

I kept staring at him, feeling my stomach beginning to clench. "You're going to suggest something totally crazy, aren't you – like breaking into Richard Cross's office, or kidnapping the grandma, or something?"

To my dismay, he took me seriously. "I don't know. Something... But it's got to be something that'll stir things up for the killer and we just don't know enough yet to know what would do that." He gave me a weak smile. "That's why I need to think."

"While I carry on plodding through the busy-work."

He grinned, probably because I was talking now as if I accepted his conclusion. "We each have our different strengths." He stood up. He looked happy that we'd sorted things out. "I'm off for a piss."

"As you said, we each have our different strengths. I'll see you at the office, later."

I stood up, too, as he walked away. But, before he left, he turned back and said, "You're a fucking idiot, by the way, for whatever stupid thing you did with Megan today instead of getting back with her."

* * * *

"Did anybody ever consider the possibility that Harry Cross stuck the knife in his own chest?"

Harper and I had finally called it a day on the phone calls and she seemed to be regretting her desire to work on our exciting murder investigation.

"Yes," I said. "The pathologist. She reckons it's possible but unlikely. All the detail's in the report, if you want to see her reasoning."

"Yeah, nah. I'll take her word for it. Look, I'm going to shoot through, if that's OK. My dogs could do without me putting in another late night. I worry that one day I'll walk in on them and they'll start screaming, 'Oh my God, who's that strange lady?'"

"Yeah, you go on. Thanks for your help today."

"Do you think Ronnie's ever going to turn up?"

"Nah, reckon he's gone home. And I'm going to do the same."

We walked to the lift and travelled down together, chatting about the pandemic and the vaccines and the latest outbreaks. She got off at the ground floor and I carried on down to the basement where my car was parked.

The first thing I noticed when I reached the car was the gigantic thug leaning against the bonnet. I stopped dead, still a few metres from him. He was at least my height – which is 185 cm – but probably twice my width and depth. He wore a singlet and boardies and his massively muscular arms were folded across his barrel chest. He stared at me through eyes that seemed too small for his face, sunken below heavy brows and a shaven head. His mouth turned down, as if from a habitual distaste for all things human and me in particular. I studied this menacing apparition for some time, trying to decide whether to run for the exit, or try to make it back into the lift. I had no doubt at all if I stayed there I'd get stomped on.

It was as I deliberated my best escape route, taking in as I did, the elaborate intertwining of mawkishly sentimental and blatantly fascist symbols tattooed all over his arms, chest and neck, I saw something that froze me to the spot. On his right forearm – a canvas large enough to accommodate the complete works of van Gogh – was a grinning skull, surrounded by flames, with a banner beneath it that seemed to be a motto but which I couldn't read from that distance.

"You're Death's Head Guy?" I asked. If Bigfoot himself had manifested in my office car park, I couldn't have been more astonished.

One corner of the man's mouth twitched into a smirk.

"You was warned," he said. His voice was deep and gravelly.

"What's going on?" I asked. "Who are you?" He pushed himself upright. Maybe I'd underestimated how big he was. "What have you got to do with the murder?" He took a step towards me. Stupidly, I stood my ground. I wanted answers. This just didn't make any sense.

"Who do you work for?" I demanded, even as he walked towards me. "Is it Novak? I asked, naming the gang boss Grigor Mostek worked for, but it got no reaction. "So who sent you?"

"You was warned," he said again and swung a fist at my head. I'm proud to say, I remembered the self-defence lessons Ronnie had given me and threw up an arm to block the blow. Sadly, even though I got the block in place in good time, my arm might as well have been a small twig in the path of the giant log that was swinging at me. When his arm connected with mine, it threw me sideways, so when his fist hit my face, it probably wasn't quite as deadly as it might have been. All the same, it still knocked me to the ground. I didn't really understand that I was falling until I hit the concrete floor. I looked up at Death's Head Guy, my vision sliding across him in a way that made me feel sick. He leaned down, grabbed me by the shirtfront and pulled back his fist for another blow.

Chapter Twelve

I woke up in Princess Alexandra Hospital, groggy and panicked. I struggled to sit up and saw a woman throw aside a magazine and leap up from her chair.

"Megan?"

Nothing made sense. Until I remembered Death's Head Guy. And then nothing made sense again.

"He shouldn't be real," I said.

Megan pressed me back into the pillows. "You just stay still. I'll get the nurse."

"What the hell is going on?" I demanded and my head exploded with pain.

"They said you'd probably have a headache," she said. "Just stay put and I'll get someone."

Headache? It was like saying an amputated arm was a small scratch. I stayed still with my eyes screwed shut until the torture subsided. Then I peeped out at the room. It was empty. Had I imagined Megan being there? Had I imagined Death's Head Guy? It all seemed possible. In fact, it would make a lot more sense than that this was really happening. But the pain in my head felt real enough.

"Thus I refute you!" I said aloud, quoting Johnson's spurious argument against solipsism. Just because my pain was real, didn't mean anything else was – or wasn't.

"Do you indeed," said a portly young woman in a nurse's uniform, entering the room and moving towards me like a shark scenting blood.

"It's all right, he's a philosopher," Megan said.

"Don't worry, darl, we get all sorts in here." For a while, I was pulled and prodded, sheets were straightened and pillows plumped. I complained about my head and she gave me two pills. Eventually, she said, "Doctor will be along in a while. Do you feel like eating?" She pulled over one of those trays on wheels that fit around a bed. "Breakfast menu's on here." She added a glass of water and a TV remote.

When she left, I took the pills and stared at Megan. I suppose I was waiting for an explanation.

"Ronnie called me," she said.

I looked around, suddenly wondering what time it was. Breakfast? The nurse had said breakfast, right?

"How did I get here?" I asked.

Megan sat on the edge of the bed. "I don't know all the details. Someone found you in your car park and called an ambulance. You were out cold. They took scans and there wasn't anything bad, just a small contusion on your brain. No broken bones or skull fractures or anything. Seems you have a good, thick skull. Which is obviously useful in your line of work."

A small contusion on my brain? Nothing bad?

"Why did Ronnie call you? Never mind." I already knew. It was his ham-fisted way of match-making. I felt my irritation growing and, with it, the pain in my head. I tried to calm myself. I could tell Ronnie what I thought of him when I felt better. In fact, it would give me something to look forward to. "Who else did he call?"

"No-one, as far as I know."

"Not my mum and dad? Please say no." They worried so much about me anyway, especially after the plane-ramming incident last year, that I didn't want them even to suspect I was being beaten up in car parks again.

She shook her head. "I don't think so. Only Ronnie was here when I arrived last night and no-one else has been since."

Ronnie was my emergency contact. I carried an ICE card in my wallet naming him just so my parents wouldn't be the first to know, in case something really bad happened.

"Why did you come? I haven't seen you for months and now you're at my bedside?"

"I – I was worried." She looked upset, distressed.

"Well, I'll be fine now, thank you. No need to hang around."

Her eyes were suddenly full of pain. She got up off the bed as if I'd poked her with a stick. It made me feel cruel and mean. I wanted to be kind but there was a giant boulder of hurt and anger inside me that, once set rolling, could not be stopped. Some part of me was enjoying seeing her upset and humiliated. Some part of me wanted to see more.

"Goodbye," I said and stared into her eyes until she turned away and hurried out of the room.

I lay back and closed my eyes. The pain in my head was a metal spike being twisted and turned. The pain in my chest was new and yet familiar, a hand, squeezing my heart. Her hand. Squeezing hard.

"So, how are you, Mr. Kelly?"

The doctor was a woman, tallish, with smooth brown cheeks. She had on a professional smile, which faded as she studied my face. I wiped at the tears with quick, angry strokes.

"I'm fine. Just a headache. Can I go now?"

Whatever she thought was going on, she didn't mention it. She picked up the chart from the foot of my bed and scanned it. She came close, took a little torch that looked like a pen out of her pocket and got me to follow it with my eyes. Then she turned on the light and flicked it into my eyes a few times, making me flinch because of what that did for my headache. She started asking me questions about what day it was, who was the Prime Minister, and such, then got me to count backwards from a hundred in sevens. I struggled with some of the questions and the counting thing was nearly impossible. At the end of it, I felt frustrated and annoyed, knowing I'd done badly.

"You have a quite a bad concussion," she said. "Unless you have someone who can be with you full time at home and keep a close eye on you, I'd like to keep you here under observation for another day."

"I need to go," I told her. "I'm fine."

She rolled her eyes. "No, you're not. You need to rest physically and mentally for a couple of days – especially mentally. What do you do for a living?"

"I'm a detective."

She seemed surprised. "A cop? Actually we get quite a few cops in here with concussions. It's a dangerous job. Did you get injured making an arrest?"

"I'm a private detective. And, no. I was attacked in a car park. A lot of the people I investigate seem to consider me a bit of a pest."

She nodded as if she could see how that might be. "In which case, I think I'm even more inclined to keep you here."

A voice came from the doorway and we both turned to look. "It's all right, I'll look after the stupid sod."

Ronnie walked into the room and stared down at me with a grim expression.

"Are you his father?" the doctor asked.

"Christ no! And, if I was, do you think I'd admit to it? Nah, love, I just work with him."

She spent a few minutes explaining to Ronnie just how much care I was going to need – which seemed to include waking me up while I was sleeping, just to make sure I could wake up properly! He yeah-yeahed his way through her spiel, which seemed to irritate her a lot. In the end, though, she said I could go home with him and left us alone.

"Come on then," he said, when she was gone. "Get your arse into gear." He ratted through the cupboards and found my clothes. "Let's not hang about, hey? I hate these places."

* * * *

"I don't believe it," he said after he'd parked me on the sofa at his place.

"You want to see my bruises?"

"I can see someone tried to remodel your face. What I don't believe is that it was Death's Head Guy. It just doesn't make sense."

"Yeah, that's what I told him."

"And, anyway, just 'cause the bloke had a skull tattoo doesn't mean a thing. Half the bikies in Brisbane have them. It's like six-year-old girls with unicorns on their backpacks; it's a cultural thing."

I was already getting tired from talking about it. Maybe the doctor was right. Thinking seemed to be much harder work than it should be.

"All right, so I was beaten up by a random six-year-old and her unicorn. Aren't you the one who's always telling me there's no such thing as coincidences in a murder investigation?"

"Yeah but…" He looked unhappy.

"And he only said three words to me. 'You. Was. Warned.' Three words. And he said them twice, just in case I found the concept difficult to wrestle with. 'You. Was. Warned.' So what was that if it wasn't a reference to the letters I got?"

"All right. All right. It's not a coincidence. But I'm still not happy."

I sat back and massaged my temples. "Yeah, well, your happiness is not my biggest concern just now. Whatever this is about, Death's Head Guy seems to want me off the case and, to be honest, he made some pretty persuasive arguments. And why is it always me that gets beaten up? You're the bloody annoying one. And why won't our building services people install cameras in the car park? That spot, right outside the basement lift, is the scene of at least three assaults that I am personally aware of. They could halve violent crime in this city just by pointing a camera at my car."

Ronnie sat down facing me in his favourite armchair. He unscrewed a stubby and took a long swig. I sighed. The doctor had recommended no alcohol for a couple of days. "Actually, you don't want to go there, mate. I raised the matter with building services last year after those bozos kicked your arse – twice – and they seemed a lot more concerned that your business was attracting unsavoury types to the building than they were about your safety. I had the strong impression they were going to look at the contract to see if they could give you the elbow."

I shook my head in despair and immediately regretted it. Whatever the hospital had given me as pain killers seemed to be having no effect at all.

"I might just curl up under the doona until this headache goes away," I told Ronnie.

"Good idea. Then I won't have to watch you wallowing in self-pity all day. The spare room's free. You know where to find it."

I did, sadly, it had often been my bolt-hole in times of life-threatening thuggery.

"That was a fucking stupid stunt, calling Megan," I said.

He scowled at me. "Just fuck off and lie down."

"It's none of your business. Just keep out of it."

"Yeah, no worries. I won't try and do you any favours again. Stuff up your life any way you like."

He got up and took his beer out onto the patio. It was winter and the days were getting cooler but a winter's day in sub-tropical Brisbane enjoyed the kind of temperature lots of northern countries would endure in a normal summer. Most people I knew didn't even heat their homes at night. I watched as he settled himself on his favourite sun-lounger. Carefully, trying not to move my head too quickly, I got up too and went to bed.

* * * *

I woke up in the dark, with a shadow looming over me. I cried out and struggled to get up. A hand pressed against my chest, forcing me down.

"Jesus fucking Christ, mate, get a grip!" It was Ronnie. I stopped struggling. "I'm just waking you up like the doctor said." He let me go and stepped back. "The good news is, you're going to live. The bad news is, you're going to live."

I reached over and turned on the bedside lamp. Ronnie was in his pyjamas.

"What time is it?" I groped for my phone as I asked.

"It's about ten. I'm on my way to bed."

"What? I slept all day?"

"Like a log. How's your head?"

I suddenly realised it was way better than it had been. "Great," I said. "But now my face hurts where he pummelled it."

"Yeah, well, that's my duties as medic complete. If your brain turns to soup in the night, it wasn't my fault." He turned and left.

As he closed the door, I remembered my manners and called out to thank him. He didn't respond. I settled down again but, after about half-an-hour of trying, I realised I wasn't going to get back to sleep. I went downstairs and turned on the TV but nothing caught my interest. I wandered around, looking for a book that wasn't military history or a sports biography but didn't find anything. I went into Ronnie's office and looked at the picture on the wall – all pictures of his dog club friends and their dogs, with just one image of him as a young man with a handful of other soldiers. It was a fascinating picture just because it was the only one that seemed like a genuine memento rather than careless decoration. Again it struck me how much of Ronnie's life seemed to be a front, a disguise he was wearing to conceal something no-one else must see, or even suspect.

I'd asked him about the soldier picture once and he'd shut me down with a tirade against "stickybeaks" whose lives were so dull they needed to seek vicarious thrills by poking around in other people's stuff. *Camouflage and smokescreens*, I thought.

Was that part of his black ops training, or was it just part of Ronnie's nature? I suspected it was both.

I took the picture off the wall and looked at the back. There was nothing but the hardboard backing of the frame. So I took the frame apart and got the photograph out. There was no revealing text on the back, just a single date: 1/11/1991. I made a note of it in my phone and reassembled the picture and frame. I hung it back on the wall as carefully as I could. For a while I studied the background of the shot – sandy, blurry, rocky. It could be the Middle East, I supposed, but it could just as easily be a beach in the UK for all I knew. It was frustrating that I couldn't ask him about the date without confessing to my snooping.

I looked around for a computer but Ronnie didn't own one, as I well knew. He used his phone for everything. He was scarily proficient with it, too. Even though he was twice my age, I felt like the old boomer, with my preference for nice, big screens and real keyboards, while he could type faster with two thumbs than I could with both hands.

With a sigh, I went to sit in front of the TV again. I put on a Start Trek: Voyager re-run on Netflix and didn't watch it. I was thinking about what Ronnie had said in the pub, about the investigation needing a shake-up. Well, if Death's Head Guy actually showing up wasn't that, I don't know what was. It meant the notes were legitimate. It meant we had a whole new area of investigation that the cops never had after the murder. It meant…

It meant that someone with access to up-market women's magazines was worried enough about re-opening the investigation that they would risk exposing themselves in an attempt to scare us off – an attempt which had seemed silly and trivial but was obviously deadly serious. It also meant there was a party to this whole affair – Death's Head Guy – that no-one had even suspected existed until now.

I frowned at the images of aliens and ray guns. Ronnie was right. None of it made sense. I mean, the case, not the TV, although I was finding that hard to follow too. There was something vaguely ridiculous about what had happened in the car park, even though my attacker might have killed me.

I started working through it again, this time from the position that Death's Head Guy was just a stooge, hired by the real killer. I pictured Jennifer, Richard and Cassandra Cross in turn, imagining them hiring a thug to beat me up. I couldn't make it seem real. None of them were the kind of people who had access to blokes like that. I tried to imagine Claudia Knecht doing it. She certainly had the balls to go into the sewers and find herself a thug but what I couldn't imagine was her pulling such a half-arsed stunt as sending those letters. She was more the nerves of steel type. It was much easier to imagine her sitting back with a smirk while our pathetic investigation foundered on the same rocks the cops had hit. June Onbekend? Well, I didn't really know her well enough to be sure but she seemed too *nice* to try to have me killed. Too nice to kill Harry Cross for that matter.

The show had reached a point where the protagonists were conducting some protracted argument with the bad guys via their wall-sized shipboard TV screens. *Teleconferencing*, I thought, idly, *like people in a pandemic*. I leaned back and closed my eyes.

"What happened to curling up under the doona?" Startled, I looked around. It was Ronnie. The TV was off and there was light outside. "Sorry, did I wake you?"

"I… What?"

"The Genius Detective, on the ball as usual. Fancy some toast?"

I blinked a few times. "Yeah. And coffee."

He disappeared into the kitchen and I got up and padded after him. The wall clock showed six thirty.

"I couldn't sleep so I got up to think things through," I told him.

"Yeah? Shame you didn't work it all out."

"How do you know I didn't?"

"Because you'd have been pounding on my bedroom door like an ankle biter on Christmas morning, all bouncy and excited and wanting to show off how clever you are." He did a little bouncy and excited mime that I assumed was supposed to be me.

I flopped into a chair at the kitchen table. "I don't show off. Anyway, I got as far as realising the guy who clobbered me is the big shake-up you wanted. Yay! Then I must have dozed off."

The toaster twanged and Ronnie brought over a pile of toasted white bread and a tub of cheap margarine with a table knife stuck in it. He put it down in front of me and I tried not to wince. I'd gone on at him so often about the crap he ate that he must know my complaints by heart.

"Get that down you – if you can bear to sully your body with my imperfect offering – and I'll tell you want happened yesterday while you were idling in bed."

I thanked him weakly and began spreading the trans-fats. I was actually famished and, despite the pain in my jaw, my swollen left eye and the cut on my lower lip, I felt like I could eat a horse and then chase the rider. Conversation ground to a halt as we ate, then, over a disgusting cup of instant coffee, Ronnie said, "We're seeing Bertolissio at half eight." I glanced at my phone. Loads of time yet. "She came to see you in the hospital to get a statement but you'd already gone when she got there."

"The early bird…" I said. The coffee, whatever it tasted like, was working its magic and I was starting to come alive.

"Yeah, well, she rang me to get an appointment and I reckoned today would be right."

"Yeah, no worries. Thanks for keeping her at bay."

"The hospital said forty-eight hours but what do they know, right?"

"Right." I couldn't tell if he was joking.

"She wants you to go through some mugshots. You up for that?"

"Sure. I don't think this bloke's going to be hard to spot. He actually had a swastika on his left earlobe."

"Sounds like a charmer. Have you given any thought to which of our potential suspects hired him?"

"So you think that, too?"

"Well, my first though was that it was Mostek's mob. It would be all in a day's work for them. But – I don't know – it all seems a bit amateurish for that lot. If it wasn't for the letters, maybe… Anyway, who do you reckon?"

I shook my head, sadly. "None of them. I'm not saying none of them would have me beaten up, just that I can't see how they'd have found Death's Head Guy. They could have used your mate Barry McGuire, I suppose." McGuire was a local entrepreneur who rented out thugs for little jobs like that. A kind of Uber for contract killers and standover men. During our last murder investigation, the killer had used him to target us and, when Ronnie beat up his heavies, McGuire sent an assassin, on his own initiative, to finish me off and restore his street cred.

"Yeah, nah," said Ronnie. "He wouldn't be that stupid."

Which was probably true. Ronnie had got McGuire off my back by sending him pictures of McGuire's wife and children with some barely veiled threats that McGuire had taken very seriously. To this day, I still feel slightly queasy at the possibility Ronnie might not have been bluffing.

"Which only leaves the Cross family and their employees as suspects," I said. "Can you see any of them hiring Death's Head Guy? 'Cause I can't."

Ronnie shrugged it away. "You never know with these things. He could have been one of Cassandra's old boyfriends – or her brother for all we know." I made a mental note to check out her background. "Or Claudia Knecht's, or even June Onbekend's, or any one of the XtraVirtual employees. There could easily be some weird connection to the killer and we'd never find it. But…" He raised a finger and smiled. "We have two small clues. One: the killer knows Death's Head Guy and he knew him at the time of the first letter."

"She."

"Yeah, yeah." He put up a second finger. "Whatever the relationship, it isn't so close that he – or she – isn't willing to risk exposing him, either because they don't care about him, or because they think he can't be tied back to them." He pulled a sour face. "Or because they're really, really close and they know Death's Head Guy would never dob them in."

"So that's just one clue, really," I said, just to tease him.

"Yeah, all right smartarse, let's hear your insights, then."

I put my cup down with the drink only half finished, deciding I couldn't torture myself with it any longer. I grinned at Ronnie. "I don't have insights. I leave that to my employees."

He grinned back, eyes narrowing. "Well, your employees

aren't doing much of a job. I spoke to Harper yesterday evening. She finished off all the calls to absentee witnesses and came up with nothing at all. She'll get it all written up today but she seems to think all the stories are consistent with their original statements and there's nothing new to change anybody's alibis or timelines."

"Sounds like she did a great job." I don't know why Ronnie was always making me feel so defensive about my two employees. Maybe he was resentful because I was making a go of my detective agency and he had failed so badly at his own. "Anyway, at least all that crap's out of the way. It's kind of nice to know the cops did a solid job."

"Yeah, so solid they've left a killer on the streets for more than a year."

Chapter Thirteen

Meeting Detective Sergeant Alexandra Bertolissio at police headquarters in Brisbane was quite a different experience from meeting any of her colleagues. She didn't keep us waiting, she was polite, she got us coffee, she found us a comfortable meeting room.

She looked at the bruises on my face and winced. "That must have hurt," she said.

"Still does," I assured her.

"I like it," Ronnie said. "Adds character."

She had a folder with her from which she extracted the statement form. "OK, lets get the formal part out of the way first. Why don't you tell me what happened?" So I did. She wrote it down, I read it, and signed it. She put the form away in the folder.

"Thank you. Now tell me what you think is going on because, honestly, this doesn't make much sense to me."

"Nor to us," I said.

"We haven't even got a working theory," Ronnie added. "Looks like there's someone – possibly a woman – who doesn't want us investigating the murder. She sent some silly letters, then hired a heavy to beat Luke up." He shrugged and looked away as if the whole thing was too ridiculous for words. Bertolissio nodded.

"You'd recognise this man if you saw him again?"

"Definitely," I said. "As it says in the statement, he had several distinguishing marks and, well, you just don't forget the face of a bloke who nearly killed you."

"What about the voice? Anything distinctive about it?"

"Nah. Lousy grammar but that's hardly distinctive, is it? He only said three words."

"Like he was sending a message he'd rehearsed?"

"Could be."

She opened her folder again and pulled out a photo. It was a head-and-shoulders shot of Death's Head Guy. She placed it on the table for me to study. It looked as if the photo had been taken from a distance, outdoors in a crowd.

"Was that the man?"

"Oh yeah. He's younger here, maybe not so many tats, but that is definitely the guy." I looked up at her. "Who is it?"

"No idea."

"What?"

"Let me guess," said Ronnie. "It's a picture taken by ASIO at some kind of right-wing rally."

"Good guess," she said. "They've spotted him at several get-togethers of alt-right groups over the years but they don't know his name and he's never been arrested. He likes to hang around what you might call white supremacist politicians but you know what they're like, they never admit to knowing the fascist thugs who turn up to their rallies – even the ones who are seen on stage with them."

"Do you know what groups he belongs to?" Ronnie asked.

"I'm meeting ASIO this afternoon to see what they've got. The files I have access to are rather limited."

"How did you find him?" I asked.

"Ronnie gave us the description you'd given him. He wasn't in our own database, of course, but once I started spreading the net, he soon popped up."

I pushed the photo back towards Bertolissio and sat back in my chair. Ronnie grabbed the image and began studying it.

"I can't tell if this is good or bad," I said. "I was nervous enough when I thought he was some dickhead hired off the street but now I find out he's a right-wing crazy who hangs out with politicians. What the hell does that mean? And what does it mean for the Harry Cross murder?"

"He might still just have been hired off the street," Bertolissio said. "Even right-wing crazies need to pay the rent."

"Any chance he was spotted on Murdock Island that day?"

Bertolissio smiled. "It was the first question I asked Trevor. The answer is, no. It might be worth going back to everyone who was there and showing them this photo but I doubt it. The Murdock Island resort is a pretty genteel sort of place. I doubt that someone with Nazi tattoos on his face and neck could walk around there without being noticed."

"What about known associates?" Ronnie asked, not looking up from his scrutiny of the photo.

"There are a couple of people he's been seen with more than once. People we know. We hope to get more from ASIO. We'll be interviewing his friends as soon as we can, now that Luke's confirmed his attacker's identity. What have you found?"

Ronnie looked up, grinning. He pushed the photo across the table to Bertolissio. "Right forearm, partly obscured by his shirt sleeve."

For a moment, Bertolissio squinted at the image. Then she

looked up at Ronnie. "You think that's a gang mark," she said.

"Yes and you know which one."

She turned to me, looking unhappy. "You're not going to like this."

I took the picture from her and stared at it. All I could see under the sleeve was a red and blue smudge. It could have been anything but my stomach sank, knowing exactly what it was – the feet of a little red devil, a logo belonging to my old friends the Devil's Playthings.

"Jesus," I said, feeling my blood turn chill.

The last time Ronnie and I had met the Playthings in person, the notorious bikie gang had been trying very hard to tear us to pieces. We'd then spent more than a year testifying against their leaders during a long, drawn-out legal process that had seen half-a-dozen of them end up behind bars.

"Well," said Ronnie, cheerfully, "that explains why Death's Head Guy was so enthusiastic about meeting you."

"Christ," I said. I wanted to get up and leave the room, just get moving and keep moving until I was far, far away.

"We don't know for sure," said Bertolissio. "We'll get forensics to enhance this and do a proper match. Meanwhile, I think that's probably enough for now. Luke, if you think you might need protection, I can… Well, you know there's not a lot I can do, really. But I'll make sure the local uniforms check on your house whenever they can. You know Tim Pearce I think. I'll ask him to keep an eye on things."

"Luke will be fine," Ronnie said. "Won't you, mate? I'll keep him at my place until we find out what's going on. The bikie thing might easily be a coincidence."

Bertolissio stood up and so did I. My legs felt weak. A few minutes ago, I was dealing with a heavy hired to scare me.

Now it was all about organised crime and Nazi thugs. Oddly, these revelations seemed to have cheered Ronnie up no end.

"There's got to be connections between the Playthings and other major crime figures," he said, to Bertolissio. "Like Grigor Mostek and his mob. Also, I'm betting the pollies that Death's Head Guy was working for as a minder had connections to Harry Cross, and maybe now to Richard."

Bertolissio nodded her agreement. "I'll start looking into all that as soon as we're finished here." It was a hint that we should bugger off. She suddenly smiled. "You two certainly have a knack for shaking the branches and making strange things fall out."

They were both excited, like kids who'd been told they were off to a theme park.

"So," I said, sounding more bitter than I intended. "We're all agreed it was a good thing that I got beaten up."

They both stopped smiling and looked at me. Ronnie grabbed my upper arm and steered me to the door, saying, "Don't mind him, concussion always makes him cranky."

"I'll call Tim Pearce right now," Bertolissio said by way of a goodbye.

* * * *

I went with Ronnie to my house and packed some things. It struck me that I should have a "go bag" ready all the time, like some nutty American survivalist, not because I thought the collapse of civilisation was imminent, but because it looked as if having to run and hide was becoming a fairly regular event. As I packed, Ronnie roamed around the house, peering into rooms and opening cupboards. I caught up with him in the family room, making himself a sandwich on the kitchen counter.

"Make yourself at home," I said.

"I thought I'd use up some of this grub before it goes off. It could be a while before you're back again."

"Good point." I went to the cappuccino machine and switched it on. "I should get myself a decent cup of coffee while I have the chance."

"Nice place," he said, looking around. "I know I've seen it before but I've never really given it a good look." He gestured through the window with a buttery knife. "Quarter acre plot, too. You don't see that much any more."

"Yeah, well…" I said. Owning the house gave me a twinge of guilt every time I thought about it. I'd always lived in rented units small enough to fit several times over into the place I now owned. "My financial adviser reckoned I should, you know, invest." It seemed like a pathetic reason to own four bedrooms, three of which I didn't use.

Ronnie shook his head in dismay and got on with his sandwich.

"I mean," I went on, talking more to myself than to him. "Have you counted how many chairs there are on this property? I have. How did I end up with nearly twenty chairs?" It was my turn to point at the garden, where four of my chairs were visible. "I sit out there and imagine I'm in Walden but I'm just kidding myself. I'm not Thoreau, I'm bloody Donald Trump!"

"Mate, you're talking bullshit, as usual. You've got to have chairs. What are you going to do, just have one chair and carry it with you from room to room? Ask visitors to bring their own?"

As usual, he was deliberately missing the point. "It's not the chairs. It's just… everything. It's all so… excessive."

Ronnie put the top on his sandwich. It was almost as tall as it was wide. He managed to cram a corner into his mouth and take a bite. "I'll tell you what's excessive," he said, around the mouthful. "That bloody thing." He waved his sandwich at my huge, gleaming cappuccino machine. "I've seen CBD cafes with smaller ones than that."

I walked over to the fridge to get the milk. "That's different. It's like whatshisname, you know, the Scottish writer."

"Sir Walter Scott?"

I blinked in surprise that he could name one but then I guessed that Scott was probably one of Ronnie's childhood favourites.

"No, the other one. Anyway, there's some story – probably apocryphal – that, when he got married—"

"Is this going anywhere soon?"

"Just eat your sandwich. Anyway, he had a budget to furnish their new home but—"

"But he spent it all on a cappuccino machine the size of a small car?"

Through gritted teeth, I said, "No, he spent it all on a beautiful Persian carpet."

"Bet his wife was pleased."

"The point being—"

"That just because he was as mad as a bag of frogs, you're allowed to be, too?"

I gave up. "Something like that."

I finished preparing my drink while he finished his sandwich and started making another.

"Let's talk tactics," he said. He slapped the massive slab of a sandwich down on a plate and brought it over to the table. We both sat and he pushed the sandwich over to me. "Here.

You need that more than me. I think you're getting skinnier."

I pushed it back. "Thanks but it'll spoil my lunch. What do you mean, tactics?"

I had to wait while he made his assault on the second sandwich.

"We need to find Death's Head Guy," he said, when he could. "He connects us to the bloke – or bird – who sent the letters and he – or she – connects us to the murderer."

"Yeah, personally, I'm not so keen to meet him again. I think we should let the cops do that."

"We can get to him first."

I didn't like the excitement in his eyes. Angrily, I said, "You remember the part about him being associated with the Devil's Playthings? Of course you do. You made the connection. Well, I know you're old and senile but, you may recall, the Playthings had us locked up in a room in their clubhouse while they chatted about where to dump our bodies. It was so long ago now but, you know, I remember it as if it was just a couple of years ago. Oh wait! It was just a couple of years ago. And do you remember how many of those charming young men and their strapping, Amazon girlfriends swore and spat at us during the court case and told us how much they'd like to cut off parts of us and feed them to their big, slavering dogs? Because I do. It was all of them. And if you think I'm going anywhere near that clubhouse, or any one of its smelly, bearded, bloodthirsty denizens ever again, you are mistaken my friend."

Ronnie smiled at me as if he'd enjoyed my little monologue. "You make a very good point, O Fearless Leader. If Death's Head Guy really is associated with the Playthings, I reckon that's exactly where he'd go for help in avoiding the cops. It wouldn't be too big a stretch to think he might be hiding out at the very clubhouse you remember so fondly." He took another giant bite of the giant sandwich. "But that's not what I had in mind."

Watching him eat was making me hungry. I went to the counter and started work on my own, human-sized sandwich. "I'll be sorry I asked this, but what did you have in mind?"

"Nothing much, just talking to a few people."

"Which people?"

"You'll see."

I started to protest that I wasn't going to be dragged into stupidly dangerous situations without even knowing who, where and why but I gave up mid-sentence. If he didn't drag me with him, he'd go alone. There was no point arguing with him. Not only did he always think he knew best, he actually did know best most of the time.

"All right," I said, raising my arms in surrender. "Suppose we get to Death's Head Guy before the cops – a giant thug and part of an organised crime gang that has sworn to kill us both, a man who almost beat me to death with less effort than I'd take to swat a fly, a man with so little regard for the social niceties, he wears Nazi tats all over his head, a man who—"

"Luke?"

"Yes?"

"Shut the fuck up, mate. If I find the bastard, I'll ask him a few questions, that's all."

I remembered the last time I'd seen Ronnie ask a hostile thug a few questions; he'd left the man on the ground nursing several broken bones. I'm not saying for a minute that the man didn't deserve what he got. He had been trying to kill me just prior to Ronnie's interrogation. I'm just saying Death's Head Guy would make at least two of that other thug and he looked a lot meaner and tougher. I know Ronnie was as tough as a ute full of Mallee roots – as he himself might put it – and he had all that special forces, twenty-ways-to-kill-a-man-with-an-empty-crisp-bag training, but the bloke was getting on. He was sixty five and had already had a hernia operation. Yes, he was a gym junkie and had those psychopathic grey-blue eyes and could probably crack walnuts with his buttocks and all that but even a man like Ronnie could be outmatched by a bigger, stronger, meaner, younger man. Someone like Death's Head Guy, for example.

"We should probably think this through," I said.

"Fair enough," he said, reasonably, standing up. "Grab your bag. You think, I'll drive."

Chapter Fourteen

There are few things as depressing as a city centre nightclub in the middle of the day. The approach was dismal, a concrete, traffic-filled canyon that connected two thoroughfares, the door was dismal, a battered, steel slab in a brick wall, surrounded by dead lights and tattered posters, and the deep-set, hollow eyes that studied us through a jail-cell peephole in the door were so dismal I felt like curling up and dying on the spot. Ronnie said the right things to get us inside where we could savour the scuffed paintwork and the brutalist lighting gantries and cinderblock textures.

The hollow-eyed door keeper led us across a stained dance floor to a group of three men sitting in plush seats at a round table. They all watched us in silence as we approached. One was a big, bald-headed man of around fifty, whose tastes ran to bright, floral shirts and heavy gold jewellery. On either side of him, were bigger, younger men.

"Two blokes," Ms Hollow-eyes said when we stopped. "Said they wasn't cops."

She spoke to the older man. He didn't take his eyes off us as he said, "Ask Rob and Chris to join us."

Our escort nodded and slouched off into the shadows behind the bar.

"You've got a fucking nerve, you cunt."

"No need to be scared, Barry," Ronnie said, smiling. "I haven't come for you."

My insides dropped at the mention of the name. I had no doubt this was the same Barry McGuire who had tried to have me killed – twice – and had finally backed off when Ronnie threatened his family. I wanted to shake Ronnie by the throat and demand to know what in God's name was wrong with him.

McGuire looked gobsmacked at Ronnie's effrontery. He looked first at one of his companions, then at the other, in a theatrical show of disbelief. When he looked back at Ronnie, he burst out laughing.

"Come and sit down, mate. I'm guessing this is your buddy, Luke. Lucky Luke, I call him. The man who can dodge bullets."

Ronnie took a seat opposite McGuire and, reluctantly, I took one beside him. Two more big, young men came hurrying out of the back and joined us, standing behind me and Ronnie, scowling down at us. I remembered Ronnie telling me McGuire always kept a bodyguard of four ex-military mercenaries. That meant the gang was all there.

"I know it was just business, Barry," Ronnie said. "No need to apologise."

McGuire shook his head in amazement. "How the fuck do you walk around with balls as big as that?"

Ronnie kept on smiling. "Tell me it's personal and I'll piss off right now."

"Mate, if it was personal, my guys would be rolling youse two up in a rug by now."

"That's good," said Ronnie. "'Cause I need your help with something."

McGuire spluttered in amazement. "You need my help? Are you fucking joking?"

"Do you want us to chuck these fuckers out, boss?" one of the men behind me asked.

McGuire raised his hands as if to stop an immediate assault. "No, no. I want to hear what this comedy duo has to say." The thug next to him burst out laughing. McGuire turned, irritated. "What's so fucking funny?"

The man blinked, nervously. "Nothing. I just thought 'The Two Ronnies'. You know, 'cause you said 'comedy duo', hey?"

"More like one-and-a-half Ronnies," the man on the other side of McGuire said, eyeing me nastily.

McGuire held his arms out across them. "Just shut the fuck up, everybody." He waited a beat, to ensure he was being obeyed. Then he said to Ronnie, "Right-o, mate, you've got the floor."

Ronnie was unperturbed by it all. "Thank you," he said, as if he'd been waiting impatiently for the kiddies to settle down. "I'm looking for a bloke who's been freelancing as a heavy for hire. Not one of your contracts." I saw McGuire's eyes narrow. I supposed it was because he didn't like the idea that there were independent rent-a-thugs operating in his town. "I don't know his name but he's made himself visible at several – what would you guys call them? – 'alt-right' rallies? Anyway, he's some kind of Nazi shit-stirrer. He looks like this." He reached into a pocket and all four of the bodyguards drew guns, levelling them at Ronnie's head. I stopped breathing but Ronnie just smiled at McGuire. "Please, if I was coming for you, the likes of this mob wouldn't even know I was there."

McGuire waved a hand impatiently and the goons re-holstered their weapons. I breathed again, even though one or two of them seemed extremely reluctant. Ronnie pulled out the photo of Death's Head Guy and passed it across the table. Even I could tell from his expression that McGuire knew the man in the photo. So did the blokes sitting beside him.

"What do you want him for?"

"I need to ask him a few questions about a case I'm working on."

"The Harry Cross thing?" I almost asked how he knew but, of course, it had been all over the news.

"That's the one," said Ronnie.

"Did he do it?"

"I don't think so. But he might know who did. That's why I need to find him."

McGuire handed the picture back. "Doesn't look familiar."

"Really? I thought he might have worked for you. In the past, maybe."

"Is that what you told the coppers?"

Ronnie grinned. "No need to bring them into it. And there's no reason they should even know that we've had this chat."

"The papers said you're working with them."

Ronnie dismissed the idea with a gesture. "Sometimes we can help each other. Sometimes we find our objectives are just a bit different. It's like you and me in that way. Sometimes things get a bit tense between us, things get said, guns go off... Other times, we can be mutually supportive. Like, I can give you a heads-up on some dickhead who's moonlighting and cutting you out of your percentage and, in return, you can let me know how to reach him and maybe give me a couple of hours to put a few questions before you send your friends here to discuss his licence to operate." He sat back, relaxed. "What do you reckon?"

"I reckon you don't listen too good, mate. I said he didn't look familiar. So, are we done yakking?"

Ronnie's face darkened. "Hang on. I've given you some valuable information. All I'm asking for is a bit of *quid pro quo*."

"Yeah? Well that sounds disgusting. You should be ashamed of yourself. If you're going to talk dirty, maybe you and your rent boy should take it elsewhere."

The henchmen sniggered. Ronnie surged to his feet, fists balled. In an instant, the sniggering stopped and the guns were back out.

"OK," I said, also hurrying to stand up. "Thanks very much for seeing us, Mr. McGuire. We appreciate your time." I glanced at Ronnie who was standing rigid, glaring at McGuire. "So, we'll be on our way. Won't we, Ronnie? Come on, mate. We don't want to overstay our welcome." McGuire didn't help matters by grinning smugly up at Ronnie. However, our situation seemed to seep slowly into Ronnie's awareness and he turned, at last, to look at me. I smiled and nodded encouragingly.

He looked back at McGuire. "I'll remember this," he said. He stepped back, threw his chair across the floor and stomped off across the dance floor. Finding myself alone in the middle of four armed men, I gulped and ran to catch up with him. He marched with his head down and didn't say another word until we were outside.

"Right-o," he said. He turned to me, a small smile on his face, and winked. "We need to get to the car and fast."

"What? Are they coming after us?" I looked back, stumbling because we were walking so fast. There was no sign of pursuit.

"Don't be a plonker. We're going after them."

"What?"

We reached the car and after him insisting he drive, we climbed in. We were facing back down the way we'd come.

"Keep watching," he said.

"What?" We sat there for about two minutes. "What's going on?" I asked as the mysterious vigil stretched out.

"There we go." Two men came out of the club and made for a car parked outside. It was the pair who had stood behind us: Rob and Chris.

And, suddenly, it was all clear. "He wanted Death's Head Guy for himself! And you knew he would. That was your plan all along: get him to send his thugs after him, so we could follow them and find him." It was amazing. And horrifying. "Why didn't you tell me?" But, of course, he wanted me to act like a scared rabbit, to convince McGuire it was all going horribly wrong for us. "Those blokes could have shot us!"

"They might still," said Ronnie, pulling out from the kerb. A silver Mercedes with the two bodyguards in it was moving up the road far ahead of us. "If they catch us following them. So less chat and more keeping your eyes open, hey?"

We wound through the town, heading north, through Fortitude Valley, eventually hitting the Airport Road. When we turned off this onto Gympie Road, my stomach sank. The suburb of Chermside was almost certainly our destination and that's where the Devil's Playthings clubhouse was located. The traffic on Gympie Road was as dense as ever and it was hard to keep sight of the car we were tailing. Despite my urging, Ronnie wouldn't get any closer. Even when he had to run a red light to avoid losing them completely, he wouldn't close the gap.

"Traffic's good," he said. "Keeps us invisible."

My heart was still in my throat from the fierce acceleration and the sight of cars closing on us from both sides of the junction, so I didn't say any of the many things I wanted to.

To my intense relief, we drove past the turning to the Devil's Playthings' clubhouse and kept on up the road. We turned off into a pleasant little suburb – not exactly leafy but quiet and well kept, with open spaces and rows of single-storey homes with wooden fences and tiled roofs. We had to hang back even more in these quiet streets, so much so that we lost them almost straight away. We were then cruising up and down the empty streets, looking for their car. Fortunately, there were almost no cars parked on the roadside, and our quarry's silver Mercedes stood out like a sore thumb when we found it.

Ronnie pulled up almost out of sight around a corner. I swallowed hard.

"Are we going in?"

"No," he said, as if I'd said something really stupid.

"But what if they kill him?"

"No-one's killing anybody," he said, again with contempt in his voice. "McGuire is a businessman. He's not going to kill someone for cheating him out of a few bucks in commission. Just take a deep breath. All that's happening in there is McGuire's men are reminding Death's Head Guy that freelancing is frowned upon. They might be asking a few questions about who he was working for and why but I doubt that they'll even rough him up unless he's stupid enough to argue the point."

I thought about it. Organised crime seemed so reasonable and civilised the way Ronnie explained it.

"So, we're just waiting until they go?"

"And then we'll nip in and ask him a couple of questions of our own."

"Right. And no-one's going to get beaten up or, you know, tortured, or anything."

"You mean by us?"

"I mean by you."

"Please! What do you take me for?"

"And you didn't bring your gun?"

"That was once. Are you never going to let that drop?"

"Nope."

We sat in silence and watched the house. After about ten minutes, McGuire's henchmen came out, got into their car and drove away.

"Right-o," said Ronnie. "Our turn." He drove up to the house and parked outside, saying, "You can wait here, if you like."

"No way! I want to get a good look at this bastard." It wasn't something I'd realised until then but I really did want to look this bloke in the eye and tell him what a scumbag he was. Ronnie just shrugged and we got out.

The garden was overgrown with weeds and the garage beside the house was open to reveal a large motorcycle. Unlike everywhere else in the street, this house needed a paint job. It was a mild, winter's day, with the temperatures in the low twenties and the skies clear and blue. Yet no amount of sunlight could lift the air of neglect that hung over the property.

We stopped at the front door. Ronnie said, "There's no way he'll answer the door a second time." Then he kicked the door in. Just like that. He strode ahead of me into a daggy hallway. I heard noises and cursing from a room to the left of us. Ronnie heard it too and barged straight in. Death's Head Guy was fumbling in a corner to retrieve the shotgun he had stashed there. In a couple of strides, Ronnie was beside him. I couldn't see quite what happened but Ronnie struck out at the man, twice, and Death's Head Guy was on the floor, yelling in pain.

"That's for fucking with my friend," Ronnie said, standing over him. Which surprised me. A lot. Then Ronnie sort of swivelled his body, side on to the fallen man and kicked him in the head. It wasn't a kick like you see in fights on the telly. This was a quick bending of one knee and a swift, hard jab with the sole of his boot. "And that's for trying to pull a gun on us," he added but the man was barely conscious and I doubt he heard it.

Ronnie pulled a length of rope out of his pocket and, rolling Death's Head Guy onto his belly, tied both his hands behind his back. Then he tied his hands to his feet. It looked painfully uncomfortable. A part of me was feeling sorry for the big bikie – it was obvious he had already been beaten by the men who were there before us – but another part of me was glad the big fella was securely trussed. I have to admit, there was even a small part of me that didn't mind at all that he was having such a bad day.

"What do youse mongrels want?" Death's Head Guy was already recovering enough to get angry.

"Just a chat," said Ronnie, calmly.

"Yeah, well, untie me and we'll talk."

"Mate, you are in no position to make demands. Now listen. As you've probably guessed by now, you've got yourself into something way bigger than you ever imagined. There are forces at play here that will chew up a little grub like you and spit you out. You've already met McGuire's men, and now you've got us. Next comes the cops, and, after that, there are plenty more waiting in line for a piece of your sorry carcass."

In response, Death's Head Guy thrashed violently – and uselessly – and bellowed furious threats at the pair of us. Ronnie kicked him in the ribs and said, "Stop being a dickhead." Our prisoner seemed to see the sense in that because he stopped thrashing and glared at Ronnie in silence. Ronnie sat down on one of the armchairs in the room. I was too agitated even to pretend to be relaxed. I walked away from them both and leaned against a wall beside a small bureau. There were opened letters on the fold-down top, along with bills, bank statements and the like. I looked down at them, mostly so that I didn't have to look at the man on the floor, but I took in very little of what I saw.

"Right-o," said Ronnie. "We'll start with the easy ones first. What's your name?"

"Fuck off."

"It's Thomas Thackery," I said. They both looked at me and I held up an electricity bill.

"Thomas," said Ronnie, to the bound man. "What shall I call you? Tommo? Is that what your friends call you? Or do you have some kind of nickname, something your white supremacist thug friends call you? Nothing? OK. I'll call you Tommo. So, tell me, Tommo, did you kill Harry Cross?"

Thackery seemed genuinely shocked. "What? No! Why the fuck would I kill Harry?"

"Harry? You were on first-name terms with the famous Harry Cross? How would a low-rent scumbag like you know the rich and powerful CEO of XtraVirtual?"

The question seemed to set Thackery off thrashing again. Ronnie waited while he tired himself out. The baleful expression on the man's face as he glared up at Ronnie had grown sullen. Perhaps he was beginning to realise he wasn't getting free until Ronnie had finished with him.

"Harry Cross was one of us. He was a good bloke. He put up the money for loads of election campaigns and stuff, paid for rallies and looked after brothers. If you want to find who killed him, go lift a few rocks where the antifa shitheads hang out. It'll be one of them bastards for sure."

Ronnie studied him in silence for a moment. My head was still whirling from the revelation that Harry Cross was funding white supremacist groups and their politicians. But Ronnie had moved on.

"Who paid you to kill Luke Kelly?"

Thackery looked at me. "I wasn't supposed to kill the cunt, just rough him up. It's not my fault if he can't take a thumping."

"Who paid you?"

"That's my business."

Ronnie snorted with laughter. "You really think so, do you? Look at you. Do you think you're not going to tell me anything I want to know? Anything at all?"

"Fuck off."

"McGuire's men asked you the same questions, didn't they?"

"I've got friends. Brothers. They won't stand for this. You're a fucking dead man."

"Yeah, yeah, you're a big scary bikie, with swastikas on your face and motor oil on your jeans. I bet ninety-nine per cent of the people you meet are scared shitless. But McGuire's men weren't impressed, were they? It took you all of five minutes to tell them everything you know. And the cops won't be impressed, either. I bet you'll sing like a fucking magpie. And, guess what, I'm not impressed either. I'm not impressed by you. I'm not impressed by the Devil's Dickheads. And I'm not impressed by a bunch of wannabe Master Race wankers and their pathetic plans for racial purity. Jeez, mate, the very idea of a thing like you breeding pure makes me want to puke. What do you think, Luke? Are you impressed?"

I did not want to be dragged any further into Ronnie's little torture session. Just being in the same room was bad enough and, if I could have thought of any reason to leave, I would have. However, I felt the need to help Ronnie bring this to as swift a conclusion as possible. I took my cue from something Ronnie had said earlier.

"I'll tell you what impresses me. Tommo, here, has no idea how much trouble he's in. I mean, how can anybody be that stupid? Like you say, McGuire's men, us, the cops, we're all going to be asking questions, threatening, beating, all that, but it's the others who are coming after us who will really play rough. And then there's the one who hired him to bash me. That one isn't going to ask questions at all. That one will only want a quick, quiet kill. It doesn't matter who Tommo talks to or what he tells them. There's a killer out there who has to assume the worst. It won't matter what Tommo says, how much he pleads, the only safe and sensible thing for the killer to do is to eliminate him."

Ronnie nodded, pretending to mull it over. "So, the best thing Tommo can do is give us the name of whoever hired him because the sooner we catch the killer, the sooner Tommo can stop looking over his shoulder and waiting for that knife blade to slide in between his ribs? I see what you're saying. What do you think, Tommo? Are you going to help us save your worthless life? Oh, and I just thought of another thing. What if the killer is watching Tommo's house? They've seen McGuire's guys go in and come out and then us. You can imagine what they must be thinking. Now, I know I said the cops would be along after us but what if the killer gets here first? What if we leave you all tied up on the floor like that and go on our way and then the killer strolls in when we've gone?" Tommo gritted his teeth and heaved at the rope. "I'm not saying that's going to happen. Probably the cops will get here in time, But, even if they do, it's just a temporary stay of execution."

"You're so fucking full of it!" Tommo shouted and thrashed around again. He was red-faced and panting when he finished. He lay on the ground with his eyes closed as many, long seconds ticked by.

"All right," he said at last. His voice was weary and resentful. "I was hired by a bloke called Angus Hudson. I never met him. He called me out of the blue. Said we had mutual friends. Paid me in Bitcoin. I didn't even know it was really anything to do with Harry Cross until those fuckers turned up this morning. And then you."

Ronnie thought about if for a moment.

"I believe you," he said with a finality that said the whole, miserable affair was over.

He stood up and pulled a folding knife from his pocket. With a flick of the wrist, a long, fat blade appeared. Thackery's eyes widened. I pushed myself off the wall, my stomach clenching. Ronnie leaned towards our prone prisoner and Thackery flinched away. Calmly, Ronnie pushed the blade down and cut the rope that connected Thackery's feet to his hands. The bikie groaned as his legs and back straightened.

"Right, mate. Since you've been so cooperative, I see no

reason to hand you over to the cops, or anyone else who might be on their way. Now you're more mobile, you can hop your way to the kitchen, find a knife and cut yourself free. I reckon it'll take you about five minutes if you're quick. After that, it's up to you but, if you want my advice, I'd jump on that big penis-substitute you keep in the shed and ride it out of here as fast as you can."

Thackery stared at Ronnie from the floor without saying a word as we left his house.

We walked up the street in silence until we reached the car.

"You said you were just going to ask him a few questions," I said. I sounded pouty, even to myself.

"Yeah, well, that's all I did, mostly."

"You took that rope with you. You knew what you were going to do."

"Mate, get in the car and stop being such a sook."

He climbed in the driver's side and I went round to the passenger side. I thought, briefly, about storming off in a huff but the idea of roaming those dismal outer-suburb streets was too depressing for words. So I got in.

"Keep low," Ronnie said, sliding down in his seat.

"What? You don't really think the killer's out here watching us, do you?"

"Don't be a bell end. Any second now, Thackery's going to—"

A roar from up the street told me Thackery was already free and had reached his motorcycle. I slid down until I could just see over the door sill. The big bike rolled down the drive and into the street. Revving like a madman, Thackery, tore down the street and past us on his way to god-knew-where. We sat up and watched his bike disappear around a distant bend in the road. We sat like that for quite a while.

I drew a deep breath. There was no point haranguing Ronnie about the unacceptable levels of violence he constantly resorted to. There was no way I could change him. I thought he was a thug. He thought I was a wuss. And, I had to admit, he'd got the result we needed.

"OK," I said. "I suppose our next step is to find this Angus Hudson bloke. Whoever the hell he is."

"No need," Ronnie said, setting the car in motion. "Angus Hudson is the name of a character in an old TV soapie called Upstairs Downstairs. My wife used to be a big fan."

"I've never heard of it. I don't suppose Thackery ever heard of it, either. Why would he pick that name to feed us?"

"He didn't. The killer chose it. It does give us another clue, though."

"What? That the killer likes obscure soapies?"

"It's not obscure. It was bigger than covid back in its day. Anyone from my generation would know it instantly – and the names of the main characters. Mr. Hudson was the butler."

"Yeah, all right, but there could be a real Angus Hudson. It's not that rare a name, I bet."

"They paid in Bitcoin, Luke. They were trying to be anonymous."

I considered that. It made sense. "So we're looking for an old man who knows how to use Bitcoin."

Ronnie bridled. "He doesn't have to be that old! Someone my age would fit the bill."

I grinned at him. "Exactly. What about the Bitcoin? I wouldn't have a clue how to buy it, or transfer it. Would you?"

"Yes. And any idiot could google it in about ten seconds. And, before you ask, yes, it's untraceable and a lot easier than setting up anonymous offshore accounts to do money transfers."

I should have known that making anonymous payments would be among Ronnie's core skills. "So, an old bloke who knows how to google," I said, feeling flat.

"Or a woman. She could have used a proxy to make the deal."

"Wow. So, after all that, we've narrowed it down to anyone who can google."

"The glass is always half empty with you, isn't it? I don't know how you ever get up in the mornings. In fact, we got some useful info out of that. For one thing, Thackery didn't know this was about Harry Cross."

I frowned. "And yet he actually knew Harry."

"Yes, he did, because dear old Harry was a right-wing nut job who liked to put his money where his prejudice was."

"So there's a connection. Someone else, who was also probably a part of Harry's crypto-fascist secret life, connects to Thomas Thackery. And, when they needed some muscle to scare me off, they remembered the bodyguard thugs that used to hang out at the rallies and the meetings and gave one of them a call."

Ronnie sounded doubtful. "Yeah, it was a bit more specific than that. They knew about Thackery before they sent the first letter."

"Which was actually trying to use him to send the investigation off in the wrong direction. So, when that didn't work, they set Thackery on me so we'd be more motivated to focus on him?"

"Yeah, I reckon. They probably thought we'd find Thackery and he'd kill one or both of us, the cops would go after him, and the whole investigation would turn into a big ball of confusion."

And, of course, that nearly happened. I remembered Thackery scrambling to get his gun when Ronnie burst into his house. It could easily have worked out that he got to it before Ronnie stopped him. Then things would have been very different.

"It's a bit cold, isn't it?" I said. "What kind of person does that kind of calculus? I mean, sacrificing us to derail an old investigation? If the original murder of Harry Cross was a crime of passion, you'd think the killer might not be a total psychopath, wouldn't you?"

I noticed we'd reached Toowong. Ronnie was taking us back to the office.

"Yeah…" he said, thoughtfully. "Fifty-fifty on that one, mate. In my experience the kind of person who kills someone in a moment of so-called passion, is already someone who doesn't value human life all that much. I wouldn't expect them to be any more considerate of others when it came to saving their sorry necks afterwards."

Chapter Fifteen

It was a full house back at the office. Desi was waiting to ambush me with a handful of telephone messages and both Noah and Harper were at their desks, trying to catch my eye. Ronnie hurried away as soon as Desi blocked my path.

It was always disconcerting to see Noah and Harper hanging around the office. I'd done a calculation earlier in the year that we needed seventy per cent utilisation to be a viable business. That is, Noah, Harper and I all needed to be on charge to clients seventy per cent of the time. Even with things as good as they'd been lately, that level of utilisation seemed like a mad fantasy. The main effect of doing the calculation had therefore been to give me a spike in anxiety every time I saw them.

I took Desi to my office and we sat down to review her messages. She had a couple of promising new clients in her fistful of notes and an old client who wanted to give us some more work. I took a calming breath and told myself everything would be fine. As the calm descended, I was able to see that Desi was looking quite agitated. I apologised to her for neglecting things and promised I'd spend the rest of the morning focused on the business. It seemed to unruffle her feathers a bit and we soon settled down to some serious admin.

I kept noticing Ronnie prowling around outside. He stopped first at Harper's desk, then at Noah's. Then he wandered out of sight and Harper and Noah got together. They kept glancing my way and it was making me nervous again. Desi, having worked through the list of things that she needed to get me to do, had started to chat more widely about cases and people, as was her way.

"What's Noah doing back in the office?" I asked, cutting across her.

"Finished his job. Waiting for another. You could sling him that new misper, He likes them."

"Yeah, I need to check that out, first." Missing persons cases were tricky, I'd discovered. They often involved a lot of travel and other expenses that clients liked to quibble about, the missing person, if we ever found them, didn't often like to be found, and the client was usually disappointed, either because we didn't find their missing child or husband, or because they didn't like the fact that the child was now living as a transvestite in Sydney, or the husband and his new girlfriend were now taking out a restraining order against his "stalker" wife. Or whatever. I definitely needed to vet misper clients very carefully, or risk losing money on the job.

"I'll set up an interview," she said, helpfully.

"Great. And would you ask Noah to come in as you go out, please?" She was clearly taken aback at being dismissed. "Busy, busy, busy," I added, smiling as regretfully as I could.

Noah didn't hang about when Desi stopped by his desk. He bounced out of his chair, grabbed up a folder and swerved around the furniture as he hurried to my office. Seeing him in energetic motion, I remembered he was a keen soccer player. I wondered if he was regretting giving up his life as an apprentice electrician for one as an underpaid, underappreciated junior detective at the Featherfoot Agency. Probably, I supposed. Yet he was a positive, cheerful type. It might take years before he became disillusioned and bitter.

"Hey, Luke," he said as he dashed in and took a chair. "How's it going?" He was only a few years younger than me but so much about him made me feel old.

"Finished with the fraud job?"

"Yeah, poor bastard was faking it after all. I hate when that happens."

"You've filed your report?"

"Yeah, now the wheels are in motion to grind his bones, I reckon." He put the folder on my desk. "Do you want to see?"

I looked at the manilla jacket and shook my head. "I'll read it online. You get all your receipts and everything?" I knew he would have. Noah was pretty good about that kind of thing.

"Look," I said, without letting him answer. "Do you still want to work on the Cross murder?"

"Bloody oath, mate!"

"Good. In that case, I've got some research for you to do." I ran through some of the key people in the case and our recent discovery of the connection between Harry Cross and far right political figures. "I want you to find everything you can about Harry's dealings with neo-nazi groups, white supremacist pollies, bikie gangs and mob bosses. He's been funnelling money into some pretty evil causes and there may be some crossover between those causes and Harry's organised crime connections." Noah was blinking, wide-eyed. "I'm not saying there is, it's just that we may have stumbled on a great steaming pile of crap here and I'd like to get as clear a view of it as we can, as soon as possible, before we dive in."

"O-kay…" he said, slowly. "Isn't this more kind of yours or Ronnie's sort of thing?"

"I'm also not saying you need to go interview bikies and pollies. Just do what you can online and in the library. I think we've had enough violence already on this case without you wandering into any bear pits."

He seemed to remember the beating I'd had. "Yeah, right-o. How're you doing now?"

"I'm good. So, are you right? Got any questions? Everything's in the files if you need more background on the case."

He didn't get up and go. "There is one other thing." It was obviously something embarrassing from the way he squirmed in his seat. "What's the company policy on employees seeing each other?"

I blinked at him for a moment as my brain slowly caught up with what he'd said. "What? You and Desi?" I couldn't imagine a less likely pairing but each to his own, right? He frowned at me as if I were being deliberately obtuse.

"Nah, mate. Harper."

So, my imagination had failed miserably. There was a less likely pairing, and Noah and Harper was it. I forced myself to show no reaction. I clamped my jaw down on the words, *But she must be twice your age!* I tried to get my brain to stop imagining the impossible – Noah and Harper holding hands, Noah and Harper snuggling on the sofa, Noah and Harper in bed – and focus on the question I'd been asked.

"We, er, we don't really have a policy on that. To be honest, it's not something I've given any thought to." He watched me carefully with an earnest and slightly anxious expression. It hit me hard that my answer was actually important to him. Really important. "Look, my first reaction is to say 'Who cares?' As long as it doesn't interfere with your work – any more than any other relationship would... You're both grown ups." *Well, she is, anyway.* "So, as long as you behave appropriately and all that crap, it's up to you. And, anyway, what right does an employer have to control the lives of his employees? I don't hold with all that rubbish about censoring your social media and your fashion choices and your political activity and everything. I pay you to provide a service for a few hours each day. That's all. As long as the quality of what I'm buying is up to scratch, the rest is all your own business."

I realised I'd gone off on a bit of a rant but Noah didn't seem to mind. He gripped the chair arms and prepared to raise himself.

"So, we're all good, then?"

"Yeah, no worries." He bounced to his feet and headed to the door. As he left, I said, "Oh, and, er, congratulations, or whatever."

He gave me a grin and bounded away to his desk. I sat for a while and marvelled at the strangeness of what had just happened, not just the Noah and Harper strangeness but the making up rules that affect people's lives and happiness strangeness. In what possible sense was I qualified to do that? Well, I had actually studied ethics for three years as an undergrad, which, I supposed, might make me way better qualified than almost any other manager on the planet. But even so...

I was still in a morally stunned state when Ronnie came piling in.

"On your feet, Lukey boy. We're off to see our friends at

the cop shop."

"We're…? What?"

"While you were handling your HR problems, I was talking to Bertolissio on the phone. I told her we had new developments to report and she extended an invitation to QPS Headquarters. You coming or what?"

I glanced at Desi who was frowning my way with what looked like a premonition I was about to break my promise.

"Yeah, no worries," I said.

* * * *

We drove to the CBD without a lot of conversation. Ronnie rarely volunteered information and would probably have sat in silence the whole way if I hadn't had questions I needed answering. The first was, "Did you know about Noah and Harper?"

"What about them?"

"That they're…" I realised I didn't know quite what it was they were.

"You mean that they're bonking? Buffin' the muffin? Banging like a dunny door in a hurricane? Playing hide the sausage? Horizontal dancing? Shagging? Rooting like rabbits?"

"I wish I hadn't asked."

"Yeah, I knew. Everybody knows but you, mate. Do you want to know why?"

"I don't want another lecture about how I don't have any interest in other people's lives."

"Suit yourself."

"So, how long have they…?"

"Why didn't you ask Noah when he was right there in

front of you?"

"I – I was just so surprised. Is it serious?"

He scoffed. "What do you think?"

"I don't know what to think. It doesn't make any sense."

He looked at me as if I was a lost cause. "Mate, Noah's a dumb kid who's getting all the sex he wants from an experienced older woman. He's in Freudian heaven. Harper's got an enthusiastic toy-boy to play with any time she cares to whistle for him. She's living the dream – or at least the cougar fantasy. Is that serious? I don't know. Probably as serious as anything ever is."

Ronnie was always so cynical about these things and I could never decide if he was saying what he felt or trying to wind me up. Or both. I settled back to driving and brooding. The other question I wanted answering bubbled up.

"And why did you call the cops? You know we broke into that man's house and beat him up. How's DI Reid going to take that? He already wants your head on a platter. Doesn't this just deliver it to him? With a bow on it?"

Annoyingly, Ronnie laughed. "So, in this scenario, Reid is King Nebuchadnezzar, I'm John the Baptist, and Bertolissio is Salome? Or are you Salome? I'm not sure."

"Very funny. But it was Herod, not Nebuchadnezzar."

"You're such a fucking smart arse."

"Smart being the operative word. Unlike some."

"Listen. We went to see a confidential informant, who gave us Thomas Thackery. We went to see him and found him tied up on the floor. We untied him, asked him a few questions and left. We then called the cops to report what we'd learned. What could be more innocent than that?"

"Oh, I don't know. Not lying to the cops, maybe?"

"You think Thackery is going to contradict us? The

chances are he won't say a word. If they pick him up, he'll lawyer up and tell them to go root themselves. What can they touch him for? He doesn't care about the cops and nor should you. We have other worries."

My stomach was already doing that thing where it seems to be in a death struggle with my intestines. Now it sank. "What worries?" I asked, although I could see a few.

"Let's see…" He held up the index finger of one hand and tapped it with two fingers from the other hand. "One: Thackery is a fascist thug with lots of big, burly friends. I think we can expect them to come looking for us pretty soon." He put out his middle finger and tapped that one. "Two: whoever hired Thackery saw him as disposable but once he—"

"Or she." It was kind of a reflex after so long working with Ronnie.

"—*or she* finds that he's been talking to us, *they* will most likely put out a hit on him and on us." He tucked his little finger under his thumb and held up his ring finger along with the other two. He didn't bother to tap it. "Three: Reid isn't stupid. No, let me rephrase that. Reid is stupid but even he will see that his promotion is in dire straits if he passes the news up the chain that several of his suspects and the murder victim may well have close ties to an Australian Senator and the Senator's party. Now, being noble and honest, Reid will… Oh, hang on. No. Being a miserable little toad, Reid will immediately try to shut down the investigation. In particular, he will try to shut us down and erase any trace of his cooperation with us."

I turned it all over in my mind. None of it was good. I was going to be murdered by bikies – something that had been hanging over me for a couple of years now – or I was going to be killed by an assassin – also something I'd lived with for some time. Worse still, the murderer would go free because Reid wanted to be Chief Inspector. The fact that I thought this last was the worst case didn't strike me for several seconds. When it did, I had my sanity to worry about as well.

* * * *

We parked and went to the Police Headquarters building. Like the regular I was, I went straight to the counter and asked for Reid. DS Bertolissio appeared within a couple of minutes and led us through the labyrinthine interior to a comfortable little meeting room with a nice view of the Brisbane River, almost completely blocked by an ugly great office building. Bertolissio called Reid as soon as we arrived, using a speakerphone on the desk, and he said he'd be "right there".

"How's it going?" Bertolissio asked pleasantly while we waited.

"Oh, you know," I said. "Beatings. Threats. Just the usual."

"How's your head?"

"Still attached. Which has to be a good thing, right?"

She laughed. "Cheer up, Luke. Life begins on the other side of despair."

I laughed too. "Everything has been figured out except how to live."

Ronnie looked from one of us to the other. "What the fuck?" he asked. Clearly quoting Jean-Paul Sartre at one another was a behaviour he disapproved of.

Bertolissio smiled politely. "Trevor won't be long."

"Any progress at your end?" Ronnie asked.

"Let's wait for Trevor before we start talking shop, shall we?"

And, right on cue, in walked the man himself.

"You know, I hate to see you two tossers in my place of work without any cuffs on. Al says you've got new information. So let's have it."

He said all this while he was taking a seat. Ronnie looked at him with mild amusement.

"I'm fine DI Reid. Thank you for asking. And how are you? Still using the haemorrhoid cream?"

"If you're going to piss about, Walker, you can leave now."

Ronnie stood up, smiling. "As ever, it was a pleasure to meet you. We must catch up again soon."

Bertolissio spoke to Ronnie as if he were a naughty schoolboy. "Ronnie, I'm sure Trevor didn't mean any offence. So why don't you just sit down and tell us what it is you've discovered?"

Still smiling, Ronnie took his seat again. "For you, darl, anything."

Bertolissio looked at me. "Luke, why don't you start?"

I felt suddenly flustered. Had she asked me on purpose because she knew I wouldn't be able to lie convincingly? But why would she even think we might lie? I needed to get a grip. This was just paranoia. I couldn't start at the beginning. There was too much to hide. Where should I begin?

"Is there a problem?" Reid asked.

"We heard today that Harry Cross was a major sponsor of certain right-wing political causes. I mean, really right-wing. Like Nazis."

Reid and Bertolissio exchanged frowns. "Where did you hear this?" Reid asked.

"From a man called Thomas Thackery. He's the one who beat me up the other day."

Reid looked at Ronnie. "And what state is Mr. Thackery in now?"

"I don't know what you're trying to infer," Ronnie said.

"Imply," Bertolissio and I said in unison. Ronnie ignored us.

"We found Mr. Thackery in his home," Ronnie said. "He'd been beaten and tied up. It was lucky we got there when we did. When we released him, he told us all about Harry Cross and his support for white supremacist causes."

Reid nodded. He could obviously tell the story was bullshit but chose to ignore the fact, for the time being.

"How did you find him?" he asked.

"Sources," Ronnie said.

"Confidential sources," I added.

Again, Reid nodded. "And were they tied up and beaten, too?"

"You're a very cynical man," Ronnie said.

"Did Mr. Thackery tell you who had hired him to assault you?" Bertolissio asked.

"No," I said. "That is, his client used a false name. Thackery doesn't know who he really is."

"He?" she asked.

"The voice on the phone and the name he gave were masculine. It may have been an intermediary."

Reid seemed angry. "So what if Cross was some kind of alt-right supporter? What's his politics got to do with anything?"

His tone, rather than the question, made me wonder what Reid's politics were. Ronnie fielded the question while I mused.

"Thackery knew Harry Cross. There's an association. Thackery was described in the threatening letters. There's another one. Cross knew bikie thugs like Thackery. That puts the Devil's Playthings in the frame for the killing, plus others."

"What others?" Reid asked.

"We're still working on that."

Reid huffed. "Is there a Playthings connection to Grigor Mostek?"

"We should ask Organised Crime for that intel," Bertolissio said.

I had expected Ronnie to pipe up and tell Reid he was obsessed with Mostek but, of course, it suited him that Reid had gone off at a tangent, so he'd stayed quiet. The "others" Ronnie had been referring to were a certain Senator and his party but we didn't want the cops to go there. Not until we had hard evidence. And maybe there wouldn't be any evidence. There was no point getting Reid off-side if that lead was a dead end.

The conversation went back and forth for a little while after that but it was clear we'd thrown Reid all the fresh meat we were going to. He said he was going to have Thackery brought in for questioning and Ronnie suggested he might have the bikie's house searched first in case there just happened to be, for example, an unlicensed shotgun lying around there. Reid grunted his acknowledgement and Bertolissio took us back down to the foyer.

"What's going on?" she asked, as soon as we were reasonably private.

"What do you mean?" I asked.

"I mean, what are you hiding from Trevor?"

"Nothing," said Ronnie, trying to sound hurt.

Bertolissio didn't look happy.

"You two need to remember who your friends are," she said. "I went out on a limb to get you the virtually unprecedented level of cooperation you currently enjoy. So did Trevor. If this all goes sideways because you concealed information vital to our investigation – information you promised to share – you won't have any more friends in the Service. Do you understand me?"

I looked at Ronnie. She was right. We had promised. Ronnie ignored me.

"There is something," he said. "But it's probably nothing. If Reid caught wind of it, he'd pull the plug. It's better to accept the risk that you won't give us enough rope, than the absolute certainty that Reid will cut us off and do what he can to close down our investigation."

She studied Ronnie in silence, lips pursed, a small frown of concentration creasing her forehead. "Somebody important..." she said, thinking aloud. "A senior police officer? Maybe... A prominent businessman? No... A politician? A right-wing politician. Someone a thug like Thackery might have served as muscle for? Here in Brisbane. Or nearby. State, or Federal?" She turned her gaze on me so suddenly I almost jumped. "Warm, aren't I?"

Ronnie was smiling. "If it was something like that but it was an incredibly remote possibility, don't you think it would be better to keep it to ourselves – at least until we had some tiny shred of evidence?"

I jumped in. "And we'd come to you with it, of course, the minute there was something concrete."

She thought about it. "Do you have a name?"

I considered denying it but Ronnie just said the name without hesitation. Bertolissio didn't flinch. On the other hand, she certainly didn't laugh.

"You need to verify or eliminate that connection as fast as you can."

"As I said, we're working on it."

"Work faster. We don't want that kind of possibility hanging over the case for a second longer than it has to."

"And if it turns out to be a solid lead?"

"Yes, well, we'll face that apocalypse when the time comes. Do I have to tell you not to mention this to anybody?"

"Like my staff?" I said.

She took a breath through her nose. "Like your client. Like the Cross family. Like XtraVirtual employees. Like the press."

I nodded. "Right. Of course. No worries."

"I started the day with no worries. Now I've got a big one. What about mob connections to… anyone on the case?"

"Just the one you know about – Harry and Mostek's lot. Trust us, we'll be discrete."

That seemed to be it. "Do you want to join us for lunch?" I asked the detective.

She looked at her watch, surprised. "I had mine about two hours ago."

"Lucky you," said Ronnie.

Chapter Sixteen

We drove to Ronnie's favourite hotel in Jindalee. It was the place where we'd met. It felt like a lifetime ago. Everything about the place looked the same including the menu and the food. After eating some of it and passing the rest to Ronnie to finish, we went to the saloon bar to have a beer. It was a nice day – a typical Brisbane winter's day of blue skies, bright sun, and the temperature hovering around twenty-five. I'd have liked to take our drinks out to the beer garden but Ronnie was a creature of dim interiors and comfortable fug.

At least... sometimes. There were so many contradictions in Ronnie's personality I was becoming increasingly convinced that I didn't know the real Ronnie Walker at all. The brooding, ex-special forces, geriatric ninja, didn't square with the sociable old duffer who hung out with The Dogsbodies – a club for fancy dog breeders. The sharp, driven detective, skilled at getting people to open up to him, didn't square with the brooding recluse who'd sit on his patio in the dark, nursing a beer, or at a bar like this one, swirling a shot of rum in his glass and never taking a sip. The true blue, dinky-di, ocker, daggie, Aussie bar-fly image he presented to the world, didn't match the well-travelled, highly-trained background of the undercover agent he once was. The cocky, belligerent, violent man with whom I'd hunted killers across South-East Queensland, wasn't the tortured, guilt-ridden soul who had opened up so briefly to me on the Murdock Island ferry.

With all of this buzzing in my head, I looked at him, nursing his stubby and watching me in silence.

"You're a complete fraud, aren't you?" I said.

He grinned. "Don't tell the tax office."

The grin and the joke were more evidence. He might have pulled back in shock and surprise, saying, "What do you mean?" or somesuch, but he didn't. He wasn't at all surprised.

"*Parle-tu française?*" I asked, remembering my earlier speculation about his time undercover in North Africa.

"*Bien sûr. Pourquoi demandes-tu?*"

"I knew it!" I couldn't be sure, of course, my own French was strictly high school, but his accent sounded excellent. "You speak Strine like a native, too, don't you? It's all part of the camouflage."

"If I do, I'm missing the mark. I'm supposed to be speaking Australian with just a hint of a lingering Leeds dialect."

"If you even come from Leeds. If you were ever in the SBS."

"What's so wrong about picking up the local lingo? I like Strine. It suits me. Better than French, hey?"

"No! I mean, probably, yes. But that's not the point. The point is, I don't even know who you are. I don't know if I can trust anything you've ever told me. It's like… It's like half of you is just a cover. Like you're on a mission. Like… The Dogsbodies. That's got to be cover, right? And hanging out in bars, drinking with the flies like an old derelict."

"I don't know what's gotten into you."

"Oh, now we're acting surprised?"

"Luke, I've never told you a single thing about myself that wasn't true. Honest, mate. I've got a birth certificate, marriage certificate, divorce papers, passports – two of those – anything you want to see."

"Yeah, I bet you have. And you'd know all the right people to have them made to fit whatever your story is this week."

"Luke, this is getting stupid."

"Is it? I remember last year when you helped Karen out with her little problem. All it took was a couple of phone calls and you had a fucking MI6 agent stealing data from a Hong Kong office! Who has that kind of clout?"

His tone had been one of slight amusement but now it turned harder. "Me, Luke. I lived in that world for a very long time. I was one of the best. I worked with a lot of people and I've got a lot of close mates. There are people who would do me favours because we were all like brothers back then. There are other people who would do me favours because they owe me. Big time. Some would even do me favours just because they respect what I did and what it meant. Don't go making a mountain out of a molehill, mate."

I don't really know why but I felt anger bubbling up inside me. I stood up. "Maybe you have told me the truth. Maybe. But maybe it's all the stuff you left out that worries me. You work so hard to pretend you're some washed out old has-been, just another old Aussie battler, propping up the bar in his local." I noticed that people were looking at me. In fact, everyone in the bar was looking at me. I lowered my voice. "Well I'm sick of it. I don't want to see you again until you decide to come clean about…" I didn't actually know what I needed him to admit to. "…whatever the hell you're hiding."

And then I flounced out. It wasn't the first time I'd stormed out of that particular hotel because Ronnie had upset me. In the car park, I stood in the sunshine and remembered. It was here that I'd asked him to help me find my girlfriend's murderer and he'd suggested that maybe the man she'd had dinner with and who had taken her to an alley and stabbed her to death might have been her lover. Looking back, I could see it was a reasonable line of enquiry. At the time, he'd seemed like a mad, boorish old bastard who was deliberately being obnoxious. So why was I standing out in the car park now full of barely-controlled rage at him. Because he hadn't told me everything about his past? Because his entire personality was some kind of front? Because it had taken me more than two years to realise I didn't know him at all? Was I simply angry with myself?

I put my feet in motion again, got in my car and drove to the office. Ronnie could find his own way home. Sod him.

In Toowong, I looked around the car park, feeling suddenly vulnerable. My little fit of pique now meant I couldn't stay at Ronnie's place. I felt a shiver run through me. I had to admit, I felt a lot safer with Ronnie around. Irritated but safer. For a moment, I even considered going back and apologising. After all, how he lived his life was his own business. What right had I to demand that he show me his true face?

Because we work together! I thought, angry and hurt again. *Because we've fought together, struggled together, saved each other's lives, depended on each other.* We weren't just colleagues, we had been through more together than most people ever would. We were partners. Hell, I was only in the detective business at all because of him. Knowing Ronnie had profoundly changed my life. And even though we could barely be civil to one another most of the time, even though we led almost separate social lives, even though we really didn't like each other all that much, there was a bond between us, a deep, important bond, the kind on which you could trust your life.

At least, I thought there was.

* * * *

The office felt busy and bustling even though there were only four people in it. Most of the time it felt huge and empty, with me in one corner and Desi far away in the opposite corner. But, seeing it now with Harper and Noah at their desks, I could see it wasn't a very big space. And then I wondered how Desi coped with it. A lot of the time, she was there alone. That must be really hard for such an outgoing extrovert. Maybe she spent the time talking to friends on the phone. I kind of hoped so. It would make me feel less guilty.

Everyone said hi as I made my way to my desk. From the corner of my eye, I saw Noah grab a piece of paper and get to his feet. By the time I'd sat down, he was in the doorway.

"Got something," he said, holding it out to me and coming in. What had I set him working on? Ah yes, the connections between Harry Cross and far right groups. So whatever he was holding was probably not something I'd be pleased to see.

It took the sheet from him. It was a printout of a photograph. It showed people at a party, women in ball gowns, men in tuxes. At the centre of the shot was the fascist senator Harry Cross had been funding. On his arm was a svelte young woman, who was either his grand-daughter, or something far worse. Talking to him were Harry, Jennifer and Cassandra Cross. Everybody looked happy.

"It was a fund-raiser," Noah said. "Raising money for the senator's last election. This was from two years ago."

I handed it back to him. "Great. Nice to know the White Australia Movement has so much support. And that the senator has such excellent taste in hookers."

Noah blinked, as if he didn't know whether I was joking or not. He didn't take back the picture.

"Look at the bloke at the back, on the right," he said.

I did. There were lots of people in the background and it took a bit of squinting before I finally saw it: Death's Head Guy, Thomas Thackeray, wearing a black suit and tie, scowling at the other people in the room.

"Crikey," I said. "How the hell did you spot that?"

Noah smiled. "I've got a good eye for faces."

"Useful skill." I was still studying the photo. There was something aloof, perhaps a little grumpy about Thackery. He wasn't part of any group, just standing among them, scowling.

"So, he was working security for this little shindig," I said, thinking aloud. "Can we get the guest list? Can we find out who else the senator paid to guard him? I want to know if Richard Cross was there. I want to know if there were other Devil's Playthings members on the staff. What do you think?" I looked up at Noah. He had the drowning man look of someone feeling out of his depth. "Yeah, right," I said. "Not easy. Look, send me the photo – by email, don't put any of this in the case file – and I'll send it on to DS Bertolissio. She can get all that information for us. A lot quicker and easier than we could, anyway. Thanks, Noah. Keep digging. This is great work."

I sent him away and sat back to think about how I was going to ask Bertolissio to get what we needed.

"Ah hem."

I looked up to find Harper standing in the doorway.

"Yes?"

"Noah tells me he… said something."

"About you and him."

"Yeah. Look, I don't want you to go making a big thing out of this. We just…" She seemed to struggle to explain whatever it was they had been doing. I held up a hand to stop her.

"Whatever it is, it's none of my business. You're here to do a job and I trust both of you to do it. If I didn't, you wouldn't be here. So just forget about it. All right?"

She looked pained. "It's just that I don't want you to think—"

I stopped her again. "Mate, I don't care. It's your life. Not mine. Like I said, I trust you both to do your jobs like professionals. OK?"

She didn't seem completely satisfied but she agreed it was OK and left. I reached for the desk phone to call Richard Cross. Bertolissio could wait. I'd realised I needed to talk to everyone in the family again and, given that we hadn't left Cassandra and Jennifer on the best of terms, I thought I'd start with Richard and maybe get him to smooth the way. Of course, I hadn't left him on particularly good terms either.

Just as my fingers touched the handset, it rang.

"Vincent Aikenhead on line one for you, boss," said Desi.

"Aikenhead?" I asked, stupidly. "What does he want?"

"He just said he'd like to talk with you."

"Ah, right. Put him on." I heard the call connect. "Mr. Aikenhead. Luke Kelly. How can I help you?"

"Is your partner with you?"

"My p—? Oh, Ronnie. No, he's out just now. Did you

particularly want him?"

My momentary hope was dashed. "No, no. You'll do fine. I just wanted to check in and get a bit of an update."

We chatted for a while and I tried to keep it vague, stressing the large number of interviews we'd done and the necessity to confirm the honesty of our witnesses and the quality of the police investigation. Not that I had anything to hide from Aikenhead. I just didn't want to get into the strange new direction the case was taking. Talk of white supremacists and bikie gangs would sound great to the tabloids, but to Aikenhead it might sound more like some kind of conspiracy theory. I didn't want us taken us off the case before we saw where all this was leading. On a sudden impulse, I asked him if he'd been at the senator's fundraiser that night. It was possible he'd seen things that could help. He said he'd check his calendar and came back a few seconds later.

"I – em – I was somewhere else that night. The senator isn't really my kind of politician." He sounded shifty. I wished I could see his expression. "Why do you ask?"

"No particular reason." I tried to sound breezy but probably sounded as shifty as he did. "Harry Cross was there. We think there might have been someone else there too. Someone we'd like to interview." His reaction made me push it a little farther. "Did you know that Harry Cross supported a number of extreme right-wing causes?"

"Yes, well, he was never shy about sharing his political views – or his social ones."

"So you knew him quite well, then?"

"No, hardly at all. But, well, he was a man other people often talked about. Some liked him. Most didn't."

I told him I was about to re-interview the family and we

wound down the conversation.

Afterwards, I started up a new case file: one for things I couldn't yet show to DI Reid, and made a note of the phone call in it. I also added the photo Noah had just sent me by email and made a note about that, too. Finally, I gave access to Noah, Harper, Desi and, after a second's hesitation, Ronnie.

Then I called Richard Cross.

Claudia Knecht seemed rather cool when my call reached her desk but, after a short delay, she put me through.

"Dr. Kelly, I wasn't expecting to hear from you so soon. I heard you were in hospital. I hope you're all right now. Has there been a development?"

"I'm fine, thank you. Did you hear why I was in hospital?"

"Yes. Terrible business. I didn't know such things happened here in Brisbane."

"Oh, it's more common than you might think. Can I just ask, who told you about me?"

"Right. I forgot I was a suspect for a minute there. Well, as it happens, it was Tom Willoughby – you know, the Police Commissioner? We had lunch yesterday."

I clamped my mouth shut to stop myself saying what I thought about the Police Commissioner having lunch with a suspect in a murder investigation and keeping him up-to-date on how the case was progressing.

"So?" Richard asked as I took a deep breath.

"I need to talk to everybody in the family again. There have been developments and I need to discuss them with you, your mother and Cassandra."

"What kind of developments?"

"A completely new line of investigation. One the cops did not explore. One I'd rather not talk about on the phone."

"Is this to do with the bloke who put you in hospital?"

"As I say, I'd rather do this face-to-face."

"OK, well, you should talk to Claudia and set up a meeting. I'll switch you back to her."

"No, wait. It isn't quite that simple. I need you to talk to your mother and your sister-in-law and get their co-operation. I don't think either of them is keen to talk to us again."

"Yes, I know. You seem to have a knack of rubbing people up the wrong way. I really don't see how I could—"

"I'd rather not ask the cops to do the interviews. I think your family would be even less thrilled about that starting up again."

"I think my mother would bring out grandma's gun if the cops showed up at the farm again."

"Your grandmother has a gun?"

"Great, great grandmother, actually. It's a family legend. My mother has a story about how, when she was a bub, her own great grandma used to sit out on the verandah with a big Colt 45 revolver and take potshots at the skinks. Mad as a hatter. Lived to be ninety-seven."

"Different times," I said, drily.

"All right, I'll talk to them but I can't promise anything. Will that do you?"

"Yes, thank you."

"Anything else?"

"If you could pass me back to Claudia now, that would be great."

Claudia gave me a half-hour slot with Richard for the next afternoon. She didn't exchange pleasantries, despite my attempts.

* * * *

Desi was waiting at my office door when I hung up and made me sit with her and do admin jobs for the next hour. It might have only taken half an hour if she hadn't wanted to tell me all about a new covid-19 lockdown in Melbourne, her sister's boyfriend's car troubles, and something to do with a dog and a pop singer that made no sense at all. I finally shooed her out and shut the door after her with most of the working day gone. As an afterthought, I called her on the phone and asked her to book me into a hotel for the night.

I needed to think. The case had become dangerous and complicated, fraught with political minefields, and full of hostile suspects – one of whom was probably trying to have me killed. Ronnie and I had fallen out. Again. And I'd been shitty to Megan after she'd tried to extend an olive branch. If I could just take each problem in turn and work on it, I might get somewhere, but they were all clamouring for attention and demanding that I do something about them right now.

I went to stand at the window, looking past the rooftops of Toowong to the hills beyond. In the past, I'd have taken a walk out to the cemetery and sat down by Chelsea's grave. I'd had plenty of long talks with her – well, with my memory of her – and it had always seemed to help. But that wasn't working any more. My memory couldn't conjure her up the way it used to. I couldn't hear her voice. I couldn't imagine the good sense she used to offer me. One day, sitting beside her grave, I'd realised that she was gone for good, that I had finally, truly lost her forever.

Of course, there had been other people I could talk to – Ronnie, for example, and Megan – but they weren't there for me now. It had been a very long time since I could talk to my parents about anything other than the most superficial stuff. And that wasn't entirely bad. There was a comfort in it. Just being near people who loved you like that was a balm for the soul, even if we only talked about work and relatives and household problems.

I'd come to the conclusion sometime in the past year or two that I wasn't the kind of person who had friends. Not close, intimate friends. It had been shocking to me to realise it at first but I soon got used to it. My university friendships had faded to an occasional catch-up level. The friends I'd shared with Chelsea had turned out to be hers, not mine. And now I was left with a handful of friendly acquaintances – Alexandra Bertolissio and Tim Pearce, both cops, and Kazima, the CEO of my software company – people I turned to for advice or exchanged pleasantries with, but with whom I never just went out with for a drink, or called up to spend an idle weekend.

I thought about going to see Ronnie. I probably needed to apologise to him. So what if he wasn't telling me everything? He didn't owe me his life story, any more than I owed him mine. I should go and say I was out of line, let him take a few cracks at me. I smiled, thinking he'd probably suggest it was my time of the month. He was full of sexist crap like that. After that, we'd be OK again.

Except… It was more than just him not mentioning a past girlfriend, or some job he once had. He had systematically hidden his true self from me. Our whole relationship was a lie. Ronnie was not who I thought he was. When he'd spoken to me in French, my blood had run cold. Not only had he sounded like a fluent French speaker but there was a change of tone. Just for a moment, the crusty old digger facade had dropped and I saw a man of sophistication and poise. Someone who might actually have read Sartre after all. In the original French.

It stung that he would deceive me like that. And yet, when I thought about the extent of the deception, it filled me with awe. The meagre collection of books he had – all military histories and biographies – the daggy dad outfits he wore, the Dogsbodies club, the beat up old Volvo he drove, hell, even the décor in his home! It all went way beyond hiding his past, way beyond what I'd heard about people on witness protection programmes. This was a man who was acting a part, unremittingly, day in, day out, for his whole life, whether there was anyone around to see it or not.

What kind of man did that? What kind of a man could do that? In the realisation of the enormity of what was going on, my upset about my injured feelings fell into perspective. In fact, seen in that light, the fact that Ronnie had let the mask slip for just a few seconds was shockingly significant. He'd actually lifted the curtain for me, just briefly, and I hadn't understood it at all. I'd stormed off in a sulk.

Jeez, I needed to get out there and find him.

I whirled around, ready to rush out, and there was Ronnie standing in the doorway, watching me.

"We need to talk," he said.

* * * *

We went down to the mall under the office and settled at a table in the food hall. It was busy and noisy and smelled of fried food but that was OK. The ghost of my last meeting there, with Megan, hovered at the edge of my memory, but that was OK too.

"I think I owe you an explanation," Ronnie said and took a sip of his coffee.

"No, you really don't," I said. "I owe you an apology."

He looked at me over the rim of his cup, as if to say, "Go on."

"It's none of my business," I said, trying to keep it simple. "Your life is probably beyond my comprehension. Your motives will probably never make sense to me. And, as for who you are… Well, you're a miserable old bastard who's leading a double-life so complete it makes those stories of Russian sleeper agents in the cold war suddenly seem totally credible. But you're also the miserable old bastard who has saved my life too many times to count—"

"Five"

"—and, at some deep, unfathomable level, I trust that, whatever you're up to, you'd never let it hurt me."

He kept on looking at me until I felt really uncomfortable but I held his gaze. Eventually, he put down his cup and said, "So you don't want an explanation, then?"

Shit, yes! But I tried to keep my cool. I was pleased with myself for being so big about it and didn't want to lose all my kudos points. "Yes, of course, but only when you're ready. Just because I have a hissy fit, doesn't mean you have to do anything you don't want to. As you can see, I'm over it."

I saw a tiny flicker of an amused smile on his lips, which was really bloody galling after how magnanimous I'd just been.

"Right-o, then, let's get back to work, hey? Plenty of hard yakka for us before we can solve this bugger."

I said, "You can drop the act when you're around me, you know. You don't have to be all ocker and blokey all the time."

He treated me to a confused frown. "I don't know what you're on about, mate."

I clamped down on an angry retort and he grinned, seeing

it. "Fine. Let's just go back up."

* * * *

"So, Noah found this?" Ronnie asked. We were back in my office and he was studying the picture of Thackery at the senator's do.

"You don't have to sound so surprised. He's a good bloke."

"He's got a good eye, I'll say that for him. What do you make of it?"

"Not a lot. We already knew Harry Cross was a big fan of sticking minorities in concentration camps. Now we know his mother and wife didn't find the idea unappealing either. As for Thackery, well, it gives us a bit of evidence connecting him to the senator and, now, we have a link to two of our suspects."

"And the third member of the surviving Cross family?"

"Richard? No sign of him in the photo. Noah's trying to find out where he was that night."

"We need to interview the lot of them again."

"Already on it." I looked at my desktop calendar. Desi had been busy. "I'm seeing Richard tomorrow morning, then Cassandra, then going out to the farm in the arvo to see Jennifer. I should probably do that one on my own."

He nodded. "Yeah, you got that right. What can I do?"

I couldn't swear to it but I believe that was the first time Ronnie had ever asked me for direction in a case. I found I couldn't speak for a moment as I got over the surprise. But by hesitating, I lost my big chance.

"Tell you what," he said. "I'll go and see the mistress. She's the one major player we haven't spoken to yet."

To be honest, I'd actually forgotten all about Carla Ventura, Harry Cross's bit on the side. I dredged my memory for what I'd seen in the police files.

"She was on the set of some TV show in a studio in Hemmant at the time of the murder. About a thousand witnesses agree, and her alibi is confirmed by time-stamped video recordings. There's a good reason she wasn't on our suspect list."

"It's all right Luke. There's no need to be defensive."

"I'm not being—" I took a breath. Jeez, did I have to fall for his wind-ups every single time? "It's a good idea. She might be able to give us some useful background."

"Yeah, plus, have you seen her? Ripper, mate. A real stunner."

"Yeah, right, she'll probably think you're a total cutie, too."

"You should come along. She might have a thing for scrawny, pallid types."

"Here's an idea, why don't you take Harper? When Ms Ventura sues us over your inappropriate and – and I can't emphasise this enough – disgusting old man sex overtures, it would be nice to have a witness who can testify in court that the restraining order was well deserved."

Ronnie just grinned and said, "No problem. It'll give me a chance to catch up on all the goss about her and Noah."

After that, we spent some time at the whiteboard working through the connections between all the people we knew about in the case. It was a tangled network that reached out to organised crime, a bikie gang, and a federal politician. After we'd stared at it for a long time and added the odd line here and there, Ronnie suddenly said, "Also…" He added two more people to the board: our client, Vincent Aikenhead, and his company lawyer, Victoria Finn.

"No connections to anybody," I said, seeing where Ronnie was going with it.

"Not yet," he said.

Chapter Seventeen

Ronnie and I were back on our usual more-or-less even keel, so I cancelled the hotel and went back to his place. We went via a Mexican restaurant where we continued to chat over plates of sticky, thick, almost unidentifiable dark stuff with cheese and guacamole, stuffed into tacos. I managed about a third of mine and Ronnie scoffed the rest. To complete the ethnic experience, we drank some truly awful margaritas and Ronnie talked about soccer, prompted by the many photos and fan merchandise on the walls.

To lead the conversation toward more interesting topics, I asked, "What exactly is a football team?"

Ronnie scowled at me. "A bunch of blokes in short trousers," he said. There was a warning note in his tone.

"I mean, the players change from season to season, the management changes, the stadia are built and rebuilt over the years. Why is this year's team considered to be the same team as the one from twenty years ago? It's the Ship of Theseus problem, really. What is it that fans are loyal to all their lives?"

Ronnie didn't answer me. Shaking his head, sadly, he said, "Let's go Philosophy Boy, before you start asking the waiter what the meaning of life is."

"Seriously, it's a fascinating subject. What makes a thing a thing? If I teleport you from here by disassembling you and reassembling you elsewhere, are you still you? Or did you die and something new got made? And do you know that every cell in your body dies and is replaced by new ones every... I don't know, every few years or something. So what makes you you?"

"Are you going to pay for this, or what?"

"And there's this joke about brooms..."

He stood up and went to the counter to pay, saying, "All right, I'll get it. But it's going on expenses."

I watched him settle the bill then followed him out into the street. It was cool and I wished I had a jacket.

"Doesn't that kind of thing interest you at all?" I asked.

"What kind of thing? Jokes about brooms? Teleporters?"

"Just... ideas. You know?"

"Not your kind of ideas. Crap that doesn't matter." We reached the car and he held out his hand. "Give me the key."

"I'm not drunk."

"Mate, you're a two pot screamer. Just give me the key."

I handed him the fob that enabled the engine. He took it from we without a word and got in the car. I got in the passenger seat and frowned at the road ahead.

"I thought philosophy was going to be my life, you know." Ronnie drove off in silence. "You may think footy and two hour workouts are how a person should fill their life but there have been many brilliant thinkers down the ages who would disagree. I thought I'd spend my life immersed in the great mysteries of the universe, teasing apart subtle and complex ideas, being a part of that great chorus of debate and discussion, adding my own little light to the illumination of this vast puzzle we all inhabit."

I fell to brooding, feeling the weight of the world's proud

ignorance and careless rejection of one of the noblest and most difficult of all endeavours. Resentment bubbled up in me.

"Now philosophy is like a hobby or something. I revisit the big ideas in my spare moments, if I remember, never making any progress in understanding, not even keeping up with the reading in my field. Or what used to be my field. Now, I'm a detective, a gumshoe, a featherfoot, a private dick... I fill my head with terrible crimes and petty misdemeanours, with the dreadful, sordid motives of horrible people, the lies and evasions and misrememberings of witnesses and enablers, worrying if they know something I should know, if they're trying to mislead me to protect themselves or someone else, or if they're just plain wrong. There's an epistemological swamp for you! A pointless, stinking swamp that I wallow in every day. Or, more to the point, that I try to wallow in but can't half the time because I'm sorting out stupid, mindless management issues, or doing stupid, mindless administration."

With a sigh, Ronnie pulled into his drive.

"Thank God we're here," he said. "One more minute of that self-pitying whining and I'd have pushed your head through the windscreen."

I glared at him and got out. That's when I noticed someone standing on the doorstep. It was a woman, tall and in her sixties with long grey hair. For an instant, I thought it was Jennifer Cross and my heart skipped a beat. Did she have a weapon? Was she pinning a note to the door?

"Maggie!" Ronnie called. The woman smiled and the illusion vanished. "Sorry I'm late. I've been babysitting young Skywalker here." I was pretty sure Ronnie had never seen a Star Wars film in his life but he had learned that I didn't like the endless jokes about my name that everybody made.

"Hi, Luke," Maggie said. "Don't let the old bugger wind you up."

"I try not to but he is so very irritating."

We joined her in the porch and Ronnie let us in.

"Maggie and me are going out for a few drinks. You'll be all right for a couple of hours won't you?"

"Yes. Yes, of course. No worries. Have a nice time."

"We'll take your car, hey?" Ronnie said, steering Maggie towards it. "Bit nicer than mine. My keys are in the hall if you need to go out."

I watched them get in the car and reverse out of the drive. I was a bit miffed. I was supposed to be staying with Ronnie because of the imminent danger of bikie thugs turning up to murder me, not to be a house-sitter while he went off carousing with his woman friend. Then I remembered Ronnie telling me that most bikie killings are actually drive-by shootings at the victim's home. I looked around quickly and hurried inside.

It wouldn't be so bad. It would actually be nice to get some time alone. I could watch the news and read a book or something. Ronnie didn't have any decent music and his antique hi-fi system didn't even have a place to plug a phone into but I had my ear buds with me and I could chill out to something relaxing. I had a stack of books on my Kindle app I'd been trying to get around to for weeks. Now was the time to make a start on it.

I went to the kitchen to get a coffee. The doorbell made me jump like a startled roo. I'd seen thugs from the Devil's Playthings do exactly this: go to a victim's door and, when he answered, push him inside and kill him. I'd literally sat outside a victim's house in a car and watched them do it. Now they were at my door, ready to kill me. My first thought was to hide but that was no good. They knew I was in because all the lights were on. My next thought was to run. Ronnie had a back door but what if one of them had gone round to wait for me there. Besides, Ronnie's back yard was like a fortress, walled in by an impenetrable bougainvillea hedge. The only way out from there was to go round to the front. No, what I needed was a weapon. There were knives in the kitchen drawer. Big ones. I opened the drawer and looked at them. The sight made me quail. Could I really stand in front of two big blokes and fight them off with a knife? And wouldn't they have guns? They did that time I watched them murder Simon Anning.

Guns! Ronnie had a gun, upstairs in his bedroom somewhere. The doorbell rang again and again I jumped. "Just a minute," I shouted, to stall them, and ran upstairs. Two paces into Ronnie's bedroom and I dropped to the floor, remembering the last time I'd run in there and a sniper had fired at me from across the street. I crawled on all fours to the bedside table on the right of the bed. That was the side Ronnie slept on and the place he would keep his gun. It wasn't in the top drawer, or the bottom one. It wasn't under the bed. It wasn't under his pillow.

The doorbell rang again, several times. They were getting impatient. How long before they kicked in the door? I thought about hiding in a closet, about climbing out the window. Where was the fucking gun? Between the mattress and the divan, I felt something hard and cool. Almost sobbing with relief, my fingers closed around the stock of Ronnie's pistol. I pulled it out and stared at it. It was brutal. Functional. Steel and plastic. Could I shoot a man with it, even a man who had come to shoot me?

Damned right I could!

I crawled back to the door then hurried down the stairs as quietly as I could. I kept low. A plan formed as I crossed the hall to the door. I'd keep low, pull the door open fast, stay behind it and, when they raised their weapons, expecting someone to be standing there, I'd take them both out. Two shots. Bang, bang. Then I could call the cops.

My heart leapt into my throat when they started banging on the door with me just a couple of metres away. Not breathing – barely able to move – I reached for the latch to open the door and realised it opened the wrong way. The hinge was on my right. When it was open, I'd have to shoot left-handed, or expose myself. It didn't make any difference. I'd just have to risk it. Hopefully, my ruse of being on the ground would have them looking the wrong way.

I turned the latch with my left hand, threw back the door, and dropped to the ground. I swung the gun across and up to aim for the killers' chests but the barrel of the gun hit the edge of the door and twisted the pistol out of my hand. I landed painfully on my left elbow, shocked by the pain and the horror of lying there on the floor empty-handed with two armed thugs about to shoot bullets into me.

One of the killers screamed. Not a big scream. More a cry of surprise and alarm. Blinking into the dim light, I realise there was just one of them. And it was a woman. With her hands to her mouth.

"Oh my God, Luke, are you all right?" the killer asked, stepping towards me.

"Megan?"

She stopped and looked down at me, concern slowly being replaced by incredulity.

"What are you doing?" she asked.

"I thought – I mean… What are you doing here?"

"Who were you expecting?"

"I – No-one. I was just…"

"Did you fall over? How did you…?" She noticed the gun. "What the hell, Luke? I mean, like, what the holy fucking hell?"

I got to my feet. My heart was starting to slow down but my breathing was still ragged. The hand I used to hold the door to steady myself was trembling. "You'd better come in," I said. "It's not safe out there."

She looked behind her. "What? Are you in trouble?"

"Yes, I am. Do you want to come in?"

For a moment, she hesitated, then she gave a quick nod and walked past me. I took a look up and down the street and closed the door. I picked up the gun and followed Megan through to the kitchen. I put the gun on the counter and switched on the kettle.

"Coffee?"

"What's going on, Luke?"

I felt wrung out and weak. "There's some blokes who sort of want me dead – bikies, fascists, rich people… The usual crowd." I gave her a five-sentence run-down of the Harry Cross case and how I thought one of the family had done the murder, probably Jenny, and now wanted me dead. "I thought maybe you were one of her standover men, come to, you know…"

"Which explains the gun, I suppose." She stepped over to it and looked down at it like it was a nasty stain on the worktop. "But why were you rolling about on the floor?"

"All part of my cunning plan."

I was after a smile but I saw her frown. "Do you know the safety is on on this thing?"

250

Shit! "No. I don't actually know much about guns. That one belongs to Ronnie."

She looked up at me, the frown still in place. "Go and sit down. I'll bring you a drink. You look like you just ran a marathon."

I looked down at myself and saw my shirt was wet with sweat. I nodded and went out onto the patio. I sat in one of Ronnie's sun-loungers, laid back and closed my eyes. She arrived soon after with a couple of coldies.

"Thanks. I'm sorry about… that."

She shrugged and took a pull on her bottle. "So, people are trying to kill you. Again."

"Yeah, you'd think I'd be used to it by now."

"I can see why it would never get old."

I nodded to myself and stared up at the stars.

"Shouldn't Ronnie be here to look after you?" she said, breaking a long silence. It wasn't what every man likes to hear from his former lover but it was true and Megan and I had never been dishonest about such things.

"He's out on the piss with his fancy woman." It struck me that Megan's presence and Ronnie's absence were not a coincidence. My jaw set. "He told you to come round, didn't he?"

"He suggested you might like some company."

I kept my eyes on the stars, not on her. Bloody Ronnie. Bloody Megan. Why couldn't they both just leave me alone? "I'm sorry about how I acted."

"You mean throwing yourself around in the hallway while trying to point a gun at me?"

"I mean when we met earlier and I stormed off in a huff. That was…" I didn't really know what it was. Maybe it was the only thing I could have done after hearing about her and her husband splitting up. Maybe staying there and ranting and screaming would have been worse. Even so, I regretted it. I closed my eyes again, feeling the urge to get away. "You should have told me."

She didn't speak for a long time. Then she said, "I was an idiot to go back to Donny. It was the most stupid thing I've ever done. More stupid even than marrying him in the first place. And the consequences – hurting you and wrecking what we had, and hurting myself, and even hurting Donny – well, the consequences were commensurate with the crime. And I really, really wanted to run back to you and beg you to forgive me but I knew you'd be angry and you'd hate me and I hated myself more than enough already... I just couldn't face it. I couldn't face you. And by the time the guilt had stopped paralysing me quite so much, a week had passed, and then two, and I had the extra problem that I hadn't told you and I'd made things even worse. And, after a bit longer, I thought maybe it was for the best. I'd live with the knowledge that I'd wrecked my best chance for happiness, and you... You deserved the chance to move on and get over it."

She fell silent again. So I prompted her, my words being drawn from a deep well of bitterness. "But fucking Ronnie wouldn't let it go, would he? He kept on at you like he kept on at me. How long has he known about you and Donny breaking up?"

"Don't blame Ronnie. I told him not to say anything. I wanted you to, you know, forget."

"But it was his stupid idea for you to come into the office."

I couldn't see her but I felt her nodding. In a small voice, she said, "He told me you wanted to see me again."

A flame of anger kindled inside me. Through gritted teeth,

I said, "He lied."

The words seemed to hang in the night air, echoing, filling all the space around me. Through their noise, I heard Megan put her bottle on the ground, stand up and walk back towards the house.

"I'm sorry," she said.

I wanted to get up and run after her. If I let her go, I knew she would never be back. And yet my body wouldn't move, my voice wouldn't call out. I just lay there, my heart thudding, and listened as the front door opened and closed and Megan went away forever.

By the time Ronnie got home, I was falling-down drunk. I remember shouting at him. I remember taking a swing at him. But I don't remember much else.

* * * *

I woke up on the sofa, fully clothed, with a blanket over me. An empty bottle of Ronnie's best rum stood on the coffee table nearby.

"Morning, sunshine." Ronnie was standing in the door to the kitchen. Just moving my eyes to look at him was something I deeply regretted. "You'll feel better after a good feed," he said and I heaved at the thought of it. The air smelled of puke, I realised, making me heave again. Ronnie went back in the kitchen and I settled in for a good wallow in my misery. Five minutes later, he turned up and put a mug of coffee on the table nearby. "Get that down you. Then you might think about showering."

I lifted the blanket and looked at myself. The smell of puke wasn't in the air, it was coming from the stains on my shirt front. I moaned and sat up. I had to keep my eyes closed to stop my head exploding.

"Don't worry," Ronnie said. "You made it to the loo but you still managed to get it all down you. Neat trick."

I began to remember. "You told Megan to come round, you fucker."

"Yeah," he said and actually sounded sheepish. "That might have been a mistake, hey?"

"You think?"

"There's a bottle of aspirin there next to the coffee."

I squinted at the table and found them. It took everything I had but I got a couple into my mouth and washed them down with the scalding hot coffee. "I think I need a doctor," I said, honestly concerned that I might be dying.

Ronnie shook his head and went back to the kitchen. I watched him go and drank some more too-hot coffee. It was execrable but it seemed to be helping. Another mouthful and I managed to get to my feet. The stairs looked like the north face of the Eiger but I managed to get up them – sometimes on all fours – and make my way to the bathroom.

By the time I came out, I was feeling merely terrible, not like the walking dead. I put on clean clothes, deciding I'd just throw away the ones I'd been wearing. Ronnie was still in the kitchen when I came down. He pulled a plate out of the oven – fried eggs, bacon, sausages, grilled tomatoes, and some kind of crispy potato fritter things that came from a packet. At first I picked at the food. The tomato was the only thing that was half appetising, but the more I ate, the hungrier I felt, until I'd wolfed down the lot and mopped up the grease and tomato juice with a slice of bread. Having a full stomach really did make me feel a lot better.

Ronnie had been reading the morning paper while I worked on the meal. He was the only person I knew who still got his news printed on sheets of paper.

"Better now?" he asked setting the paper aside.

"Much. Thank you. Was I really bad last night? I don't actually remember much."

He grinned at me. "A few things were said."

I was torn between guilt at being such an arsehole, especially when I was his guest, and righteous indignation at his inexcusable interference in my life. "Yeah, well, you probably deserved it."

"Yeah, maybe I did. I don't suppose you remembered we're seeing Richard Cross in an hour's time?"

I checked the kitchen clock and cursed. "I don't think I'm up to it."

"Rubbish. You'll be right. Another cup of coffee and you'll be fit as a Mallee bull."

I did want another coffee but not the crap Ronnie made. "All right but we leave now and get a proper coffee on the way."

He shook his head again. "You're the sort that gives inner-city, latte-sipping elites a bad name."

I think he was only half-joking.

"I should probably call Megan. You know, to apologise. I was kind of shitty with her."

"Yeah, you told me all about it. You're a fucking dickhead. I'll drive, you can call her."

For all his griping about my electric car – still a rarity in Australia if you can believe that – he always chose it over his own old Volvo, so I had a nice quiet ride in which to make my call.

"Heart of the Matter Media," Megan said. I almost jumped into the apology I'd been rehearsing, when she went on, "You've made the right choice. Leave your details and I'll get back to you, or call my mobile on—"

"She's out," I said to Ronnie. "It's the answering service."

"So, call her mobile."

The beep went and I hesitated. Maybe leaving her a message was not such a bad idea. I still felt hungover and, if she was mad, I didn't fancy my chances in a shouting match.

"It's me," I said. "Luke. Look, I just wanted to say I'm sorry about last night. I'm a complete fucking drongo. I just…" I stopped myself before I could launch into some pathetic self-justification. "Anyway. I wanted to say I was sorry. That's all."

I hung up. I didn't look at Ronnie but I could hear him recounting my character flaws under his breath.

"Why do you want me to get back with Megan anyway? What the hell do you care?"

He turned to stare at me. I squirmed, wanting to tell him to keep his eyes on the road, but the last time I'd said that to him, he'd kept staring at me on purpose, telling me with a grin, as he watched me freaking out, that he was a better driver on his peripheral vision than I was with both eyes forward. I learned my lesson: Ronnie is as mad as a fiddler's bitch and it's best not to give him any opportunity to prove it while he has my life in his hands.

"You're my mate," he said, quietly. "I want what's best for you."

Now it was my turn to stare. Did he mean that? Did he think we were mates?

Chapter Eighteen

Claudia Knecht was cool and unapproachable when Ronnie and I got to Richard Cross's office. She asked us to wait and rebuffed my attempt at conversation with a firm, "He won't be a minute." It was about five minutes before Richard buzzed her to let us in.

"Teleconference with the Melbourne office," he said by way of explanation. "Poor sods are in lockdown again." Last time I'd been there, I'd assumed the massive screen on one wall of the massive office was just a big TV. My assumptions were not keeping up with the times. No-one shook hands and, thank God, Richard didn't try to elbow bump me. "I hope this isn't going to take long. I had to do some reshuffling to fit you in this morning. It would be nice if I didn't have to offend too many people. Coffee? Tea?"

"We've just had one, thanks."

We sat on a pair of sofas and Richard waited expectantly.

"Thanks for talking your mother and sister-in-law into meeting us again," I said. "I hope that wasn't too difficult."

"We all want to see this thing resolved," he said. "However painful it is."

Ronnie pulled the party picture from his pocket and laid it on the coffee table between us. Richard looked at it without speaking. I thought I saw him stiffen.

"Do you remember this event?" Ronnie asked.

"Fundraisers for Nazis were more Harry's thing than mine."

"Were you at this particular event?"

"No."

"It was on the eighteenth of March the year before last."

"No, I wasn't there?"

"Don't you want to check your calendar?"

Richard drew a deep breath. "Harry's politics are not mine. I don't support fascists."

"So it wasn't just to win favour and get access to a senior politician, for the sake of the company?"

"If that was it, there would have been plenty of less obnoxious political parties to suck up to. The company donates generously to the Liberals and not quite so generously to the Labor Party. This was Harry's personal project."

Ronnie nodded, understanding. "And your mother and Cassandra? Was it their personal project too?"

"Yeah, look, what's all this about? That do was a long time ago. Why's it so special?"

Ronnie held up a hand. A plea for patience. "I'll come to that in a sec. Can I just ask you, if you weren't at that little Nazi Party shindig, where were you that evening?"

Richard looked unhappy but went to his desk and spoke to Claudia over the intercom. "Where was I on the evening of…?" He looked at Ronnie, who supplied the date, loudly enough for Richard not to need to repeat it.

"You were in Sydney…" Claudia's disembodied voice said. "…visiting the office. You had a dinner appointment in the evening and came back the next morning."

"Thank you." He came back to the sofas and sat down. "All right? Carry on."

Ronnie reached across to the photo and tapped his finger on Thackery's face. "Do you know this bloke?"

Richard picked up the picture and studied it closely. "Looks like one of the bouncers. Who is he?"

"He's Thomas Thackery, a local bikie gang member. A couple of days ago, he put Luke in the hospital after Luke had received threatening letters. Of course, Luke attracts enemies like a sheep's arse attracts flies, but the fact that the bloke trying to stop us investigating Harry's murder also appears to have connections to the family, is just too much of a coincidence, don't you think?"

He gave Ronnie a long look. Wheels were clearly turning in his head but all he said was, "It's a bloody tenuous connection, hey?"

"Is it? You can see what kind of questions this raises. Here we have your brother associating with radical right-wing elements—"

"Elected politicians, actually, from a registered political party."

"Yeah, yeah. Elected politicians who employ criminal thugs to do their strong-arm work. We know your brother also associated with notorious organised crime figures. Did your brother cross one of them? One of these fascist bigwigs he loved so much? Or maybe one of his crime boss mates?"

I thought Ronnie was drifting away from the main point. "The key factor here," I said. "Is that someone we know is connected to your brother's murder, is also connected to your mother and sister-in-law: two of our main suspects. We haven't shown a connection to you, yet but, if there is one, we'll find it."

It came out sounding a lot more threatening than I'd intended. All I'd meant to do was point out that the family was firmly back in the frame because of Thackery. Although, seeing Richard's face fall and nostrils flare, I had to ask myself what I'd hoped to achieve by that.

"Here we go with the accusations, again," he said, directly to me. "What is it with you? Your mate here can see that crims and Nazis make much better suspects than we do. I'm a businessman. I've done all I can to support this investigation. My mother may be many things but she's not the kind of woman who would kill her own son, for God's sake. And Cassie… Well, you've met her, does she look like a woman who would run her husband through with a knife? She wouldn't harm a fly."

"We have to ask the difficult questions," Ronnie said. Far from backing down, the firmness in his voice told me he was getting angry himself. Of course, that might just have been because I'd pissed off our suspect. "We've already uncovered lots of stuff the cops never found. If you want us to find who killed Harry, you might want to put a lid on your injured pride routine and start cooperating." I saw Richard's eyes widen in outrage but Ronnie pressed on. "It may be that crims and Nazis had some good reason to kill your brother and, I agree, if they did, they'd make great suspects. But most of the people were talking about aren't Queensland Senators, they're grubby little mongrels who would do anything for a quid. And, let's face it, your family is rolling in the stuff. If any one of you wanted someone dead, and you happened to know, say, a bikie thug that you'd met at a social occasion like this one…" He tapped the photo again. "…the actual price would be trivial. It'd be loose change."

Richard stood up and paced away from us. I expected his

next words to be an eviction order but to my surprise he said, "Why would I kill my brother?"

"I don't know. Why would you?"

"I wouldn't! It's crazy."

"He beat Cassandra." Richard just stood there, his nostrils flaring. "Did she want revenge? Did you?"

"You are so up the wrong fucking tree. There's nothing going on between me and Cassie."

"Why didn't you go to see your mother after you saw Harry's body?"

"Cassie needed me."

"And your mother didn't?"

"Cassie needed me more?"

"You know how that sounds?"

"I'm sure you're going to tell me."

"It sounds like you and Cassie are lovers. Or it sounds like you hate your mother."

"All right, that's it. I want you two out of here."

Ronnie, his face set into a pugilistic scowl, stood up without argument. I got up too but a question popped into my head. "Richard?" I said, as if we'd been chatting amicably all this time. "What's your connection to Victoria Finn?"

It took him by surprise. "Who?"

"She's the Head of Legal Affairs at Eastern Island Resorts. Was she the one you had dinner with that night in Sydney?"

Again his eyes gave away something. Anger? Fear? "I've never heard of her. Now, if you don't mind."

He literally showed us the door.

* * * *

We left the car where it was and walked through the CBD

towards Cassandra's place. On the way, we stopped at an outdoor cafe in Elizabeth Street and ordered coffee and a pie. The pie was some fancy, gourmet treat that tasted crap. The coffee was excellent. Ronnie and I had barely spoken. I was feeling quite shell-shocked after our confrontation with Richard.

"I reckon I could have handled that better," I said.

"You did great. That bloke's got a broom so far up his arse you can see it when he yawns. He needed a good shake-up."

It wasn't exactly my intention, but I took the compliment.

"What made you ask about Vicki Finn?"

"I don't know. There was something shifty about him when you asked him about the night of the fundraiser. And I remembered you putting Finn and Aikenhead on the board back at the office. We still don't know what their real motive is for hiring us."

"Yeah, well, nice try but I don't think that's it. It looked to me like he'd never heard of her."

I had to agree. "Yeah, but something about the question rattled him. He'll never talk to us again, will he?"

Ronnie sighed. "It was easier as a cop. People had to answer your questions – even if all they'd say was 'No comment.' I just hope he hasn't phoned ahead to the other two to tell them to give us the cold shoulder."

"Do you really think he hates his mother?"

"Looks that way to me. Maybe they can't agree on politics."

I thought about my own parents, habitual Liberal voters. I'd started arguing with them about it from about the age of fifteen but nobody changed their minds and we sort of all got over it and accepted it after a few years. It still galled me that they'd occasionally spout garbage from the *Courier Mail* and other News Corp media about unions and immigrants but they tried to keep it to a minimum and I tried not to quote Marx and Engels back at them, so we mostly got along just fine. But if one or both of them were out-and-out white supremacists, how would I cope with that? Would I still be speaking to them? Would I hate them?

"It's a question for Jennifer this arvo," I said. "Maybe I'd best save it for last, in case she gives me the boot."

He pressed his lips together. "I wish I could come."

"You don't trust me?"

"About as far as I can throw you, mate."

"So, quite a long way, then?"

We exchanged grins.

"Anyway, you'll be cozying up to Carla Ventura. That should compensate. Do you suppose it's her real name?"

Ronnie looked up, startled. "Fuck. I never thought of that? What's Harper doing?"

"Harper? Nothing much. Writing up her interviews. That kind of thing."

He pulled out his phone and poked at it. "Harper? I want you to look into Carla Ventura. By the time we meet up to interview her this arvo, I want a full background – including her real name and any associations between her, her family, her lovers, her business associates, her pets, her hair products, and the Cross family. Anything at all. Also any connections to organised crime and the Devils Playthings bikie gang. No. No. Yes, I was joking about the hair products. And the pets. Right. See you."

He put away the phone. "I don't think I've ever met a woman so literal-minded."

"Do you really think we might have missed something?"

"Us and the cops. There was nothing in their files about her background. Once they had an airtight alibi for the murder, they just stopped looking at her."

"But she could have hired Thackery as well as any of the Crosses. I know they checked her finances and there was no hint of any payments to hit-men but that might just mean she's clever enough to hide it. And she's a woman. She might well have copies of high-end women's magazines lying around to make anonymous letters out of."

"We do not need another suspect," Ronnie said. "Let's hope Harper draws a blank."

We both sipped our coffees in silence for a while, until Ronnie said, "I don't like this case."

"You mean in absolute terms, or compared to other murders?"

He scowled at me. "I mean I don't like it. It's got too many suspects with too many alibis and no witnesses of anything useful. It's got tentacles into all kinds of nasty, criminal groups. It's a big, blurry mess and nothing will ever resolve into a clear line of investigation."

"You know, the last time you got all broody about the case, you said we needed something to shake it up and I got beaten to a pulp by Thomas Thackery. Which was good, I suppose. It led to all kinds of new information. Only I can't help feeling a bit nervous about what would have to happen – to me in particular – to resolve the blurriness you don't like."

He grinned at me. "Mate, if I thought it would clear things up, I'd give you a good thumping myself."

I gave him a tight smile in return, not at all sure he didn't mean it.

"Time to go," I said.

* * * *

Cassandra's maid greeted us with a friendly smile and led us from the lift into the glorious vastness of her mistress's home. The space, the whiteness, the tumbling vistas of the city below, awed me all over again. The lady of the house was arrayed on a snow-white sofa as if she were posing for a photo shoot. She was holding an iPad and, when she put it down to greet us, I noticed it was displaying a copy of *Vogue.*

"You don't read paper magazines?" I asked.

"Why is everybody so interested in my reading habits?"

"Who else is interested?"

"That funny little policewoman with the big brute in tow."

I had no doubt who she meant. "And what did you tell her?"

"I told her I'm twenty-five not ninety-five."

"So, only old people still read magazines on paper?"

"What was the woman's name? It was Italian, I think. You and she should get together. You obviously think the same way. Anyway, I know what you're going to say next, because it's what she said."

I couldn't help smiling. Cassandra could have had no idea what a compliment she'd paid me. Ronnie understood, however, judging by the grumpiness in his voice when he said, "Let me guess. She said, 'Old people like your mother-in-law?'"

Cassandra was leaning forward, fascinated. "Yes, that's right. What's going on here? Why does it matter if Jenny reads paper magazines. I'm sure most people over thirty still do."

"Does she?" I asked. "Just to be clear."

"Well, yes, but—" A bell chimed. "Yes?" she said, to no-one.

A voice came out of the air. I looked around but the speakers, wherever they were, were well hidden.

"Mr. Silverberg is here for you, Mrs. Cross."

"Send him up." To us, she said, "Aaron is my lawyer. I asked him to come for the meeting. I hope you don't mind."

"Not at all," said Ronnie. "Jewish, is he?"

Cassandra smiled. "I really don't know. You should ask him."

Ronnie smiled back. "Let me guess, you took on Mr. Silverberg after your husband died."

"What on earth are you suggesting?"

"I'm suggesting your husband would not have approved of a Jewish lawyer – given his political views – and you were after a tiny bit of payback."

She inspected Ronnie with a tilt of her head and a little frown of concentration, as if he had become an interesting puzzle. Noticeably, she did not contradict him or throw us out.

The lift door opened and we waited for the maid to bring the lawyer to us. I watched him approach. He was short and round and sleek, like a fat, happy cat. He wore a waistcoat under his expensive-looking suit. There was something so very wealthy about him that I immediately felt dowdy and irritated. We all said our greetings without handshakes and resumed our seats.

"Mrs. Cross has asked me to sit in on your little chat today," Silverberg explained.

"Cassandra has no need to be nervous," Ronnie said, managing to sound quite ominous. "We just want to ask a few questions."

"Are you recording this conversation?" the lawyer asked.

"I am," I said.

Silverberg gave me a tight smile. "Would you mind turning off your device?"

"I'd rather not. It helps me when I write up my notes afterwards."

Ronnie gave me a look. "Just turn it off, mate. Mr. Silverberg, here, will stop the interview if you don't. Isn't that right?"

Silverberg kept smiling. "Indeed. So many things end up on social media these days. I'm sure you understand." I understood he had just insulted us but I let it pass and stopped my recording app.

Ronnie turned to Cassandra. "I don't mind him being here, but why do you feel you need a shyster? We're not the cops. You can't incriminate yourself?"

"Mrs. Cross feels, as do I, that it is always best to err on the side of caution in these matters," said Silverberg. I could see this was going to be a very tedious interview.

To Cassandra, I said, "You've been talking to Richard, haven't you?"

"Shall we start?" said Silverberg, assuming the chairman's role.

"Sure," said Ronnie. "Cassandra, we know your husband used to bash you. Did he beat the kids as well?"

Cassandra went rigid. She was about to speak but Silverberg cut in. "You don't have to answer questions like that, Mrs. Cross. I'm sure Mr. Walker understands that some topics are off limits."

Ronnie turned to the lawyer. "Why? This isn't a public hearing. It's a chat, with no official standing at all. We're trying to find out why Cassandra's husband was murdered and who did it. Why would she want to hide the truth about anything?"

Silverberg sighed heavily. "Can we just get on with it?"

Cassandra looked from one to the other as they spoke. She seemed anxious. Ronnie pulled out the fundraiser photo and put it in front of her.

"That was a fundraiser you attended with your husband and your mother-in-law. Do you remember the occasion?"

"I think so. It was before the election. Harry's man got re-elected."

Silverberg picked up the picture and studied it. His forehead creased into a frown, probably when he recognised the notoriously antisemitic Senator.

"Everybody's smiling," Ronnie said. He reached for the photo and took it back. He placed it in front of Cassandra again. "Was Richard at the same party that night? Only he's not in the picture."

"I don't remember. I don't suppose so. Not with – It's not his kind of thing. You'd have to ask him."

"We did. What about this man?" Ronnie tapped Thackery's face.

Cassandra looked genuinely confused. "I've no idea who that is."

"Look carefully. Maybe you met him, spoke to him?"

"Mrs. Cross has already said she doesn't know the man." said Silverberg but Cassandra continued to stare at the picture and I thought I saw recognition dawning.

"You do know him, don't you?" I said.

She looked at me and, just for an instant, her expression was hunted. Then she sat back and composed herself. "No. I don't. I've never met him. I've never spoken to him."

"Maybe not," said Ronnie. "But somebody did? Was it

Harry? Or Jennifer?"

She looked at Silverberg, commanding him to step in. Which, of course, he did.

"Are we finished? I have to say, it feels like we've finished."

Ronnie threw up his hands in defeat. He clearly thought we weren't going to get anything else out of Cassandra. "Sure," he said. "Luke?"

"I have one more question."

"Just one?" Silverberg asked. "Very well."

"Cassandra, after your husband was killed, Richard joined you in your chalet on the island and stayed with you, In fact, he went back to the mainland with you."

"You want to know if we were having an affair," she said. "Well, we're not. Nothing could be farther from the truth."

Silverberg stood up with a look of distaste on his chubby features.

"No," I said. "That wasn't my question. What I wanted to ask was, why does Richard hate his mother?"

It caught her off-guard. "She never app—" She stopped dead and looked down at the photo in confusion.

"That is clearly a question for Mr. Cross and his mother to answer. Now, gentlemen, I think we'll call it a day."

"Righty-o," said Ronnie, standing up. "Lovely to meet you, Mr. Goldberg."

"It's Silverberg."

Ronnie picked up the photo and held it so Silverberg could see it. "Wouldn't matter a bit to this lot, I reckon. They've probably got loads of different names for you." I had no idea what Ronnie was doing but I hurried to get moving towards the lift. "What do you reckon, Cassandra? What would Harry have called him? Or Jenny?" He turned so she could see the picture. "What were you all laughing about, hey? Did the senator make one of his famous jokes about Muslims? Or was it Asians? You seemed to be enjoying yourself."

Cassandra's fists clenched. "You don't know what you're talking about. You don't know what it was like living with—"

"Mrs. Cross!" Silverberg was looking angry too. "It's time you two left. Or do I need to call building security?"

I was already half-way to the lift. Ronnie sneered in Cassandra's face. Then he looked slowly around the magnificent apartment. "Yeah, it must have been awful."

I ducked my head and hurried to the door. It opened as soon as I started hammering on the call button. I ducked into the lift and out of sight. I heard Cassandra saying things like, "How dare you, you vile little man?" and "Get them out. I don't want them here. Sandra, call security."

Ronnie strolled into the lift, grinning from ear to ear. I took my finger off the button that was keeping the doors open and pushed the "G" button about ten times before the carriage started to descend.

"Fuck, man!" I said. "What the actual fuck?" Ronnie seemed pleased with himself. "Was that just, like, fun for you? What is your fucking problem? You want the whole lot of them refusing to talk to us?"

"Mate, that was the last time Richard or Cassandra would ever see us anyway. It was worth stirring the pot a bit to see if they'd say anything juicy."

The doors opened and the reception guy was standing in the lobby with another bloke, also in uniform. They both looked unhappy and nervous. As well they might. I could have taken on the two of them myself and made a good show of it. Ronnie could have tied them into a ball and bounced them around the room. I headed for the door at a brisk walk with Ronnie sauntering along behind me.

Chapter Nineteen

Lunch was in a mall in the CBD. It was busy and noisy. I vetoed Ronnie's idea of finding a hotel and "getting on the grog" as he put it. I didn't want to turn up at Jenny Cross's place reeking of booze. So I had a soggy quiche and a salad swimming in so much balsamic vinegar it should have been sold as a chemical weapon rather than food. Ronnie had burgers and chips which he wolfed down while I prodded and poked at the quiche.

I tried to call Megan again but again I got the voicemail. I didn't leave a message.

"So," said Ronnie, punctuating his words with a chip on a fork. "We now know that Richard and Harry didn't see eye-to-eye on Harry's right-wing politics. However, their mother was all in. Cassie, bless her cute little butt, was only there for Harry's money."

Harsh but fair, I thought and then felt guilty that I was being un-feminist. "And we have evidence that everyone in the family might have known Thomas Thackery, except Richard."

"Which doesn't mean he doesn't know him."

"True. What did you think about Cassandra seeming to know one of the others had spoken to Thackery?"

"Not a lot. It was either Jennifer or Harry. But maybe it happened on some other occasion and it was Richard. So it could still be any of those three with the Thackery connection. Your reluctant witness on the island nearly ran into an old lady. Maybe you were right all along and it was Jennifer."

I didn't feel at all pleased about the possibility of validation. "But... his mother? Even for the Cross family it seems unlikely."

"I don't know. You reckon Richard hates her. Maybe he has good reason. Maybe Harry and his mother were enemies too. Maybe she's an old witch. We know she's a Nazi. And Harry had to get his sociopathic tendencies from somewhere." He studied the chip he'd been waving about, then popped it in his mouth. "Maybe I should go with you this arvo after all." He grinned and prodded his fork at me. "In case she gets all stabby on you."

"I think I can handle it." But that was just bravado. The idea was creepy as hell. I could just imagine her coming at me with a huge kitchen knife. "Anyway," I said, trying to dispel the vision. "We have no actual evidence against Jennifer. And no actual motive, either. In fact, what we do have is a solid alibi that she was miles away at the time of the stabbing."

Ronnie looked speculatively at my quiche and, without thinking, I pushed it towards him. He pushed it straight back with a wince of revulsion, saying, "Yeah, nah. You keep it, mate."

We sat in silence for a while.

"There's a lot of work to do," Ronnie said. "You're right, we've got nothing against Jennifer. But we've got nothing against anyone else, either."

"We've firmed up some of the motives of some of the

family," I said, defensively. He pulled a face that showed how little he thought of that. "We've identified a couple of other possible suspects: Claudia Knecht and June Onbekend." That earned me an eye roll. "And we've made connections to the Devil's Playthings and to neo-fascist politics."

Ronnie shook his head in apparent despair. "All of which makes my point. We're just getting started on this and we've got a ton of work to do."

The silence descended again. "You know," I said. "Richard is still our best bet. His alibi is piss-weak and his antagonism towards his brother is strong, even now. We still can't rule out a romantic entanglement with Cassandra and he obviously hated Harry's politics. He had a lot to gain from Harry's death, even without the inheritance, and it could be he hoped to get the widow and the business anyway."

"And the Thackery connection?"

Trust Ronnie to go straight for the weak spot in my argument. "Yeah, well, as you said yourself, just because he didn't go to the same white supremacist fundraisers, doesn't mean he didn't know him."

He checked his watch. "If we leave now, you can drop me off in Hemmant on your way out to the farm."

"What? It's right out West, practically at the beach. I'm going East. Can't you catch a train or something? I'll drop you in Roma Street."

He stood up. "Jeez, you're such a whinger. Nobody likes a whinger, mate. Come on, we can pick up Harper on the way."

* * * *

The phone rang as I drove out along the motorway towards Toowoomba. The display told me it was my client.

"Mr. Aikenhead, how are you? Surviving the new lockdown, I hope."

"Luke, I just got off the phone with Richard Cross." *Shit.* "He was telling me about a visit you paid him this morning. He had also spoken to a lawyer called Silverberg who says you and your partner seem to have set out to deliberately upset Richard's sister-in-law, Cassandra."

"It's in the nature of the business that this kind of thing happens, Mr. Aikenhead. We have to ask a lot of very sensitive questions and people, quite understandably, become upset about answering them."

Hang on, said a little voice in my head. *Something's not right, here.*

"I didn't take your company on so that you two could go around throwing out wild accusations and offending people."

"If you're worried about the legal ramifications, I can assure you your company and you personally are quite safe."

"That's not my concern, Luke. I'm concerned that your idea of investigating a case seems to amount to throwing lots of mud around to see if anything sticks. Have you made any progress at all? Richard seems to think you're just thrashing about aimlessly."

Richard?

"I'm sorry, do you know Richard Cross personally?"

"What?"

"You keep calling him 'Richard'. Is he a friend of yours?"

He sounded flustered. "I've – I've met him a few times. The business community in Australia is quite small, above a certain level. You'd be surprised."

"And did you tell him you'd hired us to look into his brother's death?" *No,* I thought. *There's more.* "You did it as a favour, didn't you? He asked you to hire someone to re-open the investigation. That's why you did it."

It all made sense now. All those bullshit stories Aikenhead had told us about falling profits and media lawsuits were just a blind for this. Richard Cross had asked him to help find out who killed his brother.

Aikenhead had gone quiet, so I asked another question. "Is Richard footing the bill? Or XtraVirtual, maybe?"

"What?" He seemed to recover himself. "That's none of your business. Look, I want a lot more visibility of your investigation from now on. I want a detailed report every evening of each day's activities and your plans for the next day."

"Of course, if that's what you want, but—"

"No buts. That's how this will run from now on. And I reserve the right to veto any interviews or lines of investigation that don't look fruitful."

"I really don't think you'd be the best judge of—"

"I don't care. That's how we're going to do it. If it wasn't for this damned lockdown, I'd be up there on the next flight, to supervise things personally."

"Really? It's that important to you?"

Again, he sounded flustered. "I don't like to see my money being wasted."

"I assure you, we—"

"A full report tonight. And every night. Do you understand."

"Of course. I just—"

The line went dead.

I pulled off the road onto the hard shoulder and thought about what had just happened. The only conclusion I could reach was that Richard Cross and Aikenhead were close. Very close. Richard had called Aikenhead after I upset him and

Cassandra – not just because he already knew Aikenhead was our client but because he knew Aikenhead could and would do something about it.

But where did that lead me? Could Richard and Aikenhead have acted together somehow to kill Harry Cross? Aikenhead ran the company that owned Murdock Island. He might have known anybody there – including June Onbekend, who was probably the only person with a clear and simple means to have done the murder. Had Aikenhead paid, or persuaded Onbekend to stab Harry to help out his good mate, Richard?

I wanted to call Ronnie and talk it through but he'd be too busy drooling over Carla Ventura to spare me the time. Instead, I called Noah at the office.

"Noah, you did such a good job finding that photo of the Crosses at that fundraiser, I want you to repeat the miracle. Get me everything you can about a possible friendship between Richard Cross and Vincent Aikenhead, CEO of Eastern Island Resorts."

"Vincent Aikenhead our client? That Vincent Aikenhead?"

"That's it and, Noah, don't put anything about what you're doing into the files."

"Because you don't want our client to know we're investigating him."

"That's the go, mate. Catch you later."

* * * *

"Where's the rude one?" were Jennifer Cross's first words when she opened the door to me.

"He, er, sends his apologies for how he behaved last time. He's, um, very ashamed that he let his curiosity get the better of his good judgement."

277

Jennifer gave me a taut smile and let me in. "And does he send his apologies to Richard and Cassandra, too? Cassie's in a terrible sulk since your visit this morning."

I spoke slowly, choosing my words carefully. "Ronnie sometimes lets his passion for the truth lead him to be a bit aggressive in his questioning. I promise you, all he wants to do is find your son's killer."

She pursed her lips and nodded. "Sit down and ask me your questions."

I sat down in a big armchair in front of the gigantic stone fireplace. Jennifer took the seat opposite me, so far away that I had to raise my voice a little. It struck me again what a handsome woman she was, tall and straight-backed and still strong and vigorous. She'd been a model when she had first met her late husband, Harry's father, and she still had the grace and poise. It was odd to think that under that broad brow lurked the mind of a racist bigot.

"I'd like to ask you about a fundraiser you attended with your son a couple of years ago," I began and went through the same process we'd been through with Richard and Cassandra. I showed her the picture, and asked her whether Richard had been there. It elicited a derisive snort.

"Richard has other interests. He never goes to political dos."

I wanted to pursue the obvious disdain in her voice but I stuck to the plan and asked her if she remembered Thackery from the event. When she saw the face I was pointing at, she went still and silent. It was several seconds before she looked up at me and said, "No, I don't know him."

"You didn't speak to him that night – or maybe at some other event?"

"I told you, I don't know him."

She was lying. The sight of Thackery had upset her. I was sure of it.

"His name is Thomas Thackery. He's a member of the Devil's Playthings motorcycle club. He often worked security for the senator, I believe."

"So?"

"So you might have run into him – checking invitations, maybe, or standing near the stage during speeches."

"How many times do I have to tell you? I don't know him."

"Only, I've been receiving anonymous letters about him – from a woman, the cops reckon – connecting him to your son's death. Then, a few nights ago, he ambushed me outside my office and gave me a rather painful walloping. And then this picture turns up, with Thackery standing there just a few metres away from you, your son and your daughter-in-law."

"There must have been hundreds of people at that event."

She was still holding the photo. I got up and took it back from her, returning to my seat as I put it back in my pocket. It gave me time to think about where to go next with my questioning. However, Jennifer pre-empted me.

"Richard never went to any of those events. He couldn't have met Thackery."

"Sorry? What?"

"I know you think he killed his brother. Well, that picture won't help you pin it on him. If anything, it proves he had nothing to do with it. Maybe it was Thackery who did it. Have you even thought about that?"

"Yes, for about five seconds. Thackery's got no motive and no-one saw a bloody great bikie thug covered in tats on the island that day. And, even if he did kill your son, someone else would have been paying him to do it. Even Thackery

279

isn't the kind of bloke who goes around killing people just for the fun of it."

She shut her mouth tight. Her eyes flicked around. She was angry but also scared. Slowly, she composed herself enough to say, "I won't have you persecuting my son."

"I thought you and Richard hated each other."

Her eyes widened. "How dare you say that? Is that what he told you? What kind of man are you to think such a thing? Do you even have a mother? Haven't you ever had disagreements? Of course you have. Children sometimes get confused about… things. But a mother's love transcends all of that. One day Richard will…"

She turned sharply away from me, perhaps to hide tears. She seemed seriously upset but I couldn't just stop asking her questions. I might not get another chance. I tried to placate her.

"I'm not trying to pin anything on Richard, I promise you. He seems like a decent sort of bloke. I can't really imagine him killing anyone."

There was a shout from upstairs, a woman calling someone's name. We both looked at the staircase. There was an old woman in her nightdress standing half-way down. She looked frail and was holding the banister for support. Her grey hair was a tangled mane around her thin, wrinkled face. She was barefoot – probably why we hadn't heard her coming down.

"Richard's the only decent one of the whole lot of 'em," the old woman said.

Jennifer leapt out of her chair. "Ma! What are you doing up? Angela! Angela!"

An Asian woman in a nurse's uniform appeared at the top of the stairs and hurried down to retrieve her charge as

Jennifer rushed up from below. I stood up. The old woman had transfixed me with her little dark eyes.

"This family is rotten," she said. "Festering." She pointed an arthritic finger at Jennifer. "She should never have married that man. Those poor little babies."

She couldn't say anything else because Jennifer and the nurse were fussing around her and steering her back up the stairs. They disappeared, still fussing and cajoling the old woman and were gone for several minutes. Then I heard Jenny chastising the nurse in a low, angry voice. Eventually, she reappeared.

"I should get a proper, white nurse," she grumbled as she flopped into her seat. She glared up at me. "Have we finished with all this? Because I certainly have."

I didn't think I'd be able to get back to any semblance of a proper interview from there, so I just nodded and thanked her for her time. She raised a long-fingered hand and waved it wearily at the door.

"You know the way out."

"Yes, thank you. Oh, just one small question before I go. Do you know a Vincent Aikenhead?"

Her weariness vanished in an instant. She glared at me wide-eyed and thin-lipped in rage. "You little bastard. Get out. Get out! And don't come back."

I got out and shut the door after me. Then I stood on the porch, looking out across the brown paddocks, wondering what the hell had just happened.

* * * *

I drove to a small town near the highway and found a scruffy little café-cum-newsagent-cum-general-store. They were no longer serving coffee or food – it being about three P.M. – but they didn't mind if I sat at a table and drank an iced tea from the fridge and ate a Kit-Kat from the counter. They even offered me a straw, which I declined because it was plastic. It was dark, wooden and ramshackle in the shop. The perfect metaphor for my state of mind.

I called Megan again. She didn't answer. This time I left a message to say I understood why she might be avoiding my calls but I just wanted to apologise for last night and I wouldn't call again. The man and woman behind the counter watched and listened. A stranger in the shop was the most interesting thing to happen all day, I supposed.

Then I called Ronnie. At least he answered.

"How'd it go with Curvy Carla?" I asked.

"Ripper, mate. What a woman!"

"Stimulating conversation about world affairs, I suppose."

"You're a bloody snob, mate. I'll tell you, she could have sat there and recited her times tables and I'd still have had a bonzer arvo."

"Yeah, well, I might be a snob but at least I'm not an old perv. Did she say anything helpful for the investigation?"

"Nah, mate. She thought Harry was the ant's pants. Told me he bought her loads of stuff. So that proves it, hey? They never talked about politics – or anything much – just went at it like rabbits whenever they got the chance. Why did I never meet a woman like that?"

"I can't imagine. So, a complete bust then."

"No pun intended, right?"

"Right."

"What about the world's oldest supermodel? You get anything out of Jenny Cross?"

"Yes. But first I should tell you about a call I received

from Aikenhead." I gave him the gist of the call and he listened in silence.

"What the hell's going on there?" he asked when I'd finished.

"That's what I thought. It's weird, right?"

"Bloody oath, mate. So Aikenhead and Richard Cross are old pals and Richard got Aikenhead to light a fire under the investigation again."

"We don't know that for sure but that's what it looks like. Do you reckon it rules Richard out as a suspect?"

"I don't know. Maybe. What did his mother say?"

"She thinks we're hatching a plot to pin the whole thing on Richard." I told him how the interview went and, again, he listened attentively.

"Damn! I wish I'd been there. I love it when they go off like a frog in a sock. It's only when you get right under their skin that you can really see what their hiding. And it was when you mentioned Aikenhead that you got the elbow?"

"Oh yeah, definitely."

"Now, why would she know him? And why would he piss her off so much?"

"And what's it got to do with Richard?"

"Anything else?"

"Not in the interview, as such, but there was a creepy incident." I told him about Jennifer's crazy old mother standing on the staircase sledging the family and lamenting the poor children before being manhandled back to her room by Jennifer and the nurse.

"It'll come to us all sooner or later," he said.

"I thought you said she was *compos* when you spoke to her."

"Yeah, she seemed all right. Maybe she's off her meds.

Anyway, go over that interview with Jennifer again. I want it word for word this time."

"I've got the recording."

"Yeah, yeah. Just tell me. From the top."

So, I told him all over again. This time, he kept interrupting with, "Were those her exact words?" and similar, to which I eventually started replying, "It's on the bloody recording if you don't believe me."

* * * *

"Is it just me, or is the Brisbane traffic worse since covid than it was before?" I asked as I entered the office.

"It's the busses," said Desi, grabbing up a handful of message notes and following me to my room. I flinched. It would be nice to come into the office just one time and not have a load of messages to deal with. "No-one wants to go on them any more. I think it's great. I go everywhere by bus and they're always half-empty now, even in the rush hour."

"Is Ronnie about?"

"He came in half an hour ago then shot through." She shrugged, as if the comings and goings of Ronnie Walker were one of life's mysteries. "He looked really miserable. But he always does, really. Said he'd see you at home. Are you staying at his place?"

"What're all those?" I asked, pointing to the messages.

"Oh, just the usual. There's a lot of journos, though. Seems the cops released a POI on Thomas Thackery and said it was in connection with the Harry Cross murder. You can imagine them waking up in newsrooms across the country. Sitting up and sniffing the air like meerkats." She did a quick impression. "My guess is they gave the media your name to get rid of them. Do you want to talk to any of them?" She pulled out one of the slips of paper. "This one's from The Guardian. That's the one you read, isn't it? She seemed really nice. I mean, for a journo." She put the message on my desk.

"Just leave them all, please. I'll take a look. Thanks." It took her a moment to realise I was suggesting she leave.

When she went, I worked through the messages. There were a couple of prospective clients and I set them aside, promising myself I'd spend a couple of hours tomorrow making sure we lined up some new work. It had bugged me that Aikenhead had been such a dick on the phone. If he had pulled the plug today, I'd have been scrambling to get new work going. It made me realise I'd been neglecting things. I needed to get Noah and Harper working on other projects right away.

Speaking or which… Neither of them was in the office. I called Desi and asked where they were.

"Smoko," she said.

"Since when did they take breaks?"

"They're entitled."

"Yes, I know. It's just that…"

"They just need a bit of alone time. You know?"

"Right. Yeah, of course."

The scene in my imagination, of Harper and Noah exchanging sweet nothings across a coffee table in the mall below, was too disturbing to dwell on. To distract myself, I set about writing my evening report to Vincent Aikenhead. It was easy enough, although I had to bear in mind all the time that he was a close friend of Richard Cross, so I had to be careful what I said.

When it came to the section on what my plans were for the next day, I stopped dead. I didn't actually have any plans.

What I wanted to do was explore the connection between Aikenhead and Richard. I needed to look for motives they might share for killing Harry Cross – and then for re-opening the case a year later. I looked up to find Harper and Noah at their desks. I went to the door and called Noah over.

"Anything yet?" I asked, by way of greeting.

He shook his head. "Nah, bugger all really. Richard Cross is pretty low-key for a bloke in his position. Doesn't get his piccy taken much. His social media posts are all pretty bland. Same for Aikenhead, really. Quiet type, I reckon. Harper's trying to put together a timeline for both of them – to see what days they were in the same place, what events they were both at. You know. I've been concentrating more on mutual acquaintances, shared interests, that kind of thing."

"Sounds good. Anything unusual yet?"

"Nah. If anything jumps out at me, I'll let you know."

"And Harper? Has she got anything?"

"Well, there's lots of times Aikenhead came to Brissy and lots of times Cross went to Sydney but they've both got legit reasons to do that, yeah?"

It was true. If there was ever a pair of conspirators who could cover their tracks in a cloud of legitimate business, it was these two.

"OK, thanks Noah. When you've got as far as you can with these two, expand the search to include June Onbekend."

"The manager at Murdock Island Resort?"

"That's the one. I need to know if either Aikenhead or Cross met her at any time in the months before the murder. Also, any relationship she might have with either man. Is that OK?"

"Sure. No probs."

"And keep an eye open for Claudia Knecht in all that. She was Harry Cross's personal assistant and now works for Richard. She would have made all the arrangements for the island retreat."

He looked sceptical. "So, we're talking about a four-way conspiracy?" He grinned. "Maybe everyone was in on it, like *Murder on the Orient Express*."

"You know, I wouldn't be at all surprised. I think if I'd known Harry Cross myself, I'd have conspired to murder him, too."

I watched him go over to Harper's desk and tell her what we'd just said. He sat beside her and looked over some documents she was showing him. They sat too close together, their shoulders touching, either deliberately or because that's the way they were now. Unbidden, Megan came to mind. She and I could be like that again, I thought, casually intimate, closer than ordinary people. All I had to do was to stop being angry with her.

Chapter Twenty

By the time I left the office, it was dark outside. Harper and Noah were still at work but Desi was long gone. The thought of going down in the lift to the basement car park was weighing heavily on my mind. The chances of being jumped by Thackery and his mates – or Harry Cross's murderer – were far too high for my liking. In fact, I'd resolved to see building management the next day and insist they install security cameras and, if they refused again, I'd find a safer place to work. So I stopped at Harper's desk on the way out and, feeling like an idiot, asked her if she carried mace.

"You mean, like, a pepper spray?"

"Yeah, that kind of thing."

"Why?"

Well, you're a woman. I just thought you might." She looked as if she was on the verge of being offended. "I should have bought some while the shops were open. I'm just worried I might get jumped again. In the car park."

"Do you want me to go down with you?"

"No, no. I'll be fine. It's just nerves."

I started to go but she said, "Hang on," and reached into her handbag. "This might help." She handed me a small metal cylinder that might have been a lipstick.

I looked at it. It had a nozzle at one end and was obviously a spray of some sort. I put a finger on the top to give it a squirt.

"Don't!"

I froze. "What is it?"

"It's a rape alarm. You'll deafen half the building if you set it off."

I looked at the little gadget with new respect. "Right-o. Thanks."

"Sorry I didn't have pepper spray."

"She'll be right."

I didn't think a super-loud horn would do much to deter Thackery or his mates, but I pocketed it anyway and tried to look grateful. As it happened, I needn't have worried. I got to my car without incident and reached Ronnie's in one piece.

* * * *

Ronnie was in a bad mood. As soon as I got in, he marched me over to the security monitor on the sideboard in the lounge room. It was the most sophisticated piece of technology Ronnie owned, apart from his phone, and oddly anomalous in his low-tech life. The six panels on the screen showed views from four external and two internal cameras. The front door was clearly visible. The moment I saw it, I realised what he was going to say.

"All right, all right. I should have checked the monitor when I heard Megan knocking."

"That's very true," Ronnie said. "Instead of running around like a blue-arsed fly, grabbing guns and falling about like a one-man clown show, you could have just taken a quick look at this and saved yourself the embarrassment. And if you ever go in my room again and take anything, I'll break your arm. Yeah?"

"Yeah, right. Sorry."

"But that's not what I was going to say."

He hit a few keys and pulled up a window. A few more and a recording began to play. It was from a camera mounted at the front of the house that showed the street. I saw Megan get out of her car and walk down the street to the drive, stand still for a moment, then square her shoulders and walk down the drive. Ronnie tapped the controls again and the point of view changed to the interior of the hallway and the front door. I watched myself run into the hallway with a gun in my hand, open the door, knock the gun out of my hand, and fall on the floor. Megan stepped into the shot, looking down at me as if I'd gone mad.

"You're bloody lucky you didn't shoot yourself. Or Megan," Ronnie snarled, tapping again at the keys.

"The safety was still on," I said, earning myself a look of disdain from Ronnie. "Can we just eat? I feel guilty enough already without you rubbing it in."

"Shut up and watch."

The POV went back to the hallway. The door was closed. Megan walked quickly down the hall towards the door. The scene must have been from later, after I'd upset her and she was leaving. She pulled the door open and stepped through. It was hard to tell quite what happened next but she seemed to stumble on the doorstep.

Ronnie switched again, this time to an outside camera, one covering the porch and the door.

My breath caught. A big man, dressed in a black hoodie and jeans, walked down the drive. He reached into his pocked as he walked. He pulled out a small rod. I was just beginning to wonder what it might be when he gave it a flick and a blade sprang out. He walked right up to the door and looked like he was about to knock. Then the door swung open and Megan stepped through it. She collided with the man. He grabbed her and clamped a hand across her mouth, lifting her off the ground so that her struggles were ineffective.

"Fuck!" I said. I knew the man. It was Thomas Thackery.

Thackery, massive and powerful compared to his struggling victim, shook her violently until she stopped struggling. He put the knife-blade against her throat and spoke into her ear, uttering god-knows-what threats. With her subdued, he calmly reached out and closed the front door. He set Megan down on her feet and removed his hand from her mouth, placing it instead around her throat. Holding her by her neck, his knife against her ribs, he led her out of Ronnie's drive and across the road to a black van. He opened a side door and shoved her inside, climbing in after her. For a long, long time, nothing happened. Then the van pulled away from the kerb and moved off, out of the shot.

While I sat on the patio brooding and feeling sorry for myself.

I felt sick. My legs were weak. I went over to a chair and sat down.

"Why?" I asked aloud. "Why would he take Megan?"

"Because she almost fell over him. What could he do? He didn't want to be identified."

"Will he…?" I couldn't bring myself to say it.

Ronnie came and sat down too. "Kill her? He might. If he's going to, he's already done it by now. If not…"

"That's right! He might keep her as – as leverage, to keep us off his back."

"I wasn't going to say that."

"But he could, hey?"

Ronnie's face was grim. It was obvious he didn't agree with me. The brief hope that had flared, died away. Why would Thackery keep Megan alive? The cops were already after him. Whatever we did, didn't matter to him any more. Unless…

"What if he was involved with the murder? Or, at least, the murderer? What if he really wants us to shut down the investigation?"

"Look, mate, I don't think he gives a stuff about the investigation. He came here to kill us. Either he's pissed off with us for causing him so much grief, or someone is paying him to do it."

I closed my eyes, trying to take it all in, trying to see what it might mean for Megan.

"My guess is it's the latter," Ronnie said. "Somebody else, someone who really does care about the investigation, wants us gone. Thackery is up to his neck in crap anyway, so a nice big score, like two hit jobs, would fill his pockets for a trip to somewhere he can lay low for a while."

My head felt like it was in a vise. It was almost impossible to think. Thackery had grabbed Megan almost twenty-four hours ago. There had been no contact, no ransom note. Nothing. I found myself praying to a Universe I knew didn't care. *Please, please let her be alive.*

"Who?" I asked, forcing myself to focus. "Who wants us dead? It can't be Richard Cross. He was the one who set the whole investigation going again. If he'd killed his brother and literally got away with murder, it would be insane to make Aikenhead start it all up again after so much time had passed."

"Maybe he's got a guilty conscience." I gave Ronnie a baleful look. This was no time for humour. "Trust me," he said, "murder of a family member can twist the perpetrator up like a pretzel. I don't think we can rule him out just because re-opening the case would be nuts."

I didn't agree. I'd spoken to Richard more often than Ronnie and I couldn't see him as a madman, hell bent on self-destruction.

"It's his mother," I said. "It has to be. He hates her. Her alibi for the murder was always dodgy. The maintenance guy on the island saw her on the road after the killing." Ronnie started poking at his phone. It sent a rush of anger through me. "Am I boring you?"

He held up his phone so I could see the screen. There was a picture of a beautiful woman I didn't recognise.

"It's Cindy Crawford," he said.

"Who?"

"Jeez, mate, one of the original supermodels. She's fifty-five in that picture. Would you describe her as an old woman?"

"What are you talking about?"

"I'm saying some of these models age very well. Now, Jenny Cross is ten years older than this, I admit, but, if you saw her in the street, would you describe her as 'an old biddy'? Because that's what your man Maury Ludgate called the woman he almost ran over." He poked at his phone again, obviously to fetch up the record of Ludgate's interview. "He called her an 'old biddy', a 'ditzy old bitch' and 'a real crumbly'. Now, maybe there are plenty of sixty-five-year-old women he'd have described like that but not Jenny Cross. Not in a million years."

I remembered my interview with her from earlier in the day. Ronnie was right. Jennifer Cross was a good-looking woman who still had the style and graceful movements of a woman half her age. To clinch the argument, Ronnie pulled out the photo of the fundraiser and held it for me to see. Jennifer Cross was in a clinging evening dress that a great many women of all ages would have been reluctant to be seen in. "That is not an old biddy," he said.

"All right, the maintenance guy evidence is a red herring. But there's still the weak alibi and the crappy relationship with Richard."

"You reckon? Richard hates his mother so much he wants her convicted of his brother's murder?"

"Maybe. I don't know. She might have confessed to him for all we know."

He threw up his arms. "All right! It's Jenny. How does that help us get Megan back?"

"I don't bloody know! We go out to the farm and search it. There's loads of places you could hide someone in a place that big. Sheds and bush and all kinds of places. The farmhouse alone is as big as a bloody shopping mall."

He shook his head, angrily, and flopped back in his chair. "This is getting us nowhere. We know Thackery took Megan. We need to focus on him."

I screwed my eyes shut and pressed my palms against my forehead. Between the fear and frustration filling my mind, there wasn't much room for cogent thought in there. But I had to find room, somehow. Megan's life might depend on it.

The sound of the doorbell made me jump to my feet. I stepped to one side so I could see the security monitor. *Why didn't you do that last night?* I asked myself.

"You called the cops?" I demanded, outraged at the sight of the uniformed officer standing outside.

"Of course I did. Get a fucking grip. We need to get this reported and out of the way, then we can go find Megan."

I set off for the door. Ronnie called after me, "You never know, it might even help."

∗ ∗ ∗ ∗

"Luke!" Sergeant Tim Pearce pulled his head back in surprise. He reached for his notebook. "I thought this was the home of…"

"Ronnie Walker. It is. Come in. That's Ronnie over there. We work together."

"Right. Al mentioned a partner." He moved past me to greet Ronnie, holding out his hand for a shake. Ronnie looked at it but didn't take it. "Right, sorry. Old habits." A frown crossed the young sergeant's brow. "Is this something to do with the Harry Cross case?"

I let another cop in and went to join them.

"Yes, it is," I said. "Very much so. My ex-girlfriend, Megan Thomas, has been kidnapped."

"Look," said Ronnie. "Before we get into all that, the front porch out there is a crime scene. A woman was abducted from there about twenty-four hours ago. You need to get forensics in and cordon off the area. We've got the whole thing on video and we know who the kidnapper is. We've also got video of the vehicle he took her away in. I can't make out the rego but you can easily see the make, model and colour. You should probably get onto that right away, too, hey?"

One of the things I liked about Tim Pearce was that he had none of that arrogance I've so often encountered in cops. He looked at me and I realised he was asking me to vouch for Ronnie. I nodded quickly.

"All right." To the other cop, he said, "Chen, get out there and set up a crime scene around the porch area and the drive. Then take up a position at the end of the drive and make sure nobody comes in or out without my say-so." Chen disappeared with a "Yes, Sarge," and Tim pulled out a mobile phone. He stepped away from us and made a call to Detective Sergeant Bertolissio, telling her almost word-for-word what Ronnie had told him. After that, he made another call, on his radio this time, explaining what had happened, stating that this was related to an ongoing homicide investigation, that the investigating officers had been informed, and requesting a forensics team and more cops.

"Al will be here in half an hour," he told us, when it was done. "I'd better see that video now, if you don't mind, sir."

"Call me Ronnie." I could tell from his tone that he approved of Tim.

He ran through the video clips again for Tim's benefit and the sergeant made notes of times and names in his notebook as the show unfolded. We filled in details of who the players were as they each appeared.

"And you were here when it happened?" Tim asked me.

"Yeah, out there on the patio at the back."

"You didn't hear anything?"

"Not a damned thing."

"And why was Ms Thomas here? I thought you said she was your ex-girlfriend."

"Ronnie asked her over. She thought we might get back together."

He looked at Ronnie, then back at me. "And did you?"

"No."

"Did you have a blue?"

"No. Not really. I was just… unkind."

He nodded and wrote something down. To Ronnie, he

said, "And you were out on a date with…" He flipped back a couple of pages.

"Maggie," Ronnie said. He gave Tim her phone number. "You'll want to check."

"Yes, I will."

He asked a few more questions about our movements since the abduction. He was just saying, wide-eyed, "What? *The* Carla Ventura?" when there was a knock at the back door screen and DS Bertolissio let herself in.

"I didn't want to come through the front," she said. "Trevor's on his way. He might be another half-hour. Hi, Tim."

We went through the video again and Bertolissio asked many of the same questions Tim had already asked. I was beginning to feel agitated. This was all taking so long and Megan was out there somewhere, a prisoner, or worse. If we had to show the video and answer all these questions again for Reid when he arrived, I thought I might explode.

Bertolissio went with Ronnie to the video console and worked with him to take copies of the recordings. At the same time, Tim went to his car and brought back a clipboard with forms so that Ronnie and I could give him formal statements. The forensic team arrived and Tim went out to supervise them. Shortly after that, Detective Inspector Reid came in. Bertolissio spared me a repetition of the video-and-questions routine by giving Reid a quick, clear summary and telling him she'd have the video and our statements on his desk in the morning.

"So you reckon it was Thomas Thackery?" Reid asked me. His tone suggested there was probably some mistake but he'd get to the bottom of it.

"It was Thackery," Ronnie said, drawing the big cop's

attention. "You might even get a rego from the video if your people are good enough."

Reid glanced at the console. "That's a lot of security for a suburban home."

"Yeah, well, shit happens and the cops need all the help they can get."

Reid nodded to himself in silence. He turned to me again. "Why would Thackery kidnap your ex-girlfriend?"

"I think he came here to kill Ronnie and me. Megan got in the way and he… I don't know. The guy's as thick as pig-shit. Maybe he thought he could use her somehow. As leverage."

"Leverage? That's what the Genius Detective thinks, is it? Wouldn't it have made more sense for him to kill the girl and then finish the job he came to do?"

I wanted to hit him. Suppressing the urge, I said, "Yes, it would. That's why I said I don't know why he took her. I'd be happy to hear your theories, you being a professional and all."

He gave me a smile. "Well, it's yet to be established that Ms Thomas is even missing. If she is, it's yet to be established that the kidnapper was Thomas Thackery. And, even if it was Thackery, it's yet to be established that he had any motive in coming here other than to kidnap Ms Thomas."

Astonished, I looked at Bertolissio. She was looking away, studying the wall. "That's ludicrous! It's complete bullshit. Ronnie, show him the video."

"Mate, he's just winding you up, But he's right. All that crap has to be established because your true blue copper is only thinking about making a watertight case that will stand up in court. He's not thinking about getting out there and tearing down fences and kicking in doors to rescue some poor innocent woman who's in danger of being killed by a psychotic thug at any moment."

Reid's nostrils flared and he worked his jaw like he was grinding rocks between his teeth. But he turned to Bertolissio and said, calmly enough, "Finish off would you, Al. I'm going to shoot through. I don't think there's anything else I need here. I'll see you in the morning."

He walked out through the front door and across the "crime scene". Bertolissio hurried after him and they talked outside, out of earshot. Tim Pearce shifted his stance, looking embarrassed. Feeling he needed to say something, he stepped closer.

"We'll be out of your hair as soon as forensics have finished," he said.

"Thanks, Tim."

I went to sit on the patio and stare at the sky. Reid was a total bastard and a useless pile of crap, but he was right about the kidnapping. It didn't make sense. Yet I needed it to make sense real quick, for Megan's sake.

I could hear Ronnie and Bertolissio talking for a while and then she left. I could see the red-and-blue lights of the cop cars flickering in the leaves of the taller gums around me. After a while that stopped, too. Ronnie came out and handed me a beer.

"They're gone."

"Good," I said. "Useless pricks."

"I don't know." To my surprise, he sounded ambivalent. "The cops are doing what they can. And Reid's team is pretty good at what they do. There's just something wrong with this case."

"I don't want to hear all that crap again!" I realised I was shouting. I wanted to throw the furniture around and smash things. But that was not going to find Megan. Forcing myself to calm down, I asked, "What do you mean, wrong?"

He laid back in his sun lounger and took a long pull. He didn't seem like he was about to say more, so I prodded him with, "What's wrong with the case?"

"Everything," he said. "The murder, for example. Why do it there? Why, of all the places on God's Earth, pick a room in full view of the hotel reception desk staff, during a company junket, on an island? It narrows down the suspect list to virtually no-one. It increases the chances of being spotted to almost certain. It decreases the window of opportunity to practically nothing and makes the time of death easy to calculate. If this was a premeditated killing, the murderer must have been a complete drongo because there must have been a thousand better times and places to kill "Harry Cross.""

Of course, we'd had this conversation before and I'd gone through the same thoughts myself, over and over. "A crime of passion would make much more sense," I said. "Except for the fact the killer stole a knife from the restaurant and took it to the meeting room to stab Harry." A stupidly obvious thought struck me. "Unless…"

Ronnie sat up and said, "Go on."

"Unless it was a bit of both. Something upset someone while they were all on the island, not before. That person determined there and then to kill Harry. They took the first weapon they saw – the knife – and then did the deed at the first opportunity that presented itself."

He didn't laugh or scoff. He went still, thinking about it. Eventually, he said, "We need to know who said what to who at the restaurant the night before the murder. Someone confessed something to the killer, or they let something slip. A secret about Harry, perhaps."

I could see already that, while this made a lot of sense, it didn't get us much closer to a solution. In fact, it opened up a world of extra interviews and investigation about what might have happened at dinner that night. And, with the family not speaking to us anymore, our prime suspects were out of bounds. Of course, the police might do the work for us. I was sure Bertolissio at least would see the need. But with the family lawyering up, they might not get very far.

"And all this stuff with the fascist senator, and the bikies, and organised crime connections, and a secret plot between Richard and Aikenhead, and Claudia Knecht and Cassandra, and everything else we've found, is all just a steaming heap of red herrings?"

Ronnie scowled at his stubbie, still deep in thought.

"Not everything," he said after a while. "Not Death's Head Guy."

"Thackery? What do you mean?"

"I mean, whoever set Thackery on us is either the murderer, or they know who is."

"All right," I said, cautiously, not sure how this was a revelation since it's what we'd thought from the beginning.

"There are only two people in the family who we can be sure could have known Thackery: Jennifer and Cassandra."

"And they both have alibis. So…" But I began to see where he was going.

Ronnie finished my sentence. "So neither of them committed the murder. But, it was someone they loved. Someone they were eager to protect. Someone they were willing to commit crimes for – like having you beaten up and maybe killed."

"Richard."

"Who else could it be?"

"He's just about the only person on the island that day who didn't have a good alibi. In fact, it's always bugged me that he didn't seem to remember all the tree felling going on near him that day, which is pretty suss."

Ronnie waved that away as if it was an annoying mozzie. "We don't have a real good motive, though."

"Unless somebody said something to him at the dinner the night before that set him off." Ronnie pulled a face, probably thinking how hard that would be to establish. "Jennifer said we were trying to fit up Richard for the murder. She seemed very protective, even though she doesn't like him for some reason."

That evoked a thoughtful nod from Ronnie. "It's probably Jenny who hired Thackery. If the killer is Richard, Thackery's paymaster is Jenny. She's trying to protect her remaining son."

"Even though he killed Harry? Wouldn't Cassandra be a better bet? She might even have put Richard up to it. God knows she had plenty of motive. And, after that, she'd have a vested interest in keeping him out of jail. Also, just because Jennifer thinks we're after Richard, doesn't mean she thinks he did it."

"But it still means she'd try and protect him."

I liked my Cassandra theory better, even though it did hang on them having conspired to murder Harry. "Don't you think it was odd that Cassandra lawyered up so quickly?"

"You think that suggests guilt? What if it just means she feels helpless and vulnerable?"

I'd been leaning forward, eager and excited but suddenly the wind went out of my sails. I flopped back and sucked on the bottle. "All right. We can't tell which of them it is. How do we find Megan?" I checked my phone. It was nearly eleven o'clock but I couldn't imagine sleeping that night. On impulse, I called Noah. It took him several rings to answer.

"Luke?"

"Sorry to bother you at home but something's come up. Did I wake you? Is Harper with you?"

There was a pause, probably while they decided whether to say yes or no.

"Yeah, she's here? What's up?"

I explained quickly about Megan's abduction.

"Holy crap! What can we do?"

"Nothing. It's OK. I just want to know what you two found out today about Richard Cross. It looks like he's just become our prime suspect for the murder."

"You think he took Megan?"

"No. Look, it's complicated. Thackery took Megan. We don't know why but we need more information to help us understand it. So, Richard Cross…"

"Right. Yeah. Hang on."

I heard a muffled conversation between Noah and Harper. After a while, Harper said, "You're on speaker, Luke. Is Ronnie there too?"

I put my phone on speaker and Ronnie said, "Hi, Harper. Do you want to put some clothes on, or are you OK talking naked?"

I was horrified but Harper just laughed. "In your dreams, you old perv. What do you two want to know?"

Ronnie took over the conversation, as he usually did. "What was the connection between Richard Cross and Vincent Aikenhead for a start. Did you find anything at all?"

"Nothing conclusive," Noah said.

"They're lovers," said Harper.

I looked at Ronnie and he at me.

"We don't know that," said Noah.

"Aw come on. We've got pictures of them together all over Sydney, they often stayed at the same hotel for various functions, and, here's the cincher, they were in Sydney together for the Gay Mardi Gras. We haven't got pictures of Aikenhead in leather shorts or anything but the man and his company are frequent donors to LGBTQ causes and he was an outspoken supporter during the gay marriage campaign. I don't think he's out or anything but he might as well be."

"Just because he—" I began but Ronnie spoke over me.

"Good work, kids. Enjoy the rest of your night." He signed for me to hang up.

"Wait a minute," Harper said. "Isn't there anything we can do about Megan?"

"Not tonight," said Ronnie. "You've been very helpful. Thanks." He signed again, more forcefully.

"Yeah, thanks, guys," I said. "See you tomorrow."

"So," said Ronnie. "I was right. It's Jenny."

I forced myself not to object that I'd said it was Jenny all along and he'd done nothing but argue. Instead, I tried to stay on topic.

"Wait a minute. You're saying that because now you think Richard couldn't be having an affair with Cassandra? What if he's bi? What if they're just really close friends?"

"It's Jenny." His tone said that was final. "She sent Thackery and I reckon she knows exactly where Megan is."

The evening had grown cold as it edged into night and I was vaguely feeling the need for a jacket. But I didn't want to break the flow of the discussion. It was the first time in ages I felt we were actually getting somewhere with understanding the case. I tried to summarise what we now thought we knew.

"So, Richard finds out something about Harry at the

dinner on Murdock Island and decides there and then to kill him. He grabs a knife and makes his plans. He knows Harry will be alone before the wrap-up meeting the next day when he'll be rehearsing his speech to the staff. So, when the time comes, he sneaks down to the hotel, somehow slips past the staff and any witnesses, stabs his brother, then sneaks back to his chalet, also without being seen."

"When you put it like that…"

"I know. It sounds impossible. But somebody did exactly that, so why not Richard?" Ronnie gave a shrug of acquiescence so I went on. "He doesn't have to dispose of a murder weapon because it's still in Harry's chest. All he has to do is give it a wipe, wash off any blood on his hands and clothes and he's home and dry. He then waits for someone to come and break the news, goes to look at the body and then disappears into Cassandra's chalet until they can all go home. And maybe he did that because he hates his mother or maybe it was because Jennifer might be the only person there who could look into his eyes and know what he'd done."

"Because Mother always knows your secrets. Nice one. But I reckon it's simpler than that. His mother probably knew he was a poofter and hated him for it. His brother too. It wouldn't sit well with their notions of Aryan purity or whatever crap they believed."

"You can't say 'poofter' any more."

"What would you call it?"

"Gay."

"And what's the difference?"

"You know the difference."

"Freedom of speech?"

I clenched my jaw in frustration. "Do you really believe everyone has a right to be a bigot, or are you just winding me up? 'Cause, if it's the former, you're no better than Harry Cross and the neo-Nazi trash he supported. And, if it's the latter, I don't think that scoring cheap points at the expense of entire oppressed minorities is a fit pastime for a supposed grown-up."

His wicked grin told me all I needed to know.

"It's fucking difficult working with you, you know. It's like… I don't know what it's like. I've never had to deal with anyone who thinks it's fun to be so bloody obnoxious all the bloody time – even when we're trying to save Megan's life. You do remember that that's what we're trying to do here?"

He looked at me with a steady, serious gaze. God knows what he was thinking. I hoped he was re-calculating his estimate of just how far he could push me.

"OK," he said. "You're right. I'm sorry. Carry on. You were just about to get to the best part."

"The best part?"

"Where you explain why Richard talked Aikenhead into re-opening the case. After a year, it was pretty obvious he'd got away with it. So why start it up again?"

"I thought you agreed it was Richard?"

"All we agreed was that Jennifer or Cassandra are the only ones we know *might* have an acquaintance with Thackery, they probably didn't do the murder because they have alibis, so, if one of them hired Thackery, it's probably to protect someone. Richard is the only reasonable candidate – even though he has no motive and we've got no particular reason to suspect him. And I reckon it's Jennifer who's trying to have us killed because she's Richard's mother, she thinks we're out to get her son and there's good reason to believe Richard isn't getting his rocks off with his sister-in-law."

"Jeez," I said, feeling disheartened all over again. "Talk

about coming at the thing sideways."

"I told you, there's something wrong with this case."

"But," I said and I had a feeling I was clutching at straws, "you definitely think Jenny is the one pulling Thackery's strings. So that's who we need to go see to get Megan back."

"Definitely."

"What?" I had been so sure he'd give me some more hedging and prevarication, that I wasn't ready for the certainty of his response.

"I say we go out there tonight." He glanced at his watch. "Order in some food. I'm starving. We'll eat and then go out to the farm."

"You think she's there?"

"Where else would she be?"

It caught me off guard. "I – I don't know. Thackery's place?"

"The cops will have gone straight there. Same with the Devil's Playthings clubhouse. They won't make the connection with Jennifer Cross though."

"So we should tell them."

"Yeah, nah. Jennifer Cross isn't some scumbag bikie whose civil rights can be trampled on at DI Reid's pleasure. She's part of one of the richest families in the State and Reid is up for promotion. Involving the QPS in a lawsuit would not be his wisest move just now. Even if he thought it was, I can't see how he could persuade a judge to give him a search warrant on the massive lack of evidence we can give him. No, it looks like we're going to be doing some of what you call my 'special forces shit'. I.e. going out there and taking a look, then calling the cops if we actually find anything."

I stood up, eager to get on with it. "We can get you a Maccas on the way. Come on."

"Hold your horses, Padawan. Let's give them all time to get into bed and fall asleep before we go tramping around the place. Farmers have guns, don't forget. And, if Megan is there, Thackery and his mates might be standing watch. I'd rather they fell asleep at their posts than that we turned up while they're all freshly coked up."

It made some kind of sense, I supposed, but the idea of Megan being in the hands of those people a second longer than necessary, made my stomach knot. I sat down again and pulled out my phone.

"Chinese," Ronnie said, anticipating my next question.

Chapter Twenty-One

As we drew closer to the farm, the peaceful protest in my stomach gradually became more strident until it became a full-scale riot. Ronnie was right, I should have eaten. It would have given my gastric juices something to do other than burn holes in my guts. *Next time listen to the old bastard*, I told myself.

"At least the car's quiet," I said, thinking aloud. "You'd think armed forces would consider that when they buy Jeeps, or Humvees, or whatever they call them now."

He didn't respond.

"I mean, why go roaring around with a massive diesel engine hammering away and pouring out smoke, when you could just sneak around in an electric vehicle and surprise the enemy?"

"Mate, shut the fuck up."

"You know, it wouldn't hurt you to be a bit, I don't know, compassionate, or something. We can't all be battle-hardened veterans. Yeah, maybe I babble a bit when I'm nervous. Would it be so difficult just to humour me? Even once?"

He pursed his lips, angrily. "Mate, I look at you and I think, 'Why has no-one hit this bloke with a shovel yet?'"

We travelled in silence for a while. It was about two A.M. and we hadn't seen another vehicle since we left the main road. I was driving and Ronnie was navigating. He reckoned he'd found a way to get us close to the house without going through the main gate. That meant us weaving along single-lane roads – some just dirt roads – with no street lights and sudden, unmarked turns. The constant danger of driving into a ditch, or a tree, or a roo, was wearing me out but I resisted the urge to keep asking Ronnie if there was much farther to go.

"Why did Thackery take Megan?" I asked. I didn't think Ronnie would know but the question just kept echoing in my head.

"That again?"

"Does it make even a little bit of sense to you? If you were on a mission to kill a couple of blokes and some stray woman turned up, would you just grab her and run?"

"No but I'm not some dumb fuck with swastikas tattooed on my face."

"So, you're saying he just panicked and did the first thing he thought of?"

"All I'm saying is he had the choice to kill her on the spot – which would have probably ruined his chance to surprise us – let her go and run – which means she could tell us all about our surprise visitor – or take her with him and work out what to do with her later."

I mulled the options. It was a while before I realised that Ronnie had implied he wouldn't have taken her, meaning he'd have let her go or killed her. I resisted asking him which it would have been. As so often with such questions, I wasn't sure I wanted to know the answer.

"So, he takes her," I said, still worrying at the same bone. "He sticks her in his van, ties her up, probably, and drives off. Then what? As you said, he can't go home or to the clubhouse, because the cops are looking for him." I didn't like where my own thoughts were going. I swallowed hard and kept straight on. "Why would he bring her out here to Jennifer Cross? It would have been a lot easier to finisher off and stick her down a gully in the bush somewhere."

Ronnie was silent for a long time. When he spoke, his tone was unusually soft. "You're right. He should have just killed her and dumped the body. I'm sorry. The most likely outcome of this night is that we won't find anything at the farm. But there's two possibilities that give me hope. The first is that he probably questioned Megan and she told him everything she knows about our investigation."

"What? How does that help? She doesn't know anything."

"Yes, she does. I filled her in when she came to the office. Then you told her about it when she came round. Remember? And one of the things you told her was—"

"That we thought Jennifer Cross had hired Thackery!" God, I was so stupid! I hadn't even remembered that Thackery didn't know who was paying him. He thought it was a bloke called Angus Hudson. The only way he'd possibly know about Jennifer Cross would be if Megan had told him.

"Jeez, I hope you're right."

"Me too. But, if she told him – and why wouldn't she? – I reckon he'd want to sheet the whole problem straight off to Jenny. The way he'd see it is, Jenny Cross got him into that mess, she has more money than God, and, if she wants it cleared up, she is going to pay through the nose. Never mind twenty-K for a killing – or whatever he was getting from her – knowing who'd secretly hired him would add a couple more zeroes, easy. And double that for disposing of the girl. And double it again for him disappearing and keeping his mouth shut."

"If Megan told him. Otherwise, this trip is all for nothing."

"Yeah, nah. She told him all right. I have a lot of time for Megan but, tied up in a van with a two hundred pound gorilla, she's going to answer any questions he asks."

I tensed up so much I almost drove us off the road. "I'm going to kill that bastard." Ronnie didn't say anything and it made me feel silly and childish. "All right. But I'm going to lock him up. I can do that."

"And Jenny," Ronnie added. "And whoever killed Harry Cross."

* * * *

We pulled in at a farm gate on a dirt road. Ronnie studied his phone for a minute then put it away.

"Right-o," he said. "Through that gate and over that hill. We're about a kilometre from the main house. No talking once we crest the hill. All right?"

I nodded my agreement. I got out of the car and fetched our packs from the back seat. We'd made a stop at the office to pick up some surveillance equipment – a parabolic mic, some binoculars, some little radio mics we could stick to windows, a little periscope with a flexible tube, and so on. I'd bought most of this stuff a couple of years ago when I first set up the company, along with digital recorders, bullet-proof vests, walkie talkies, passive and active bugs, cameras with four hundred mm lenses... anything that seemed like cool "spy stuff". At the time, it made me feel like I was gearing up for a big and exciting adventure. The reality was that nobody in the company used any of it much – or at all, if truth be told – except the cameras. So it had just been sitting in the storeroom all this time – until now.

"I hope Noah's been keeping this stuff charged," I said, handing a pack to Ronnie. It hadn't occurred to me to wonder until that moment. As our resident sparky, Noah had been given the job of making sure all the electronic gear stayed in working order.

"I checked everything as I packed it." Ronnie sounded irritated. "You need to get your head in the game, mate. This could be dangerous. Thackery was a big enough worry before there were millions of bucks at stake. As for Jenny, don't think graceful old GILF, think lioness protecting her cub."

"GILF?" I asked. "Is that, like, a military term?"

He looked at me as if to check I wasn't joking. "Google it when we get back," he said.

We trudged off across the field, climbing the low hill in silence. It was a clear, cool night. There was no Moon but the Milky Way stretched in a broad swath of silver across the whole sky, giving us plenty of light to see by. Even so, the ground was bumpy and treacherous and I stumbled more than once. It took us about ten minutes to reach the brow of the hill. Ronnie signed for us to get down as the farm house came into view. He crawled forward, with me following suit, until we had a clear view of the whole complex.

He took off his backpack and pulled out a pair of binoculars, so I did the same. The farm buildings were lit up by security lights and the whole thing had a surreal appearance, as if we were looking down on a model farm in a shop window display. The farmhouse itself was a big, sprawling affair with a large two-storey main building and a couple of T-shaped single-storey wings that had probably been tacked on later. The house faced away from us. There were paddocks and a large dam in front of the house with a sprinkling of small sheds and animal houses around them. On our side of the house, at the back, were a couple of very large sheds and, to one side a concrete apron against one wall of a truly massive shed. There were several vehicles sprinkled around the site – tractors, quad bikes, cars and utes. On the gravel apron in front of the main house were two, very interesting vehicles. One was a rather smart silver Jaguar XJ – a luxurious electric model I'd been coveting for some time. The other was a black van.

"He's here!" I said, a little too loudly.

Ronnie hissed back at me like an angry cat. "I told you no talking."

Whispering back, I said, "But the van, look."

"I can see the fucking van."

I didn't care how rude he was, I was too elated to care. Thackery was there. Maybe Megan was there too. I scanned the rest of the buildings. Where would they put her? In the main house? In one of the outbuildings? Or was she still in the van? The thought of her tied up in the corner of some stinking animal shed made the binoculars tremble in my clenched fingers.

"We need to get down there."

"Just—" He turned on me angrily but immediately softened. "Relax. If she's there, we'll get her out. Have you got a phone signal?"

I pulled out my phone. I had one bar of 4G. "Just."

"Call Bertolissio. Tell her where we are and to send the troops. Tell her Thackery is here with at least three of his bikie friends and we suspect they're holding Megan, too." He hesitated. "Tell her we might need an ambulance. Don't let her talk you into waiting in the car."

"What do you mean? Where's his three mates?"

"I don't know, but there are three motorbikes parked over

by that shed." I followed the direction he pointed in and wondered how I could have missed three stonking great bikes standing out in the open like that.

"And that's why we don't go rushing down there," he said. "Make the call."

I scrambled back down the hill a way so no-one at the farm could see the light from my phone. I made the call to Bertolissio on her private number. She didn't give me a hard time about how it was after two, or about waking her up. She just listened to what I had to say and told me to go back to the car and wait for her to arrive. In my turn, I didn't waste time arguing with her but just asked her to hurry. Even if she thought I might do as she asked, she surely didn't imagine that Ronnie would.

I rejoined Ronnie. "What's the plan?"

"We go to the bikes first and disable them. Then we do a quick tour of the sheds and try to get a good angle on the house to see what's going on in there and where everybody is."

"What about the van?"

"What about it?"

"What if Megan's in there?"

"It's too hard to get to. You'd be seen from the house."

"Maybe not."

"And maybe you would. Do you want to face four or more bikies with guns? 'Cause I can't see how getting yourself killed helps Megan."

"I'd be careful."

"Look, why don't you just stay here and keep an eye on things? I'll do the recce and you can be overwatch. I'll take a radio and you can tell me if anyone starts looking around."

"No, I'm coming. Did you bring your gun?"

"No, I didn't! We're not shooting anybody."

"But you said they'd have guns."

"Yes, they will. And if they point one at you, you put up your arms and surrender, right? The cops will be here in an hour, hour and a half tops. Our main objective is to stay alive until they get here. Secondary objective is to find where Megan is. Tertiary, gather any fresh evidence we can in the Harry Cross case."

"But surely—"

"Luke, we can only help Megan if we stay alive. You can see that, right?"

I screwed up my eyes in frustration. "All right. We'll do it your way. But what if she is in the van?"

"We'll figure it out when we get down there. Come on. Stay low until we're well down from the crest of the hill, otherwise we're too easy to spot from the house."

He crawled forward with me behind him for about twenty metres before getting up into a crouch and running. He'd just come fully upright when all hell broke loose to our right. At first it just seemed like a bedlam of screaming and shouting and drumbeats. Ronnie grabbed my arm and pulled me to the ground.

"Fucking cows!" he hissed. "Lie still."

It was only then I realised we'd practically run into a herd of cattle. The beasts were blacker than the night itself and were now bellowing and running about like the Devil himself was chasing them. Luckily, they were all running away from us because I was feeling very vulnerable lying there in the middle of a field with crazed, half-tonne animals pounding the earth with their hooves.

A couple of dogs joined in the commotion, their violent barking coming from one of the sheds at the side of the house. A door opened at the back of the house and two men walked out into the yard. They held torches and flicked the beams left and right as they looked for whatever had spooked the cattle. We were too far away for the torchlight to reach but we lay utterly still as they paced back and forth, probing the darkness. Jennifer Cross appeared in the doorway and for a while, she too peered into the night.

"Probably just a dog," she called out to the two men. "If you see one, shoot the damned thing. Ours are all chained up."

Good to know, I thought.

The commotion from the cattle had subsided, only the dogs kept up their shouting. The men gave up their ineffectual search and went back to the house. However, they shared an inaudible conversation and only one went back inside. The other pulled a gun from his waistband and set off round the house, looking for intruders.

Ronnie nudged me. "I'm going after that one," he said. "You get to those bikes and slash their tyres. Let me see your knife."

"What knife?"

"You didn't bring a knife?"

I started to protest but he put up a hand to silence me. From somewhere, he produced a nasty looking blade. It was short and fat, sharp on both edges, with a narrow, curved handle. I took it from him carefully. It looked horribly cruel.

"Front wheels. Through the side wall. One quick stab," he said. "You'll hear the air coming out. Try not to knock the bikes over." I glared at him in silence. "When you're done, signal me on the radio." He held up his walkie talkie. "Two presses on the speak button, like this." He pressed his button twice, rapidly, and my handset made two quick hisses. "Then meet me at that shed over there." He pointed and I nodded.

Without another word, he rolled away from me, got to his feet and ran off across the field. I watched him for a moment, astonished at how fit and strong he was for a man who looked like such an old wreck, then I also got up and headed across the field, vectoring away from Ronnie towards the right-hand wing of the house.

I could see the bikes and there were no obvious obstacles between me and them. Except, I suddenly realised, there must be a fence, something to keep the cattle away from the house. I stopped. I couldn't see a fence at all. I looked across at where Ronnie must be but he had vanished into the darkness. I edged forward. Surely I'd see a fence before I walked into it. The lights on all around the house would reveal it, even if the starlight wasn't enough. I heard a snort behind me and almost fell over spinning round to see what it was. About five metres away was the enormous black bulk of a cow, its wet nose glistening in the dim light, its eyes two tiny points of light. There was a shuffling and huffing behind it and I realised there was a small mob of them sizing me up. I stepped back from them and they shuffled forward.

Now, I'm a city boy and the closest I'd ever come to a whole cow was the giant slab of scorched meat my dad would wrestle with on our Australia Day barbie. However, I knew a few things about cattle that I'd picked up from books. One is that this herd was either a dairy herd, in which case it was full of gentle, curious souls who just wanted to get a closer look at me, or it was a beef herd, in which case it was full of steers, castrated bulls who were also likely to be sweet-natured critters. The only thing I really had to worry about were so-called intact bulls. They might not be quite so forgiving of strange humans wandering around in their field at night. The urge to turn on my torch and take a peek between the animal's legs was almost irresistible.

I also knew that the best thing to do was to be bold and confident and shoo them away, just like a farmer would. But that was out of the question. The next best thing was to avert my eyes and make myself look small and non-threatening. It was tempting but I had to get to those bikes and then find Megan. I couldn't stand in a field all night appeasing a bunch of cattle.

I turned and ran. I ran full pelt. It took the cattle a moment to realise what had happened but then they lumbered into motion after me. Heart pounding louder than the hooves behind me, I headed straight for the house, reckoning that was the shortest distance to the fence. At great risk of stumbling on the rough ground, I looked over my shoulder. About a dozen of the monsters were chasing me and, very obviously, going a hell of a lot faster than I was. I'd be trampled to death in just a few seconds.

Some part of my brain registered the fence. Or, rather, not a fence but some kind of diabolical trip-wire, a single strand of glinting metal at about knee height. There was no avoiding it. Even as my conscious mind caught up with the danger my eyes had seen, I was leaping as high as I could in the hope of clearing it.

I came down hard at the other side of the wire and tumbled to the ground and down the slope. I looked back at my pursuers. They'd be on top of me in a second. Literally on top of me. But it didn't happen. They all stopped dead at the wire and stood there calmly watching me, huffing through their giant noses and staring with their pinpoint eyes. It was ridiculous. A single strand of fence wire should have been no impediment to those brutes. They should have torn through it like it was cobweb.

An electric fence, my brain said. I breathed again. Their lifelong subjection to electric shocks had trained them to stop rather than take another jolt, even in hot pursuit of me. It was a kind of miracle. I lay in the coarse grass, thanking the gods of farming technology, while my heartbeat slowed and I remembered to get on with my mission.

I realised I was quite close to the house now and ran at a crouch to get away from any eyes at the many back windows. The shed with the bikes parked near it was not far beyond the end of the wing I was following. There were no lights on in that wing and I hoped it was all bedrooms and no-one was in them, or awake if they were.

The bikes were in a tight group. I remembered Ronnie's warning not to knock them over. The clatter from three of these big, heavy machines falling against each other was scary to imagine. They smelled of oil and leather and metal. I shuffled close to the front wheel of the first one. The tyre smelled of rubber. I put a hand on it and it felt hard, imposingly solid. I still had the knife in my other hand. I put the nasty little blade against the wall of the tyre and pushed. The wheel turned a little and the bike rocked alarmingly, but the blade didn't penetrate. I pushed again, harder, and the bike rocked even more, but the knife still didn't go in. I cursed whoever designed those things to teeter on pathetic little kick-stands. If I pushed harder, the bike would topple over for sure. What the hell was I going to do? For a moment, I considered letting down the tyres using the valves. The thought of sitting beside the bikes for however long it would take for the tyres to deflate made me queasy. The idea of Ronnie mocking me for it made me dismiss the idea.

No, I had to stab the tyres, quick and hard. It was the only way to get the knife in. So I stabbed, thrusting the blade as hard and fast as I could. This time it went in. Air came hissing out. Then, with majestic slowness, the whole bike fell sideways. I grabbed at the seat to stop it but the damned thing weighed far more than I did and it simply pulled me over on top if it. On the way down, it hit the bike beside it and that started falling too. That one hit the third and they all ended up in a tangled heap of metal with me spreadeagled across the top of them. The noise was probably not as bad as I'd thought it would be but it was still pretty bad. If I'd decided to dump a tonne of scrap metal on the ground outside the house, it probably wouldn't have been any less noticeable to the people inside.

Within seconds, three men came running from the front of the house. I scrambled to get to my feet and managed to pocket Ronnie's knife as I did so. The three men – one of whom I immediately recognised as Thackery – were armed with guns. Two had pistols and one had a rifle. They didn't waste any time looking around but made a bee-line for their precious bikes. As soon as they saw me, they raised their weapons. I remembered Ronnie once saying the best thing to do when being approached by a man with a pistol was to run. The chances of anyone with a handgun hitting you from any distance other than very, very close, were slim. If the man was running, the chances were zero. Rifles were more accurate but, even so, if the shooter was moving, they would most likely miss. The only weapon I should really fear in that situation, would be a shotgun because the shot spread out after leaving the barrel to form a large bolus that could be lethal at short range and cause injuries at surprisingly long ranges. Accuracy wasn't all that important with a shotgun.

If I'd been Ronnie, no doubt I'd have dashed off into the

darkness with bullets zipping through the air all around me and then circled round to finish off my attackers with a few well-placed kicks or a garrotte. However, I'm not Ronnie. I stood up and raised my hands high over my head. Actually, I remembered belatedly, that was exactly what Ronnie had said I should do just before we split up. The three bikies came up to me, pushed their guns into my face, told me how much I was going to pay for fucking with their rides, knocked me down, kicked me a few times and dragged me back to the house.

Chapter Twenty-Two

"The other one." Jennifer Cross didn't seem surprised to see me standing in her lounge room in the grip of a big man with black ink on every visible scrap of skin and a large pistol in one hand. I'd been in that same room just a dozen hours ago, having an almost civilised chat with the woman. Now, it seemed, I was her prisoner.

And so was Ronnie.

My partner in crime prevention was sitting on a dining chair that had been placed in the middle of the room. His hands were held behind his back with a plastic zip tie and the back of his head was a bloody mess. He looked pale and haggard. He gave me a baleful sideways glance and went back to hanging his head and breathing loudly through his nose.

Apart from Jennifer, who was standing in front of the oversized hearth, the only other person in the room was Richard Cross. He'd been sitting in an armchair when Mr. Body Art dragged me in but had jumped up in alarm at the sight of me. As I glared at him, he sat down again and put his head in his hands.

"Where's Megan?" I demanded. "Why isn't she here?"

Jennifer spoke to Mr. Body Art. "Bring our new guest a chair, would you, and make sure he's comfortable."

Body Art dragged me with him to the dining table, dragged me and a chair back to where Ronnie sat, and plonked me in it.

"Aren't you going to tie his hands?" Jennifer asked.

"Jase's got the ties," Body Art said, defensively.

"Where's Megan?" I said again, more loudly.

Body Art cracked me across the side of my face with his open hand saying, "Shut the fuck up."

"Megan's safe," Ronnie said. "For now. Mrs. Cross was just in the process of negotiating with her bikie friends how much to pay to make us all disappear. I think you turning up just doubled the price again."

Body Art snickered. Richard made a groaning noise which seemed to enrage Jennifer.

"And you can shut up, too," she said, turning on him. "This is all your fault. All of it."

Richard looked up angrily. "I didn't tell you to go and hire a bunch of criminals. I didn't tell you to go around kidnapping people. For God's sake, Mother, what were you thinking?"

Jennifer threw up a hand and stalked across the room. "I'm not going to go over all this again. You know why I did it. I think gratitude would be more appropriate than whining and recriminations. Take some bloody responsibility for once in your life. God, I wish your brother was alive!"

"Instead of me? I bet you do, you old hag!"

"How dare you?"

She looked like she was going to fly at him and beat the crap out of him but, at that moment, the door opened and Thackery and Jase came in. Thackery looked around the room as if he was checking that no-one had run off.

"I need a tie," Body Art said and Jase went to hand him

one. As he fitted the plastic ring around my wrists and pulled it so tight I winced, Thackery walked up to Jennifer and sneered in her face.

"The price just went up, Grandma."

Jennifer, almost as tall as he was, glared back into his eyes. Her expression said, "Fuck you," but she didn't actually say it, and Thackery took that as acquiescence.

"Thackery," I said. "Where's Megan?"

He turned to me with a grin. He was clearly feeling fully in control of the situation.

"You mean the cute chick with all the black hair and the nice tits?"

I felt a coldness in my stomach. There was something in his tone and expression that scared me. "If you've hurt her…"

I got another backhander from Body Art that made my right ear ring like a bell. Ronnie's knife was in the back pocket of my jeans. I used the pretence of cowering from another blow to start fishing it out.

"Stop that," Jennifer said, meaning the hitting me, I hoped. "Let's get this deal done so you can all get out of my house."

Thackery sent his two mates outside to, "make sure there's no other fuckers creeping around," and went to sit down with Jennifer to talk terms. Richard went back to holding his head. No-one was watching me or Ronnie. I managed to pull the knife free of my pocket easily enough, but turning it and pressing the blade against the plastic tie hard enough to cut it was really tricky and took a long time. By the time I finally severed the tie, Thackery was standing up again, saying, "As soon as you make the transfer, we go, and you'll never see us again,"

Unfortunately, the tie came apart with a loud snick! I froze. Thackery looked sharply at me. I looked back, arms behind my back, pretending I was still tied. Nothing to see here. But his eyes went to the floor under my chair where, no doubt, the plastic tie was plainly visible where it had fallen. His eyes flicked back to mine again and he reached for his gun.

I needed Ronnie.

In a clumsy, sideways lurch, I threw myself off the chair and grabbed Ronnie's wrist tie with one hand as I sliced it with the knife.

"Stop!" Thackery shouted. I couldn't see him but that gun must have been pointed straight at me by then.

"Oh my God!" I heard Jennifer cry and then there was a massive explosion.

Richard screamed, "No!"

I swear I felt the bullet tear through the air just above me. It should have torn through Ronnie, too, except he was no longer there. I looked and found him on the ground nearby. He'd rolled off his chair and pulled it along with him. To my astonishment he heaved the chair, from a half-sitting position, up into the air and towards Thackery. It was a pretty good throw, too. It didn't hit him, or even reach him, smashing to the ground at Jennifer's feet, but it made him step back and stop shooting and the racket Jennifer was making was a great distraction. Richard had also jumped to his feet and was shouting at Thackery. It gave Ronnie the chance to get to his feet and charge at the big bikie.

I got up, too. I still had the knife in my hand. If I could get to Thackery before he shot someone, maybe I could do something to stop him. I ran at him, yelling in a kind of wild, wordless frenzy. He looked away from the silent but much more dangerous Ronnie and swung his arm and the gun towards me, the one making all the noise. He fired too soon and the bullet went smashing into a glass cabinet far behind me.

I was a couple of paces behind Ronnie and I could see all his moves as he closed on the bikie. Ronnie's right hand was across his own chest, fist clenched, like he was an American about to sing an anthem. As he neared Thackery, the arm swung out and Ronnie's knuckles connected with the back of Thackery's gun hand. The gun flew from the bikie's stunned fingers. But that wasn't the end of the manoeuvre. Ronnie opened the fist that had struck Thackery's hand and pushed it hard towards the big man's throat, striking him just below the jaw as Ronnie stepped past him, moving his leg behind Thackery's legs. Disarmed, choking and now off-balance, Thackery toppled over Ronnie's leg and was forced to the floor by my friend's relentless thrust against his throat. His head hit the floor with a sickening bang.

Which was actually really cool to watch, believe it or not. Ronnie had been incredibly fast and accurate. It had been like watching a virtuoso musician doing impossible things on their instrument. Which made Ronnie a sort of virtuoso of violence. Which was also cool, except his impressive take-down had left a big void where Thackery had been standing just a moment before. I charged into the void, unable to stop myself, tripped over Thackery's legs and, saints be praised, collided with the big, overstuffed armchair Jennifer Cross had been sitting in.

I scrambled to my feet, a bit dazed. Thackery was out cold on the floor. Ronnie was still kneeling beside him, checking the bikie's pulse. Jennifer Cross was actually struggling to get to Ronnie but was being held from behind by her son. The door opened and Jase and Body Art tumbled in, guns ready. They stopped dead, astonished by what they saw. Still running on some kind of adrenal jet fuel, I dived for the gun that Thackery had dropped. Somehow, I fumbled it into a two-handed grip, aiming at the two bikies.

"Don't move! Drop your guns!" I shouted. The gun went off, shocking me as much as it shocked my two targets. The shot went over their heads, splintering the lintel over the door. "The next one's in your chest!" I yelled, as if I'd meant to do that. They both threw down their weapons like they were burning their hands. I almost sobbed with relief. Ronnie stepped up from behind me and took the gun from my trembling fingers.

"Jase," he said, quite calmly. "Would you zip-tie your friend – hands and feet – and then do the same for Sleeping Beauty here?" He meant Thackery. "Then do your own feet. Got it?" Jase nodded and pulled out his bundle of ties. "Nice and tight, now. I'll be checking your work. Luke, would you pick up those guns, please? We don't want anyone getting silly notions. You know I don't like shooting people."

I was still on the ground. I got up and went to collect the rifle and handgun that the bikies had tossed. I didn't feel quite right, sort of giddy, and everything sounded a bit distant and echoey. *Just shock*, I told myself. *The after-effects of the adrenaline.* But my heart was still hammering in my chest and showed no signs of slowing. I suddenly remembered Ronnie's knife and looked behind me. It was sticking into the back of the armchair I'd landed in. My legs were wobbly and I needed to sit down. I took the weapons to the dining table and put them on its bright, polished surface. I pulled out one of the dining chairs and sat down heavily.

Ronnie was finishing off tying up the crims we'd bagged,

tightening Jase's ties and adding one to Jase's own wrists. Jennifer Cross and her son were having a heated argument in hushed voices. That is, Jennifer was exhorting him to do something to save himself and Richard was telling her it was all over and she should just calm down and tell the truth.

"Right-o," said Ronnie, getting up after tightening his last tie. "Youse two, shut the fuck up."

He had the gun in his hand again and I suppose it added a bit of weight to what he was saying. Richard and Jennifer stopped arguing and turned to face him.

"You vile little man!" Jennifer said. It seemed gratuitous but I could see why she'd be upset.

"Yeah," said Ronnie, drawing out the syllable. "I've been called worse. Look, you're both under arrest."

"Who do you think you are?" Jennifer sneered. "You can't arrest us. You're not a cop. You're nobody."

"Any citizen can make an arrest," I said from my fuzzy isolation at the far end of the huge room. They all turned to look at me. "Everyone has the same powers as the cops in that regard, except cops can arrest you on suspicion of committing a crime. The rest of us have to actually witness one being committed."

Ronnie gave me a small frown. It shook my confidence. I thought about getting my phone out to google "citizen's arrest" and check my facts. But I found I was more interested in what Ronnie was saying.

"Before the cops get here, I've got just one question I'd like you to answer: which one of you two was it that killed Harry Cross?"

"Mum, don't say a word," said Richard. "I'll call the lawyers. Don't tell them anything until they arrive."

He pulled a phone out from his packet but Ronnie waved

the gun at him and said, "Put that thing away. We've got enough crooks and scumbags in this room without you bringing lawyers here. Look, just tell me. It's all going to come out now. We've got you on kidnapping, conspiracy to obstruct the course of justice… a dozen charges, easy. And don't think your friends on the floor are going to keep quiet when the cops start applying the thumb screws."

"Mum," Richard said in a warning tone. "Don't say anything."

Jennifer looked at him and tears welled in her eyes. "No, he's right. This whole awful thing is over. Don't you want it to be over Richard? Hasn't a year of this been enough?"

Richard took her by the shoulders. "Please, Mum. Don't tell them."

She stepped back from him, her expression hardening. "You always were a weakling. Harry was worth ten of you, you bloody queer."

Richard recoiled but he kept trying to persuade her. "Mum, think about what you're doing."

Jennifer straightened her shoulders and lifted her chin. She turned to Ronnie. "Richard did it." He killed my son."

"What?" Richard's amazement sounded completely genuine. "What the hell are you talking about. I didn't kill Harry. I always thought…"

Now it was Jennifer's turn to be amazed. "What? You're saying I did it? You're saying I killed my own precious son?" She shook her head vigorously. To Ronnie she said. "No, he did it. He murdered his brother."

Richard was growing angry. "What are you trying to do you vicious old hag? You did it. You know you did. Tell them. Do you hate me so much you want to get me locked up for something I didn't do?"

"Me? Why would I kill Harry? I loved him. You were the jealous one. You were the one who couldn't stand that he had everything you didn't."

Ronnie looked over at me. My head was clearing and the weakness that had overwhelmed me was passing. I got up and walked back towards the three of them. As I did, I noticed someone on the staircase. I looked up at her and so did Ronnie. After a while, so did Jennifer and Richard.

"Mother?" Jennifer said. "Whey aren't you in bed? Where's the nurse?"

The old lady in her white nightie and wild hair didn't answer. She just kept looking down at us, her face slack.

"Gran?" Richard asked. "Are you OK?"

The old lady shook her head. "What a family," she said. She fixated on Ronnie. "You're that cop."

"I'm an ex-cop," he said. "We did talk a few days ago."

"I did it," the old lady said. Just like that. "I killed Harry. I stabbed him while we were on that island, with a knife from the kitchen. I used to be a nurse, you know. Long time ago. So I knew just where to find his shrivelled little heart."

"What?" I think all four of us might have said it at the same time.

"The Asian bitch is hiding in a cupboard upstairs," the old lady said. "Panicked when she heard the shooting." She turned and started walking with painful slowness back up the stairs.

"Excuse me," said Ronnie. She stopped and turned to look at him. "If you killed your grandson, why did you do it?"

"It was the children. Cassie told me at dinner. Harry had started bashing them too. She couldn't stop him, she said. Useless cow. Well I could stop him. And I did. That boy was a bad 'un. Always was."

With that, she carried on up the stairs. No-one spoke. No-one tried to stop her. Richard and his mother exchanged looks that were hollows filled with guilt and horror.

"Fucking hell," said Ronnie. "What a case."

I don't think anyone there had any doubt that the old lady's confession was true. I certainly didn't. So, that was it. Case closed. I felt no sense of triumph at the revelation, just an emptiness, like the book we'd all been reading from had finally closed but I couldn't remember why we'd been reading it or what it was about.

"Where's Megan?" I asked.

"Outside in the van," Ronnie said. "I heard them say she's OK."

I ran.

It was almost a day-and-a-half since she'd been taken. Had they kept her in that van all this time? I wanted to go back and stomp all over Thackery. I wished I'd stuck him with Ronnie's knife and not just that ugly old chair.

I threw open the back doors and a man fell on me. It was another bikie. I jumped back in shock and he fell to the ground. I scuttled farther back as he tried to grab me. In the van, I could see Megan. She was sitting on the van's floor, tied up with duct tape. She had a gun in her hands. It was pointing at me.

The bloke on the ground was cursing and getting up. I still had my own gun, so I pointed it at the him and shouted, "Don't move. Stay down." It's all I could think to do while my brain caught up.

Of course there were four bikies. There were three bikes plus the van. One bikie for each. We knew that but, somehow I'd forgotten. God, I'd been stupid. Ronnie too. I looked into the van.

"Megan? What's going on?"

She lowered her gun. There had been tape across her mouth at some stage but she'd pulled it aside and now it hung under her chin. Her eyes were red and swollen with crying. She was pale but her expression was mostly anger. "That one got a bit gropey after they left me with him. I got the gun off him and held him until you got here. As soon as I heard the gunshots, I knew you were here." Her voice broke in a sob. "I kept telling myself you'd come."

I wanted more than anything to run to her and hold her but the creep on the floor was still standing in the way of setting her free. I put my gun in his face and shouted, "Try and take it off me, you bastard. Give me a reason to shoot your fucking head off." His wide-eyed fear was very gratifying. He must have seen that I meant it. I stepped back again, breathing heavily.

"Get up." As he climbed to his feet, arms raised, I said to Megan, "I'm taking this piece of shit to the house. I'll be back in two minutes, I promise." She gave a quick nod. Her eyes said she could probably hang on two minutes but not a second longer.

My prisoner preceded me to the house without any drama and I kept the gun on him while Ronnie tied him up with the others. Jennifer and Richard Cross were sitting far apart and neither spoke nor looked at the other.

"I called Bertolissio just now," Ronnie said. "She's just a few minutes away. There's a SWAT team and an ambulance with them." He glanced at Thackery who was still unconscious.

"He's last in the queue for medical care," I said. I was so full of anger about Megan, I wanted them all to die, all the bikies, Richard and Jennifer, even the old granny. The minute the fourth bikie was secure, I grabbed Ronnie's knife from out of the chair back and rushed out to free Megan.

I cut the duct tape as carefully and gently as I could and peeled it off her. She let me do it in silence. As I worked, her demeanour slowly changed from rigid defiance to a tired relief, to utter physical and emotional exhaustion. I kept up a steady stream of babbled explanations, assurances and endearments. I hardly knew what I was saying. I just wanted her to know she was safe now, that I loved her, and I was so sorry for sending her away that night. When I finally cast aside the knife and held her against me, she was limp and sobbing weakly. She smelled of urine and sweat and it broke my heart. I'd just decided to carry her into the house so she could shower and find some clean clothes – and Jennifer Cross had better not utter one syllable of objection – when the police convoy arrived.

Chapter Twenty-Three

When Ronnie and I walked into the office after lunch the next day, Desi, Harper and Noah stood up and give us a round of applause. The news that the "Genius Detective" had solved the infamous Harry Cross murder had not made the morning papers but it had made the lunchtime TV news and was all over the Web. There had been a crowd of reporters besieging Ronnie's house when we left – after getting just four hours' sleep and a quick breakfast – and they were clogging the entrance to the office building when we arrived. The Building Manager gave us a tight-lipped smile as we walked past the Building Services offices on the way in. No doubt we'd be hearing from her soon about all the inconvenience to the other tenants.

"Tell us all about it," Desi said. Ronnie seemed ready to oblige but I had to dash. I wanted to get to the hospital to sit with Megan. The ambulance paramedics had taken her there after treating her at the farm. They didn't think there was much wrong with her besides exhaustion and dehydration. They seemed far more concerned with Ronnie's head wound and my bruised ribs. They took us both in for scans but it turned out that Ronnie's skull was tougher than the length of wood he'd been hit with, and my ribs were so used to being pummelled by then that they just took the new kicking in their stride. Ronnie did have a sprained thumb from hitting Thackery in the throat so hard.

We'd all got off lightly.

Thomas Thackery, not so much. He'd been rushed into theatre with a fractured skull and brain haemorrhaging. They thought he'd be fine but they needed to operate to relieve the pressure on his brain. The broken bones in Thackery's gun hand were just icing on the cake. The cops asked lots and lots of questions about how it happened but there were plenty of witnesses who all told the same story, so even DI Reid had to let it go in the end. He'd no doubt find some other opportunity one day to lock up me and Ronnie.

Megan had been kept at Princess Alexander hospital for observation. They put her on a drip to help rehydrate her and Bertolissio assured me she'd sent someone to Megan's home to fetch her some clean clothes. Ronnie should have stayed in bed too but they'd have had to fight him to make him stay. So I told them I'd look after him and they let him go.

I'd driven him home from the cop shop against the flow of the morning commuter traffic.

"I should have remembered to warn you about the fourth bikie," he'd said after a long silence.

"Mate, you'd just had your skull bashed in."

"Yeah, even so. I could have got you killed."

"Megan had it all under control." The image of her face, pale and grim in the back of that van would stay with me forever.

"You're not going to do anything stupid, are you?"

"Like what?"

"Like carry on sulking and drive her away."

I gave him a grin. "Not again."

Never, ever again.

"Good, because I hurt too much to give you a thrashing just now."

"What do you mean, you hurt too much? Do I need to take you back to the PA?"

He shook his head and winced. "I mean, all that leaping about and throwing chairs around was a bit more than this old body can take. I need a week in bed. Minimum."

"No worries," I'd said, smiling magnanimously. "Take a few days off. We just cleared our schedule for the next couple of weeks. By the way, You didn't tell me how you got that bump on the noggin."

He looked out the car window and sighed. "You know I went off to track down the bloke on guard duty? Well, I was so busy stalking him, I walked right past another one who stepped up behind me and clonked me. How stupid was that?"

"Pretty damned stupid." I smiled happily, enjoying the rare chance to gloat at Ronnie's incompetence.

"You did…" he'd said, after a long pause, and stopped.

"What did I do?"

"I'm just saying, you did all right. Cutting me free. Charging at that dick like a berserker while he shot at you. Collaring the arsehole in the van. It was all… you know…"

"All what?" I was grinning again, enjoying his discomfort.

"Like, you know, marginally competent."

"Wow, that's really big of you, mate. Of course, I wouldn't have had to rescue you if you hadn't got yourself caught in the first place."

"And you wouldn't have been there, tied to a chair, if you hadn't knocked over all the bikes. What was the last thing I told you before you set off?"

Yeah, I should never have told him about that.

He grinned. "Mate, when I write my memoirs, every section involving you will start with, 'I just looked away for two minutes and he…'"

I grinned too. Of course, neither of us would have been there if I hadn't let Megan get snatched from right under my nose. And that wouldn't have happened if Ronnie hadn't talked her into coming round to see me. Wisely, we had both decided not to go there.

"In the *Nicomachean Ethics*," I had said, my thoughts wandering on to the general problem of making mistakes and avoiding them in the future, "Aristotle said we should—"

Ronnie shut me up with a stream of loud and enthusiastic cursing. When I looked at him, he was still grinning.

"I still can't believe the granny did it," I said.

When I'd told DI Reid during my early morning interrogation, he'd said, "Fuck off. You're telling me that doddery old woman sneaked through a hotel foyer full of people, stabbed her grandson and then sneaked out again with no-one seeing her? She's having you on, mate. What do you reckon, Al?"

Bertolissio had none of his scepticism. "No-one sees old ladies," she'd said. "As women age, they become invisible."

It was as good an explanation as any of us was going to get for how she'd pulled it off.

If she'd been eighteen, I'd have had a good look. That's what Maury Ludgate had said. I had no doubt by then that it was Granny that he'd almost hit with his ute on the day of the murder.

As we pulled into the office car park, I'd said, "Do you suppose she expected to get away with it?"

Ronnie shrugged. "She wiped her prints off the knife."

It had been the tiniest of precautions and yet it had been enough to leave the police – and us – floundering, with no suspects and little evidence.

"She won't go to jail, will she?" I said. Bertolissio had told me the old woman wasn't expected to live more than a few more months. Even if the Crown Prosecution pushed for it, there wouldn't be time to complete a trial.

"Do you mind?" I asked Ronnie.

He thought about it for a long time. "Yes," he said, at last. "Yes, I do,"

"Even though Harry was an evil bastard? Even though she probably saved those two kids from a lifetime of abuse?"

He didn't answer me, just looked out at the parked cars, his jaw stubbornly set.

* * * *

The hospital was a maze and I'd just about decided Megan was lost forever and no-one would ever find her again, when I stumbled on her ward. To my surprise, she was dressed and just about to leave. She was in a public ward and there were people all around us. I'd envisaged a scene where I'd sweep her into my arms and pledge my undying devotion but, instead, I just stood there, awkwardly holding the flowers and chocolates I'd bought from the gift shop.

"Hi," I said.

"Luke."

She offered me a nervous smile.

"Is this the one?" the woman in the next bed asked.

"What? The Genius Detective, fella?" asked another.

"Came riding to her rescue like a knight of old," sighed a third.

"Doesn't really look up to it, does he?"

"I don't know, I've always liked the Guy Pearce type."

"I'm more of a Chris Hemsworth girl, myself. If you know what I mean."

The ward erupted into laughter. Megan was laughing too, although I was feeling a little bit got at. She spoke to the crowd.

"Yes, everybody, this is Luke, who saved my life. Now I'm going to return the favour by getting him out of here before you all embarrass him to death. Bye bye, everyone. It was a pleasure meeting you all."

She took me by the arm and steered me out into the corridor with people shouting "Bye, love," and "Be gentle with him."

We stopped at the nursing station. I put the flowers and chocolates on the counter and asked the nurse there to give them to someone who needed them.

"That'd be me, I reckon," she said and winked to let me know she was joking.

We moved away and stood out of earshot.

"Are you mad at me?" I asked.

"I was, when that big bastard threw me in his van while you sat and sulked just ten metres away." I winced, feeling the justice of the complaint. "But I forgive you."

I nodded. It would be a long time before I could forgive myself.

"It was a miracle I found you," I said, thinking out loud.

She smiled. "The first time you found me was a miracle. This time, I suspect it was a bit of clever detective work."

"Yes, that, but also a miracle."

She was about to speak but I stopped her. "I just have to get this out before the moment's gone and it all seems too melodramatic or something." She waited. I swallowed. "I love you. I knew it the minute Thackery took you. No, I knew it the minute you left me." I realised that was ambiguous. "I mean, the first time. When you went back to your husband." It was her turn to wince. "It's that old don't know what you've got till it's gone, thing. I'm kind of an idiot like that. So, what I want to say is this: I know I'm not much and you're so…" I was choking up, so I cut myself short. "Will you have me back? Please."

With a sob, she threw her arms around me. The nurse behind the desk looked up at us and grinned. Megan sobbed into my chest for so long I began to worry that she hadn't actually answered my question. On the other hand, she'd just been tied up and locked in a van for a day-and-a-half with a bunch of thugs, knowing those might be the last few hours of her life, so I supposed she had the right to a good, cathartic cry.

I was about to suggest I take her home when I heard a voice nearby.

"Luke? Megan?"

Detective Sergeant Alexandra Bertolissio was watching us with her big, intelligent eyes.

"Maybe this isn't the best time…" I began but Bertolissio put up a hand to stop me.

"I'm not here on police business. I just wanted to stop by on my way home to catch Megan up on how things were going."

"On your way home? You mean you've been working ever since I saw you last?"

She smiled. "No rest for the wicked. Especially with you

and Ronnie delivering bad guys to us trussed up like bales of wool. Anyway, this is good. I can bring you both up to speed at the same time."

Megan finally released me and stepped away, her attention was squarely on the smart little detective now, not the scruffy, lanky one.

"Thanks to Luke and Ronnie, we've been able to make a series of arrests. Gloria Foster has been—"

"Who?" I'd never heard the name.

"Harry Cross's grandmother. She's been arrested for her grandson's murder. We also arrested Harry's mother, Jennifer, for… well, a load of things, not least of which is kidnapping. Thomas Thackery will be charged – when he gets out of the ICU – with kidnapping, aggravated kidnapping and various kinds of assault and extortion. So will his bikie friends. The real beauty of it all is that we have confessions from everybody and Jennifer and the bikies have all dobbed each other in. We also have a statement from Richard Cross indicting his mother and her hirelings."

"Have you arrested Richard?" I asked. His role in the affairs of the previous night seemed to have been limited to being at the wrong place at the wrong time and having the wrong family.

"We've charged him with failure to report a crime and stuff like that. It looks like he wasn't an active participant but he knew for several hours after he went to his mother's house that Thackery had Megan outside in the van and he did nothing. Even when they tied you and Ronnie up, he didn't try to stop them, or call the police. They made a deal, in his presence, that would have resulted in three deaths. He was practically a co-conspirator at that point."

And yet I couldn't help thinking he'd been in an

impossible situation.

"Did he tell you why he had me and Ronnie open an investigation?"

Bertolissio shrugged in a very Italian way. "He told us he couldn't live with the suspicion that his own mother had killed his brother. He wanted to know the truth, whatever the consequences."

"You don't believe him?"

"It's possible. It's also possible he just hated her."

"Thackery," Megan said. It was the first word she'd spoken since Bertolissio had arrived. "Will he get bail?"

"I don't think so. We'll oppose it. We'll make the case that he's a flight risk. My experience tells me he'd be very unlikely to be on the street again for many, many years."

"How many?"

Bertolissio glanced at me. She'd heard the fear in Megan's voice as clearly as I had.

"Megan, I can't say for sure. But there are so many charges against him – including for beating up Luke that time, evading arrest, stealing a van, carrying and using an unlicensed firearm, attempted murder, kidnapping, extortion, assault, and various conspiracy offences, it's almost certain he'll do ten years without parole and, if we're lucky, it'll be closer to twenty. It's up to the judge. Everyone will do their best to put him away for a very long time."

Megan nodded but did not seem reassured.

"I should probably let you two go. I must say, I'm ready for my bed."

"Of course," I said. "Thank you for dropping by."

"There are reporters outside. Would you like me to go down with you and get you to your car?"

"No, we'll be fine," said Megan. "Can I just ask... Luke

and Ronnie are OK, right? I mean no-one's coming after them, or anything?"

"We'll be fine," I said. It was pretty obvious that the dartboards in the Devil's Playthings clubhouse would be replaced by pictures of me and Ronnie but I'd lived with that for a couple of years already. Either bikies had short memories or, more likely, vengeance against law enforcement – even fringe dwellers like me – was not considered a good business model. Most likely, they'd consider the loss of Thackery and his mates as the cost of doing business and move on. It would probably help that Thackery had been freelancing and none of this had been official club business.

"I'll keep an eye out for any trouble," Bertolissio said. "But Luke's right. I don't envisage any comeback."

Megan nodded silently. I pulled her close. "It's all over now. It really is."

Bertolissio took a business card from her pocket and pushed it into one of Megan's. "That's a counselling service. Those guys are great. I've used them myself."

I wondered what kind of trauma could ever have been sufficient to shake the unflappable DS Bertolissio. Maybe I'd ask her one day.

She went off and Megan and I ran the gauntlet of shouting reporters – several of whom followed us all the way to the car, badgering and bullying us to make a statement. They didn't usually bother me but that day, feeling protective of Megan, I hated every loutish one of them. I remembered I had the contact details for a Guardian reporter on my desk and thought maybe I'd give her a call, later. I needed to make the point to someone that the promotion-hungry Detective inspector Reid had been an invaluable help in solving the case. It might stick in my throat but I owed him that much.

I had planned to take Megan back to the office but she seemed too fragile to face the questions or even the cheerfulness of a group. So we went to her unit in Kelvin Grove and we sat on the sofa and drank a cup of coffee. The place was a bit of a dump and very small. I'd never been there before. She'd given up the very nice unit I remembered when she went back to her husband, she told me. Then she'd had to find the new place in a hurry when she moved out again. There were still boxes of stuff unpacked on the floor and an air of camping out about everything. I saw her looking around at the boxes and the piles of folded clothes as if she were seeing it all with fresh eyes. It brought a pained expression to her face that broke my heart all over again.

I took her hand and said, "I guess the last thing you needed after all this was for me to be such a sook."

"It was all my fault."

"You tried to do the right thing, that's all."

"No good deed, hey?"

Goes unpunished. Was that what I'd been doing? Punishing her?

"Megan…" I wasn't sure what I was going to say but I pressed on, hoping I'd say something sensible. "I'm a fool." Maybe not sensible, but at least it was true. "I've kind of bumbled through life, sort of letting things happen to me. Letting people happen to me, too, if that makes any sense. I've been, I don't know, passive, I suppose."

Passive, soft, disengaged, remote.

She watched me with a kind of nervous curiosity. I was hoping she might jump in with a comment but her silence meant I needed to say more – maybe actually find a point to make.

"The thing is, I don't want to be like that. Not with you. I was like that with Chelsea. I can't tell you how guilty I've felt since she died – how I've despised myself. It's a selfish, lazy, even cowardly way to be. And I want to stop. Right here. Right now. I want to be fully engaged, fully present, carrying my share of the load. Do you know what I mean?"

"I think so." She sounded cautious.

"The thing is, I love you. And that has to mean something more than just 'you give me warm fuzzy feelings.' It has to mean I care about you, how you feel, what you need, who you are. And it has to mean I care for you, too. That I look after you, that I do what I can for you, that I help you and know you and support you."

Her lips twitched into a smile. "Jeez, does that mean I have to do all that as well?"

I smiled back. "Bloody oath, mate! Of course, you can have a couple of days off, until you get over the shock of me not being a useless pillock any more."

"That might take a long time."

"Maybe I could help you sort this place out while we're waiting."

She looked around. "Nah, I don't like this place. I'm moving on soon. If you really want to be useful, come here and give me a cuddle."

Thank You

Thank you for reading *Bright City Dark Love*, the third of my Luke Kelly crime novels. I really hope you enjoyed it as much as I enjoyed writing it. If so, I'd be grateful if you'd leave a review on one of the book retail sites, your blog, or pasted to a wall on the nearest underpass. There will be more books about Luke's adventures. To stay informed of when new books of mine are about to appear, please visit my website and sign up for my newsletter.

About the Author

I am a writer living in Queensland, Australia. A former research scientist, IT consultant and award-winning software designer, I now live and write – mostly science fiction and crime – in a quiet corner of the Australian bush with my wife, Christine, and a Tonkinese cat called Minsky.

Other Books By Graham Storrs

Crime Stories
Sisters: The Complete Short Story Collection

The Luke Kelly Crime Series:
Bright City Deep Shadows
Bright City Lost Souls
Bright City Dark Love
Bright City Old Wounds

Science Fiction
Cargo Cult
Heaven is a Place on Earth
Mindrider
Time and Tyde

The Timesplash Series:
Timesplash
True Path
Foresight

Novels in the Placid Point Universe
(in chronological order):

The Rik Sylver Trilogy:
The Credulity Nexus
The Sentience Machine
The Dissonance Factor

The Canta Libre Trilogy:
Emissaries
Supplicants
Warriors

The Deep Fracture Trilogy:
Loner's Deep
Omega Point
Nadezhda

Contact the Author

I am always happy to hear from readers, so don't be shy. And if you enjoyed this book, don't forget to post your review.

Follow me on Twitter: @graywave

or on Facebook:
facebook.com/GrahamStorrsAuthor

For an up-to-date list and full details of all my novels and short stories, visit cantalibre.com

www.ingramcontent.com/pod-product-compliance
Lightning Source LLC
Chambersburg PA
CBHW071229250626
47163CB00001B/104